Black Camelot

Black Camelot

DUNCAN KYLE

ST. MARTIN'S PRESS
NEW YORK

Library of Congress Cataloging in Publication Data

Kyle, Duncan.
  Black Camelot.

  1. World War, 1939-1945—Fiction. I. Title.
PZ4.K989B [PR6061.Y4] 823'.9'14 78-3964
ISBN 0-312-08301-7

In gratitude
for
DAVID

Black Camelot

Chapter One

He lay in the back of a field ambulance as it bounced agonizingly over the rutted, slush-bound, shell-pocked roads of the Ardennes forest, on its way back to an emergency treatment station. His clothing had been cut open, to allow a dressing to be strapped over the large wound, still bleeding freely, in his thigh. Even the injection of morphine, which had rendered him almost but not quite unconscious, had not been sufficient to deaden the pain.

When, after thirty-two racking kilometres, the ambulance halted outside a farmhouse which was being used as a field dressing station, he was lifted out with care and gentleness. He was laid on a table and the medical orderly looked at him in surprise and said to the doctor, busy at another table, 'This one, sir, wears two uniforms.'

'Eh?' The doctor straightened and moved across to look. Having looked, he inspected. On the patient's sleeve were the inverted chevrons of a sergeant in the United States army. The battle blouse, however, had been opened, and another uniform was visible beneath it. It bore the insignia of a captain in the Waffen SS. Carefully the doctor rolled back the sleeve, looking for further indications. In silver thread the Führer's name was worked into the material.

'Leibstandarte,' the orderly muttered. 'Is he a spy?'

'I don't know.' The doctor went to a field telephone, spoke into it, waited, spoke again and returned. 'Not a spy,' he said. 'He was on special duty.'

Together they began to cut away the clothing, and in doing so made another discovery. The man on the table was, as a member of the Leibstandarte, among the elite; but he was more: he held Oak Leaves to the Ritterkreuz – the Knight's Cross of the Iron Cross. They did their best for him,

7

then sent him back to a military hospital near Cologne.

Three days later a huge man arrived at the hospital. He was an SS Colonel, a national hero, instantly recognizable to everyone who saw him, even though one eye was covered in bandages. He was six feet six inches tall and built in massive proportion. On one cheek lay the deep etching of a duelling scar.

'You have a wounded officer here – Hauptsturmführer Rasch?'

'*Jawohl*, Herr Obersturmbannführer!'

'Take me to him.'

He sat quietly by Rasch's bed, waiting for the wounded man to awaken, impatient but controlled. After a while his presence communicated itself and Rasch's eyes fluttered open. Instinctively his body straightened and he grimaced at the resulting pain.

'Gently, Franz,' Skorzeny said, a hand moving to the patient's shoulder. He nodded at the wound. 'How bad is it?'

'I'll recover. Give me a couple of weeks and – '

'Good. I'll be glad to have you back.' Skorzeny opened his briefcase and removed a bottle wrapped in paper. 'Whisky,' he said. 'American, unfortunately, but . . .'

Rasch accepted the bottle. 'Thanks. How are things going?'

Skorzeny grimaced. 'Over. They're fighting still, but the attack is finished.'

The two looked at each other. Rasch had been with Skorzeny through three desperate actions. Together they had parachuted to the mountain heights of the Gran Sasso in 1943 to rescue Mussolini; a bare three months earlier, Skorzeny had led the surprise attack on Admiral Horthy's palace in Budapest, with Rasch beside him. Both adventures had been spectacularly daring and spectacularly successful. The third, the attempt to break through the thinly-held Allied lines in the Ardennes, was a failure.

Rasch said, 'Why?'

'Supplies,' Skorzeny said. 'If we'd captured one petrol dump! But we didn't. We hadn't enough tanks or armour or

8

guns. But even then, if we'd got the petrol, anything might have been possible, even Antwerp.'

'And now?'

Skorzeny's hand plucked at the bandage round his head. 'I had the honour to meet the Führer on December 31st. The fight goes on, on all fronts. He remains confident.'

'Do you?'

Skorzeny said, 'He is a genius. I am not.'

He rose to leave and Rasch said quickly, 'The Eastern front?'

'The Soviets are concentrating great strength on the Vistula. Get well quickly and come back, Franz.' Skorzeny saluted formally and departed.

The door, clicking as Otto Skorzeny returned to continue Hitler's fight, was a punctuation mark in Rasch's life and he recognized it as such. In that moment he knew he would not see Skorzeny again, that the war's excitements were over and only its horrors remained. The Vistula river might delay the Russians for a little, but the momentum behind their long and increasingly commanding advance would carry them across it, sooner rather than later. And what was true of the Vistula was true also of the Rhine; one day the Americans, the British, the French and the Canadians would drive across it and Germany would be meat in a vast military sandwich.

Franz Rasch was not an emotional man; the farewell to Skorzeny moved him not at all: Otto Skorzeny was a man easy to admire, but hardly to be liked. He was too big, too hard, too demanding, too relentless. Rasch was, in any case, attached to very few things in life. He had loved his wife, but she had been killed in an air raid on Berlin almost a year ago. He had loved the Führer, if that was the word. Certainly his feelings had once been strong and deep, but the military miscalculations had begun his disillusionment, and the dreadful butchery after the attempt to kill Hitler in July had almost completed it. A boyhood friend, von Talenburg, had strangled slowly, dangling at the end of a piano wire strung from a meat hook, because he had been ADC to a general

9

who was implicated. Worse, Rasch knew Fritz von Talenburg's long agony had been filmed for the Führer's pleasure.

The cigarette Skorzeny had half-smoked still smouldered in an ashtray beside the bed and a trace of sour smoke caught Rasch's nostrils, provoking a cough that sent pain through leg and hip. Rasch thought angrily that of the two things that still mattered in his life, one was already as good as lost.

For centuries Rasch's family had owned a small estate in East Prussia. By the standard of some of their neighbours it was little more than a large farm, but it was the place where he had been born and had grown up. It had always been his hope that he would eventually return there to live out his days as his father, his grandfather and generations of Rasch forbears had done. But with the Russians on the Vistula, with Marshals Rokossovsky and Cherniakowsky poised for a new offensive, the estate was as good as lost. It would be two or three weeks before Rasch could leave the hospital and by that time the Siberian savages would have drunk his wine, eaten his livestock and smashed everything he possessed.

Of the things he loved, only his horse remained, and the thought of Grenadier could still bring a smile to his face. Lying in the hospital bed, his forehead sweating from that last sharp pain, Rasch reflected that perhaps the only wise thing he had done had been to pack Grenadier off to Sweden when Donnelly, the Irish trainer who looked after him, had decided to leave an increasingly dangerous Germany for safely neutral Sweden. It seemed unlikely he would ever again sit on Grenadier's back, feeling beneath him the rhythmic power of that tremendous stride, but it comforted him to know that the animal would not end up being grilled on some Russian bayonet. Grenadier, at least, had a future. He, on the other hand, had not. Or not, at any rate, a future of any worth. When the war ended, as it must, in Germany's defeat, he would be penniless, a refugee who would never see his home again.

Lying there, after Skorzeny's departure, staring at the ceiling's flaking paint, Franz Rasch made a decision of sorts.

He would withdraw from the war. Any chance that was offered to him, he would take. Any chance at all. Not that chances were likely to be offered, but that wasn't the point. That he should have thought in that way when the future so clearly held no new opportunities for men like him was, in a strange way, prophetic.

Huge red fingers lay clasped on the blotter like a hillock of raw sausage. Beneath them lay a slim folder and from time to time the hands lifted and fell, tapping at the cardboard and discolouring it with perspiration. The air in the office was thick with cigarette smoke; a large ashtray on the desk flowed over with squashed cigarette ends. The hands unfolded, took a cigarette, worked a lighter, and reclasped.

They belonged to SS Obergruppenführer Dr Ernst Kaltenbrunner, chief since the death of Heydrich of the Reichsicherheitshauptamt, the complex apparatus of state security. Like Hitler, Kaltenbrunner was Austrian. He was very tall, with big bones prominent in a face like an axe blade, a powerful build and a fanatical commitment to the Führer's beliefs. It was of Adolf Hitler that he thought as smoke wreathed round him and his hands moved sweatily against the file.

Two days earlier, Kaltenbrunner had listened as the Führer, drawn and dismayed by the failure of the great gamble in the Ardennes, by Montgomery's subtle containment of the massive German thrust, had stared into the future and forecast its course.

Two lieutenants on Keitel's staff, armed with trays of small flags and crosses, arrows, tapes and numbered cards, had been working at the map table, updating the strategic position in line with the latest intelligence reports, and Hitler and Kaltenbrunner had watched as the Eastern front moved a few inexorable kilometres west, and the Western front was positioned eastward. Afterwards, with the two officers gone, Hitler had launched into a historical survey.

The topic was familiar to Kaltenbrunner, a subject central to Hitler's philosophy: the absolute inability of capitalist and communist states to achieve a permanent rapprochement. The American/British/Russian Alliance was incomprehensible to him. How was it possible for Stalin the revolutionary and Roosevelt the millionaire to conduct a practical relationship? How was it possible for Churchill, the aristocrat and Bolshevik-hater, to behave as Stalin's friend? The answer was that it was not possible. The answer was that it was the merest accommodation, that the Alliance was infinitely fragile and would inevitably disintegrate.

Hitler's vision of the future showed Britain and America and Germany allied against Russia. The study of history allowed no other possibility and realignment *must* therefore happen. But when? If it happened soon, if it happened *now*, if the Western Allies saw *sense* before it was too late, then together America, Britain and Germany could roll back the Russians to the Urals and beyond, and prevent the creation of a Bolshevik Europe. But they were insane, the British and the Americans! They couldn't see what was plain for everybody to see: Russia, not Germany, was the enemy of Europe and of civilization. The Alliance would crack, and with that crack it would fall apart, but the crack was not yet in sight.

'Germany's greatest need,' Hitler had said, just before Keitel, Jodl and Guderian returned to resume the strategic conference, 'her *greatest* need, Kaltenbrunner, is for one small crack to be made in that Alliance!'

Kaltenbrunner's mind had returned to the Führer's words when, a few hours earlier, he had received the papers in the folder which now lay beneath his hands. They came from the briefcase of a Cologne banker who had been killed in the street in a daylight raid. By some small miracle, the briefcase had accompanied the body to hospital, then to the mortuary. When the body was identified, the briefcase had swiftly found its way to RSHA headquarters in Berlin because the banker, Freiherr Heinrich von Klaussen, was a close friend and supporter of the Reichsführer-SS, Heinrich Himmler.

Was it possible, Kaltenbrunner asked himself, that the means to create the small crack in the Western Alliance which Hitler wanted so badly, had been delivered to him? The big, red hands continued to tap restlessly at the folder as he thought about it, chain-smoking. Appointments were broken, callers sent away, urgent administration postponed.

Finally, late in the evening, he sent for SS Brigadeführer Walter Schellenberg, chief of both espionage and counter-espionage since the arrest the previous August of the venerable intelligence chief Admiral Canaris. Schellenberg had, in fact, to be summoned from his home, a fact which itself gave Kaltenbrunner minor pleasure. There were two things about Schellenberg of which he strongly disapproved: first, the taste he showed for relaxation, which accorded ill with the demand of his job for vigilance; second, and infinitely more important, was the contact Schellenberg appeared to maintain with the Swede, Count Folke Bernadotte. Kaltenbrunner believed Schellenberg was working to persuade Himmler to displace the Führer, assume the leadership of the Reich, and sue for peace. If true, and Kaltenbrunner didn't doubt it *was* true, it was certainly treason; it was also the vilest kind of disloyalty to the Führer and to the oath Schellenberg had taken of eternal loyalty.

The knowledge infuriated Kaltenbrunner and his helplessness in the matter magnified his fury. He could not accuse Heinrich Himmler of disloyalty; not, at any rate, if he wished to stay alive. Perhaps, one day, with Bormann's aid, and if Himmler took one step too far . . .

To Schellenberg he said, 'You are aware that the Führer believes there must be a radical rearrangement of international alliances?'

Schellenberg lit a cigarette. 'I know his view about natural war between West and East, yes.'

'He believes it will happen soon.'

'Tomorrow morning would be convenient,' Schellenberg said.

'That's defeatist talk,' Kaltenbrunner snapped.

'No. But it's only of value if it happens *before* foreign armies occupy German soil.'

'They must never do that.'

Schellenberg said coolly, 'The Russians have been advancing for too long to be easily halted. The British and Americans have most of France and endless supplies. It's a matter of time.'

Kaltenbrunner controlled his temper. Much might depend on Schellenberg's knowledge of international information channels. He lit yet another cigarette, picked up the file and tossed it across his desk. 'Look at that!' He watched as Schellenberg leafed quickly through the few papers. Then: 'Well?'

'A moment more.' The younger man read on. Kaltenbrunner knew the paper was not easy to comprehend but Schellenberg had read law at university. After a moment he said, 'You have difficulty in understanding?'

'Not in understanding,' Schellenberg said. 'Believing. This appears to mean that a major American business corporation had – '

'*Has*. An American corporation *has* holdings in German industry.' Kaltenbrunner finished the sentence for him.

'These papers came from the Administration of Enemy Property?'

'No.'

'No? And profits have actually been remitted?' Schellenberg whistled.

'To Switzerland. And perhaps from there to Spain, and from Spain . . .' Kaltenbrunner grinned.

Schellenberg finished the pages swiftly. 'Messerschmitt, I. G. Farben, Untersee Elektrika?' He looked up. 'Is this genuine, or is somebody playing games?'

'It's real,' Kaltenbrunner said. 'Always handled privately, you see. Always under Swiss instructions.'

'Where did it come from?'

'From a mortuary. But its place of origin is impeccable.'

'How has it escaped notice for four years?'

'I don't believe it has. I've been making some inquiries. Three days after the Führer became Reich Chancellor in

1933, he received an American businessman, and that man was the president of this corporation. The Reichsführer-SS was also present.'

'Special arrangements, then?'

'Through the Bendler Bank in Köln.'

'Bendler? Then it's von Klaussen!'

Kaltenbrunner nodded. 'The late von Klaussen. He was killed yesterday by a bomb. The Reichsführer's first backer, and one of his closest friends. *Of course* there were special arrangements.'

After a moment Schellenberg said, 'Interesting,' on a rising inflection.

'An opportunity, eh?'

Schellenberg blinked rapidly several times, refocusing his mind and wondering whether Kaltenbrunner contemplated using the documents in some attack of Himmler. But that was impossible with the Führer apparently involved. He said, 'You intend to use them?'

'If anything can demonstrate to the Bolsheviks the treachery of their capitalist American allies,' Kaltenbrunner said, 'these papers can do it.'

'Publish them, then?'

'Of course. Stalin will go mad. It confirms all his suspicions. This is the worst kind of duplicity, and since it's the kind of thing he expects, he'll find it easy to believe.'

'Agreed,' Schellenberg paused. 'This is why you spoke of forcing a crack in the Alliance?'

'Certainly. It's bound to!'

Enthusiasm, as always, made Schellenberg wary. 'Not bound to, but it might, though in my opinion it's quite a long shot. It also needs a lot of help. Where will you publish?'

'Newspapers, where else? Sweden, Spain, Portugal, Switzerland. They'll love it!'

'According to informed sources inside Germany, it has been revealed that . . . Something along those lines?'

Kaltenbrunner frowned. He disliked being opposed, particularly by smart young men.

Schellenberg hesitated. 'They would be suspicious of the

source if we simply published. I believe I might be able to find a better way.'

'Find one, then,' Kaltenbrunner said. Adding, as Schellenberg was leaving, 'Quickly – and in your office. Not at home!'

Schellenberg saluted.

Chapter Two

In late January 1945 life was complicated for SS Brigadeführer Walter Schellenberg. He had dreams and schemes. He had powerful friends and powerful ambitions, and there were powerful enemies, too, anxious to see his applecart upturned. Also, time pressed him. Sometimes he felt like one of those nightclub jugglers who spin twenty plates on twenty canes and rush from one to the other to keep them spinning.

From the time of the surrender of Field Marshal von Paulus's Sixth Army Group at Stalingrad, ten years and a day after Hitler's first assumption of power, Schellenberg had recognized that Hitler's dream of conquest must ultimately fail. But he had had a career to foster, and had done it with concentration and success. He had been Heydrich's protégé; following Heydrich's assassination, he had become Himmler's. He was head of the Ausland SD, the overseas intelligence organization of the SS, and, following the fall of Admiral Canaris, had taken over the Abwehr, the military intelligence organization, too. The latter had presented difficulties of digestion; old loyalties and new masters go together badly, but the process was at least partially complete.

It was, however, a lonely position. When, in 1943 and 1944, Himmler's star had climbed ever higher in the firmament of Hitler's favour, jealousies had arisen. Martin Bormann in particular resented Himmler's position, had long sought to undermine it and had allies in Kaltenbrunner and Müller, head of the Gestapo, to help him. It was Bormann who had persuaded the Führer that Himmler should be given high military command (and thus the opportunity to make a fool of himself) and Himmler, lacking both the necessary ability and the experience, had duly done so in the Oberrhein, with the result that Alsace would soon belong to the Allies. Now Himmler was to take over Army Group Vistula, facing the Russians, and similar consequences could be expected.

So Himmler was away, difficult to reach and of diminishing value as a protector. For months Schellenberg had been using all his persuasiveness to plant in Himmler's mind the need for Hitler to be replaced by a man with whom the Allies might negotiate somewhere short of unconditional surrender: ideally Himmler himself. But the Reichsführer-SS had always vacillated, was vacillating now and would continue to vacillate. Accordingly Walter Schellenberg had quickly appreciated that in Kaltenbrunner's scheme lay good possibilities for his own ambitions. A major intelligence coup would earn the gratitude of all sides: of Himmler, of Kaltenbrunner, even of the Führer.

When he had told Kaltenbrunner he thought the odds were long against making any breach in the wall of the Alliance, he had been speaking the truth as he saw it. The misbehaviour of a corporation, however important, was really a quite minor revelation, though there was no doubt it would anger the Soviets, or that they would make use of it to exert pressure upon their ally. But if there were a way to anger them further – another revelation, and about the other ally, Britain, the odds would shorten appreciably. It was still only a slim chance, but worth the effort, and Schellenberg had an idea: something he'd thought of, wondered about occasionally, but never acted upon.

He therefore had a great deal to think about and on that day, because the water supply in his apartment was uncertain, and he thought best in the bath, he drove to the SS barracks in Potsdam, borrowed the commandant's bathroom, spent two hours brooding in plentiful hot water, and returned to his office with his thoughts in something approaching order.

He took a piece of paper and wrote:

1. Bohle.
2. Canaris.
3. Who?
4. How and where?

He then telephoned the Foreign Ministry, was informed that Bohle was at home, and drove to see him, ignoring the message on his desk instructing him to telephone Kaltenbrunner at once.

Gauleiter Bohle was not pleased to see him but Schellenberg, in uniform and exuding urgency, was not easily to be fobbed off. He was admitted with a certain reluctance and said at once, as they sat down before an electric fire, 'I'm here to pick your brains.'

'What about?' Bohle asked cautiously. Bohle, for many years responsible for the Nazi Party organization and membership abroad, was notoriously protective about his Auslandsorganization, and had always striven to keep people like Schellenberg at arm's length.

'About nineteen-forty.'

Bohle frowned. 'It was a long time ago.'

'It was the turning point of the war,' Schellenberg said earnestly, knowing Bohle's views. 'We should have finished Britain before turning east.'

'You should have given the Führer the benefit of your advice,' Bohle said sourly. Hitler's decision to abandon Operation Sea Lion, the projected invasion of southern England, still rankled with Bohle. He had been born in Britain and would have ruled it had the invasion succeeded.

'I'm interested in might-have-beens,' Schellenberg said.

'Here to reminisce, perhaps?'

'No.' Schellenberg lit a cigarette. 'I'm working on something for the Führer personally.' He could afford the lie direct, since neither Bohle nor his out-of-favour master Ribbentrop was in any position to check the statement. 'And it occurs to me that at that time, while you were waiting in Paris with your bags packed, you must have known more about Britain than any man in Germany.'

19

'Perhaps.'

'You must,' Schellenberg said, moving from the general to the particular, 'have had a list of the people who might be expected to welcome you and co-operate.'

Bohle gave a tired smile. 'I wondered what you wanted.'

'Had you?'

Bohle shrugged. 'Yes.'

'Have you got it still?'

'No.'

'Where is it?'

'I don't know. It went to Heydrich.'

'To Heydrich! But that must have been – '

'A long time ago. I know, but that's what happened.'

'How many copies?'

'To my knowledge only three.'

'Your certain knowledge?'

Bohle nodded.

'Who had the others?'

'Heydrich and Canaris.'

Schellenberg's sigh was almost a groan. 'All right. Tell me how it was assembled.'

Bohle gave a grim smile. 'It was in the bright years. Would you like a drink?'

'Very much.' Schnapps was poured and Bohle emptied his glass with giveaway suddenness.

Schellenberg sipped at his own and said, 'If I may say this in the friendliest way, you should be careful. When you talk about the bright years, I understand. Others might not. And while you're about it, don't overdo the schnapps. Now, how was the list assembled?'

'About the schnapps. I've had a cold.'

'Never mind the schnapps. Go on.'

Bohle sighed. 'We had three principal sources. The first was the embassy in London. Ribbentrop ran it well. It was always full of important people and a lot of them were impressed. We sounded out their views systematically and quite often we invited people to Germany. You'd be surprised how many prominent British people preferred Hitler to Baldwin and Chamberlain.'

'What categories of people?'

'Politicians, civil servants – Foreign Office particularly – social butterflies, musicians, actors, journalists – '

'The embassy spectrum. I understand. What were the other sources?'

'Businessmen. Heads of companies. After the depression years we found they were very impressed by the way German industry was humming after only a few years of the Third Reich. Within the usual business exchanges, our people over there and theirs over here, a great deal was learned about a lot of people.'

'Did you ask the direct question?'

'Whether they wanted a similar regime in England? Sometimes we did. Not often. The British like oblique approaches. But the man who says he'd like to put the trades union leaders against the nearest wall, if he means it, could reasonably be held to have some sympathy. Businessmen like strong, stable economic systems they feel are well disposed towards them.'

'And category three?' Schellenberg asked.

'Tourists. People who came and saw and liked what they saw. Mayors of decaying industrial cities who looked at Essen and wished it could be moved to Lancashire or Durham. Provincial newspaper editors, city administrators who liked the way we actually did things while they could only hope.'

Schellenberg said, 'Quite a list. How many?'

'About two thousand.' There was a little flick of resurrected pride in the way Bohle spoke.

'Two thousand you could rely on?'

'Probably not all. But most.'

Schellenberg said, 'I'm grateful. I'm sure the Führer will be, too.' He emptied his glass and left, and drove away pleased with his instincts. He'd been right about Bohle. But he was a good deal less pleased with his knowledge of where the lists had gone. Heydrich had had two, Canaris one. Now Heydrich was dead and Canaris in a Gestapo prison and in what condition it was difficult to imagine. But far worse than that was his personal knowledge of the files of both men's departments. He himself now controlled all Canaris's Abwehr files. After the absorption of the Abwehr into his own department, they had been delivered to a warehouse in four removal trucks, and after months of work were still about as orderly as a pigsty, thanks to the Admiral's loyal staff who had accidentally let two of the huge card index files fall open. The cards had been recovered, but it was as though they had been expertly shuffled and as a result the whole system was appallingly difficult to use, and the cross-indexing was effectively wrecked.

But at least he knew where the Admiral's files were. Heydrich's records were an altogether different matter. Within both the Party and the Schützstaffel, Heydrich's files were privately known to be the most dangerous storehouse of information in the country; for Heydrich, it seemed, had not restricted his assemblage of damaging evidence to enemies or potential enemies of state and party. It was widely believed those files contained unpalatable facts about the entire leadership of the Party from Hitler downwards. Schellenberg remembered vividly a conversation he had had with Felix Kersten, Himmler's Swedish masseur and closest confidant. Kersten said Himmler had shown him a document showing not only that Hitler had once undergone treatment for syphilis, but that the treatment had been insufficient and unsuccessful. Kersten believed that document had come from Heydrich's files and was now in Himmler's.

Schellenberg knew the story of Heydrich's papers. After his death in Prague in 1942, the filing cabinets had been sealed on Himmler's orders and driven, at high speed and in SS trucks, escorted by an armed Waffen SS detachment, to a secret hiding place. There, Himmler himself had spent two weeks alone going through them. When he had finished, a number of files dealing with citizens of foreign countries had come to Schellenberg's own department. Those on military, naval and air force officers had been released to Gestapo Müller following the July 20th attack on Hitler's life. The rest, in fact the great bulk of Heydrich's papers, had remained accessible only to Himmler himself. It was, to Schellenberg, an interesting question why Adolf Hitler, who must know the explosive nature of the files, had allowed them to remain in Himmler's sole possession.

But he had. And there was no possibility of gaining access to them. In earlier times it might just have been feasible to ask the Reichsführer if he knew where the lists had gone, but Himmler was now in command of Army Group Vistula, as well as being the focus of Schellenberg's other plans, and Schellenberg much preferred that he should remain in ignorance of this one – at least for the time being. With Heydrich's copies unavailable, there remained only Admiral Canaris and his copy, which might or might not be somewhere in the confused mass of the Abwehr papers.

To find out, he must see Canaris and he did not relish meeting the old Admiral. Schellenberg had himself carried out Canaris's arrest, the previous August, acting on Kaltenbrunner's orders and bitterly resentful because Canaris was a friend. Now Canaris was a prisoner in the fearsome Gestapo cellars in the Prinz Albrechtstrasse and Schellenberg wondered what the months of imprisonment and interrogation had done to him, and whether the fine intelligence had survived kidney punches and truncheons. Even if it had, Canaris was walking dead and knew it, and so might resist . . . information might have to be beaten out of him. That prospect degraded them both and Schellenberg visited the Prinz Albrechtstrasse full of distaste and apprehension.

He drove away astonished: Canaris had been instantly forthcoming, informing Schellenberg, with a direct simplicity that brought a lump to the younger man's throat, that after forty years of serving Germany, he would serve while there was breath in him. He remembered the document well and knew where it was. The price was a cigar; Schellenberg promised a box, doubtful as he spoke whether they would reach the old admiral.

Two hours later, rummaging through the dusty mass of Abwehr information, sweating and covered in dust, Schellenberg unearthed it. He spent the remainder of the night at his desk, trying to find the answers to the questions posed in items 3 and 4 of his aide-memoire. By morning he was more or less satisfied that he knew how and where to make use of his two paper weapons. Certain inquiries must be made first, but the essence of the procedure was clear.

What he needed still was the answer to item 3. *Who* was to be the means?

Next day he pursued his inquiries and what he learned seemed to confirm the soundness of his plan and he was almost ready to lay it before Kaltenbrunner, but still it was proving impossible to find the right man. Schellenberg racked his brains and failed to come up with a name. More accurately he thought of a hundred and rejected them all.

In the end it was his secretary who unwittingly solved his problem. As she brought him a cup of tea substitute in the afternoon she said, 'You'll never guess who I saw in the street at lunchtime! Hauptsturmführer Rasch. Poor man, he's been wounded.'

'Really,' Schellenberg said, with a sudden interest that was far from feigned. 'I hope it isn't too severe.'

'He was walking with a stick.'

'If you see him again, give him my good wishes.'

Schellenberg sat and thought about Franz Rasch. After ten minutes he sent for his secretary. 'Do you think you could find out where Rasch is, and ask him to come and see me?'

'Of course.'

Rasch, Schellenberg gloated to himself, fitted every requirement. There remained the problem of persuasion. Orders would not do; you cannot order a man to be a traitor.

If Walter Schellenberg was now ready to present his plan to his superior, Kaltenbrunner was more than ready to hear it; he was impatient and angry that Schellenberg had ignored several urgent demands to report to him. But Schellenberg, playing several games at once, had been careful to ensure that it was known that Himmler had been making demands upon his time. As chief of the Reich Security Office, Kaltenbrunner's authority, and the fear of it, extended into almost every corner of the nation's life. It stopped short, however, of Heinrich Himmler. As Kaltenbrunner was well aware, questioning the actions of the Reichsführer-SS could endanger more than just his job.

None the less, Schellenberg was very much the junior and could be treated as such. When he presented himself with his briefcase at Kaltenbrunner's office, he was stood to rigid attention and given an angry dressing down. Nor was Schellenberg made happier when, before he could begin to outline his plan, the door opened to admit SS Gruppenführer Heinrich Müller, head of the Gestapo, who took a seat with the obvious intention of listening. He thought of Canaris, in a cell a short distance away; in the presence of this blood-stained pair, it seemed only too possible that he could join him.

Kaltenbrunner, moreover, was clearly determined to make the presentation difficult. Schellenberg began by saying he proposed that the scheme should be effected in Sweden.

'Why just Sweden?' Kaltenbrunner demanded.

'The reasons are good,' Schellenberg said patiently. 'I will enumerate – '

'They had better be good. Considering the time you've wasted, the whole plan had better be good!'

'I believe it is. It has been broadened to take in other matters.'

'Never mind the jargon. Get on with it!'

Schellenberg began again. 'The intention is to provoke a major disagreement between the Soviets and the United States, by delivering to the Soviets a report of American industrial holdings in the industry of the Reich.'

'Is this what you've spent so much time doing?'

'With a further intention,' Schellenberg persisted, 'of sowing discord also between the Soviets and Britain and between Britain and the United States.' For the first time he was not interrupted.

He opened his briefcase and removed two folders. 'These papers are the ones which you have already seen. The second folder contains the list, prepared for the invasion of Britain, of important British citizens who were to become our collaborators.'

'Show me,' said Müller in his thick Bavarian accent.

Schellenberg handed it to him and Müller riffled the papers. 'Is it genuine?'

'Yes.'

'Were you aware of this?' Müller asked Kaltenbrunner.

'No.'

'Nor was I. How did *you* know that it existed?'

Schellenberg said, 'I guessed. It was prepared for the Foreign Ministry by Gauleiter Bohle. Something like it was bound to exist. I asked Bohle and he confirmed it.'

'This is a valuable document,' Kaltenbrunner said. 'Valuable to our intelligence services. Use could have been made of it.'

'We're going to use it now.'

'The only copy?' Müller demanded.

'I understand Reichsprotektor Heydrich possessed one.'

Kaltenbrunner said, 'Go on.'

'My belief is that the Soviets, confronted by proof of American participation in our industry throughout the war, will accuse the United States of treachery.'

'If you remember, Schellenberg, that was *my* idea. What you were supposed to do was to develop it. Come to the point.'

'I believe,' Schellenberg said, 'that the Soviet reaction will be immediate and angry, on the highest level, Stalin direct to Roosevelt. However, we have evidence which suggests that there is some kind of rapport between Stalin and Roosevelt. It is possible that if Roosevelt says, as he must, that this is an isolated case and that the United States Government did not know, and that prosecution for treason will follow at once,

26

Stalin will accept his word, however reluctantly. In that event, nothing would have been achieved.'

Müller said, 'Why should there be some special relationship between Roosevelt and Stalin? One's a multi-millionaire aristocrat, the other a revolutionary.'

Schellenberg said, 'Roosevelt has always been nervous of British influence. Perhaps he's agreed that Stalin can have certain territories.'

'You mean, do you,' Kaltenbrunner asked dangerously, 'when Germany has lost the war?'

'I mean,' Schellenberg said, 'that Italian communists, and French ones, might be allowed into Government.'

'That isn't what you said.'

Schellenberg said, a little desperately, 'It's what I meant. But the point, which you insist I reach, is that the relationship between Stalin and Churchill is very different. They distrust each other profoundly. Churchill is everything Stalin detests and Churchill loathes everything Stalin stands for. Their relationship can only be uncomfortable, a matter of chance not of choice. When the Soviets learn that this list exists, and that important people in many spheres of British life were actually prepared to collaborate with us, Stalin simply will not believe the British Government knew nothing of it.'

'Why shouldn't he believe it?' Kaltenbrunner said. 'Such things are always possible. We ourselves have routed out more than five thousand traitors, many of them officers, and senior officers at that, of the Wehrmacht itself. Five thousand! And all of them since the traitor von Stauffenberg tried to murder the Führer on July 20th.'

'He won't believe it for three reasons,' Schellenberg said. 'The first is that the reputation of the British Secret Service is excellent. Stalin will be certain that they would know. Secondly, the names in this list are not those of a clique in the army, or in industry; they are spread widely through the population. Political and business leaders in important cities, politicians, industrialists, writers and academics. They are spread just as widely geographically, too, from Scotland to the south of England. If you study Bohle's list, it is most convincing.'

'Is it true, though?' Müller said. 'If there is one thing the Foreign Ministry is not, it is realistic. If a pig told Ribbentrop it was an elephant, he would admire its trunk.'

'Defining truth is not easy,' Schellenberg began.

'Spare us philosophy.'

'It was a statement of fact,' Schellenberg said. 'The truth, such as it is, is that the list was compiled with great care over a period of several years of intensive activity by the embassy in London and by the Foreign Organization of the Party. The people listed are admirers of the Reich and people who expressed sympathy with our aims.'

'A long time ago,' Kaltenbrunner said.

'Five years. The point is not where their sympathies lie now, but the effectiveness of the list as a weapon. The Soviets will believe because they wish to believe.' He thought of adding, 'Like Ribbentrop,' but decided against it. 'Everything we know suggests Stalin is chronically suspicious. His actions over many years, for example in the purges of the Red Army, demonstrate very clearly that he distrusts even his own immediate circle.' This was sailing very close to the wind, and Schellenberg knew it. Müller and Kaltenbrunner did not so much as glance at each other, but suddenly the air was thick with all three men's knowledge of the Führer's own pathological suspicion, and of the brutality of the purge of the German army.

Kaltenbrunner merely said, 'For the sake of making a little progress, we'll assume you're right about Stalin. Come to the practical matters.'

'Very well,' Schellenberg said. 'The question is how best to arrange that these papers reach the right quarter in such a way that their authenticity is accepted. There must be no suspicion that they are a device of German intelligence.'

'There *will* be suspicion,' Kaltenbrunner said. 'It is impossible that there could not be suspicion.'

'Then it must be minimal. Along with the documents, it is

necessary to supply a wholly believable and circumstantially acceptable explanation. The Soviets will test it, as far as they are able. It must stand up to the testing.' He paused and took a photograph from his briefcase. It had been cut from a newspaper and showed a smiling elderly woman wearing a striped silk dress. She was clearly at some kind of formal party.

'This,' Schellenberg said, 'is Alexandra Kollontay, the Soviet Ambassador to Sweden. I imagine you must know of her.'

'All I want to know,' Kaltenbrunner said. 'She's a sick old woman.'

'Sick, certainly. She has been ill for years. But her mind is unimpaired, as, I might add, is her strong personal friendship with Stalin. If these papers were to reach him via Kollontay, with her assurance of their validity, he would be already half-way convinced. That is one reason why Sweden is the logical place. There is no other Soviet ambassador Stalin trusts so much. Secondly, Sweden is accessible easily from our own territory. It is possible to effect delivery of these papers quickly. The problem I had to solve, therefore, was to find a way of arranging for the papers to reach Madame Kollontay in a wholly convincing way. I believe I have found it. I suggest we use a traitor.'

Kaltenbrunner's mouth tightened. The big hands clasped on the desk in front of him. 'If that's the quality of your thinking, Schellenberg, you should be relieved of your duties! Who do you suggest? Your friend Canaris, perhaps? That's why you've been paying him social calls and sending him good cigars – so you can deliver him to the Russians!' He paused, then added quietly, 'When you use the word traitor, Schellenberg, be careful. It can come back, like a boomerang.'

'He's altogether too thick with the Swedes anyway,' Müller growled. 'All this soft talk with Bernadotte and the Swedish Red Cross. That's just about your mark, Schellenberg – negotiations to release Jews!'

Schellenberg said, 'My contacts with Count Bernadotte

have been made on instructions from the Reichsführer-SS alone.'

'Don't ever exceed those instructions,' Kaltenbrunner warned grimly. 'Not by a millimetre.'

Schellenberg tried to ignore the flat stare. 'I suggested we should use a traitor. I should perhaps have said we should manufacture a traitor. The individual chosen should be, in fact, a loyal German. His background will be such as to convince all of us that he is utterly reliable; it will also convince the Soviets that he would have natural access to these documents.'

'And you propose,' Kaltenbrunner's voice had an edge of sarcasm, 'that this paragon will be manufactured? That kind of nonsense would not stand up to five minutes of expert interrogation, and whatever else the Soviets are, they are not fools in such matters.'

'It will stand up,' Schellenberg said steadily, 'to any questioning, because it will be true. The man exists. The background exists. The treachery will be manufactured around him.'

For the first time, he saw a trace of response in Kaltenbrunner's hard eyes. The technique of the frame-up was well-understood in this office.

Kaltenbrunner said, 'So we let it be known he is a traitor, and kill him?'

'No,' Schellenberg said, 'we let him live. And when he arrives in Sweden, we make certain arrangements for his reception. He will be guided, but subtly, so he is unaware of it.'

Chapter Three

Franz Rasch had not believed it could happen. All the careful orders, the farewell salutes, the good wishes, had done nothing to destroy his feeling of unreality. The tri-motor Junkers 52 into which he had climbed at Tempelhof, and in which he now sat, was so familiarly the plane in which one flew off to war that his mind somehow found it unacceptable as a vehicle of escape. Rasch was in that curious state of mind when feeling contradicts intellect. The plane *had* left Berlin, *was* now heading for Stockholm, *would* soon land him on neutral soil. Those were facts. It was also a fact – no, it was a miracle! – that having decided to get out of Germany, he was not only going, but going in style. In his pocket was the visa obtained for him by the Foreign Ministry; behind him were the goodbyes of high-ranking officers. It was all true, yet in some curious way it was unreal; only the past was real: yesterday and the four thousand or so other yesterdays of the Führer's rule.

Pressure on his eardrums told him the plane was losing height and he glanced out of the window at the snow-covered ground beneath, where the only thing moving was the aircraft's own shadow. He watched it idly: the distinctive tri-motor shape of the Ju-52, skimming over whiteness. Recollection stirred. He'd seen the film so many times in so many places: Hitler's own Junkers flying into Nürnberg for the Rally, the sunlit earth below, music in the air and ahead what the film-maker Leni Riefenstahl had called *The Triumph of the Will*.

Rasch's smile was brief and wry. The hundred thousand throats were already silent in history, the will had faltered too many times, now there was no careful orchestration of the Horst Wessel song to hymn a Junkers to its landing. For a moment he was gripped by a kind of sadness for the years and the people he had known and he shook his head in irritation. Then he blinked. He had actually seemed to *feel* the shackles of the past give way, somewhere in his brain. He looked again out of the window, able now to accept what he saw. It was Sweden below, and he was *free*! All he had to do was to get off the plane, present his passport and visa, and walk into his new life. There was nothing in the way. Though, as it happened, the Junkers' captain proved to be in the way: Lufthansa, punctilious as ever, waiting to speed the distinguished passenger.

Rasch extended his hand. 'Thank you. A good flight.'

The captain shook it. 'A privilege,' he said. 'It is not every day we carry Oak Leaves to the Knight's Cross.'

'Fly safely home,' Rasch said solemnly, thinking of Mustangs and Spitfires. The captain doubtless intended to fight Ivan to his last breath for Volk, Führer and Vaterland. He climbed down to the tarmac and stamped his foot, partly because the wounded leg had stiffened during the flight, partly to feel Sweden beneath it. The flight steward jumped down and handed Rasch his small suitcase. He began to walk with the straggle of other passengers across the apron to the airport building. One suitcase, one walking stick, one successful escape; Rasch's face always looked severe and was usually an accurate reflection of the man. Today the expression was a lie.

Just before he entered the building, he turned and glanced back at the Junkers. The captain, framed in the doorway, raised a hand in salute and an uncharacteristically generous impulse almost sent Rasch back to talk to him. Why on earth would a man who was already safe in Sweden choose to go back to a tottering Reich? He stared for a moment at the saluting figure, raised his stick and turned away. There was now only the remaining duty to be done and it was scarcely onerous, therefore he would do it, if only as a kind of thankoffering for the chance of freedom. His mind went quickly over the instructions Schellenberg had given him. A car would take him from the airport to the Grand Hotel, where he was to register and wait. When Count Folke Bernadotte was free to see him, he would be informed, and Rasch was then to present himself, and the two envelopes he now carried in his pocket, to the Count. That was all. Here you are, sir, with the compliments of all concerned, and now, if you'll forgive me, the lights of Stockholm beckon. Salute and withdraw.

The Swedish immigration official did no more than glance at passport and visa; Customs didn't want to inspect his bag. Ignoring the slight but ever-present ache in his wounded leg, Hauptsturmführer Franz Rasch strode towards the exit and the car that would be waiting to take him into the city. Several private cars and taxis stood on the little curve of road beside the airport entrance, obviously waiting for new arrivals. Rasch put down his bag and waited for one of them to approach.

None did. They approached other people. Passengers' bags were taken and stowed and their owners were whisked off in a puff of exhaust gases. Rasch was left where he stood. The last car vanished and with his high spirits a little lower, he began to realize that it was very cold. Where was that damned car? Typical of the Foreign Ministry that it couldn't even arrange for a car to be at an airport on time! He'd just have to take a taxi. But all the taxis had gone and he realized suddenly that he did not have money for a taxi. They'd told him in Berlin that he would be given Swedish kroner when he got to the hotel; there'd been some nonsense about a shortage of currency. All he had, as a result, was a very few Reichsmarks – those and Lisel's two brooches, and you didn't pay taxi fares with diamond jewellery. Rasch picked up his suitcase, intending to go into the airport building and either wait there for the embassy car, or persuade somebody to change his few Reichsmarks.

He was walking towards the swing doors when a voice said in slightly accented German, 'I'm going into Stockholm. Is that any use to you?'

Rasch turned. The man was somewhere between thirty and thirty-five, sandy haired, smiling hesitantly. 'I'm to be met,' he said. 'But the car has not turned up.'

'Too cold to stand waiting,' the stranger said. 'My car's just round the corner. Where do you want to go?'

'Grand Hotel.'

'Really!' The man laughed. 'I'm going there myself. If you'll wait a moment I'll bring the car round. No sense in carrying suitcases.'

'Thank you.' Rasch watched him walk away. He had a suspicion the man was English. The German was good but the accent odd, and something in the clothes was neither German nor Swedish. On the other hand the plane had come from Berlin and the man must know that. Anyway, what did it matter, Rasch thought to himself, since he was no longer a loyal officer but merely a man in need of a car? If the Englishman didn't object, then neither did he. This was a new world.

Rasch was not precisely correct but nearly so. Joseph Conway was English in everything but the technicality of his Irish passport. The accented German he spoke had been learned in the beginning at a school called the Royal Liverpool Institution; the tweed coat he wore had been bought in a sale at Austin Reed in Regent Street. His English held some traces of Lancashire but none at all of Ireland, and his mind held no trace at all of loyalty to any country. Conway's loyalty was all directed inwards. Accordingly he would not have had the smallest objection to filling his car with Germans, Japanese or headhunters from New Guinea, for that matter, so long as they suspended their warlike activities until they got out again. Also, there must be something in it for him.

He had no idea what was in it for him on that cold Stockholm day. Had he known, or even guessed, that he was about to become involved in events that were to give him first a dream of wealth, and then, in bewildering succession, a series of experiences that were to terrify him, to put him more than once in danger of his life, and ultimately make him seek to vanish forever, he would have driven the little

Opel as fast as he could in the direction of Lapland. But Conway had no way of guessing. He had spent the previous hour or so, as he often had to at the airport, just keeping warm. He had arrived at Bromma cold, frustrated and worried. The cold he dealt with by entering the comfortable little airport restaurant, ordering hot coffee which was in fact a coffee substitute made from barley, cupping his hands round the mug, and sipping quickly at the scalding fluid. His frustration, or some of it, would disappear with the arrival of the expected, but late, Junkers passenger flight from Berlin. The worry, which was entirely justified, was destined to increase and, save for a single brief period of optimism, to remain with him.

Joseph Conway was thirty-five years old, a journalist and a citizen of one neutral country working in another. For more than three years he had made an excellent living free-lancing from what was effectively the only available window on Nazi Germany. Careful reading of German newspapers was his main source of information, and he had become adept at translating small clues, which evaded the censorship, into stories for the world's press. There was the time, for instance, when he noticed that a leading article in the *Berliner Zeitung* referred not, as it usually did, to 'the European fortress' but to 'Fortress Germany.' Conway's interpretive article, suggesting that this indicated growing defeatism within the Third Reich, was published from London to New York to Valparaiso and New Delhi, earning him both good money, which he needed, and a sharp increase in his reputation, which he needed even more.

Conway's principal talents as a reporter were his alertness and his imagination. He could put the pieces of a news jigsaw together more quickly than most, and often with less regard for the fidelity of the resulting picture. If a diplomat cleared his throat before offering a good morning, Conway was ready to interpret the hesitation. His sources included tipsters, whom he paid when he could not avoid it, travellers to and from Germany, the reports of Swedish correspondents in Germany whose work he milked unhesitatingly, and any

Swedish or neutral diplomats still willing to talk to him.

Principally, however, he relied on his now-practised study of the German press, and it was to collect a bundle of papers that he waited on that day at the airport. Though every correspondent in Stockholm received the German papers, Conway had found that few were prepared to come out to Bromma Airport to collect them. Most of his competitors were staff men, salaries paid monthly on the dot, and content to wait in their comfortable offices until the papers were delivered. He had discovered that by meeting the plane he could often beat even the news agencies by two or three hours. It was time that meant money.

He sat by the window sipping his coffee substitute, looking out at a runway across which light snow flicked in a gusting wind. The plane would get down, no problems there. It was just the usual dreary business of having no idea when it might arrive. The Junkers pilots invariably and sensibly kept radio silence until they were well across the Swedish coast, and since there was no way of knowing even if the plane had taken off, he could only sit and wait for the loudspeaker to announce an arrival which would, by then, be imminent.

Alone with his coffee in the small deserted restaurant, Conway worried. In recent days he had worried increasingly and with excellent reason. For as long as the war lasted, there was a living to be made in Stockholm. The war, however, could not now be expected to last for long. Adolf Hitler's great gamble in the west, that desperate thrust through the Ardennes in the hope of bisecting the Allied armies, had been held and turned, and the American and British steamrollers were moving again. In the east, the Russians crashed inexorably forward, announcing new advances daily. The war would be over in a few months, possibly even in weeks, and with the end of Hitler and his Reich would come the end of the importance of Stockholm as a clearing house for news – and other, more furtive varieties of information.

Conway knew he had somehow to get out, to guess where the next great news centre would be, and to go there. But that kind of move was never easy. There would be plenty of news in Germany, but there would also be armies of newsmen chasing it, with the resources of their papers behind them. Alone, he would be at a terrible disadvantage and though he was self-confident enough to believe he could survive, the prospect of arduous news-chasing in a ruined country was not attractive. Recently Conway had concluded that the answer to his problems lay in a regular job with one of the great newspapers in London or New York, but such a job was easier to want than to get. He had no delusions about his reputation: there had been, over the years, too many carefully-confected stories which had collapsed upon examination like expiring soufflés. What he needed, and needed badly, was a really big, utterly exclusive news break, and such things were not easily achieved. For several days now, however, he had been further unsettled by the fact that an Irish ship was due to arrive in a couple of weeks at Gothenburg to pick up, of all things, a cargo of telephone poles. It sounded like the beginning of a joke, but Conway had a chance of getting on that ship, and none at all of getting aboard one of the British aircraft that ran the risky and crowded service to Stockholm.

Recently, too, he had suspected that the big story he wanted so badly might be in the offing. A curious smugness about the Foreign Ministry spokesmen suggested something in the air. A tipster with mysterious and probably phoney central European contacts, had whispered to him (and to how many others?) a rumour of an imminent deal between high officials of the SS and a leader of world Jewry. Half of Conway's mind said, believe that and you'll believe anything; the other half told him the SS would be running round like trapped rats, doing anything that held out some slender promise of salvation when the collapse came.

He had long made a habit of watching passengers disembarking from the Junkers. There was always the chance he might recognize somebody and grab a quick interview or at least draw a conclusion. Lately, because he needed money and therefore news, he had taken to watching the passengers with greater care, through binoculars. And today, though he placed no faith in it, he had additional reason to look at them carefully. The previous night an anonymous telephone call had told him there would be a remarkable passenger – he remembered the phrase – on the Berlin plane. Not that Conway nowadays took much notice of anonymous calls; there had been too many and they had been too fruitless.

When at last the plane's arrival was announced, Conway waited until it was actually visible on its approach before getting up and leaving the restaurant. He stood where he could watch the passengers as they climbed one by one out of the door half-way along the Junkers' fuselage. It was always passengers first, luggage second, cargo third. Today, as had become usual, most of the first group of people to appear were women and children. Conway's experienced eye told him they were Swedes who had decided that life in Berlin had become altogether too uncomfortable and dangerous. As if to confirm that, he saw a woman he knew slightly, wife of one of the Swedish correspondents in Berlin, leave the plane. He recognized one other person, an official of the German timber purchasing company, but nobody else, and it seemed to him unlikely that any of them were of great importance. He was thinking of replacing the binoculars in their case and going indoors again when he realized that one, at least, of the passengers merited another look. 'A remarkable passenger,' he thought, and smiled to himself. Maybe the anonymous tipster did know something. Resting one elbow against the side of the building to steady the binoculars, he looked at the man again, carefully. 'German,' he thought to himself. Swedes tended to look relaxed, simply pleased to be home. Germans looked around them in a slightly puzzled way, as this man was doing now, as though unable to believe that the sound of war had stopped.

The German wore a leather coat, dark brown or black, and was hatless. Unwise of him in this wind, Conway thought. The man stood with squared shoulders, back straight and held a walking stick. 'How old?' Conway asked himself, and guessed at mid-thirties. The man's face had a slightly pinched look, but perhaps the cold was responsible. Then, as the passengers began to walk slowly towards the Customs shed, Conway saw the limp. 'Wounded soldier,' he speculated, and wondered why he might be in Sweden. Not that it was unusual for German soldiers to arrive in Sweden; the Nazis had long ago negotiated transit rights through Sweden for their troops stationed in Norway. But those troops wore uniform and did not limp.

Conway was frowning as he watched the man. It was often impossible to know what alerted his instincts; all he knew was that they were alerted now, and that they were right often enough to be taken seriously. It might be worthwhile, he decided, to watch the man go through Immigration and Customs and see who met him. No time would be lost; it would be a little while before the newspapers came through. Conway put the binoculars away, went into the airport building and looked out through the main entrance to see what cars were waiting. Apart from the taxis, there were only three, one a Mercedes. Perhaps that was for the intriguing visitor? At last the Junkers' passengers began to straggle out of Customs. A woman and child were collected by the Mercedes' chauffeur and driven away. Others got into cars or taxis. A dozen or so emerged before the leather-coated man.

Conway watched him halt in the hall and look round. There was no doubt now that he was or had been a soldier. His lapels bore no insignia now, but had certainly done so: the leather was punctured where the devices had been. He had one small suitcase and a briefcase. The walking stick, now tucked under his arm, was presumably useful but not vital.

There was no one to meet him inside the building. Perhaps outside? But no, the private cars had gone. Yet the German clearly expected to be met. Conway's own elderly Opel was parked round the corner, out of sight but not far away. He'd got interviews before by offering people lifts. Sometimes he'd say he was a newspaperman, sometimes not; it depended who he was talking to. His instincts twitched again as he watched the last of the taxis pull away. Conway believed in luck.

The German, disappointed, went awkwardly through the swing door. After a moment, Conway followed and said in German, 'I'm going into Stockholm. Is that any use to you?'

He walked briskly round to the car park and was again favoured by fortune: the car started, uncharacteristically, first time. Damn – he had not collected the papers! Should he go back? It would mean missing the German. If the German turned out to be a non-starter, the day would have been wasted. Yet he had a feeling the German was very much a runner. In spite of the limp.

To hell with the papers! He put the Opel in gear and was moving out of the car park as another car, a Citroën, passed the entrance, going rather too quickly. It braked sharply in front of the main building and a man got out in a hurry, crossed to the German and spoke to him. Coming closer, Conway saw the startled look on the German's face, then the shake of the head. The other man spoke again, pointing to the car peremptorily, obviously giving orders. The German shook his head again; it was equally clear he was refusing. Conway, thoroughly fascinated, pulled in behind the Citroën and quickly got out of his own car.

'I repeat: it is an order!'

The German said, 'I have other orders!'

'You refuse?'

'Certainly I refuse.'

The other man hesitated, then saw Conway approaching, climbed quickly into the Citroën and drove away.

'Still want a lift with me?' Conway asked.

'Thank you.'

'Then get in.' Was he mistaken, Conway wondered, or had this tough-looking German actually looked a little afraid? As he put the Opel into gear and moved off, he said, 'Your friend didn't look very pleased.'

'No.' A single, determined syllable. Conway knew the signs: it would all have to be quarried from this monosyllabic member of the master race. All right, then, he'd start digging. Name first: never forget the who-when-where-why-what? 'My name,' he said, 'is Conway. Joe Conway. And I'm not English.'

The German turned grey eyes on him. They were hard, narrow eyes and they stared out over a nose of some determination, beneath which was a wide, flat mouth. 'You are what?'

'Irish.' Conway pursed rueful lips. The German had gained information and given none. He pressed on. 'Matter of fact, it's a town in Wales.'

The German said, 'What is?'

Conway stretched his hand across, offering it to be shaken. 'Conway,' he said.

There was a moment's pause before the hand was gripped, briefly, but quite hard. 'Rasch,' the German said, adding, 'you are persistent.'

'Blame my mother,' Conway said. 'Always told me people had to be properly introduced. It's a habit now.' Mentally he tucked the name away. Rasch . . . it seemed to strike some deep and distant chord but memory let nothing come up. 'Been to Stockholm before?'

'No.'

'Oh, but it's a fine city,' Conway said, laying on the Irishness. 'I hope you'll have time to look around it.'

'I hope so, too.'

'How long are you staying?' The German had turned in his seat and was now staring at him. He glanced across and saw that Rasch was smiling. Or perhaps *not* smiling; it was more a movement of the lips. 'Is this a conversation,' Rasch asked quietly, 'or an interrogation?'

'Just passing the time of day,' Conway said, moving his gaze back to the road. 'The Irish are like that, you know. Can't abide silence.'

It was plain that Rasch could not only stand silence, but liked it. Conway said insolently, 'Mind you, the Germans can be a rowdy lot,' and glanced again at his passenger, thinking that he looked about as rowdy as the scalped skull

41

in the Historical Museum.

'You know us well?'

'Lived there two years,' Conway said. 'Berlin.' Once more he'd given more than he'd got damn it! 'I hear it's a bit of a mess, now.'

'Yes,' Rasch said. 'It's a mess now. But since you wish to talk, tell me about Sweden.'

'There's a lot to tell, and it's not much farther into the city,' Conway said. 'But briefly – there's a shortage of almost everything unless you can make it out of trees. You can have a million boxes of matches, but you only get forty-five cigarettes a week. We read big fat newspapers and drink coffee substitute. But steer clear of ersatz tea. Takes your shoes off from the inside.' It was only four and a half miles from Bromma Airport to the Grand Hotel and already he had covered half the distance. He said, 'How bad are things in Berlin?'

A pause, then Rasch said, 'The people are fed.'

'They know, do they, that the war's lost?'

'Unless they're fools.'

Conway looked across at him in astonishment. No German ever replied affirmatively to that question, though he always asked it. Replies usually contained references to secret weapons and the Führer's genius. Well, at least the day wasn't wasted. He'd got his story now. Still perhaps it could be improved. 'How long will it last?'

'Berlin?'

'The war.'

Rasch thought about it. 'Three months. A little more.'

'Not a nice prospect.'

'No.'

Conway not only had his story. He now had a strong feeling that there were other treasures to be mined from this 'remarkable' German. 'Perhaps you'll have dinner with me tonight?'

'I doubt if I'll be free.'

'But if you are?' Conway pressed.

'Then, perhaps I shall do so.'

'Here we are,' Conway said as they came in sight of the Grand. 'I'll telephone a bit later to see if you're free.'

As the German went into the hotel's ornate main entrance, Conway drove round the corner, parked the Opel and went in at the side door, hurrying to the press room which the Swedish Foreign Ministry had established in two of the hotel's salons. He hung up his coat and went over to the girl secretary on duty in the centre of the room, whose charm could and often did sweep away barriers that prevented correspondents doing their job.

'Do you think,' he asked, 'that there might be a room here tonight?'

She raised an elegant eyebrow. Conway might work in the press room at the Grand Hotel; he did not look like a guest. 'You would be very fortunate.'

'They wouldn't give *me* a room at all,' Conway agreed candidly. 'But you'll get one if there's one going. Book it for me, there's a good girl.'

She picked up the telephone. 'Double?'

Conway looked offended. 'Twelve kroner for a single's bad enough.'

She spoke into the phone, then nodded at him. He went to sit at a desk, composed his cable quickly and sent it to the *Daily Express* in London.

The porter who showed him up to his room looked pointedly for a suitcase and even more pointedly for a tip and therefore had a disappointing few moments. In the room, Conway used the telephone to ask for Rasch's number and when Rasch answered said, 'I'm staying here tonight, anyway. Room 209. Let me know if you're not engaged for dinner.'

'I don't know yet.' Rasch's voice sounded angry, and having spoken, the German hung up immediately.

Conway swore. It looked as though his money might be wasted. Damn and blast the bloody German! Damn and blast Stockholm, too, and the Grand Hotel! As his eye flickered angrily round the expensive room, he thought, in for twelve kroner, in for twenty – and asked room service to

43

send up a bottle of aquavit.

Conway had avoided the hotel's reception desk; Franz Rasch approached it with confidence. The hotel clerk looked down the list of reservations and said, 'Herr Rasch? No, sir, I'm sorry. No booking.'

Rasch said, 'Look again. It was made by the German Embassy.'

The clerk looked. 'No, sir. Nothing here. I'm sorry.'

'And you are full, of course?'

'I'm afraid so, sir.'

Rasch's voice hardened. 'The manager, please.'

An under-manager appeared as if by magic, listened, and was instantly apologetic. He knew about this, he said. 'The booking is in the name of Herr von der Schulenberg. I regret the clerk was not informed of this.'

'So do I.'

'Porter!' The under-manager, apologetic and briskly efficient at the same time, wanted Rasch on his way. He turned to get the room key, but the key slot was empty.

'Where is it?' To the clerk.

'The gentleman took it. Herr von der Sch – '

Rasch said, 'He's up there now?'

'Yes, sir.'

Rasch spent a pleasant few moments at the hotel shop. He had been issued with temporary ration cards at the immigration desk at the airport, and he bought a little chocolate and a cigar and charged them to his account before following the porter to the lift and to his room.

The porter, having no key, had to knock; when the door opened, Rasch strode in. A portly man stood beside the door.

'Tip him,' Rasch ordered. 'I have no money.' He waited impatiently and, when the porter had gone, said, 'Who are you, and what is all this about?'

The man said sharply, 'You are here in direct disobedience of orders. Why did you not return to Germany as instructed?'

Rasch said, 'I do not jump every time some thug in a

raincoat tells me to jump. My orders were given to me this morning in Berlin.'

'And by that Communist journalist at the airport no doubt. They are countermanded.'

'So your thug said.'

Von der Schulenberg looked at him angrily. 'You know who I am?'

'I imagine so,' Rasch said with studied rudeness. 'You could only be the local Gestapo corporal.'

'Chief,' von der Schulenberg said steadily. 'Gestapo chief in Sweden. Now – listen to me. I have orders from Berlin that you are to return – '

'Stand to attention!' Rasch barked suddenly.

'To you?'

'To the Oak Leaves to the Knight's Cross,' Rasch said. 'As the Führer ordered.'

Von der Schulenberg put his hand in his pocket and smiled. 'You'll be stripped of it. And everything else. That is what happens to traitors.' The hand came half-way out of the pocket and Rasch glimpsed the bluish steel of an automatic pistol. He took a single pace, swung his heavy stick backhanded and heard bones crack.

As von der Schulenberg fell, whimpering with the instantaneous and hideous pain of his crushed hand, the telephone rang. Rasch, tempted to ignore it, decided not to. It would be interesting to see who was telephoning the Gestapo chief. Or, for that matter, who was telephoning the traitor Rasch!

Of all people it was the talkative Irishman, wanting to know if he would be free for dinner. What a question for a man wanted by the Gestapo!

Rasch stepped close to von der Schulenberg, kicked him deliberately and very hard in the abdomen, then bent, took the pistol and slipped it into his pocket. For good measure, he kicked the writhing figure again before he picked up his luggage and left.

Throughout, he had moved slowly, almost lazily, but accurately, with the controlled ease of a man who does

45

physical things well. Now as he strolled down the hotel corridor towards the lift, his casual appearance concealed a mind at war with itself: half of it awhirl with shock, the other half intent upon restoring order. The approach at the airport and the gabbled instructions to return to the Junkers and fly back to Berlin, had worried him not at all. The messenger had clearly been of low authority and bureaucratic mix-ups had become commonplace in recent months. But to be called a traitor by von der Schulenberg was another thing altogether. Rasch did not personally place high regard upon his decorations, but others did, including the Führer, and von der Schulenberg must have been very sure of his ground if he felt free to sneer and threaten.

As he came to the lift, Rasch halted, momentarily confused as realization struck. There was nowhere for him to go. Not just nowhere in the hotel, or nowhere in Stockholm or nowhere in Sweden or Germany: *there was*, Rasch realized in that bleak moment, *nowhere in the world for him to go*.

The Irishman! Room number what? He'd given the number . . . yes, two, zero nine! Rasch's finger was on the lift call button when he changed his mind. He used the stairs, thinking as he went up that von der Schulenberg had referred to a 'Bolshevik journalist' at the airport. Conway? Rasch halted on the elbow of the stair. Conway seemed an unlikely Bolshevik. But the Gestapo, whatever else they might be, and however inaccurate their assessment of Rasch himself, were usually well-informed. Still, Bolshevik or not, there was nowhere else to go.

Chapter Four

Hearing the knock, Conway somehow knew who was outside. When he opened the door, there was no surprise at who stood there. He had a quick impression that the big German was breathing a little quickly and looked changed from the figure he'd left not long before. Before Conway could speak, Rasch was pushing past him into the room.

'Close the door.' And as Conway hesitated, 'Close it!'

'All right.' Conway obeyed warily, watching Rasch. 'You,' he said after a moment, 'look as though you've had a nasty shock.'

Rasch grunted. He was at the window, staring out towards the royal palace.

'Bottle of aquavit there,' Conway said, pointing. 'Have one if you fancy it.'

Rasch quickly crossed to the little side table, ripped the seal from the bottle and poured. Conway, who noticed such matters, particularly when the liquor being poured was his, saw two inches of schnapps go into the tumbler and then down Rasch's throat in a single swallow.

'Have another if you want it.'

'No.' Rasch drew his hand across his mouth. 'That was good. I am grateful.'

'Anything else I can do?'

Rasch half-turned his head and looked at Conway. 'Will you lend me a little money?'

Conway grinned. 'That's how you lose friends. The answer's no.'

That grin, which bracketed him immediately with all the bar room scroungers who must inhabit Conway's world, produced a flash of fury in Rasch, as he made himself smile and shrug. 'You could give me directions perhaps?'

'Certainly. Where to?'

'I want to go – ' Rasch stopped. He didn't know where Count Bernadotte's house was, damn it, and he was damned if he'd give the Count's name to Conway.

'Difficult, is it?' Conway said. When Rasch had first brushed past him, there had been a kind of wildness, controlled but very much there, that had made Conway nervous. Now he felt a little more confident.

'No.'

'My mistake. You look as though you might be a bit out of kilter.'

'What's that?'

'Off balance.'

Rasch looked hard at him, wondering what these inanities were about. 'I'm perfectly all right.'

'Good,' Conway said. 'If you want another quadruple aquavit, just help yourself.'

'Thank you. I had enough.'

'I'll say.' Conway paused. Rasch's temper was visible, there, in the eyes. He said, 'Let me guess. That business at the airport. Whatever it was, something else has happened since you got to the hotel.'

'No.'

'Then what the hell are you doing here?' Conway said. 'You come barging into my room like the wild man of Borneo, you're all nervous and alert, you swallow half a bucket of spirits and try to borrow money and then you tell me there's nothing wrong! I didn't come across the lake on a bloody bicycle!'

Rasch glared at him for a moment, then swung his head away.

'What I don't understand,' Conway said, 'is all the melodramatics. You've got a room of your own. Why use mine? You want directions but you won't tell me where.'

Rasch's mind seemed to be flying, thoughts flashing across it like some firework display, and burning out, too, just as uselessly. He felt bereft, abandoned, helpless. His eyes fell on

48

the telephone. 'From here, can I telephone Berlin?'

Conway nodded. 'Easy. After seven o'clock it's dirt cheap, too.'

'Now,' Rasch said.

'Costs a bit more.'

Rasch picked up the phone, and Conway protested: 'It will get charged to my room.'

'I'll pay!'

'Who will you borrow the money from?' Conway said rudely. The instinct he'd first felt at the airport was as strong as ever: he suspected there was the story of a lifetime to be got out of this big German if he could find the key to it. Another instinct insisted the key was pressure. It was risky, but he was sure it was true. If he kept pushing, something would emerge.

Rasch slammed down the receiver and fumbled angrily in a pocket, bringing out a handkerchief. He unfolded it carefully and extracted a brooch in which stones glittered. 'Look.'

'Might be chain store rubbish,' Conway said.

'Damn you!'

Maybe, Conway thought, it was time to bend a little. 'I'll believe you. Officer and gent and all that.'

'Thank you.' It was half-meant, half-sarcastic. Rasch snatched up the receiver and asked for a number in Berlin.

'If it's private, I'll leave you to it,' Conway said, and went off into the bathroom.

Rasch listened to the Stockholm operator routing the call, to the clicks on the line, to the Berlin girl repeating the number, to the ringing sound.

Then: 'Yes?' Schellenberg's voice, surprisingly clear.

He said, 'It's Rasch. I'm told there's a change of orders.'

'Where are you?'

'Stockholm, where else?'

Schellenberg said clearly, 'The new orders come from the Prinz Albrechtstrasse.'

Rasch felt his heart lurch. So there was no mistake!

'You have been criminal and disloyal,' Schellenberg was saying, 'to have associated yourself with traitors like Oster and von Stauffenberg. You must, of course, return at once. Your oath leaves you no alternative. You understand?'

There was a click. Schellenberg had hung up before Rasch could reply. He stared at the receiver in his hand. That morning, God, only that morning, Schellenberg had shaken his hand. Now . . . He replaced the phone, his arm feeling leaden and slow.

In the bathroom, Conway too replaced the receiver. Excitement had brought sweat to his forehead and dried his mouth. He stood still for a moment, going over the words that had been spoken, and wishing he knew the identity of the speaker in Berlin. The Prinz Albrechtstrasse he knew all about: Gestapo headquarters. Orders from the Prinz Albrechtstrasse were Gestapo orders. Von Stauffenberg was the man who'd tried to kill Hitler with a bomb in July. And Rasch was associated with him! Then the oath? There were a lot of oaths. The German army had sworn one to the Führer, the entire army, man by man. Personal loyalty. Was that the oath? Or was it the other one, the SS oath? My Honour is Loyalty. The voice in Berlin had said, 'Your oath leaves you no alternative.'

Conway leaned against the bathroom wall and had to swallow saliva twice, in rapid succession. His mouth had been desert dry; now it was swimming. Rasch was dangerous and desperate. He had to get out of the bathroom, out of the bedroom, into the corridor and out of Rasch's way. And do it quickly. If Rasch guessed for one second that Conway had been eavesdropping . . .

He flushed the toilet cistern and went quietly into the bedroom. Rasch lay on the bed, eyes open, motionless, staring up at the ceiling. Quietly he crossed the room and went out, expecting every second that the figure on the bed would come to sudden life, seize him, silence him. Sweat coursed down Conway's back. His palm was almost too slippery to turn the door handle! But he was in the corridor, inhaling deeply in relief, hurrying along to the stairs and down towards the press room. When he'd been there earlier, he'd seen Sven Borg of the *Dagsposten* at one of the desks, and

Borg was just the man he wanted.

He looked for him hopefully, failed to see him, and felt suddenly very alone. Then Borg came back into the room from one of the washrooms. Conway crossed purposefully towards him.

Dagsposten, the Nazi morning paper in Stockholm, had very little influence but was greatly valued by Berlin because it was an authentic part of the Swedish press and could be quoted as such. Newspapers in Germany could report its shrieks of hate against Roosevelt and Churchill as 'Sweden condemns Roosevelt' or 'Sweden exposes Churchill's lies.'

Sven Borg's Nazism was, if anything, more rabid than his paper's. He behaved, and occasionally sounded, like an extension of Josef Goebbels into Sweden. A gold swastika decorated his lapel and his conversation was peppered with admiring references to Hitler. He was a walking textbook on the Third Reich and an authority on military matters.

'Hello, Sven,' Conway said.

The Swede gave him a curt little bow. Borg was used, and knew he was used, by other members of the Stockholm press corps. In a way it was part of his duties, but he didn't particularly enjoy it.

'I know I'm asking a hell of a lot,' Conway said, 'but I wondered if you had ever come across a name. A German soldier.'

Borg smiled. 'There are, of course, many millions.'

'I know. But I've an idea he's rather special,' Conway said. 'Name of Rasch.'

'Rasch,' Borg repeated thoughtfully. 'Rasch . . . let me see . . .'

Conway watched his eyes and said, '*Franz* Rasch.'

The eye flicker was instantaneous, but Borg maintained the posture of thought. He was deciding whether or not Rasch could safely be described.

'Ah, yes,' Borg said after a moment. 'Franz Rasch, you say? I have it now and he is indeed rather special, as you put it. Rasch was with Skorzeny at the Gran Sasso when Mussolini was stolen from under the Allies' noses.'

'*Was* he!' Conway injected admiration into his tone.

'A very brave soldier,' Borg said. 'He holds Oak Leaves, I think, to the Knight's Cross.'

'You wouldn't,' Conway asked, 'happen to have any cuttings?'

'I believe they might be found,' Borg said, and then, suspiciously: 'Why do you want to know?'

'I'm doing an article on war heroes.'

'For whom?' Borg wasn't going to have fun made of German heroes.

'South America. An agency in Buenos Aires. I'd heard of this man Rasch somewhere,' Conway went on, 'and I thought he'd make a change from Galland and Hannah Reitsch and Skorzeny.'

'*Signal*,' Borg said. 'There was once an article in *Signal*.'

Signal, the German army magazine, was kept on file in the Press room. Borg turned over its pages rapidly. 'Let me see. Nineteen forty-three. September was it? Perhaps October . . . yes, here.'

Conway looked at the picture. Benito Mussolini, the fallen Italian dictator, wearing a black hat and overcoat, stood with the German commando unit which had parachuted to his rescue to the top of a high mountain in the Abruzzi. Mussolini, jut-jawed and looking relieved, was shaking Skorzeny's hand. Skorzeny wore a grin of pride. Also grinning, and on Skorzeny's left, stood an unmistakable Franz Rasch.

Borg said, 'I think he was on the Budapest raid, too. The one on Admiral Horthy's palace.'

Conway looked up, smiling. 'Thanks, Sven. Very helpful. He must be a very brave man.'

'Oh yes.' Borg agreed eagerly. 'And there are many others.'

'I know.'

'If you need information . . .'

'I'll come to you, naturally.' Conway bent his head over the article. He'd picked up a bonus: Borg knew nothing about Rasch being in Sweden, or about any Gestapo involvement, and Borg would know when anybody knew. He read the article with growing interest. When he'd finished he sat in one of the armchairs and thought about Franz Rasch and about whether he dared return to his room.

Finally, he didn't. In the hall, he showed his room key to the girl at the telephone desk and asked her whether any calls had been made from his room.

She looked surprised.

'It's all right.' Conway slipped a coin unobtrusively across the counter. 'A friend's up there, and if he's made any calls he's going to pay for them. That's all.'

'I see, sir.' She checked her list. 'There was one call to Berlin.'

'I know about that. Any others?'

'Just one. Oh, I remember that, sir. He asked me to look up the number of the Swedish Red Cross.'

Conway smiled his thanks. He went back into the press room, sat at a typewriter and, after a moment's thought, began to type rapidly. When he'd finished, he put the single sheet of paper in an envelope. The secretary on duty was the same girl who'd booked the room for him. She said, 'Comfortable?'

'It's giving me ideas above my station,' Conway said. 'Listen, will you do me a favour?'

'If I can.' Her manner had at once become more withdrawn. There were a lot of bachelor correspondents in Stockholm and many of them seemed to ask that kind of question.

Conway gave her the envelope. 'It's addressed to me, as you'll see. If I don't pick it up by Thursday, will you give it to Reginald Urch, of *The Times*?'

'This is *very* mysterious, Mr Conway.' She was amused; she enjoyed mysteries.

'Wait for the dénouement! But listen, don't give it to anybody but Urch. And I'll probably want it back.'

She nodded. 'All right.'

He thanked her, went into one of the telephone cubicles and asked for his own room. There was no immediate answer and for a moment, Conway thought Rasch might have left. But then the phone was lifted and a voice said, 'Well?'

'Is that Mr Rasch?' Conway asked sweetly.

Silence.

'It's Conway,' he said. 'Perhaps I should have asked for Hauptsturmführer Rasch?'

Still silence. Conway, listening, heard breathing. He said, 'I'm a journalist. No point in my giving you away. Not yet.'

Still silence.

Conway said, 'If you need help, maybe I can help you. Maybe you can help me in return.'

At last Rasch spoke. 'How?'

'I've told you – I'm a reporter. Now listen: I know most of what there is to know about you. I know who you are, and what you are, and I listened in to your call to Berlin. Now I'm coming up to the room. But I warn you: attack me and you'll be given away instantly. Understand?'

Silence. And after a second or two, a click.

Conway debated with himself. To go into that room was a risk. Rasch was a trained killer in a dangerous situation; he was twice Conway's size, fit and strong and for all Conway knew, armed. Not that he'd need arms! Conway swallowed, and went to the lift. If Rasch decided to bolt via the stairs, that was an end of it. In a way, Conway half-hoped he would: hoped that Rasch with his temper and his SS efficiency and the danger he represented would vanish into the night, or into the arms of the Swedish police, or be anywhere but waiting silently in the room. As he came out of the lift and walked along the corridor, he felt like a man going to his own execution.

His thoughts were mirrored in the mind of the man on the other side of the closed door. Rasch felt as though he had been kicked in the stomach. Body and mind ached. Conway's words on the telephone, the extent of his knowledge, had astonished Rasch. Where on earth could Conway have found out so much so quickly? Conway claimed to be a journalist, but that was an ideal cover. In reality he could be an agent of some Swedish security department. Or, as von der Schulenberg had said, an agent of the Bolsheviks. The fact that he was Irish, if he was, had no bearing; in many countries aliens were used on security work, or as spies, for the most obvious of reasons. Conway could be anything! Even Gestapo? No, but the thought lingered.

In those first seconds after he'd hung up the telephone Rasch had indeed briefly contemplated flight. Along the corridor, down the stairs, out into the street . . . But where *then*? And who would be waiting? Von der Schulenberg *was*, as he had claimed, Gestapo, and it was more than likely other Gestapo men would be waiting for him. Not openly, perhaps, as they would in Germany, but discreetly, in cars or windows, behind newspapers. As Rasch looked around the hotel room the walls seemed to be closing in, as they'd done in a story he'd once read as a child. He was disgraced, friendless, without resources of any kind. The word suicide crept into the edge of his consciousness and he recognized it and shook his head impatiently, driving out the word and its meaning.

Then Conway knocked. Why, when he had a key, did he knock? Rasch, knowing a lot about fear, guessed the answer. The voice on the telephone had been tremulous.

Rasch opened the door. It occurred to him that the Irishman was showing courage, even if all the trumps were in Conway's hands.

'I suggest,' Conway said, 'that we both sit down.'

'Very well.' Rasch lowered himself on to the bed, leaving the easy chair for Conway.

'Now,' Conway began.

'You said "not yet",' Rasch said quickly. 'There would be no point, you said, in giving me away. Not yet. What does that mean? When will you do it? When would there be a point?'

Conway sat stiffly, upright and awkward in the soft chair. His face felt stiff, as though his cheeks had been caked in plaster and it had dried out.

'It means I won't give you away, as long as our interests coincide.'

'Do they coincide?'

'They can be made to.'

Rasch looked at the uncomfortable man in the armchair. He felt tension all over his body and resented it; in particular, he resented Conway's ability to cause that tension.

'I think not. You and I have nothing in common, Mr Conway.'

Conway watched the arrogance flowering. Always the same, these people, he thought. He said, 'You're SS.'

'Waffen SS,' Rasch was swift to correct.

Conway shook his head. 'It's a fine distinction and the Allies don't accept it. The SS has been declared a criminal organization. All of it.'

'The Waffen SS are fighting soldiers!'

Conway shook his head, smiling slightly. 'Criminals,' he said. He repeated it a second later with slow emphasis. 'Criminals. There are to be no distinctions.'

'What do you mean?'

'When Germany loses the war,' Conway said. 'That's *when*. It's also when all SS men, Waffen SS or not, turn from criminals in the state's employ to criminals on the run, because by then the state will have collapsed.'

Rasch stared at him angrily. He felt like a cat being admonished by a mouse. Conway, staring back, was conscious of the fineness of the balance.

'Not,' Conway said, 'that you need worry about that. Not yet. Your problem is to stay alive *now*.'

'I shall surrender myself,' Rasch said, 'to the Swedish authorities. They are neutral. I am a combatant. They will intern me.'

'And hand you over to the Allies as soon as the war's over,' Conway said. 'The Swedes know which side their bread's buttered on.' He was by no means certain what Sweden's attitude might be. The Swedes' independence and neutrality had been cleverly defended. He sought only to gauge the state of Rasch's mind, to pinpoint the end of temper and the beginning of bluster; it was important to judge rightly.

But there was no bluster as the German said coldly, 'Don't try to frighten me, Mr Conway. Where do our interests coincide?'

Conway said, 'You have a story I want.'

'What story?'

'The man in Berlin said you were involved with Count von Stauffenberg. That means the attempt on Hitler's life. That's the story I want.'

'It had nothing to do with me. Or I,' Rasch said with emphasis, 'with it.'

'I suppose that,' Conway sneered, 'is why they've ordered you to return. Because you weren't involved. That's why those men were at the airport. They were trying to arrest you, weren't they?'

'You don't understand,' Rasch said, and the words carried a superiority, an air of patronizing condescension, that made Conway's teeth grate.

He said, 'It's you who don't understand. You don't begin to guess what kind of trouble you're in. For instance, if Berlin formally requests your return for an attempt to murder the head of state – '

'Sweden wouldn't listen,' Rasch said.

'You forget you're a soldier,' Conway said roughly. 'You've sworn an oath of loyalty. You're different. And if they ever did get you back across the water, what then, Hauptsturmführer Rasch, Knight's Cross with Oak Leaves?'

'I'm aware of the penalties. But to return to this proposal of yours, Mr Conway, how can I tell you about the Bomb Plot when I had nothing to do with it?'

Conway said, 'We thrive on rumour. A few facts would go a long way.'

'I have no facts.'

Conway stared at him. 'Things you've been told?'

'No matter how inaccurate?'

'In Sweden for years we've had to rely on hearsay. This is no different.'

'It would be fiction,' Rasch said.

'Think about Kipling and Conan Doyle. Fiction can be very well paid.'

They sat looking at each other. As the silence stretched, Conway found and offered his cigarette packet. They were coming towards agreement.

Rasch inhaled. 'And you. What would you do for me?'

'Help, if I could.' When Rasch looked doubtful, he added, 'Damn it, that would be in my interests, wouldn't it?'

'Would there be money?'

'Certainly.'

'Which we would share?'

'Yes.'

'How much?'

'Impossible to say.'

They were silent as though by consent. Rasch was struggling with the implications of a thought that had struck him a few seconds earlier. He'd come to Sweden to deliver a packet to Count Bernadotte. Very well. Folke Bernadotte was one of the most powerful men in Sweden. If he delivered the packet and at the same time demanded asylum, could it be refused? Yet Conway seemed so sure the Swedes would hand him over, if not to the Nazis, then to the Allies, later. Would they? That might depend on the contents of the packet. Well, Bernadotte was head of the Swedish Red Cross, so it was scarcely likely to be the plans of the V-2 rocket! More likely some humanitarian information. Perhaps about prisoners. Yes, that was likely! Prisoner exchanges were exactly what Schellenberg might be working on. That would be characteristic Schellenberg, determined to finish up reeking of roses!

Rasch broke the silence. 'I'll tell you what I know. It isn't much, but I'll tell it to you. In return I shall require very little.'

'You want what?'

'A ride in your car.'

'Where to?'

'To the home of Count Folke Bernadotte,' Rasch said.

'Wasn't he at his office when you telephoned?' Conway asked quietly. And as Rasch looked surprised, 'I know most things about you.'

'The Count is a friend,' Rasch said.

'No, he's not.' Conway shook his head. 'You'd have telephoned a friend at home, you only made one phone call. To his office.'

'You seem to specialize in absurd deductions,' Rasch said. 'He would be at his office at that time.'

'I specialize,' Conway replied, 'in information. Sometimes it's news.'

'And sometimes,' Rasch said, 'you specialize in spying for the Bolsheviks.'

Conway laughed.

'You claim you're not a spy?'

'Rumours keep circulating. I was an American spy, once, so they say. I suppose your local intelligence boys saw me at the Soviet Embassy?'

Rasch said, 'You'll drive me?'

'After I get the story.'

Rasch knew a good deal more than he pretended about the bomb attack on Hitler at Rastenburg and its bloody aftermath. In telling the story to Conway, he left out most of it and invented a few titillating details, among them a beautiful blonde countess who had gone with her lover to the gallows.

Conway's eyes were gleaming with pleasure as he made notes. 'Great stuff,' he kept saying. 'Marvellous!' It occurred to Rasch that it must be easy to be a journalist.

Finally he said, 'That's all I know.' For a little while Conway asked questions and Rasch answered them. Then they were ready to go.

Conway could have double-crossed Rasch, could have given him the address and taxi fare and a fond farewell in the safety of the hotel's lobby where there were plenty of people about. He chose not to because the same indefinable instinct which, earlier in the day, had correctly sensed Rasch's importance now told him there was more, and better to come. Nor was it merely instinct. If Bernadotte was not a friend of Rasch, then Rasch must be, could *only* be, a messenger of some kind. And if Bernadotte was accepting furtive messages from men on the run, then Bernadotte had changed since Conway had last seen that patrician performer, at a news conference. Bernadotte was humanitarian, no doubt about that. But he was an aristo to his fingertips, proud as Lucifer and accustomed to the diplomatic niceties. Conway was prepared to bet that an unexpected night-time knocker on Bernadotte's door would be frostily received.

Folke Bernadotte was not in the telephone directory, but it was easy to look him up in the press room. Conway and Rasch then slipped out of the hotel via the glass-enclosed summer veranda, unused at that time of year, walked briskly in the direction of the station, and were lucky enough to find a taxi.

They sat quietly as the car wound through the streets. Twice Rasch looked through the rear window, each time shaking his head in response to Conway's glance of inquiry. They were not being followed. It seemed too easy, and it was; when they reached Bernadotte's house, a man loitered ominously nearby. There was no way of knowing who he was: Gestapo, Swedish security, police – the man could be anybody. But his presence made it impossible simply to walk up to the door.

'Find a telephone,' Conway told the driver. They should have telephoned before they'd set out and he'd said so, but Rasch obviously had wanted to do it the dramatic way, presenting himself on the doorstep.

Conway was excluded from the telephone box; Rasch merely demanded coins and went inside, folding the door closed after him. Conway, hoping to hear what was said, stood listening for a few moments in the cold, but as it became clear he would hear nothing, he went back to the warmth of the taxi.

Rasch's face, when he returned, showed his disappointment. There was little need to ask, but Conway did so, his manner deliberately needling. 'He was glad to hear from you, I suppose?'

'He's away, so they said.'

'That's what they always say,' Conway said, with the memory of a thousand brush-offs. 'Did they say where?'

'Abroad for several days.' Rasch answered almost dully.

'Is he?' Perhaps there would be a story here; Bernadotte was news. 'When will he be back?'

'They don't know.'

'They never do. Who answered, man or woman?'

'His wife.' Rasch lied. He was only half listening, and seething with anger. Bernadotte's secretary had never heard his name and no arrangement had been made for a visit from a representative of Herr Schellenberg. And Schellenberg must have known that Bernadotte was abroad!

Conway thought about his next words before he spoke. 'Hell of a way to treat your husband's friends,' he said sympathetically. 'But they say Swedish women are like that. She sounds typical.'

'She was.'

'You should have spoken to the American,' Conway said.

Rasch turned his head, eyes threatening. 'What American?'

'The one Bernadotte married. We'd better talk a bit more, don't you think – now that you haven't any friends left!'

In the corner of a quiet café they drank a fluid which tasted like beer and called itself beer but was virtually non-alcoholic. Conway had paid, as he had paid for the taxi, as he would have to pay, next morning, for the room at the Grand Hotel; he was beginning to resent it. The fact that he'd got one good story was already half forgotten. Conway was greedy.

He was also disappointed. Rasch sat morosely opposite him, staring into his glass as Conway kept probing. Often Rasch's response to a question would be no more than a shrug or an irritated glance. But the questions were having an effect on Rasch's mind. What part of Germany was he from? On the screen of his mind the scenes appeared, the East Prussian countryside, the old trees, the buildings he would never see again. The wound – where had it happened? Rasch thought of the hope there had been on the night before the push in the Ardennes forest. They'd been wearing American uniforms, driving captured jeeps, ready for murderous fun, feeling as they'd felt before the Gran Sasso adventure, keyed up and laughing and dangerous. But the Ardennes had not been like that. The Ardennes had been Russia all over again; snow and mud and an enemy of massive strength who could not be outwitted and must be fought even though he was by far better equipped. Conway's quiet question about wife and family dragged open the emotional door on Lisel, his wife, a door he had thought safely closed. She went flickering through his mind in pictures, eager, shining, golden, mangled by a bomb.

Conway, astonished to see moisture in Rasch's cold eyes, recognized despair but misunderstood his man. He was *still* concerned to defeat Rasch mentally, unaware that Rasch had already begun reforming his mental forces as though they were a shattered unit, and like a good officer, seeking sustenance and supplies for them. So that when Conway said, 'There is nowhere for you to go, nowhere to hide,' he was no longer pinning Rasch down; instead he was pushing him towards the only available sanctuary.

'I can go,' Rasch said suddenly, 'to the Russians.'

They talked about it. Conway didn't care one way or the other. Rasch could surrender himself to Saharan Tuaregs for all he cared, *except* that Conway wanted time to milk Rasch's mind, so he had to argue against, and argue hard. Russian atrocity stories came trundling out, and Conway knew plenty; there was no need to invent.

Rasch, however, had the counter arguments ready. There was hardly a need to think: they were there in his brain. The Nazis said he had tried to kill Hitler and the Russians constantly urged Germans to do exactly that and join 'the crusade against Fascism.' They would welcome a military hero who was also a proven enemy of the Führer. The Committee for a Free Germany already existed in Russia, with General von Seydlitz and many of the Stalingrad veterans ready and anxious to recruit anti-Hitler Germans! Sitting there in the Swedish café, the idea had come to Rasch suddenly, and complete. As Brigadeführer Walter Schellenberg had predicted in his operational memorandum to Dr Ernst Kaltenbrunner, realization that all the other exits from Stockholm were blocked would merely shine a spotlight brightly on the one that remained. Schellenberg had said with confidence that Rasch would soon realize he had no alternative but to surrender himself to the Russians. And already, on his first day in Sweden, Rasch had come to that realization. It was, in its way, a moment of triumph for Schellenberg. But there is a difference between a decision made and a decision carried out. Hauptsturmführer Franz Rasch was picking up his glass, intending to drain it and leave, with or without Conway, when he heard a sound and paused with the glass half-way to his lips.

Chapter Five

It was months since Rasch had seen a horse of any quality. In Berlin now there were only the nags that pulled the carts appearing on the streets as the petrol famine intensified. So that evening, he listened with real interest as outside an animal picked its unmistakably delicate way towards them along the quiet street. He knew he was not hearing the weary hooves of some dray; there was no cart, nor were the hooves heavy. He listened, revelling in the excellence of his ear. It was no pony; this beast would be big, fifteen to fifteen and a half hands, yet lightly shod: a riding horse. Police, perhaps? Possibly a thoroughbred or a hunter put to police service. How he *ached* to see a thoroughbred! He strode suddenly to the café door, Conway following as though jerked along on a string.

The police horse was coming level, and Rasch watched it with a sudden flood of pleasure: a beautiful gelding, black as coal, its neck a proud arch, its flanks gleaming even in the street lights. Conway, puzzled and watchful, heard what sounded like a sigh, and in some Irish horse-coper's corner of his brain, understood. He, too, watched as the beautiful animal stepped prettily down the street, away from them and finally round a corner. He said, 'They don't have those. Not in Russia.'

Rasch gave him a grin and Conway added it to the lengthening list of the German's emotional switches. In a very short time there had been everything from despair to delight, from indecision to resolve. You're bloody hard to follow, Mr Rasch, he thought. But I'm learning. 'Sit down,' he said. 'I'll get another beer.' And when the glasses were on the table, 'I'm fond of horses myself. Irishmen and horses go together.'

Rasch smiled. 'You saw his step? The muscles in his quarters?'

'I saw the depth of his chest.' Conway could talk horse with the best. 'Be quick on the flat. Delicate for a jumper.'

'I'd jump him.' Rasch looked at Conway. 'You know about horses?'

'I know a bit.'

'Do you know any Irish trainers?'

'A few.' He knew two, one who'd been in Germany, another who could scarcely be called Irish any more, and who had a stable not quite at Newmarket and a long record of warnings from the Jockey Club.

'Pat Donnelly?'

It was Conway's turn to grin. 'Now we *have* got something in common.'

'You know him?'

'I know him.'

'He had my horse, Grenadier.'

'In Germany?'

Rasch shrugged sadly: 'I don't know. He was in the Russian line of advance, so he was going to come to Sweden, but – '

'He's here,' Conway said. 'Came just before Christmas. He's rented some stables up by the racetrack at Ulriksdal.' Conway winced at the power of the fingers that suddenly grasped his arm, at the strength that dragged him unceremoniously to his feet. Rasch's hard eyes were suddenly blazing with excitement.

'How far?' Rasch demanded, and Conway had the feeling that if he had said Donnelly was on Mars, Rasch would have demanded to be taken there at once.

He wondered what the hell he was doing, allowing himself to remain in the grip of this madman. Either he'd been mad before he left Germany, or the day's savage twists had pushed his mind over the edge. And Rasch's strength was daunting, even terrifying. He was strong not merely in body and limb, but in his emotions and his enthusiasms. It was a little like being tied to the tail of a runaway horse, Conway thought, as he paid for the drinks, left the restaurant and found another taxi, all with Rasch urging speed and more speed.

The taxi-driver didn't want to go to Ulriksdal and Conway didn't blame him. He didn't want to go himself, though Donnelly would have whisky to dispense. But nothing would stop Rasch now and the only possible way to stay with Rasch was to go to the stables.

He said, 'There might be a bus.'

'Not at this time,' the taxi-driver said unsympathetically. 'It's half past nine. The last one's at eight.'

'Sure you won't go?' Conway said. 'We'd be very grateful.'

It sounded thin even in his own ears and the taxi-driver almost sneered as he said, 'There won't be a fare back. And I'm short of fuel. Have you any idea how little they give us? I have to make a living out of it!'

Before Conway could prevent it, Rasch had pulled the wrapped handkerchief from his pocket and was fumbling in it, dragging a diamond brooch into the light.

'Don't be bloody daft!' Conway said. He might have been talking to a wall.

'Diamonds,' Rasch said to the startled driver. 'All diamonds. Take us to Ulriksdal and you get one.'

The driver's surprise turned inevitably to suspicion, and Conway had to come smartly to the rescue. 'Drunk,' he said.

'I don't take drunks. Especially not to Ulriksdal.'

'Not for this diamond?' Rasch's urgency was almost overwhelming. His gloved finger pointed to a stone of at least a quarter carat. 'If you have a pocket knife I'll – '

Conway gave up. 'It's his,' he said. 'I suppose if he wants to give it to you, he can.'

'Ulriksdal it is,' the taxi-driver said, pulling out a penknife. 'But it's fare in advance.'

That both Conway and Rasch should have known the same Irish racehorse trainer, is not as unlikely as it sounds. The world of racing is a small one; every horse on every race-track in every country is descended from the same English thoroughbred stock, and Irishmen have looked after that stock and made their livings training and selling horseflesh for centuries in every country where racing occurs. From Dublin to New Delhi and Aintree to Albuquerque, Irish skill with horses has been enlisted by owners who want to win races.

Pat Donnelly, then, was in a sense merely another expatriate Irishman. He might have been in Kentucky or Melbourne. It simply happened that he had spent a good deal of his life in Germany, like his father before him. The senior Donnelly had opened a stable in the Prussia of the eighteen-nineties, as racing became fashionable in the Kaiser's kingdom, and had had to close it again during the Great War. But immediately after the Armistice in 1918, he'd returned to reopen it, and Ireland's status as a neutral republic had enabled him to keep it open despite the war. Given the choice, it is probably true that he would have returned to Ireland in 1942 or 1943. But he did not have the choice. While he himself might have gone, the horses would have had to stay where they were, and in any case, the racing business in Ireland was not in a particularly healthy condition.

When Donnelly opened the door of his wooden Swedish house at Ulriksdal, he found it a little difficult to believe what he saw. Conway alone would not have surprised him at all: Conway was always on the lookout for something and if it wasn't potential winners it was gossip about owners. Rasch, alone, would have been a little more surprising, at least here, in Sweden. But he knew very well, as did a great many other people, that Franz Rasch was just the man to turn up unexpectedly, as often as not with a metaphorical knife between his teeth. And sometimes, Donnelly knew, the knife might not be metaphorical.

But the two together did surprise him. 'I'm right,' he said, 'am I? It is Herr Rasch?'

Rasch grinned. 'I've come to see Grenadier.'

'Well you can't. Not tonight. I'm not letting cold air into his box. But you can come in for a minute.'

He sat them down. As Conway expected, Donnelly had

whisky, or rather whiskey, for it was John Jameson, peaty as could be, that he poured into their glasses.

Donnelly looked as though he'd been put on earth to play leprechauns. He always reminded Conway of Barry Fitzgerald, the Irish actor: small and gnomelike, with a mobile and expressive face that was wrinkled with sadness as he said, 'It's all a terrible mess, Mr Rasch. But I'm glad to see you got to Sweden. Do you have to go back?'

'No.'

Conway said, 'If he does they'll kill him. He's on the run.'

'On the – ?' Donnelly looked at Rasch, eyebrows rising on his forehead.

Conway said, 'He was one of the people who tried to kill Hitler. Or if he wasn't, the Gestapo believe he was.'

'Just tell me,' Rasch said, 'about Grenadier.'

'He's a fine big horse who's missing his best years. He could win races. And he will.' Donnelly wanted to talk about Rasch. Rasch was hard, fearless on horseback. 'What will you do, Mr Rasch?'

'I don't know.' Rasch preferred to talk about Grenadier. 'Talk about him tonight and see him, perhaps even ride him, tomorrow. How far can Grenadier go?'

'A good mile now. He's getting stronger all the time.'

'What you should be asking,' Conway said rudely, 'is how much the horse is worth.'

'A fair bit,' Donnelly replied promptly, 'even with the market low. Have you no money, Mr Rasch?'

'No.'

'No more have I, or not much. Sixteen horses to keep with barely a penny coming in.'

Conway said, 'He's got a bit of jewellery that looks valuable to me.'

'How soon can he race?' Rasch wanted to know.

'Here in Sweden? Not before May, and then it's only trotting. I've the chance to go back to Ireland, but if I take the horses the cost will clear me out and if I don't I'll have nothing to show when I get there. What will you do, Mr Rasch?'

'He's going to surrender to the Russians,' Conway said, and as Donnelly frowned in surprise, 'I told him he's mad. Maybe he'll listen to you.'

Donnelly did not much like being caught in agreement with Conway, but Conway was right. 'Don't go near 'em, sir,' he said. 'They're not to be trusted.'

'There's nowhere else.'

There was a moment's pause as Donnelly lit his pipe. Then, abruptly, he said, 'There's Ireland. How valuable's the jewellery?'

'The British would nab him in a minute,' Conway said.

'He could get a neutral ship out of Cork or Dun Laoghaire,' Donnelly said. 'There's plenty of places to go in South America.'

Rasch tried to return the talk to Grenadier and keep it there, but that proved impossible. Had he been the only one of the three with a question mark over his future, the other two might not have examined possibilities so determinedly. But all three faced difficulties.

A few minutes later, Donnelly had produced a sheet of paper and a pencil, Rasch had produced his two brooches, and rough calculations were being done, over-optimistically and under the influence of more whiskey. It was clear none of them could guess either the value of the brooches or do more than guess at the value of such horses as might be sold in Sweden.

Conway said, 'It's pointless.'

'Is that all you've got to contribute, Mr Conway?' Donnelly demanded. 'If so, go. And remember to keep your mouth shut.'

'I'm not the one with things to tell,' Conway said sulkily. 'He is. There's money in what's in his head.'

'What do you mean?'

Rasch said, 'He means selling stories to newspapers.'

'I'm talking,' Conway said, 'about you and Bernadotte and the reason you came to see him.'

'That's why you came?' Donnelly asked Rasch. 'To see Bernadotte?'

'To see if I can get asylum here.' Rasch felt an odd re-luctance to say more. He also felt tired and lethargic from the whiskey and the warm fire.

'He brought a message,' Conway said. 'Must have done.'

Donnelly frowned. 'Let me get this straight. I thought he was on the run. Then you say he came to see Bernadotte.'

Conway said, 'When he left Berlin this morning he was a messenger. When he got here they'd decided he was a traitor and they tried to arrest him.'

'Who did?'

'Gestapo men at Bromma Airport, just hours after he left Berlin,' Conway said. 'Big change of mind, it was.' He frowned and snapped his fingers suddenly. 'Hang on a min-ute. That was no change of mind!'

'If it was, then it was a quick one,' Donnelly said. 'Is that really what happened, Mr Rasch?'

'It's what happened,' Conway said with mounting excite-ment. 'Take my word for it.'

'Is it, Mr Rasch?'

'Yes.'

'Will you bloody well listen!' Conway was excited. 'How did they get the message through from Berlin? By telephone. Okay, they phone Stockholm after the plane's taken off. How long did the flight take, three hours?'

Rasch began blinking and shook his head to clear it. 'Yes.'

'They were quick, then, weren't they! Just about the second you've taken off they're on the phone to the Gestapo here telling them to arrest you. Why bother? Why not turn the plane back if you're a dangerous criminal?'

'That makes sense,' Donnelly said to Rasch.

'There's a lot more than that,' Conway rushed on. 'Look at the geography. Half the trip you're over German soil or German water and there's Denmark, which is German-held territory, to the west, and not far to the west at that. They could have radioed the plane to land at Copenhagen or somewhere. So we can assume the message wasn't sent until the plane was over Sweden, right? And in that case they really did get a move on! They'd got to find their men in the middle of the day in Stockholm and get them out to the airport. Also it's a messy way to do things. Look at it this way: they want to arrest somebody like you, a big man, tough, war hero-commando type who can handle himself. Would they try to arrest a man like you in public at an airport in another country? Why not wait until you come back, and do it then?'

Rasch, on his feet now, was hanging on every word. 'Go on.'

'Well, when they tried to arrest you, they didn't make much of a job of it, did they? What was it, please come with us Mr Rasch and naughty-naughty when you didn't? Is that Gestapo behaviour? Christ I was in Berlin in the 'thirties and I saw them at work a time or two. There was no gentle tapping of shoulders. It was knock 'em down and throw 'em in the wagon!'

The force of his own logic had been carrying Conway along, but only now, quite suddenly, did he see the destination. He almost shouted: 'You fool. You've been fixed!' He looked at Rasch's face, now stony, the eyes narrowed, and said slowly and with emphasis, 'You were sent here to be arrested. No, half a minute, you were sent here so they could fail to arrest you. So you'd think you were a hunted man. But they haven't done much hunting, have they? We haven't seen hide nor hair of them!'

'But that is *impossible*!' Rasch was almost whispering. He glared at them, eyes moving from Donnelly to Conway and back again. 'Why would they do it? Why to me?'

'Another thing,' Conway said. 'Christ, why didn't we see *this*? They've sent him over with *something*. It doesn't matter what, not for the moment. But now he knows he's a wanted man and he's on the loose with whatever it was they sent.' He turned to Rasch. 'What was it?'

Rasch said, 'But it was Schell – '

'Something for Count Bernadotte wasn't it?' Conway said implacably. 'They sent you over with the big secret to be delivered to him. Then they tried to arrest you and failed.

So now you're tearing round Stockholm thinking the Gestapo's after you. But they aren't. Not even when you leave the hotel. So what *are* they after?'

'It's crazy!' Rasch said. Fury and anguish were fizzing inside him.

Donnelly, watching and listening in amazement, said, 'I don't believe a word – '

'*He* does,' Conway said triumphantly, looking at Rasch. 'He knows I'm bloody well right.' He snapped his fingers again. 'I feel like some kind of clairvoyant. I can see the whole damn thing, clear as daylight. They've got you in Stockholm, all right? They've just told you your whole life's in ruins so you're off balance. You've got something important. You can't go near the British or Americans because you're SS. The Swedes won't want to know you for all the reasons I gave you earlier. That leaves who?'

Rasch said, 'It's ridiculous!'

'Is it? What did you decide to do?' He looked at his watch. 'An hour and a half ago, in that café, what did you decide to do?'

'I don't believe it!'

Conway slapped his forehead and laughed shortly. The whole thing was so obvious now. '*You* don't believe it, so you carry conviction. But it's not you who's intended to believe, is it? It's the people you go to. And there's *something* they have to believe! Something you know, or have been given. Something you're unlikely to give to Bernadotte because you'll be on the run. In any case you won't get near Bernadotte.'

'I tried,' Rasch said. 'That shows – '

'Yes.' Conway said. He let the sound linger. 'It shows you had something for him.'

'Nonsense!' Rasch spoke almost with passion, but his certainty was cracking under pressure. 'You speak as though it is all a plan. Yet I am here with you. Are you part of the plan?'

Conway smiled. 'You think I met you by accident?'

Rasch stared at him.

'Last night,' Conway said with relish, 'I was telephoned and told that a very interesting passenger would be on today's flight from Berlin.'

'Last *night!*'

'That's right, Hauptsturmführer Rasch. The whole thing was in train last night!'

'You're making it up,' Rasch accused him, though now with less conviction. It was his emotions that were having difficulty in accepting Conway's interpretation of the day's events; his brain saw the straight lines for what they were.

'No,' Conway said. 'Somebody calculated that if certain things happened you'd go to the Russians. Who was waiting at the hotel when you got there?'

Rasch didn't answer.

'Somebody *was* waiting!'

At last he gave in. The evidence was all there and pointed in only one direction; every objection could be met.

'Somebody predicted how you'd behave,' Conway said. 'Not very flattering, is it?'

'Who could do it?' Donnelly broke in. 'You can't say what any man will do, just like that.'

'Imagine,' Conway said. 'There's a river flowing through a valley. The sides are vertical and fifty feet high and the water's flowing at ten miles an hour. If you drop somebody in, which way would he swim? Yes, well they've dropped Hauptsturmführer Rasch in. Right in! And he did exactly what they thought he'd do. It answers all the questions but two.'

'And they are?' Rasch said.

'What were you carrying, and who gave it to you? No, there's a third question.' He turned triumphantly to Donnelly. 'Did you say I'd nothing to contribute?'

There was still a little persuasion to be done. The habits of half a lifetime tend to cling, even when their motivation has been ripped away, and Rasch found himself still reluctant to produce the two envelopes from his pocket. But as the night went on he was persuaded and the papers were examined, discussed, pored over. One set of papers was incomprehensible to them, but appeared to be a record of share deals through a German bank. They had no doubt about its importance, however, because it was apparent to all of them that the other document, a small booklet full of names, was both very important and highly dangerous. It was Rasch himself who eventually solved the mystery of why German intelligence should be supplying information to its most implacable enemy.

He cursed Schellenberg for furious and fluent moments before the others quieted him and they could all begin, again, to try to decide how to make use of the strange gift that Fate had offered them.

An hour later, heading for the lavatory, Conway saw the telephone, remembered the 'precautionary' letter he'd left for *The Times*'s correspondent, phoned the Grand Hotel and told the girl to tear it up unopened.

When he rejoined Rasch and Donnelly, the atmosphere in the room had changed. The tension was now tinged with zest. It struck Conway immediately that they must look like a group of conspirators. And he enjoyed conspiracies . . .

Chapter Six

When the Second World War began, Ireland did not have a merchant marine, relying as she did on British ships both for her supplies and for her limited export trades. By 1945 however, a small fleet of merchant ships had grown out of the necessity to maintain some sort of overseas trade that was not dependent upon the powerful neighbour across the Irish Sea. It was one of this small fleet, a fifteen hundred ton cargo vessel named *Lady Gregory* which arrived in Gothenburg to pick up a cargo of telegraph poles to replace the ones whose bases had rotted in Ireland's bogs through the years of the war.

When the *Lady Gregory* left two days later, she carried two passengers, one of whom was perfectly outfitted with an Irish passport, a Begorrah-but-it's-the-grand-mornin' manner, and a scheme he believed would make him rich. The other passenger, who limped, had boarded the ship at night, an hour before she sailed, and carried papers which would cause his immediate detention by either of the powers through whose blockades the ship must pass, if they were to find him.

The *Lady Gregory* was stopped and boarded shortly after her departure by a German E-Boat based at Frederikshaven in Denmark. Her captain, a Leutnant of the Kriegsmarine, was intrigued.

'I have not your flag before seen,' he said in English, to the *Lady Gregory*'s master, who promptly poured large glasses of a fluid named *The Paddy* and said, 'Damn the English.'

The German beamed, drank the toast, was presented with the bottle and gave the cargo of forty-foot, de-barked, pine logs a cursory examination before departing.

Several days later, the Royal Navy was just as perfunctory.

The British officer who came on board was also intrigued by the Irish ship and he, too, was happy to drink a glass before taking a quick squint at the telegraph poles-to-be and departing. On both occasions Rasch was shoved into the chain locker, which was uncomfortable and very cold, but proved to be as safe a place of concealment as the captain had predicted it would be.

It was late on an afternoon in February when Conway disembarked at Dun Laoghaire, gave a farewell wave, and went to take the bus into Dublin, where he registered at a small hotel close to the university. The immigration officers had given him ration coupons, some of which he surrendered at the hotel, having said he intended to stay for several days. At nine p.m. he was back at Dun Laoghaire to wait for Rasch to come ashore with those members of the crew who were bound for an evening's drinking ashore. There was no trouble. Rasch simply slipped past the dock gate policeman, remained with the others until they turned a corner, and joined Conway.

They had been extremely lucky. Conway, to whom luck was an unpredictable thing that seemed to come and go in more or less equal quantities, found himself slightly irked by Rasch's serene acceptance of it. The longer the luck continued, the more Conway became irritated, and Rasch more composed. The *Lady Gregory* had sailed easily through two separate blockades; in the other sense, Franz Rasch had sailed through, too. The second stage of difficulty would come, it had been expected, from their encounter with Donnelly's sister, Mrs Monaghan, who lived in a high old terrace not far from Jury's Hotel. With cheerful malice, Donnelly had painted her as a querulous old harridan surrounded by priests and deeply suspicious of anything connected with her brother. In fact they found her to be a remarkably pleasant elderly lady who spoke with affection of her brother and everybody else, with the single exception of the British, whom she hated.

The fact that Rasch was German concerned her not at all.

'I just hope,' she said, 'that you're going to do the bloody British a mischief.'

Conway assured her that was precisely their intention.

'I hope so,' she said fervently. She might, Conway thought, have been offering her hopes for the success of a church social.

'So we can stay?' he asked.

'Oh yes. Half the house is Donnelly's anyway, so I couldn't stop you.'

Rasch was installed in an upstairs room at the back of the house. He would have to remain indoors, but would be otherwise secure from any kind of prying, and seemed unconcerned. 'I shall think of myself,' he said, 'as a prisoner of war.'

The moment Rasch was safely installed, Conway left. He went to the public library, checked reference books, and departed for Belfast. The credentials issued to him in Stockholm proclaiming him to be an accredited correspondent of the Argentinian newspaper *La Prensa* successfully carried him through the border check, and on arrival in Belfast he immediately inquired how soon the next boat left for England. He took the overnight boat to Heysham and the first morning train to Manchester, and visited the *Daily Dispatch* newspaper where he talked his way into the library and examined one or two files of newspaper cuttings.

He was now ready to begin.

Keith Ulyatt, chairman and managing director of Ulyatt Bros Ltd, had had a good war, though not in the sense that he had fought hard and bravely, for in fact he had not fought at all. Ulyatt's 'good war' had been good because it had been profitable. He had been comfortably off in 1939; five and a quarter years spent manufacturing ever-increasing quantities of serge-type cloths in khaki and two shades of blue, had made him, in the words he sometimes used, 'not exactly stinking rich, but bloody prosperous.'

It was clear to him that the war would be over quite soon,

though it was not possible to put a date to it and Ulyatt faced the prospect of peace with confidence. He had made one fortune outfitting millions of men for war and was now ready, willing and positively eager to make another by kitting them out for peace. The prospect that every soldier to be demobilized was to receive a complete outfit of clothes, including hat and socks, had delighted textile manufacturers everywhere and after the war, when such things became available again, Ulyatt intended to buy himself not just a new Bentley, but one whose coachwork had been made on bespoke terms by Messrs Mulliner.

'Who is it, Susan?' Ulyatt asked his secretary with a trace of irritation, when the telephone rang. 'I'm a bit busy.'

'The War Office, sir.'

'Better take it, then, eh?' Ulyatt said good-humouredly. More orders, he thought. War Office telephone calls usually meant rush orders, urgent work, and profit. 'Hello?'

'Mr Ulyatt?' said a voice.

'Speaking.'

'Mr Keith Ulyatt?'

'That's right.'

'Can anybody hear this call?'

'No,' Ulyatt said, puzzled. 'I don't think so. Why?'

'Your secretary?'

'What's this about?' Ulyatt demanded.

'If I were you,' the voice said, 'I'd check. This is important.'

'Wait, then.' Ulyatt put down the telephone, went through into his secretary's office, gave her half a crown and sent her out for cigarettes. Then he returned to his own office and closed the door.

In the minute or so away from the telephone, he had tried, and failed, to think of a reason why this secrecy should be demanded.

'Right, what's all this about?'

'Nobody else is listening?'

'No.'

'Then *you* listen, and listen carefully. In Germany there is a list with your name on it. If it is captured you'll be in trouble. I'll telephone you again, calling myself Major Mills.' There was a click as the caller hung up.

Ulyatt's secretary, returning minutes later, found her employer sitting at his desk, staring at his empty blotter, and with his head resting in cupped hands.

She put down the cigarettes and change. 'There you are, sir.'

He said nothing, which was unusual; he was a please-and-thank-you man.

'Are you all right?' she asked, a little anxiously.

'Eh?' He looked up at her, eyes a little slack-focused. 'Oh, yes. I'm all right. Just thinking, that's all.'

Thinking was hardly the word to describe the frantic search for meanings that had been going on in Ulyatt's head. The white blotter mocked him by failing to provide words, or even hints of words. As the minutes went by, Ulyatt began to realize that the search was bound to be a failure, that no alternative existed. If the Germans merely had him on some list of textile manufacturers, it didn't matter, and they were hardly likely to keep lists of Worshipful Masters, however much they might hate freemasonry. No, there was only one list in Germany that could be dangerous to him, and Ulyatt could guess what it was. Bertram Road, he thought. Why the hell couldn't I have been born somewhere else!

Bertram Road, however, had not come into it until long after the first contact had been made. *That* had been very ordinary: an inquiry from a company agent in Hamburg as to whether Ulyatt Bros could supply some samples of barathea and doeskin fabrics of quality wool. In black. The year had been early in 1937.

Samples had been sent, the order received and attended to, the goods sent off. Everything was most satisfactory said the polite note from the firm in Hamburg, and Ulyatt replied to say that if more fabrics were required, Ulyatt's could supply almost anything in woollen cloth at highly competitive rates and faster than the opposition. There had been more orders.

He had spent the summer holiday of 1937 in Germany. He liked to take a late holiday and nose along the Rhine, drinking wine here and there. On the way back he'd called on the Hamburg agent, who told him further orders were likely to be forthcoming, invited him to dinner, and asked what Ulyatt thought about the New Germany.

'Impressive,' Ulyatt said, meaning it. He had been a regular traveller for many years and like most businessmen he approved of thrumming factories, crowded shops and the generally busy air that prosperity always had. The Germany of the late 'twenties and early 'thirties had sickened him, much as Britain in the depression years sickened him.

'And the Führer?'

Ulyatt was interested in production, not politics. 'If he can turn Germany round like this, he must be pretty impressive, too.'

After the holiday, Ulyatt returned to Bradford, and driving home from the station, saw two children playing in a street behind a mill, neither wearing shoes. The sight was not novel to him; he'd seen shoeless children daily for years, and in normal circumstances would scarcely have noticed, but he noticed that day and in a note of thanks to the Hamburg agent, mentioned the children and the contrast.

The firm received more German orders. Ulyatt was delighted. It was work for people in Yorkshire and it was evidence of greater prosperity in Germany which might, with luck, spread to other parts of Europe. In the *Yorkshire Post* he read of the squabblings within the Conservative Party with disgust. He'd no time for any of them. While they chattered and nattered and tried to kick each other's bottoms, the country was still down. Hitler, on the other hand, had really got Germany moving, and old Musso had done the same in Italy.

Ulyatt was invited to the German Embassy in London. It was the first time he'd been invited to any embassy anywhere, and he and his wife were flattered and pleased, the more so when Joachim von Ribbentrop himself shook his hand and said he had heard of the fine quality of the cloth Ulyatt made.

A little later that evening a voice at his elbow said, 'Mr Ulyatt?'

He turned. The man was tall, slim, dark, rather fine-featured.

'You're from Bradford, I believe, Mr Ulyatt.'

'Yes, I am.'

The man smiled warmly. 'Allow me to introduce myself. Wilhelm Bohle. I am – '

'I know who you are,' Ulyatt said. He turned to his wife. 'Darling, Herr Bohle is a Minister at the German Foreign Office. And he was born – ' he turned and grinned at Bohle ' – that's right, isn't it, Herr Bohle?' Bohle grinned too, and nodded. 'He was born in Bradford, in Bertram Road. Just off Oak Lane.'

Shirley Ulyatt knew Bertram Road, and wouldn't have lived there for a king's ransom. 'You weren't!'

'Oh, yes.' A moment later he was bowing over her hand, and she said, 'My husband was born there, too.'

'No!'

They discussed the coincidence at some length, and the Ulyatts were invited to lunch with Bohle the following day. Bohle had left Bradford at an early age to live in South Africa, but he said, 'What man is not sentimental about his birthplace?'

Ulyatt, who was not, agreed, and was delighted to discover that Bohle actually knew something about cricket and Rugby football, having played both at school in South Africa.

He had made a friend, a friend, moreover, in a very high position in a country that was clearly going to be massively powerful and successful. When he got home, he wrote a note of thanks to Bohle and promptly received a letter back, handwritten, on Foreign Ministry paper, inviting him to call on Bohle, if, at any time, he should be in Berlin.

He made it his business to be in Berlin within a month, and

found himself entertained lavishly. Because he was a local councillor in Bradford, he was given an extended tour of several of Berlin's municipal undertakings, and was shown the master plan for the development of the greater Berlin which was Hitler's dream.

He dined with Bohle the night before he left and was asked what he thought of the things he had seen. He said, 'Breathtaking. I wish Britain was half as wide awake.'

Bohle smiled. 'Waken her yourself.'

'Hardly,' Ulyatt said. 'I'm nobody's politician really. But when I look round here, and then go back to Bradford, I can tell you, it's enough to make you sick.'

'Perhaps we'll be able to help, one day,' Bohle said.

'Can't be too soon for me. You're the people we need.'

He found himself in steady correspondence with Bohle. Several times more he visited Germany and each time was entertained well and shown new marvels. He knew the Jews were under severe pressure, he knew there was a steady trickle of refugees into Bradford from Germany and he had met some and heard their stories. But he was dazzled. He was also mildly anti-Semitic in the joking fashion of the time. There was a harsh saying in the Bradford wool trade that if the company was called Jones and Smith Ltd, it was British, if it was called British something-or-other it was Jewish. Ulyatt, who was not a cruel man, or an uncaring one, simply shut his eyes. Nor was he alone in preferring the gleaming picture of resurgent Germany to the grubby realities of life in a Britain still deep in the inertia of the depression. He visited both Austria and Czechoslovakia after the Nazi takeovers, but by this time Ulyatt was seeing what he wanted to see, and no more.

The correspondence became more serious. Bohle began to ask for details of production capacity unused in the textile trade, for details of the new Bradford water reservoirs – a scheme in which Ulyatt had been involved and of which he was proud – and other matters. He supplied the information cheerfully. There was no question of spying; he and Bohle were merely having a discussion on paper of problems that interested them both. And then, one day, Bohle wrote: 'All Europe will come, sooner or later, to see how well the German social system works. Inevitably, they will join with us and we with them. We offer the unique mixture of Joy and Strength and we have both, in plenty. I should like to think that you will help to bring it to Britain, which surely needs the healing magic of National Socialism.'

Ulyatt, with visions of mills and sheds in Bradford humming as the factories were humming in Germany, replied that he would be only too delighted to help. Should he, he asked, join some political party to help – Mosley's British Union of Fascists for instance?

No, Bohle wrote back. It was the knowledge of Ulyatt's spiritual support that was so valuable; that and the knowledge that National Socialism had true friends in Britain.

The 'spiritual support' lasted through the rape of Poland. Ulyatt was sorry for the Poles who faced tanks on horseback but his admiration was for the *Blitzkrieg*. The sudden smash through France and Belgium in 1940 he admired even more, especially when it was contrasted with the pathetic performance of the government, the War Department, the French. If Hitler was coming, he was doing so with the maximum of rapid success and the minimum of bloodshed, and when he crossed the Channel the pattern could be expected to continue. The incompetents would be chased out, and the wheels would begin to turn again. In June of 1940 he received a postcard. It had been posted in Lisbon and was signed Bill, but he knew the sender's handwriting. It said, 'Be with you shortly.'

Bohle, however, was not with him shortly. It was rumoured that Ernst Wilhelm Bohle had been appointed Gauleiter of Britain by Hitler and was waiting in France to cross with the German invading forces. But the German invasion forces did not cross. They could not cross until the RAF had been shot out of the skies, and the RAF was very conspicuously present in the skies. It was at about this time, with Churchill in Downing Street and German aircraft dropping bombs on the crowded streets of the East End of

London, on women and children, that Ulyatt began slowly to realize that perhaps, after all, he had been on the wrong side. But not until the late autumn, when the Battle of Britain was over, and the prospect of invasion had gone, at least until the following year, did Ulyatt recover himself. Possibly the process was helped or speeded by the fact that after the postcard he never heard from Bohle again.

By Christmas of 1940 he was surprised at the way he had been deceived; by the spring of 1941 he was disgusted at the way the wool had been pulled over his eyes. From that point on, a newly-patriotic Ulyatt found that patriotism could be squared with profit. Yet the correspondence with Bohle lurked, nagging, at the back of his mind. He was terrified that one day it would come crawling out into the open. He knew he was not the only man in the British Isles who had admired Hitler, but when the nightmare occasionally visited him, he saw himself as the only one who would be punished. Apart, perhaps, from Lord Haw-Haw.

And now the day had arrived. The voice on the telephone had said, 'In Germany there is a list with your name on it. If it is captured, you'll be in trouble.' He could imagine the list; his name and address, his company's name; words like 'sympathizer,' phrases like 'promises to assist us.' Ulyatt tried to work out what Major Mills was up to. It sounded like blackmail, but was that possible? How could the list be destroyed if it was in Berlin? And if the list were not to be destroyed, if it were captured, what then? He could see himself on trial for treason.

Ulyatt passed the remainder of the day in mental agony. Every time the telephone in his office rang, and it rang frequently, his heart began to pound. Between calls he sat waiting for it to ring again. There was a time when he contemplated telephoning the police and confessing all: if he made a clean breast of everything they might be merciful, after all, it was years ago. But what if they weren't? What if they took, as the police so often did, a very serious view? There was a war on; he had supported the enemy. In his mind he could see the rope.

At half past five his secretary put her head round his door to say good night.

'Have you left the phone switched through?'

'Yes.' She looked at him in surprise. She always switched it through and had never forgotten.

'Are you quite sure?'

'Yes, Mr Ulyatt.'

'Check before you go.'

She gave him another glance over her shoulder, but his attention had gone. What was he so worried about? Maybe he'd got himself a girl friend? She half giggled to herself as she checked the position of the switching lever on her telephone.

It rang five minutes later.

'Hello!'

'Anybody listening?'

Ulyatt's heart thundered. 'Major Mills?'

'Listen to me. The price is ten thousand pounds.'

'For what?'

Major Mills said, 'Your peace of mind.'

Ulyatt, desperate to be sure, said, 'You spoke of some list. I don't know what you're talking about.'

'I'm talking about collaborators. Stay where you are. I will telephone again.' Major Mills hung up.

Ulyatt sweated through the next minutes, all his fears confirmed. It *was* some list Bohle had made! Ten thousand pounds for what, if the list was in Berlin?

Major Mills had not said when he would telephone again, merely that Ulyatt should remain where he was. Ulyatt remained rooted to his chair.

Not until just after seven did the telephone ring again, and by that time the switchboard girls at Ulyatt Bros had also left and he had had to arrange for a special line to come through to his office.

'You're alone?' Mills asked.

'Yes.'

'Tomorrow when the bank opens you will withdraw ten

thousand pounds in notes. If you are asked why you are
doing so, you will say that it is for a business transaction. The
notes should be of small denomination and for preference,
used. After that – do you know the telephone boxes by the
bookstall at Exchange Station?'

'Yes.'

'Of the two, you will go to the one nearest the platform. I
will ring at eleven o'clock with your instructions.'

'If I don't?'

'Then the document will go at once to the Ministry of
Defence.'

Despairingly Ulyatt said, 'But how do I know – '

The voice said, 'Just do as you're told.'

Ulyatt lit a cigarette. He had difficulty with the packet
and worse difficulty with the box of matches. His fingers
were out of control and so, in some degree, was the rest of
him. He trembled in sudden spasms, his shoulders suddenly
cold. His scalp sweated and crawled. His feet sweated too,
and his armpits; he could smell himself. Ten thousand
pounds was almost all he possessed and it was not, in any
case, available in cash. He would have to take the money
from the firm's accounts, then do some swift manoeuvring
immediately afterwards to replace it or the police would be
after him on another score.

He did not tell his wife, and spent an unnerving evening at
home, fidgeting as he tried to read or listen to the radio. His
wife would find some way of blaming him and the burden
was heavy enough without her further recriminations,
especially when her enthusiasm for the Germany of the
'thirties had more than equalled his own.

Next morning, the manager of the Midland Bank in
Market Street was surprised. He invited Ulyatt into his
office and asked with that undertaker's sympathy bank
managers can show, whether anything was wrong. There was
bank money in Ulyatt Bros, and the manager was concerned
to know that it was safe. There was also the safety of the
cash. It was, after all, a very large sum, and for a man to
carry it about was *most* unwise, as Mr Ulyatt would surely

appreciate. Could the manager supply some sort of escort? There were one or two burly men on his staff who . . .

But Ulyatt insisted and got his money. At eleven o'clock he was in the telephone box, deeply anxious, and embarrassed too because he'd already been in the box for five minutes, pretending to make a call, and the small queue that had already formed outside was showing every sign of impatience.

The phone rang precisely on the hour. 'Ulyatt?'

'Yes.'

'On the platform beside you is a train which leaves in two minutes. Get a platform ticket and board the train. Find a window on the right hand side. At some point on the journey you will see beside the track a man holding a small suitcase in one hand and a green trilby hat in the other. When you see him, drop the money out of the window of the train.'

Another second and Ulyatt would not have heard a word. As the voice finished speaking the vast, Victorian, girdered roof of the station echoed and shook to the blast of an engine venting steam. As the sound died away, Ulyatt said, 'Please say that again.' But the line was dead.

The red Platform Ticket machine was right beside him. He fumbled for coins, bought the ticket and went through the barrier, with the ticket inspector watching him suspiciously. The guard was already standing away from the train, ready to wave his flag. Ulyatt jumped hurriedly aboard and began to move forward through the carriage as the train moved off. Standing in the space at the end, he let the window down on its leather strap. 'Small suitcase, green trilby,' he muttered to himself. The train was climbing out of the city, going slowly. He looked forward, through the billowing smoke, feeling his eyes begin to sting. God, he might miss him! But no, there he was . . . the suitcase, the hat.

Ulyatt never saw the face: the man kept his head down, the trilby brim pulled low; but he saw him pick up the parcel, tar-paper wrapped, tied with mill-band. In throwing almost every penny he had to a stranger, Ulyatt had felt an odd compulsion to make the parcel strong, just in case. In case of what? he thought sadly to himself as the train headed for Wakefield.

Conway had watched the train labouring up the incline. If Ulyatt's heart had been thumping the night before, Conway's was thundering now. It occurred to him that the strain on the blackmailer was almost as great as that on his victim. The danger of traced calls, and waiting police, could be anticipated but not countered. He had been alone with the detail of his scheme, dependent upon it for his own safety. The idea that Ulyatt should drop the money from a moving train had been one of a number put forward by Rasch when the generalities of the scheme were being discussed. He wondered where Rasch had learned these little technical ingenuities.

The train came nearer, on a left hand curve that effectively screened the rear coaches. Damn, he thought. I should have considered that. But as it straightened, Conway could see the window down, the pale face staring out. He lifted a hand to his hat and peered through his fingers, careful not to look up or reveal anything of his features. With satisfaction he saw the parcel fall and stepped forward to pick it up, then turned and climbed over the blackened brick wall with its tin notice about the penalty for trespassing on railway property. A few moments later he was on a swaying tram, heading back to the city centre. There, before he caught the Manchester train, Conway posted to Keith Ulyatt a piece of paper cut from Wilhelm Bohle's list of British collaborators-to-be. It was part of the page containing Ulyatt's name, business and address, and the envelope was marked MOST PRIVATE AND CONFIDENTIAL. TO BE OPENED BY ADDRESSEE ONLY.

Later, in the locked toilet compartment on the Manchester train, as he struggled with Ulyatt's almost impenetrable little parcel, Conway was thinking that at least Ulyatt would feel he had something to show for his money, even if the only person to whom he could show it was himself. As he slipped the wrappers off the bundles of crackling white five-pound notes, and for the first time in his life found himself with *real* money, *substantial* money, *big* money in his hands, Conway found himself feeling powerful. The first encounter had been faced and fought and won.

He was eager for the second. But still in his mind was a tiny, nagging doubt.

He should have heeded it.

Chapter Seven

The journey was long, uncomfortable and tedious. Trains and boats were crowded, smelly and run-down through years of over-use and under-maintenance. Such food as was available was poor, and Conway regurgitated it during a particularly rough crossing of the Irish Sea. Vomiting miserably, he thought of the money in his case, and decided he wouldn't rather be dead, but it was a near thing. Once again he crossed the border easily on the Belfast-Dublin train. The journey was uneventful, merely uncomfortable.

Conway, however, was irritated that the journey had to be made at all. It was Rasch who had insisted on it, and no words of Conway's had been able to dent his stubbornness. The source of their disagreement was Conway's reluctance to keep on making crossings of the Irish Sea. It was natural enough, but it clashed head-on with Rasch's determination not to let any of the papers out of his possession.

'It's bloody silly!' Conway had expostulated. 'Every time I cross that bloody border, I'm taking a risk.'

Rasch was unmoved. 'When you come back with the first money, I give you more names and the appropriate pages of the list.'

'Yes, but it's wasting time. If I took three or four over there, I could approach them all on one trip, and – '

'And vanish with the money.' Rasch finished the sentence for him.

'I wouldn't do that!'

'You won't be able to,' Rasch said. 'The first lot of money comes here and stays here while you go back for the second.'

'And if you take the money and vanish?'

'How can I? I can not even leave the house.'

The distrust was born not of hatred, but of what they were doing. They were an ill-assorted pair in so many ways that everything about them seemed out of balance. Yet partners they must be. And in a way, there were facets of each man's character that the other came close to admiring. To Conway, Rasch's sheer strength and physical capacity were always awe-inspiring, though no longer so continuously frightening. Rasch was surprised and pleased to discover that Conway, who on their first meeting had seemed ratlike and gutless, had turned out to be quick-thinking and ingenious.

It was lunchtime when Conway reached Donnelly's sister's house, knocked and was admitted. 'Do things go well against the English?' Mrs Monaghan asked him, round-faced and beaming, with whispered malice.

'First-class,' Conway said. 'We'll make the Brits squeal like pigs before we've done.'

'Good lad.' She watched him walk towards the staircase and then said suddenly, conspiratorially, 'Do you want any help?'

Conway turned. 'Thanks, but I don't think so. I think we can manage. We have this plan, you see.'

She gave a little giggle. 'Oh, it's not me I was thinking about. There's not much a body like me could be doing. But, you see, I know some of the boys.'

Conway swallowed. He needed no one to explain who the boys were. The boys were the IRA, who had spent a frustrating war waiting to be called upon by the Germans to overrun Northern Ireland, and Conway not only didn't want to be assisted by the IRA, he prayed that they never even learned of his existence.

'Do me a favour,' he said softly. 'Tell no one. It's very important in this case that not a word should get about. People can talk, you know.'

'The boys never talk,' she insisted.

'Not even with a few pints inside them?'

'Not even then, not if they've any sense,' she said. 'Still, if you don't want . . .'

'Not, don't want,' Conway said. 'Mustn't. This has to be

two man work, one a lot of the time, with the other out of sight.' He hesitated then added, 'Trust me.'

'All right, I will. Don't you come from my own brother!'

Rasch stood at the top of the stairs. Conway said, 'Time to make my report,' and went up.

'Well?' Rasch said, as the door closed.

Conway put his suitcase down on the bed, opened it, took out Ulyatt's parcel, now retied, and said, 'See for yourself.'

A few moments later, Rasch was regarding the bundles of five pound notes with cool pleasure, passing them from hand to hand, allowing his fingers to enjoy the texture of the paper, and his ears to enjoy its characteristic crackle. He looked up at Conway. 'It was easy?'

'Easy as pie. Frightened out of his wits, I should think. He didn't even demand to see proof.'

'Surprising,' Rasch said. 'In his place, I would certainly – '

'You,' Conway said, 'have nerve. He hadn't. Must have gone straight to the bank the minute it opened.'

'And he threw ten thousand pounds out of the window of a train?' Rasch said in wonderment.

'He did.'

'After one telephone call!'

'Several telephone calls. But he had a guilty conscience.'

'I wonder,' Rasch said with rare humour, 'what that must feel like!'

The money was counted and checked. It was then placed in a safe deposit box in the vaults of a bank in Dublin before the next operation was discussed.

Rasch remained doubtful about Conway's prompt proposal that two candidates be tackled at once. 'But there wasn't any trouble,' Conway urged. 'I was there, and I know. The thought of being exposed as a collaborator turned his legs to jelly. Christ, they could hang him for it, and these people have positions to keep up!'

'Over confidence,' Rasch said.

The conflict arose because two small but splendid targets existed, virtually side by side, in Leicester and in Coventry.

To Conway here was an opportunity to remove the plumage from two birds with a single pluck. 'They're busy cities,' he said. 'It's a big conurbation, teeming with people. Nobody's even going to notice me, let alone find me.'

'Fighting on two fronts,' Rasch pointed out, 'is invariably fatal. Look at Hitler. Look at Napoleon.'

'Christ, I'm not about to invade Russia,' Conway said. 'I'm going to telephone two men who daren't own up to what they've done, and make discreet arrangements with them, that's all.'

'It is taking an unnecessary risk.'

'You're worried whether I'll bring the money back, that's all.'

'Certainly. I'm also concerned that you should actually get the money to bring back. It is too easy to make mistakes when the concentration is divided.'

'You,' Conway said feelingly, 'don't have to go backwards and forwards across the Irish Sea!'

There was no accommodation to be reached, and both of them knew it. Conway would either do as *he* wanted, or he would do as Rasch wanted; no half-way point or compromise existed. Rasch swore to himself because it was necessary to allow Conway a choice of names, but recognized at the same time that it was not just necessary but unavoidable. His own knowledge of the geography of Britain was not enough, let alone his knowledge of British life, of industry, of social patterns. Conway, having before him the opportunity to strike twice at roughly the same time, was not going to be deprived of it.

'After all,' he said. 'We agreed it's got to be a quick campaign. We can't keep it up for long, or something *will* go wrong. Let's strike as hard as we can, while we can.'

In the late afternoon and early evening he spent a good deal of time in the Dublin central public library, checking his facts. Britain and Eire might be separate countries, but much of their publishing was common to both and Britain's reference books were available in Dublin. He had a lot of checking to do and some notes to make. The notes were

93

primarily for Rasch, who remained unconvinced.

But late that night Rasch gave in, largely because he felt helpless. Conway was the man in the field; Conway was the man who *knew* the field; Conway was the man taking the risks. Above all, Conway had revealed surprising depths of shrewdness. How, Rasch felt, could he dictate the course to be followed? It was a novel experience for Rasch to be sealed off from the action, and he did not enjoy it. He felt frustrated and far from persuaded, but he conceded.

Conway left the following night carrying with him not only Rasch's good wishes but his formal agreement. Donnelly's sister had urged him, as he left, to make the English feel the pain. She surprised him, as Irishwomen often did, by the violence of their feelings about the British. Conway had no feelings at all about the British in general, though for two particular Englishmen he now entertained a certain anticipatory regard. He looked at them, he told himself, much as a man will look at a Rolls-Royce car, or a fox at a chicken.

Again he travelled by way of Belfast and it was there, as he waited for the boat, that for a little while he had a qualm. At the harbour he saw a cinema poster for an old Alfred Hitchcock film, *Blackmail*, and the word seemed to fly off the poster at him. Something about the lettering underlined the uncompromising meaning not only of the word but of what Conway was doing. Staring at it, he swallowed. Until now it had seemed merely a quick, slightly-risky way to grow rich: hardly crime at all, especially when the victims – no, not victims, he insisted to himself, the word was *targets* – especially when the targets were neo-Nazis themselves. He began to feel queasy and had to fight it. Damn it, the targets were traitors anyway. Yes, traitors! Condemning them violently in his mind, he almost contrived to feel virtuous. And he had a capacity to forget the inconvenient. As he crossed the Irish Sea, the poster's lettering faded from his mind.

He chose Leicester as a base, though not because he knew the city. Conway had been there only once before, years earlier, and remembered only being impressed by its cleanliness and self-confidence. Leicester was prosperous and had something of a reputation for smugness; people prided themselves on being self-contained. Strangers in Leicester were not immediately cross-questioned by nosey natives.

From the bus station he telephoned the YMCA, asked about lodgings and was advised that cheap ones were often to be found in the Evington district. He tried a house with a 'vacancy' card in the window, but the landlady's first question was 'What nationality?' He told her Irish, had the door closed in his face, and in a momentary flare of temper began to understand Donnelly's sister's attitude. But there was no difficulty at the next house he tried. It seemed clean and the woman who ran it was pleasant and homely. When he said, 'I'm Irish,' she smiled and said, 'I don't care if you're from Timbuctoo, me duck, as long as you've money and a ration card, and you keep your feet off the furniture.'

The house was also conveniently near to a public telephone box.

Halliday Engineering was a bigger enterprise than Ulyatt Bros. Harry Halliday, who now ran it, was a manufacturer of components for a variety of other industries. He made fuses for bombs and mines, bits and pieces that ordnance factories needed for tanks, and aircraft manufacturers needed for planes. Show him a piece of bent wire and he could tell you, more or less immediately, how much a thousand would cost, or half a million, and also when they could be delivered. He was an extremely practical production engineer. In a sense, he resembled Ulyatt in his dedication to manufacturing and machinery, but there the resemblance ended, apart from the admiration they had unknowingly shared for the methods of Adolf Hitler and the Nazi Party. Impatience with industrial recession had fuelled Ulyatt's conversion, but Halliday had come to it by a more curious route. Like Oswald Mosley, he was a Wykehamist. He had fallen under Mosley's golden spell at school and had followed him through the vicissitudes of an unusually complex political life.

When Oswald Mosley became a Conservative MP at the

unusually early age of 22, Halliday was a Tory. When Mosley turned Independent, independence blossomed in Halliday. Mosley's conversion to the Labour Party was instantly copied, as was his later adoption of Fascism. Through it all, Halliday, the disciple, remained unknown to Mosley the leader. From Winchester onwards, Halliday had worshipped from a distance. He had little time for political activity anywhere but in his mind – he was too busy manufacturing door handles and push-rods – but inside his head the loyalty remained constant. He joined no parties and discussed politics scarcely at all.

It was from Mosley he learned anti-Semitism. He read the newspaper accounts of the Fascist marches through the East End of London with a kind of sick excitement. He refused to deal with Jews or employ them, though in other respects he was known to be a good and even an enlightened employer. His attitude became known. Trades councils passed resolutions criticizing his refusal to employ Jewish people.

He was approached, inevitably by a visiting German industrialist, and the process of turning blindness to treasonable potential began. After a time, he was supplying a German contact in London with lists of Jews in prominent positions in the city. He knew most of them, some were even people he liked, but their names were listed. It was a compulsion, a putrefaction beneath the pleasant and competent appearance, but it was not a thing he talked about. In 1938 certain words were spoken to him at an embassy party in London; they rang forever in his head in some private little chamber where sounds never died away. 'When we come to England,' the blond young Aryan diplomat had said, 'we will demonstrate how to deal with them. And you'll get your chance, don't worry.'

Halliday prayed for the day.

What happened, of course, was not just that the day did not arrive: Halliday found himself, as a result of the system of direction of labour, *obliged* to employ Jews and many of them were refugees from Hitler. If there had not been two sides to his personality, as different as the head and tail sides of a coin, his mind would have been ripped apart. But when one side of his mind was dominant, the other was dormant. His anti-Semitism was to a large extent a matter for private and depraved pleasure, but it was forgotten when touching metal, examining engineering drawings, calculating rates of production. Throughout the war he worked long days and fell into bed exhausted. The anti-Semitism was there, and malignant, but Halliday was usually too tired to dwell on it as he would have liked. Sometimes he promised himself, as he climbed into bed, a private hour of hate, but usually he was asleep before more than a minute or two had passed.

Yet away from the sick dreams, Harry Halliday had a genuine idealism, without which there would have been no mainspring for his politics. It showed itself in a number of ways and he was known as a benefactor of a number of Leicester causes. He served on the governing bodies of two local schools and on the board of trustees of an old folks' home. He gave generously to the Boy Scout and Girl Guide movements and to the Red Cross and various animal charities. He was known to devote special care to the training of engineering apprentices in his company. Even when his failure to employ Jews was being commented upon in the late 'thirties, there were plenty of voices to praise him as, if not a model citizen, something very close to it.

Halliday first heard from Conway in the same way that Ulyatt had done: by telephone. There was a difference in that Halliday was more difficult to reach. Halliday spent most of his time on the works floor, yet he knew, before he spoke, that the stranger who had declined to give his name had already telephoned several times. The switchboard at Halliday Engineering was well-trained.

'If he rings again,' Halliday said, 'tell him I'll be in my office after seven for half an hour or so.' It was not unusual for people to telephone anonymously. Employees who wanted to report thefts or unjustified absenteeism often used the method and Halliday, who did not much approve, listened because he preferred to know what was going on in his factory, even if he took no action.

It was therefore in the expectation of learning about some new instance of multiple funerals for a single grandmother, that he lifted the telephone when it rang soon after seven p.m. and said, as he always did, 'Halliday.'

'Mr Henry Halliday?'

'Yes.' It wasn't often people referred to him as Henry.

'Can anybody hear what we are saying?'

'No.' It was more than any switchboard operator's job was worth to listen in to his calls and they knew it.

'There is a list produced by the Germans with your name on it,' the voice said.

'So?' Halliday was only half-listening. On his desk was a problem in metal stamping; there were savings to be made, and a good two-thirds of his attention was on it.

'Pay attention!' The voice was sharp, and Halliday blinked. He was not used to being addressed in that tone.

'I'm listening,' he said. 'What list?'

'You were one of the people who gave assurances that they would co-operate with the invading German forces. Stay where you are. I'll telephone again in a few minutes.'

It was blackmail, of course. Halliday knew it and identified it and thought about it while he waited for the caller to ring back. Like the problem in metal stamping, it was essentially an intellectual matter, and Halliday thought about it almost unemotionally. The question was how much the man wanted. He himself had a great deal to lose: freedom as well as reputation; if a government still at war chose to be vindictive, he could conceivably lose his life, though he thought it unlikely with the war so close to its end. The first question, therefore, was how much the man knew; the second, how much he would have to pay.

When the telephone rang again twenty minutes later, the voice said, 'You know what I'm talking about.'

'I absolutely deny – '

'Denials are pointless, Mr Halliday. I have original documents.'

Halliday nodded to himself. At least he knew now. 'What documents?'

'Lists compiled by Ernst Wilhelm Bohle.'

'Lists?' Halliday said. 'You told me *a* list.'

'Then my English is letting me down. Twenty thousand pounds.'

'I don't understand,' Halliday protested.

'Ten minutes. I'll telephone again. In the meantime you'd better *try* to understand.'

When the connection was cut, Halliday sat back in his chair, fingers drumming on the surface of his desk, thinking about the caller, and the demand. He could ring the police, tell them he was receiving threatening calls, and hope the police wouldn't believe what the man had to say. What, after all, could he possess – a list with Bohle's signature on it was an unlikely thing to find in a Britain at war? Therefore it was some typewritten list or other which could conceivably have been put together by an enterprising crook who had done some research.

The more Halliday thought about that, the more likely that seemed. He tried to put himself in the place of a man who saw blackmail as a swift way to a fortune, and treason as the worst of threatened charges. First Bohle. Well, he'd had enough publicity in the late 'thirites. Bohle was British by birth, had spent a lot of time in Britain, had even met and had a long talk with Churchill himself. Would the caller care to accuse Churchill, too? There was a resemblance in that in purely local terms, he too had had publicity. The *Leicester Mercury* and *Evening Mail* had attacked him for his employment policies. The more Halliday thought about it, the more he began to conclude that the blackmailer was some enterprising local with a good memory and a certain ingenuity. In that case he could ring the police; they'd intercept the call and intercept the caller, too, either at once or at some rendezvous where the money would be handed over.

Halliday had half-convinced himself of the truth of this hypothesis, indeed his hand was half-way to the telephone, when he realized that if the hypothesis were incorrect, the consequences would be disastrous. The well-nurtured Wykehamist mind recognized probabilities and could make an excellent shot at calculating them, and the probability here was that if the mystery caller turned out *not* to be an ingenious and completely phoney blackmailer, then he would almost certainly be the possessor of genuine information.

Even so, could he prove it?

Damn it, the man didn't have to prove it! He merely had to say he could: Halliday's own knowledge of the truth of what was being said was enough to bend him backwards over the barrel.

The telephone rang. 'Halliday.'

'I hope you understand now.'

'Yes I do.'

'Twenty thousand. Notes. None over five pounds. All used.'

'That,' Halliday said, 'is a difficult sum to raise.'

'You have until noon tomorrow.'

'Impossible!' Halliday said. Given time he might be able to *think* his way out of this, but that wasn't enough time. 'It can't be done by then.'

'It must.'

Did he detect a trace of uncertainty? Stand firm, he told himself. Halliday said, with deliberate hardness, 'There isn't as much as that in any account I have access to.'

'In that case,' the voice said, 'the evidence will be posted at noon tomorrow to the Home Office. You understand *that*? Goodbye.'

'Wait!' Halliday said, unable to keep the plea from his voice yet hating himself for its presence.

'Yes?'

'I'll do it somehow.'

'You'll be telephoned in the morning. The caller will be Major Mills. Be ready to receive instructions.'

The line went dead.

Halliday did not go home. An office adjacent to his own had been fitted out, earlier in the war, as a bedroom and he decided that if he slept at all that night, he would sleep there. If there was a way out of this blackmailer's trap, Halliday intended to find it and the best place to look for a solution was in the place where he was accustomed to do his thinking: his office, which was equipped with blackboard and large pads, coloured crayons, slide rules: all the necessary impedimenta.

He began by making a decision. Risk of some kind would be involved: it was unreasonable to expect to solve this problem without risk. He must therefore be prepared to take it. Equally he must minimize it.

Halliday began, in his logical way, at the beginning. The essential problem of the blackmailer was to get his hands on the money without being caught. How, in Leicester and the country round it, would an ingenious man who knew the area plan to do that? What if he *didn't* know the area?

Halliday had lied about the money. He was the kind of businessman who believed in cash and kept large quantities on the premises in a fireproof safe built into the concrete floor of his office. He had discovered in a war of shortages that the man known to be able to pay for goods, in money and immediately, was the man who got what was going. To take out twenty thousand pounds would be to make a very substantial, though not crippling, hole in his company's operating capital. But at least the money was there.

At half past nine the next morning the telephone rang. 'Major Mills. Have you made arrangements?'

'No.'

'Must I say it again? At noon the proof will be in the post, unless our business is finished.'

'I have the money. No arrangements were necessary.'

There was a pause. 'Go immediately to the Central Station. Wait in the telephone box by the ticket office. I will telephone you there with additional orders. Be there in a very few minutes.'

Halliday put on a raincoat and put the cardboard shoe box containing the money under his arm. It rode beside him on the passenger seat all the way to the station, and he kept glancing at it. His night's thinking had produced a variety of clever ploys for handing over the money, but none had included the station. He saw the possibilities quickly: the train carrying him away as the blackmailer picked up the money. Very neat!

He went to the telephone box, wondering whether he was being watched. He couldn't quite see the departures board. He'd waited two minutes when the phone rang.

'Halliday.'

'The Loughborough train leaves in two and a half minutes. There is no time to buy a ticket. Go on to the platform with a platform ticket. Drop the parcel out of the left side of the train when you see beside the track a man with a small suitcase and a green trilby. You understand? Repeat the instruction.'

'Left side. Small suitcase, green trilby.'

'For what it's worth, Mr Halliday, you won't hear from me again.' The connection was instantly broken. Halliday came out of the telephone box thinking hard. He put coins in the ticket box and went through to the train. The man had said 'me.' You won't hear from *me* again, that was what he'd said. Not *us*. One man operating alone? The local man with the long memory and the ingenious ideas?

The train left on time, leaving Halliday scarcely a moment to think, and he was a man who did very little without giving thought to his actions. All the same, the need for action was strong. He was angry that the long night had been wasted, that among all his ideas for parcels left on shop counters, in restaurants and fitting rooms, none had been as simple or as effective as this idea of using a moving train.

He stood on the left side as the train puffed out of the station, the shoe box in his hand. Where would the man be?

Conway was waiting less than a quarter of a mile up the

track. He had only to collect the parcel, scramble down a small embankment, and he would be off into the back streets. He saw the dark puffs of smoke as the engine came clear of the station roof. In a minute or so it would be alongside him, and the money . . .

Christ but the train was going slowly! He looked wildly round to see if there was a red signal, or some other explanation but could see nothing. At least it was moving though; perhaps he was panicking unduly; perhaps trains always left Central Station at a crawl. He could hear distinctly the well-spaced chuffs of the big engine, and stared at it with hypnotized eyes. *Twenty thousand pounds!*

Was it picking up speed? Difficult to tell. He looked for a face at one of the windows: it would be impossible to see, of course, until the man was actually sticking his head out of the window, but . . . Yes, there he was! Conway could see him, head and one shoulder visible as the man leaned outwards. Come on, come on! He ached to get it over.

Damn! The train was slowing again! Conway watched it with eyes that now held a flicker of fear. Should he run *now*? He tried frantically to decide. Maybe he should. There were plenty of others on the list. Being caught over Halliday wasn't worth it.

But on the other hand there was twenty thousand pounds on the train. And the train was still moving. And in a minute or so he would have the money. Conway stood trembling, poised between greed and flight.

And the train slid slowly towards him.

It was moving, but only just. Would it continue, or stop? Conway, trying to avoid showing his face, yet desperate to be able to see, looked directly up into Halliday's eyes. The box was in Halliday's hand, held out, ready to drop.

Conway nodded with what he hoped was confidence. His heart was beating wildly and sweat had broken out all over his body. He yelled, 'Drop it!' and it fell at his feet.

Conway scooped the box up and took to his heels and as he did so the train halted with a soft hiss of falling pressures. As he reached the wall he glanced back and nearly fainted. Halliday must have jumped down. The train door where he had stood was open and Halliday was scrambling down the bank. Before he was even on top of the wall he had been grabbed and swung round.

Halliday was big, glaring down at him. In that moment, Conway knew all about fear.

'Who *are* you?'

Conway stared up into the angry eyes, his own senses quickened, as they usually were, by fear. Why *that* question?

He said, 'I'm the man who'll send you to the gallows if you don't let me go.' He tried, and failed to shake himself free.

'You're working alone!' Halliday insisted.

For some reason, Donnelly's sister came into Conway's anxious mind, and with her the right words. He said, with a heavy Irish accent, 'You don't call the IRA working alone.'

'You can't be!'

'But I am.' He was still gripped by strong hands. The eyes were still threatening, but Conway knew he had won. 'And if you don't let go now, they'll see that you hang, Mr Halliday.'

From above, somebody shouted, 'Need any help, sir?' The guard of the train was watching them with concern.

Conway again tried to shake himself loose, and this time the hands released him. 'Tell him no,' Conway said.

Halliday stared at him for long seconds, aching for violence, but helpless and knowing it. Then, with a savage little gesture, he turned and climbed up the short bank, back to the train.

Conway was near to sobbing with the relief of tension, as he climbed the wall and walked away. A few people in the street looked at him curiously, but before long he was anonymous again, a figure in a crowd. Twenty thousand pounds in his bag, yet he felt strangely dulled. It had been too damned close altogether. Halliday could easily have killed him and had clearly wanted to. He got the first bus he could find, then went to his lodgings and checked the money.

All there! Seeing it restored him a little. He could feel satisfaction now, along with the aftertaste of terror.

Conway put his suitcase into the left luggage office at the other Leicester station, London Road, and took a bus to Coventry, twenty-three miles away. He had a strong sense that the moment of maximum danger had just passed. He could not have been more wrong.

Chapter Eight

In a sense it was bad luck. In another, it was bad planning. In a third, it was *The War*. Efficient travel, necessary access, accuracy of plan and execution: these are the requirements of operational planning, as Conway was later to learn. He had investigated too little, and assumed rather too much; he also made the mistake of allowing himself to begin to feel powerful. As the moment receded when Halliday's hands had gripped him so terrifyingly, Conway had begun to believe that his victims would not dare to harm him. Ulyatt had paid up without a murmur; Halliday had been furious but helpless; it all meant that the list Rasch had brought from Berlin was the real, true, authentic goods. What a weapon!

He was moving deliberately up the scale. Halliday had been bigger than Ulyatt. Powerful people lay ahead. He should have gone to London and visited Companies House, or spent time discussing the electrical engineering industry with someone who knew it; the city editor of a newspaper would have been ideal and Conway could easily have made such a contact. But he didn't go to London, he went straight to Coventry, relying, as he had relied before, on reference books which listed companies and their directors, on *Who's Who*, which had listed Halliday but not Ulyatt, on Bradshaw's Railway Timetable and the handbook of the Royal Automobile Club and the local telephone directories. They are all excellent publications, but like anything else that is produced once a year, they can easily be a year out of date.

Conway's new target was a man named Stanley Jackson, chairman and managing director of Jackson Electrics Ltd, a medium-sized company engaged, as its name implied, in the manufacture of electrical goods. Jackson's, however, were no mere winders of coils for fire elements or armatures: they were engaged in electronics and technology. Their two factories made advanced radar and listening equipment.

Conway might have found out what Jackson made. It would not have been particularly easy because by 1945 people did not talk freely about their work, particularly if it could even marginally be described as confidential.

It was almost eleven p.m. The drive from London had been, from the beginning, slow and wearisome, and Colvin had had to stop in Birmingham to collect the local man, a chief inspector with Special Branch training and in theory, local knowledge. Now, as they came into ruined Coventry, things didn't get any better. There was a detour sign on the road and having followed it, they got lost. At that time of night there was hardly anybody about: the night shifts were busy in their factories and everybody else with any sense was at home in bed. Finally they found a man, late out of a pub, and asked him the way.

He looked at them solemnly, a little drunk, and said, 'Not allowed to tell you. Talk costs lives.'

Chief Inspector Clark got back into the car and said disgustedly, 'Do I look like a bloody German parachutist?'

'We'll find a telephone box. Get a straight answer,' Colvin said.

They didn't have to, as it happened. A police Wolseley was parked a little distance down the road. Colvin halted their Humber and went over. A red glow from inside the Wolseley vanished abruptly as he approached, but there was a strong smell of cigarette smoke.

Colvin said, 'I'm looking for a factory. Jackson Electrics.'

'Are you?' The policeman climbed out. 'And who might you be, sir? Have you your identity card?'

Colvin said, 'Don't bugger about, eh?' He held out a card. 'Now show me the way.'

The policeman looked and said quickly, 'Yes, sir.' He climbed into the Wolseley. 'Just follow me, sir.'

'What's this about?' his companion asked.

'One of those fancy identity cards.'

'Which one?'

'Ministry of Defence.'

The policeman said, 'I'm glad it's not me he's after. He's a nasty-looking sod.'

'I expect,' his partner said amiably, 'that he thought the same about you.'

Colvin gave a brief wave of thanks to the police car as he pulled up at the hut. The gateman came grunting out.

'We're expected. Ought to be, anyway. Name of Colvin.'

'Yes. Mr Jackson's expecting you. Put your car over there, sir. I'll get somebody to take you.'

Jackson was thin, hollow-eyed. His collar, half an inch too big for his neck, was white and shiny with starch. He didn't get up. 'You made good time. Would you like coffee?'

'Bit later, perhaps,' Colvin said, 'thanks all the same.'

'All right.' Jackson was looking at them with an interest he didn't trouble to disguise.

Colvin, used to that look, said, 'We'd like to hear the whole story.'

'Are you both from the same department?'

Colvin glanced across at Clark. 'Not exactly,' he said. 'Why?'

'I seem to have stirred some muddy water, that's all,' Jackson said. 'People driving down from London in the blackout.'

Colvin looked at his fingernails. 'Could you begin at the beginning?' He took out a notebook.

Jackson smiled, opened a drawer in his desk and produced a small case. 'This is a wire recorder we make. It might be easier than the notebook.'

'Thank you, but I prefer the book. Would you begin by giving me your full name?'

'Of course. Stanley Fraser Jackson. I'm thirty-six, married with two children and I live at a house called Well Springs in Kenilworth Road.'

'Thank you. Now, I'm told you had a phone call earlier this evening?'

'Just after five,' Jackson said. 'Would you say that was afternoon or evening?'

'Go on, sir,' Colvin said encouragingly. For the boss of what was clearly a busy and prosperous company, Jackson seemed remarkably gentle and reflective.

'Well, it was a man's voice. He asked me if I were Stanley Jackson. I said yes. He then said that my name was on a list in Berlin.'

'Did he say what list?'

'No.'

'Did you ask?'

'Naturally. He said he was sure I could guess. Then he said that if the list got into the hands of the British authorities I would be in very severe trouble. He told me he wanted twenty-five thousand pounds.'

'A lot of money,' Colvin said. He glanced at Clark who sat immobile, no more than a pair of ears. 'Did he tell you what you'd get for it?'

'I asked him. He said peace of mind.' Jackson smiled a little wanly.

'And then?'

'He said he would telephone again in the morning with instructions about the money. How it is to be handed over and so forth.'

'And rang off?'

'Yes. Well not quite. I told him, I'm afraid, that I thought he was being remarkably optimistic.'

'And he said what?'

'He sounded rather angry. He said, if I recall his words, "Every penny. I want every penny. Otherwise the Ministry of Defence gets the information."'

'Those were his words?'

'I should have had the recorder on, you mean?' Jackson sounded apologetic. 'You're quite right, of course.'

'Probably doesn't matter,' Colvin said. 'It might have been helpful to hear his voice, that's all.'

'I'm sorry.'

Colvin scratched his chin. 'Why you? I mean, why should

he threaten you?'

'I can't imagine.'

'Could your name be on some list in Berlin?'

'I don't see why it should be, except that my name and the company's are the same. We make radar sets for aircraft. I can imagine they might want to put the firm out of action.'

'But not you?'

'They've already put me out of action, Mr Colvin.' Jackson suddenly pushed his chair away from the desk, picked up a steel ruler, and gave each of his legs a sharp bang with it. The sound was of metal striking metal. 'Anzio.'

'The list in Berlin?' Colvin was embarrassed.

'If they keep lists of double amputees they may have my name.'

'Why did you telephone us?'

'I thought I'd better tell somebody.'

'Why not the police?'

Jackson closed his eyes for a moment. 'Oh, I see. Well, because I know a man in MI5.'

'His name, sir,' Colvin asked automatically.

'You know his name, surely. He put you on to me. Mr Towers.'

'And how do you know him?'

'We produce secret instruments. I've had contact with various people.'

'No clue as to what the list might be?'

'He didn't give me one.'

'And you have no idea, none at all?'

'As a matter of fact,' Jackson said, 'I think I might have a rather unworthy suspicion.' He still spoke softly, but Colvin saw the tightness of his hands on the steel rule. 'My father's brother founded this company. He was Stanley Jackson, too.'

'Was?'

'He died fifteen months ago.' Jackson looked weary.

'Pro-German, was he?'

'In a way. He went to Berlin University in the 'nineties.

Had a good many German friends, and stayed in touch with them. In the beginning he had a lot of time for Hitler, but he was all right, really. Not the man to turn traitor.'

'As far as you know?'

'I'm certain,' Jackson said. 'But I can see how he'd give the impression.'

Colvin listened. It seemed likely that Jackson's suspicion might be correct. 'Can you,' he asked, 'provide somewhere quiet where we can talk about all this?'

'I can even give you beds,' Jackson said. 'There's an office I've had converted.'

Next morning both men were up early and were busy. When, at nine-fifteen, they again entered Stanley Jackson's office, a great deal had been accomplished. Colvin, through London, had obtained Post Office co-operation in the hope of rapid tracing of telephone calls; Clark had made arrangements with the local police, and several police cars were at their disposal. They had also made an attempt to plan telephone conversations.

Jackson was waiting for them. He asked at once, 'What do I do?'

'We're assuming,' Colvin said, 'that the telephone call will be from a public box. The job, therefore, is to trace it. We've asked every telephone operator who takes a call to this number to notify the police – there's a procedure, and it's good and quick. We have an open line rigged-up to the police, too. So with luck, once we know the right man's on the line, we can get a police car to the phone box in a couple of minutes.'

'And if it's not from a public call box?'

'Doesn't matter. The operator can keep him waiting. It might be a bit more difficult to grab him, that's all. Now then, sir, when he does come through, here's what you say.'

When Colvin had finished, he glanced at his watch. 'We should be having a trial call any minute. Just to test the system.' When it came, the trial call proved the system worked.

'We just wait, then?' Jackson inquired. 'Or can I get on with my work?'

The telephone rang several times. Normal business calls: a manager thick with 'flu apologizing for staying in bed, a breakdown in the machine shop, a shop steward with a complaint about the temperature in one of the assembly areas. Colvin and Clark stood listening to the relay loudspeaker Jackson had had rigged for them, and it occurred to Colvin that for all Jackson's mildness, he gave decisions quickly and with precision.

Between calls he asked, 'What was your outfit, Mr Jackson?'

'Outfit? Oh, I see. I was a Royal Marine.' He added, mirroring Clark's thoughts, 'You must have had some contact with the Americans.'

'Some,' Colvin said. 'They invent useful words.'

'Usually of great length,' Jackson said. 'Unit is better than outfit, I think. I find American machines a good deal more satisfactory than their language. Curious, that – '

The telephone rang.

'Hello.'

'Mister Stanley Jackson?'

'Yes.'

'Can this call be overheard?'

Jackson glanced at Colvin and Clark. 'No.'

'I told you the amount. It's twenty-five thousand pounds – '

'I can't raise it,' Jackson was saying as a red light flashed on the other telephone. Colvin picked it up, cupped his hand round the mouthpiece and grunted, then caught Jackson's eye and nodded encouragement to keep the caller talking.

'In that case some very compromising documents will – '

Jackson said quickly, 'Not instantly, I mean. I've raised five thousand and I *can* get the rest.'

'When?'

Colvin had a pencil in his hand and was scribbling.

'It'll be tomorrow. I can't get it today.'

The caller hesitated. All three could sense his tension.

'What time tomorrow?'

'I'm not sure. There's a draft being sent up from London. Until it's received, my bank won't pay.'

'Why not?'

Colvin gave a sudden thumbs up. A police car was on its way to the telephone box.

'Because we're overstretched a bit. Short of capital.'

'I'll ring you again.' They heard the click of the cut connection.

'Damn!' Colvin said. 'Another half minute and we'd have had him.' He stood listening to the telephone in his hand. 'Apparently it's Leicester Road somewhere.'

'Leicester Row,' Jackson corrected gently.

Colvin said, 'It's not one of the cars with wirelesses, damn it. The sooner every car has one, the better.' He replaced the phone with a little grimace of disappointment. 'We'll just have to wait for him to ring again. Now look, Mr Jackson, when he *does* ring again, we're going to have to work out a method of keeping him talking as long as we can.'

'I'll do my best.'

'I know you will. But if we work it out . . . Let's see if we can write it like a little play. First we've got to find out if he knows about your legs.'

'Legs, non-existence of,' Jackson said with sudden bitterness, and then apologized at once. 'I'm sorry. One hopes to become accustomed, but occasionally – '

'I'll bet,' Colvin said. The red light began flashing on his phone.

He snatched it up. 'Yes? Did they? Well, good for them. Yes, I would. HQ, where else!' He dropped the phone on to its hook, grinning.

'Well?' Clark said.

'There was nobody in the box. But they breed 'em with initiative in Coventry apparently. They saw a man scampering up a side street looking over his shoulder and they nabbed him.'

'And?'

Colvin said: 'This fella's Irish.'

'In Coventry, plenty of people are,' Jackson said.

Colvin glanced at his watch. 'If he's our man, fine. If he isn't, there's going to be another call to Mr Jackson. We'll proceed, therefore, as follows. You, Mr Clark, will stay here with Mr Jackson. Perhaps you could work on your script. I will go to Coventry police headquarters and have a preliminary talk with this man.'

Conway sat in the interview room. It was small, bleak, green-painted, and could have been nothing but a police room. In some countries such rooms are cleaner or dirtier than in others; in some there are sinister stains on floors and walls; some rooms are cold, and the chill is itself an instrument of investigation; others are hot for the same reason. What they have in common is bareness. There is always a table and a chair for the inquisitor. Another chair, on the opposite side of the table, is sometimes an indication that the room is in a civilized country.

The room in which Conway sat was centrally-heated, so it was warm; if anything it was a little too warm, but that was less a matter of calculation than of temperature build-up in a building used twenty-four hours a day. Conway sat on one side of the table. In front of him was an ashtray containing two cigarette ends which had not been removed after some previous interview. Behind him, back to the door and silent, stood a uniformed constable.

Conway was afraid yet unworried. It was a paradox he recognized and understood: the fear came from being chased by police and caught; but there was no way in which it could be proved that he had been doing anything criminal. He sat waiting for his interrogator, heart still thumping, but brain clear.

Colvin came in quietly, took the seat on the other side of the table, and said, 'Leave us, please,' to the guardian constable.

Conway said, 'I'm an Irish citizen. I have committed no crime. I protest at this detention.'

'And you demand the right to make contact with your

embassy, no doubt?' Colvin said pleasantly.

'I'm expecting to be released at once,' Conway said. 'As soon as I meet an intelligent man. I hope I'm meeting one now. If I am, it shouldn't be necessary to bother the embassy.'

'I see. Very rational.' Colvin held steepled fingers against his lips and looked at Conway thoughtfully. 'Also rather practised, it seems to me.'

'You aren't the first policeman I've talked to.'

'I'm sure I'm not.' Colvin opened Conway's passport and flicked through the pages. 'You seem to have been to quite a lot of places, Where did you meet the police?'

'Here and there.'

'Spain, I see. They can be fairly fundamental there?'

'When there's a civil war going on,' Conway said, 'the police usually aren't the most dangerous thing around.'

'No. You were a reporter there?'

'Yes.'

'On the Republican side?'

'No.'

'Germany too, eh?' Colvin's tone was of interest. 'You stayed there quite some time.'

'Two years.'

'That was after the war began, I see. Any bother with the police there?'

'Nothing much. They interviewed me occasionally. They interviewed all neutrals. I *am* a neutral,' Conway said.

'I know you are. But we're belligerents. Gives us different points of view.' Colvin's voice hardened. 'Different laws, too. Emergency powers.'

'Germany had those, too. Rather more than you.'

'And fiercer,' Colvin agreed. He was waiting for word from the police at the phone box. If Conway had used it, had smoked a cigarette perhaps, then . . . but it was no kind of proof. Even fingerprints would be no kind of proof. 'I wonder,' he said, 'if you could be some kind of spy.' He watched with satisfaction as Conway swallowed, Adam's apple bobbing conspicuously.

'The police,' Conway riposted, 'always seem to think a reporter is a spy.'

'Because you are?'

'Don't be absurd. I'm a correspondent; have been for years. Some major newspapers, most of whom will be interested in this.'

'I'm to be terrified of the *Irish Independent*?'

'I'm not *their* correspondent.'

'Why were you running?'

Always the way, Conway thought: the quick oblique question to catch you off guard. He said, 'There are two principal methods of locomotion for the human species. One provides sharper exercise than the other. I run sometimes.'

'Just like that? Sudden impulse to run and you run?'

'Yes, sometimes.'

'Particularly when you see a police car?'

Conway said, 'Not up to now. But if this is how the police carry on for no reason at all, perhaps I ought to.'

Conway was very competent, Colvin thought. Perhaps he was innocent, too. But somehow the one seemed to cancel out the other. 'Why are you in Coventry?'

'I thought I'd do a piece on the Irish who are helping the English win their war.'

'Just in Coventry?'

'No. I've been in Leicester, too. And Bradford.'

'I see. You were in Bradford?' Colvin turned the passport's pages again. 'You were in Britain, then you returned to Ireland, then came back. Why did you go back to Ireland?'

Conway said, 'I wanted some good Guinness again.'

'Man of taste?'

'I like to think so.'

The door opened. Colvin rose and left the room. Outside stood the station sergeant, shaking his head. 'Nothing at the phone box, sir. It must have been cleaned out this morning. Not even a fag end. Do you want to request a full scale forensic science job done on it?'

'No.' He went back into the room and resumed his seat

opposite Conway. 'You like Guinness?'

'I'm Irish.'

'Long way to go for it.'

'I'm Irish.'

'Must have been hard going without it for all those years.'

Conway grinned. 'I'm not guilty of anything at all. Why not acknowledge what's obviously true?'

'Answer the question.'

'About Guinness? The withdrawal symptoms were terrible. I came out in a rash of little shamrocks. That's why I left Germany.'

Colvin looked at him with hard eyes. He hadn't expected this facile, practised subject. 'One thing intrigues me about you.'

Conway waited in silence.

'Tell you what it is. I've been impugning your character ever since I sat down. I've called you a liar and a spy. I've said I don't believe a word you're saying. Yet none of it worries you. You don't take offence.'

'That's because policemen are all the same. They like people to lose their tempers. They all put on roughly the same performance and I've seen it before. This is Act One. Act Two is when you bring in the big, strong, nasty man who threatens me.'

'And Act Three?'

'You become my friend, arguing my point of view against the nasty, rough man.'

There was a knock and Clark's head came round the door.

'The nasty man in person,' Conway said.

Clark smiled at him. 'I'm not nasty. Not nasty at all.'

There was a long silence, full of frustrations. Then Colvin said, 'It looks as though we can't do very much.'

'I've done nothing. That's why.'

'Except telephone Stanley Jackson,' Colvin said. He said it very quietly.

Conway ignored him. The eyes didn't even flicker.

'I said you telephoned Stanley Jackson,' Colvin said more loudly.

117

'Who's he?'

'He exists,' Colvin said. 'Here in this city.'

'Stanley Jackson?' Conway said, eyes rolling upwards in thought.

Then he snapped his fingers. 'Got him. Cricketer, wasn't he? And an MP?'

'Isn't he clever?' Colvin asked Clark admiringly.

'Very clever,' Clark agreed.

'Too clever,' Colvin said. 'Comes into the country. Starts his little games. Causes trouble. But he's clever. Innocent as a lamb, he is. So he says. Maybe we'd better get rid of him.'

'Out of the country, you mean?'

'And damn quick at that.'

'What you mean is,' Conway said, 'that you've brought me here wrongly and without justification, that you're too small to admit a mistake, and you're going to take your irritation out on me by being petty.'

There was a pause. Then Colvin said, 'I can do it.'

Conway smiled. 'I was going anyway.'

'When?'

'Tomorrow. Like to see my return ticket?' He fished in his pocket.

'Thanks very much,' Colvin said. 'And you can show me your notes as well.'

'What notes? Oh, you mean for the article?'

'That's what I mean.'

'They're in my head.'

'Names and addresses? They're in your head, too?'

Conway said, 'In Bradford I talked to Mr Paddy Murphy in the Ring o' Bells pub. In Leicester, I talked to Mr Sean O'Connell in the Bell which is a better class of public house. In Coventry I haven't really talked to anybody yet.'

'Except Mr Jackson,' Clark said.

'Is he Irish?'

Colvin said, 'You ever met any Gestapo men?'

'I saw them once or twice.'

'It must be nice,' Colvin said reflectively. 'Sometimes, when there's a fellow like you. Awkward. Clever. You don't just sit and listen to his funny answers. You kick his teeth in.'

'Frustrating for you.'

Colvin jerked his head at Clark. In the corridor he said, 'We haven't a hope.'

'No. Yet it is his voice. Allowing for the distortion on the recorder.'

'Never prove it. We'll have to let him go.'

'There hasn't been another call at Jackson's office?'

'There wouldn't be, not with Conway here,' Colvin said. 'You know, we ought to have him escorted to the boat, but somehow I'm against it.'

'Why?'

'I don't know why. We'll let him go, and we'll follow him. If he goes direct, we lose nothing. If he doesn't, who knows?'

Conway's knees were shaking as he walked out of the police station in Coventry. He'd won, but it wasn't much of a victory. They'd pressed him, but not very hard, and that knowledge made Conway unsure of his judgment. He had been out of Britain too long to know what the war had done to the police. They *ought* to have examined his story word by word, made him repeat it, checked on repetitions and inconsistencies, and done it until he was so weary he could neither stand nor sit. So why hadn't they? Not pressure of work, if two very senior men – and there was no doubt these two *were* senior – could spend time on him. Yet they skated over it all, once over lightly, then said, 'All right. Be sure you're on the boat.'

He had been followed before and expected to be followed now, and was puzzled when a careful check revealed no one on his trail. All the same, he went direct to the station and bought a ticket for Heysham in Lancashire whence the ferry left for Belfast. That was another thing they hadn't asked: why come via Belfast and Heysham when there was a perfectly good service from Dublin via Dun Laoghaire and Holyhead? He went into the station buffet and bought a cup of tea and a Banbury cake that was all pastry like plaster and no filling, and sat down to think. He'd been blackmailing and they'd caught him. They couldn't prove anything and they let him go. In less than two hours. He'd said he was returning to Ireland and they said that was exactly what he should do. And in spite of all the tough talk about taking him to the boat and putting him aboard, they had released him into the teeming Midlands.

Conway finished his tea and decided that the whole thing stank. The police had something worked out. The best thing he could do would be to *use* the ticket he'd bought, take the first train and the first boat, and get out of Britain, which was dangerous, to Ireland, which was not; no extradition treaty existed between the two countries.

But.

He sat and thought about the but. He bought another cup of tea, and a jam tart that was half-brother to the Banbury cake. As his jaws coped with it, his mind concentrated on Leicester. Leicester was twenty-three miles away. It was also in the wrong direction. The train he was to catch went nowhere near Leicester. Dared he go there and collect the money? And if he was being followed, how could he give his followers the slip?

Conway devoted all his considerable ingenuity to the problem. He decided that since he was in a railway station, it would look suspicious if he left it, except by train. The means had to lie in that.

'Lost him,' Colvin said an hour and a half later. 'He either got on, or didn't get on, a crowded local train. It came in and disgorged a lot of people and Conway just vanished in the crush. Could be anywhere now.'

'We could have the train watched,' Clark said. 'If he got on, maybe we can find where he gets off.'

Colvin shook his head. 'It's just a local. If it halts at a village, the local bobby's off somewhere on his bike shutting farm gates. Bloody man's guilty, though. We know that now.'

Clark said, 'From the moment I saw him, I never doubted it.'

Conway, meanwhile, was sitting on a bus bound for Birmingham, west and a little south of Coventry, almost sure now that he hadn't been followed. If he had, the Birmingham bus was evidence of suspicious behaviour, not that the police needed their suspicions confirming. If he hadn't, Birmingham was big and crowded and the perfect place to lose himself. His luck at Coventry had been astounding: when the local train stopped, people came racing off it for some reason, and they had enveloped him almost before he realized this was his opportunity. In Birmingham he would spend an hour in Lewis's store, remaining in the basement among the household gadgets. People might look for a fugitive in a men's clothing department where he could be trying to change his appearance; they would look less hard among the clothes lines, spades and 'utility' teasets. In Lewis's he bought a prepared packet of brown paper and string. Then he caught the Leicester bus.

In Leicester it was child's play. He spent an hour going in and out of stores, markets and hotels until he was positive nobody could have followed him. Then he deliberately walked up to a policeman and asked the time. The policeman was polite and pleasant.

Conway retrieved his suitcase, went into the station lavatory and, using the case as a table, made a parcel of the money. He then addressed it to himself care of the News Editor of the *Belfast Newsletter*, a man whom he knew slightly. He marked the parcel *To Be Called For* and went to the post office to register it. On the grounds that a letter would reach Belfast before the parcel, he bought a letter card and wrote briefly to the News Editor explaining that he would call to collect the parcel within a day or two.

He then returned to the station to continue his journey back to Ireland. The last journey, no question about that. And there could still, he warned himself, be some danger in Belfast, but if he played the game carefully, there was a way of getting both himself and the money to Dublin in safety. It was a pity he had failed to collect from Jackson, but all the same, he and Rasch would be able to split thirty thousand pounds between them!

As he travelled uneventfully north and thought about his own share, Conway reflected that in addition to being by far the biggest sum of money he had ever earned, it had been the easiest. Ahead, and he smiled at the thought, lay a degree of comfort and a freedom from worry that he had never enjoyed before.

Chapter Nine

Colvin was blessed with the patience of a heron and shared something of its sensitivity to ripple and whorl. Had he been on the spot, carrying out the surveillance himself, taking proper pride in an ability to blend with the passing traffic while keeping an experienced watch, he would have been a good deal happier. As things stood, however, he was bored.

Conway had been spotted at Heysham, boarding the Belfast boat. No credit was due: Conway had walked boldly aboard and behaved perfectly normally throughout the crossing. There had been plenty of time to make arrangements with the Belfast police to keep a solid watch after he landed, and they had done so, apparently efficiently and unobserved, for two and a half days, during which Conway had done nothing worthy of remark. He had been six times to the cinema; eaten dull meals in duller British Restaurants and twice bedded himself down for the night at a quiet private hotel. 'He sleeps late, and he watches the silver bloody screen,' Colvin reported to his master, Mr R. H. K. Wills, 'and that's all he does.'

'And waits,' Wills said.

'Certainly. But what *for* – the chance to nip over the border when nobody's looking?'

'Possibly, but I don't think so.' Wills had a reputation for instinct. He disliked it and was inclined to distrust it, but to his mild irritation he was often right without reason.

'All right,' Colvin said. 'But that border bothers me. It's no distance away; all he has to do to cross is to take a bus somewhere and climb a wall and he's beyond reach.'

'Lawful reach,' Wills said.

Colvin grunted. 'There's this business of travel by Belfast

too. He doesn't have to enter Northern Ireland at all. He could have travelled Holyhead to Dun Laoghaire. It's easier and quicker. But no, he goes via Belfast. Why?'

'Answer your own question.'

'All right. Via Belfast, he's travelling from one part of the United Kingdom to the other. Via Holyhead he goes from a country at war to a neutral. What's the point if he's clean?'

'If he's carrying something?' Wills asked.

'He isn't.'

'Yet.'

The long watch continued, at Wills's insistence. It was Wills who had divined – rather apologetically because it was his instinct at work – that Conway might be more important than he seemed. Colvin thought of him merely as a sharp little crook. He had vast experience of criminals, far more than Wills, and thought in general that he knew one when he saw one. The list, in his view, was an artistic invention: Conway was a smart man who'd had a smart idea; he was a blackmailer, and blackmail was a weak man's crime. Ergo, grab Conway and threaten hard enough and he'd confess. That should have been the approach from the start.

'No. Let him run.' And Wills was in control.

There was an open line to Belfast, and had been since Conway landed, and Colvin had remained within snatching distance of the telephone receiver, day and night. Wills was interested in Conway's manner as much as in his movements. He insisted the Belfast detectives report how Conway looked. Was he anxious, impatient, nervous? The Belfast detectives, bored as Colvin, made a game of it. Conway had looked *anxiously* at his watch, smoked cigarettes *nervously*. Colvin brusquely filleted the fun out of it after a report that Conway had broken into a trot. Briefly much interest was generated, but Conway trotted only to cross the road to a public lavatory.

Now on the third day, Conway was moving again. Soon he'd run out of cinemas.

'Walking briskly,' the telephone voice with the soft Belfast accent said in Colvin's ear.

'I told you,' Colvin muttered. 'Cut out the adverbs. Any indication where he's going?'

'Not yet.'

Colvin pressed the intercom key. 'Sir, he's left the hotel and he's walking. Briskly, it seems. *Gone With the Wind* again, maybe.'

'Keep it open, will you. I'll listen.'

Colvin sat with the phone at his ear, murmuring 'Still there?' at intervals in case the Post Office had sabotaged his connection, and hearing the mumbled affirmatives of the police sergeant on the other side of the Irish Sea.

'Ah,' the voice said, suddenly, 'he's turning into Donegal Street.'

'Anything significant in that?'

'Well there's a newspaper office there. The *Belfast News-letter*. You did say he's a reporter.'

'Yes, I did.' Colvin leaned towards the intercom. 'Getting near a newspaper office, sir.'

'Is he? Perhaps I'll come out.'

Colvin listened, and reported again. 'He's going in.'

'Yes, I will.' A moment later Wills appeared beside him looking, as ever, like a nondescript clerk. 'On the third day,' he said.

They waited. Colvin asked and was answered. Minutes passed.

'He's coming out.'

'Yes?'

'Carrying a parcel.'

'A *parcel*?' Wills said.

'Shape and size?'

'Smallish. The size of a couple of thick books.'

'Something he's taking to Dublin,' Wills murmured.

'Back towards the hotel, it looks like,' the Belfast sergeant reported.

Wills cocked an eyebrow at Colvin. 'For his suitcase?'

'No bets, sir.'

'Customs can check his parcel at the border.'

'That's something I will bet on. He won't go within miles

of a Customs post.'

'He's in a telephone box.'

'If you can get the number he's ringing . . .?' Colvin said quickly.

'We're on to it. Trying, anyway. Stand by.'

They waited. Colvin said impatiently, 'He's making arrangements.'

Two minutes later Belfast reported with a trace of excitement. 'That parcel was with the News Editor of the *Belfast Newsletter*. It came this morning, addressed to Conway care of the News Editor. And there was a letter yesterday saying it was on its way.'

'From whom?'

'Conway himself.'

'You mean,' Colvin demanded, 'that he'd sent the parcel to himself?'

'Looks that way, sir.'

'From where?'

'The letter was from Leicester. The News Editor said he couldn't read the postmark on the parcel.' The sergeant chuckled, 'Nosey devil.'

'He's a journalist. It's a disease.' Colvin turned to Wills. 'It's all arrangements. We've got to nab him now or he'll give us the slip.'

'If he *is* going to Dublin,' Wills said mildly, 'I'm very interested to know – '

'He'll vanish. He can do it, too. Done it before.'

'The phone call, sir. It's to a Dublin number, but we were too late to listen in. He's on the move again.'

'Where to?'

'Could be the bus station from the way he's heading, sir.'

'Remember he's got a return train ticket,' Colvin said. 'And it's a very long border with a million places to cross. *Please.*'

Wills stared at him. Pleading wasn't Colvin's way at all.

'He'll find a field and climb a wall,' Colvin said warningly.

'If I agree, what do we get?'

'Him. And the parcel.'

'Let him run and we might get more.'

'Let him run and we finish up with a fistful of fresh air.'

'Reason says you're right.'

'I am right.'

Wills hesitated, then nodded reluctantly.

'Would you bring him in please?' Colvin said sweetly into the telephone.

'Be a pleasure, sir.'

For Conway the nightmare had begun. In a series of swift moves he was first thrust into a police Wolseley, taken to Belfast police headquarters, stripped and searched. His parcel was opened. Nobody said a word.

Within an hour, Conway had been taken to the Harland airfield and put aboard a DC-3 aircraft which took off immediately.

Because it was a cargo aircraft, there were no seats. Conway, in handcuffs, sat miserably and uncomfortably on the floor, tethered to a fuselage former. Again nobody spoke to him.

The aircraft landed at RAF Hounslow. Conway now found himself in the back of a plain van, unaccompanied, as it drove for twenty minutes or so, then stopped. When the van's doors opened and he climbed out, he found he was in a garage. A door was opened and he was led through it, along a corridor, into a room.

The room was empty and he was alone. He remained alone for nearly two hours. From start to finish, from the moment he was picked up in Belfast until the moment when the door of the room finally opened, Conway was engaged in what he knew to be an utterly impossible task: trying to think of an explanation for a parcel containing twenty thousand pounds.

The door's opening was silent. Conway didn't hear the lock turn, or the hinge move, but he heard a soft thump and turned his head quickly. His parcel lay in the middle of the floor! And the door was half open . . .

Conway swallowed as Colvin came into the room. He wanted words, and for the first time in his life, they wouldn't come. *The sheep before his shearers is dumb*, he thought helplessly. Colvin stared at him for what seemed like minutes. Then he said, 'I've got permission.'

Still Conway could not speak. His throat seemed to have seized up, as though all the surfaces were stuck together.

'You'll remember our last chat,' Colvin said. 'I told you then. The best way's to forget the funny answers and kick your teeth in. Well, I've got permission.'

'Christ!' Conway whispered. He hadn't meant to say anything, and now he stood listening to the word echoing in his own mind and watching the slow smile blossom on Colvin's face.

'No use appealing to Him,' Colvin said. 'He's on the side of the angels.' Colvin lit a cigarette, inhaled with enjoyment, and said, 'It can all be worked out very easily, you see. First you get smashed up physically and mentally, then you are charged with a variety of things. Some that carry the death penalty and some that don't. Spying and blackmail, for instance. After that you go on trial. The judge may decide to hang you, and we may decide to let it happen. On the other hand, you might be left in suspense – ' Colvin gave a savage little grin ' – the *other* kind of suspense, if you follow me. You could sit in a cell for three weeks waiting for the great day to dawn and then find you've been reprieved two minutes before Pierrepoint's due to let the trap drop open. It could happen. On the other hand, the trap just *might* drop open. You see? But if you're reprieved, it would be something like hard labour for life, and a little note in the Home Office file to say that life means life. No time off for good behaviour. No good behaviour even, because you'll be needled by the other prisoners, and some of *them* will get the time off, for needling *you*. I'm sure you follow.

'Then the other thing. While you're being roughed up – and I don't mean in some indeterminate future, I mean in the next few minutes – what we'll do is permanent damage. We'll ruin your hands, for a start. And there'll be some very carefully-placed kicks at the base of the spine, d'you see? That kind of approach. So if you're lucky enough to find yourself doing hard labour for life, it'll be agony every time you swing a hammer. Come to that it'll be painful every time you do anything very much.'

Colvin trod on the cigarette, grinding it slowly and deliberately into the floor. Conway stood limply, shoulders drooping, lips apart, looking at him with dread and despair.

'On the other hand,' Colvin said.

Conway blinked. His mind had so been filled with the pictures of horror that he hadn't heard the words.

Colvin knew it, and repeated them, adding a couple more. 'On the other hand we might . . .'

'What?' breathed Conway. He wasn't going to face all that. Nothing on earth was worth facing all that.

'It would depend.'

Conway shivered. 'What do you want?'

'Everything,' Colvin said. 'Every detail. Now. Here. Today.'

Conway's voice cracked on the word, but it was 'Yes.'

Colvin's hard, flat stare seemed to go on. Conway felt as though he were under a powerful lens, being dissected. Finally, 'If you've cracked, stay cracked. Don't try to put yourself together.'

'No.'

Colvin smiled without humour. 'Somerset Maugham – I think it was Somerset Maugham – he said, "Begin at the beginning, go on to the end, and then stop." Try that.'

Conway gave a helpless little shrug. 'I'm not sure where the beginning is.'

'Fine bloody reporter you are! All right, I'll help you. Let's begin with this famous list in Berlin.'

Conway winced. The list was in Dublin now, at Mrs Monaghan's and in Rasch's care. He said hopefully, 'I don't even know if it's genuine.'

'Genuine or not, tell me about it.'

Conway swallowed. 'It's a list of people in Britain who would collaborate with the Germans.'

Colvin stared at him. 'Not much future in that, surely? The war's going to be over soon.'

'You don't understand,' Conway said. 'It was made a long time ago. When the Germans were going to invade.'

Colvin said, 'I think we'd better record this as we go along.' When the wire recorder had been produced and checked, he said, 'The list. Where is it?'

'In Dublin.'

Until that moment, Colvin had doubted the list's existence. But Conway's simple answer had the smack of truth. 'You can tell me where to find it later. First, tell me about it. Lot of names?'

Conway nodded. 'Quite a lot.'

'How many?'

'About two thousand, I think.'

'Recognize any of them?'

'Yes. There's – '

Colvin, surprisingly, stopped him. 'This is just a first quick look at you. We'll wring you out later. Where did you get the list?'

'In Sweden.'

'Where?'

'Stockholm.'

'You're making me dig for all this,' Colvin said warningly. 'I want a real response, not one-word answers.'

'You asked where. I said Stockholm. That's – '

'Somebody gave it to you. Somebody must have given it to you.'

Conway thought about Rasch, secure in the house in Dublin while *he* faced this. 'I got it from a German,' he said. There was no way he could protect Rasch. Nor, he thought, any reason why he should even try.

'Name?'

Could he say he didn't know? That a mysterious German had simply handed it to him? That kind of thing happened sometimes in Stockholm, and these people must know it happened. Conway looked at Colvin's hard face and curious eyes, and felt the marrow melt in his bones.

Colvin conducted his interrogations with a mixture of instinct, experience and step-by-step logic. He now said simply, 'In two minutes I can give you injuries to last you a lifetime. Just as a beginning.'

Conway swallowed and said, 'Rasch.'

'That's his name not a description of his temperament, I hope?' Colvin said grimly.

'It's his name.'

'Go on.'

'He deserted,' Conway said. 'To Sweden. He's an SS man. Do you know about the *Schützstaffel*?'

'I know a bit.'

'He's a Hauptsturmführer. That's equivalent to captain.'

'All right. Why you?'

'What do you mean?'

'Why did he give it to you?'

'I met him. He knew I was a reporter.'

'He wanted to give the happy news to the world, is that it? And chose you to do it?'

Conway said, 'He was going to give it to the Russians. I talked him out of it.'

'I'm beginning to see,' Colvin said. 'You thought there was a quid or two to be made out of blackmail, didn't you? Nasty little sod!'

Conway sat miserably, trying to comfort himself that at least he hadn't given away Rasch's whereabouts. Not yet. He said, 'At least the Russians haven't got it.'

'They're our allies,' Colvin said, 'didn't you know? Tell me some more about this fellow Rasch. Hauptst – what was it?'

'Hauptsturmführer. Captain.'

'Captain's easier. Not a very high rank. How did *he* get hold of it?'

'I don't know. He had it in Stockholm.'

'Funny things happen, I suppose,' Colvin said. 'How much do you know about him.'

'He's quite important,' Conway said. 'He was in Hitler's Guard, the *Leibstandarte*.'

'Was he now? Real hard Nazi, eh?'

'I'm not sure,' Conway said. 'He's more than just an SS thug. He left because he hates them. He's really a kind of commando.'

'They'll need a lot of commandos to protect old Adolf in a few weeks' time,' Colvin said with satisfaction. 'But you said he was a *kind* of commando. What's that mean?'

'He was in the group that rescued Mussolini. With Skorzeny. You've heard of Skorzeny?'

'The one they call Scarface? Real butcher, they say. Rasch sounds interesting. What else do you know?'

'He got the Knight's Cross with Oak Leaves. A kind of Victoria Cross.'

'And then,' Colvin said, 'he just ran away to Sweden, eh?'

'Yes.'

'As I said, funny things happen. What else do you know about him?'

Conway took a deep breath. 'He worked for the *Ausland-sicherheitsdienst.*'

'German portmanteau words,' Colvin said. 'Now listen. I've got a bit of a smattering, that's all. When you use these long words, explain them without being asked. Understand? I know what *Ausland* means. What's the rest of it?'

'Foreign Intelligence Service of the SS,' Conway said. 'His boss was a man called Schellenberg.'

'Big stuff then.'

'So I believe.'

'What rank does *he* hold, this Schellenberg?'

'I don't know. He's high up.'

Colvin brooded for a moment, watchful eyes on Conway's pale face. Finally he said, 'Blackmail's bad. Blackmail on security grounds is a damn sight worse. But this – we're high level here?'

'I think so,' Conway said miserably.

'I'm bloody certain we are. Maybe I'm a bit out of my depth. What we're going to have to do with you, my lad, is get in some people who know what you're talking about.'

Colvin rose and left the room. He returned a moment later with a typewriter on a metal stand, and said, 'While I'm away, you can practise your trade. Start writing your statement. Details, times and places, names. All of it.'

'Scramble . . . now,' R. H. K. Wills said, and pressed the button on his green telephone. At the other end, Colvin did the same.

'Well?' Wills asked.

'Conway's not very big, sir,' Colvin said. 'But he's tied in with big fish. He's spilling things as fast as he can go, but I'm in no position to know what's valuable and what isn't. We ought to have somebody here who knows about the other side.'

'What makes you think that?' Wills asked.

'Names, principally,' Colvin said. 'Ever heard of a man called Schellenberg?'

There was a moment's pause before Wills said, 'Schellenberg?' with a surprised inflexion he could not quite control.

'He's *Auslandsicherheitsdienst*,' Colvin said in workmanlike German. 'And there's another called Rasch who's a bit confusing. Part *Ausland SD*, part Hitler Guard, part commando.'

'I think,' Wills said, 'that perhaps I'd better come down myself. What's Conway doing now?'

'Typing a statement, to keep him out of mischief.'

'All right. Let him continue until I arrive.'

As the two men entered the room, Conway picked up the typed pages and proffered them. They were ignored. He looked only briefly at the newcomer. Colvin had summoned a partner to play interrogator's games, but the man was clearly insignificant.

Wills said, 'Rasch works for Schellenberg?' Conway glanced at him with sudden apprehension. Voice and appearance did not match and the voice had clear authority.

'Yes.'

'Where is Rasch now?'

Conway swallowed, and Wills glanced at Colvin. 'You

have warned him of what can happen?'

'Very clearly, sir.'

'Then perhaps I had better underline it. Understand this, Conway.' Wills's tone was neat and clear, his eyes flat behind cheap spectacles. 'You are not to imagine that the rule of law pertains here. We can and will do with you as we wish. We will proceed without hesitation or scruple, and we will do so immediately if we suspect for a moment that you are not co-operating to the limit. Is that clear?'

Hideously clear, Conway thought, as a shiver slid coldly across his shoulders. He said, getting the words out quickly, 'Rasch is in Dublin,' and felt a sense of relief. He saw surprise in Colvin's eyes, none in Wills'.

'Address?'

Conway gave it. The wire machine was turning, but Wills took out a propelling pencil and made a deliberate note on a pad.

'Expecting you?'

'Yes.'

'When?'

'When I'd finished . . . well, here.'

'When the blackmail was completed,' Wills said. 'You were to return with the money?'

'Yes.'

'By a particular date?'

'No. Just – '

'When you've finished. But soon?'

'I suppose so.'

Wills held out a slim hand for the statement, glanced at it quickly and said, 'You were picked up with twenty thousand pounds. Is there more?'

Conway hesitated only for a second, forlornly trying to decide whether the money already in the safe deposit box in Dublin could be forgotten and perhaps collected at some future time. Colvin, standing now behind him, lashed a hard, flattened hand against the right side of his head.

Conway yelped at a sudden fierce pain which, as it ebbed, left his head ringing. Through the sounds he heard Colvin say, 'If I do that with both hands at once, your eardrums go.'

'There's ten thousand more,' Conway said wretchedly.

'Where?'

'Dublin. A safe deposit.'

'Upon what terms can you withdraw it?'

'I have to be there in person,' Conway said. He felt, but did not show, a trace of defiance. If once he got to Dublin, they'd never get him back to England. Never.

'The list is with the money?' Wills asked crisply.

'No, it's with . . .' Conway paused, then suddenly shrank in expectation of another blow.

It did not come. 'Don't worry,' Colvin's voice said behind him. 'I'm getting to know you. I can tell when you're trying to lie and when you're trying to think straight.'

'It's with Rasch?'

'Yes.'

'Then why did you hesitate?'

'I was trying to – '

'Careful,' Colvin murmured.

Conway shuddered. 'There's another paper. That's with the money.'

'What paper?'

Colvin said, 'You didn't tell me about another paper.'

'I don't know what it is,' Conway said.

'You speak German, do you not?'

'Yes.'

'And it is in German?'

'Yes.'

'What do you not understand?'

'It's figures,' Conway protested. 'Some kind of financial report. I couldn't work out what it was.'

'Rasch brought it, did he? To Stockholm?'

'Yes,' Conway said.

'He brought two documents, then. The first was the list. The white list, we might call it since it is the opposite of a black list.' Wills's eyes showed a refined amusement. 'He worked for Schellenberg who is not merely a member of the *Ausland SD*, but its head! And he went to Stockholm to give these documents to our Soviet allies. That is correct?'

'Yes.'

'Curious behaviour,' Wills said. He paused, 'Do you know why he should do this? And why, as you told Mr Colvin here, did Rasch suddenly hate the country which he had apparently served with some distinction?'

'He was double-crossed,' Conway said. 'That's why.'

'I imagined it might be.' Wills glanced at Colvin. 'You were right that he is only on the periphery of something, but he clearly has information we do not yet possess.'

'Yes, sir.'

'Get it all.'

Colvin left the room with Wills. When he returned he was carrying a vacuum flask. 'Like a cup of tea?'

Conway nodded, and watched as the tea was poured into the cup of the flask.

'Here.'

Conway drank gratefully. The tea was half cold, but his mouth was dry and he swallowed quickly. As he did so, Colvin picked up the metal wastebasket which stood against the wall and handed it to Conway. Ten seconds later, Conway began to vomit. He vomited for a long time.

Colvin, watching dispassionately, said, 'Any lies or half-truths and you'll do a lot of that.'

Much later, after the nausea had stopped and at the end of hours of interrogation, Conway received his instructions. It no longer occurred to him to think about evading them. He still wondered vaguely whether, in Ireland, he might be able to slip away. But his brain was like a pudding, and further threats accompanied the instructions: threats, and assurances of the long arm and everlasting patience of the security services.

He flew back to Belfast in the same aircraft. There was still nowhere for him to sit except the cabin floor, but at least he wasn't handcuffed this time. Beside him on the floor was the parcel containing the money, and the money was real.

The fear was real, too, and in case he forgot it for a moment, there was a slight but definite smell of vomit on his clothes to remind him.

From a telephone box near the bus station, he rang Mrs Monaghan and told her he must have eaten something that disagreed with him, and had been very sick.

'You're better now?'

'Much better,' Conway said. Beside him, in the box, Colvin gave the ghost of a smile. 'But I think I'll come through by train.'

'You'll be taking a risk,' she warned him. 'There's better ways across the border when you're carrying something.'

'I'll be okay,' Conway said.

'All right,' but with doubt. 'I'll tell him what's happened.'

He hung up and Colvin said, 'I'm glad you resisted temptation. Been a pity to have warned Rasch.'

'You'll find,' said Conway with a tiny flare of spirit, 'that he's tougher than I am.'

Colvin grinned. 'I don't mind that,' he said. 'Makes it more interesting sometimes. Get a bit bored when they crack too easily.'

Adding, 'Like you.'

Conway had the loaded gun in his pocket as he walked towards the house: it was a small, flattish blue-black automatic that weighed the jacket down only slightly, and he was wearing his raincoat, so there was no danger at all of its being seen. The money was in his suitcase, as Colvin had instructed.

He was alone now, though Colvin and two other men, singing and pretending to be tipsy, were not far behind him, swaying but keeping pace. He glanced back as he turned in at the gateway in the black iron railings and saw the three had stopped not fifteen yards away and were having an argument. Colvin had briefed him with precision, then repeated it, with such force that though Conway had heard it only twice, he knew it by heart.

Have you a key? No.

Then ring the doorbell. He rang it now.

Transfer the suitcase to your left hand and take out the pistol.

He stood waiting, suitcase and pistol in position, the pistol invisible from the street because raincoat and body were in between.

When she opens the door, say . . .

He saw the smile die on her face as she saw the pistol. Her jaw dropped.

If she's dedicated and quick she may yell a warning anyway. Be first.

Conway said, 'Be quiet. Step back. Leave the door.'

Her eyes watched him for a moment. Conway ached to glance round, to see what Colvin and the others were doing, but dared not.

Don't take your eyes off her. Guns are hypnotic. Once she's staring at it you're in control, unless you lose it.

'I said step back.'

She obeyed slowly.

'Farther. Right down the hall.'

Find out where Rasch is. Don't say, 'Is he upstairs?' She'll answer with a lie. But you can tell if they're lying.

Conway said, 'Where's Rasch?' He said it quietly and watched her eyes, saw her spot her chance.

You can see it in their eyes, in the muscles round them. They contract and widen with the lie. Be first. Make her think.

'He's not anywhere unusual?' Conway asked quickly, before she could reply.

Mrs Monaghan blinked once, then twice. 'Well, he's – '

Conway didn't even hear the feet, just Colvin's voice saying softly, 'Upstairs as usual, Mrs Monaghan?'

There was just a moment before she spat. Then she said, 'You're English!' and opened her mouth to scream. Colvin, spittle running on his face, slipped the fork of his hand in under her chin and pressed and the scream became a gurgle and a soft one at that.

'Upstairs, Mrs Monaghan?' Colvin asked again, very softly, as her face began to go purple.

She nodded and was instantly released to other hands, one of which forced a wadded handkerchief into her gasping mouth.

Colvin closed the door, then tapped Conway's shoulder and nodded.

Once she's secured, straight on up the stairs. Keep going, even if he comes to meet you. You can make him go back by going forward.

Conway felt like a zombie as he began to climb. He was remembering that Rasch had actually appeared on the stairs, the last time, when he had returned to this house. But Rasch did not appear now. Conway came to the top and turned on the landing into the short spur that led to Rasch's door.

The door opened suddenly and he was hauled into the room by the lapels. No time to get the gun out. No time to do anything. He found himself looking into Rasch's determined face. 'Those men?' Rasch demanded.

If he spots us, too bad. Remember it's your life at stake. You'll have to break his attention.

Staring into hard, bright, intelligent eyes, it wasn't easy. Rasch had the concentration of a mongoose. Conway said, 'Drunks. They've been behind me all the way – '

'They came to the door!'

Distract his attention. Remember, it's your life.

'I've got the money. Twenty thousand. From Halliday in Leicester.'

The grip on his lapels relaxed a little. Conway said quickly, 'Let go and I'll show you.'

'The men – '

'Just drunks. Mrs Monaghan will shoo them away.' Conway was bending over the suitcase, fiddling with the cheap little locks. With the lid open he took out the parcel and said, 'There!'

Rasch looked at him, then at the parcel.

You've got to be convincing.

He said, 'Will you just look at twenty thousand in notes. I had to forget the other one. Didn't smell right at all. But we've got thirty thousand between us now. Think of that!

And more to come.'

You want his hands busy and his eyes elsewhere.

Conway rubbed his hands for effect. 'Go on, open it. I'd like to see it again. The white English fiver's a lovely thing.'

Rasch went to the window and looked out. The three men were staggering down the street, having left Mrs Monaghan bound in her own hall. He returned to the bed, picked up the parcel and began to unwrap it. Conway stood, swung round as though with pleasure and said, 'Twenty thousand. In Reichsmarks that'll be . . . let me see – '

The gun was in his hand. He said, 'Keep still.'

Rasch glanced up. In an instant, as his face turned to stone, he hurled himself forward.

At the slightest movement, kick upwards hard – face, neck, whatever gets in the way.

Conway's foot, impelled by fear, swung viciously. He heard and felt it strike Rasch on the bridge of the nose, a little crunch of cartilage, and hopped two hurried steps back as Rasch hit the floor and seemed to bounce upwards again, blood cascading from the nose.

Say it and mean it. Once. So he understands.

Conway said, 'Perfectly still or I fire.' Rasch's eyes were streaming from the kick. He'd be half-blinded.

Stamp three times on the floor.

Conway stamped. Rasch's hand came up to clear his eyes. He understood what the stamps meant.

'Sit on the bed,' Conway ordered.

We'll be up the stair like rats up a hawser.

But they weren't. Conway, ears cocked for the footfall on the stair, made a second mistake. The first had been to let Rasch sit close to his stick. The second was to shift his eyes for a moment.

By the time he glanced back the stick was a brownish blur in the air between them, lifting the pistol from his grip and flicking it away, and this time Conway's reflexes were far too slow.

Rasch was on him and over him, fingers at his throat, in a moment. A second later, with the probable sequence clear in his mind, Rasch was moving, away from Conway, hunting for the gun beneath the table and curtain, where it had flown.

That second was too long, for now the door was open and Colvin was in the room, the other two behind him and, incredibly, a small table was flying through the air towards Rasch's crouching figure. Colvin had scooped it up on the landing as he heard the scuffle.

But Rasch turned, still with the gun . . .

Had he turned it on Colvin, he might have got away. Three men opposed him and there were bullets in the gun. In a sense the odds were with him. But for Rasch the target was Conway, and Conway had to be found before he could be shot, and Conway was obeying orders.

Once we're in the room, get out of the bloody way.

He was not quite under the bed, but about three-quarters of the way, before Rasch saw the wriggling leg, and by that time a heavy foot was arcing towards Rasch's hand. For the second time in less than a minute, the gun flew from the hand that held it.

Yet still Rasch wasn't finished. The table beneath which he'd dived heaved abruptly upwards and Rasch came hammering out, teeth bared with rage and determination, fists clenched, blasting for the door.

One of Colvin's men got him behind the knee, ruining Rasch's balance, and as he struggled to stay upright, a boot toe on the thigh paralysed his leg.

I'll let you know when you can come out.

'Come on out, Sunny Jim,' Colvin said. 'Everything's under control.'

Chapter Ten

The room was lined with rubber. Floor of rubber, walls of rubber, a door of steel heavily padded with rubber. Only the ceiling, fifteen feet above his head, was plain; it was whitewashed, and the bulb-holder which provided the only light was set deep into it, and covered with a wire grille.

Rasch, naked, had to sit on the floor, for there was no table and no chair; yet he looked at the room with a certain defiant satisfaction. It was a place for lunatics, or those with suicidal urges, and his incarceration there represented a small victory. His capture had been shattering; he had always sworn to himself that he would never be taken prisoner, that if the moment ever came, he would have one round in his pistol for himself. He was still angry and puzzled that in Dublin, when he had had the pistol, his fury at Conway had in some way overridden that resolve.

His fury remained, but now was walled away in his mind, to reappear upon summons. At the moment of capture, and in the hour following, it had been uncontainable and he had not stopped fighting. In Dublin he had been subjugated only by physical force. He had fought three men and hurt them all, might have beaten them all if a blow on the head had not made him unconscious. He had woken to find himself strapped hand and foot, in some kind of windowless van. At Belfast, when there had been light to see, he had found he was in a straitjacket, and despite its restrictions, had fought and kicked as they carried him to the plane; aboard it, in the air, he had tried to kick a hole through the skin of the aircraft's fuselage until a rope was slipped round his feet and they were drawn up, clear of the floor.

He had fought as they lifted him out of the plane, as they

loaded him into another van, as they carried him to a cell.

In the cell they had injected something into his arm, and when unconsciousness came, must have taken off both the straitjacket and his clothes because he had awakened naked. He had also awakened without moving, a habit he had taught himself as a soldier, coming to consciousness with eyes closed, sensing the air around him before either moving or looking. There had been a man in the cell; Rasch had sensed his presence, then heard his breathing and glimpsed shoes through a slitted eye. Rasch had struck instantly, expertly and lethally, killing as he intended with a single upsweep of his flattened hand against the man's throat, hearing the crunch of the crushed windpipe, the great gasp of agony.

He had stood, then, and watched the man die, the contorted face red and then blue, writhing into stillness, as Rasch stood over him, tense with adrenalin, daring others to come to him.

They came, but later. Firearms would have done them no good and they must have known that Rasch, as he waited, wanted the bullet, would have compelled the firing of it, but they left him with the corpse until some kind of anaesthetic gas had put him once again into safe sleep. When he woke again, he was alone and the cell was empty. The anaesthetic had left him with a raging thirst, but there was no water. He was hungry, but there was no food. There was light, there was rubber padding and there was silence. In the silence, Rasch began to think, taming his fury. He had to try to analyse, even to plan.

At first there was little in his head but despair, but it began to disappear with the thought that he had been allowed to live. If they wanted him alive, he told himself, it was for a purpose. He began to look for the purpose.

Conway had talked. He had been captured by the British, had talked to the British, had given Rasch away. The British, therefore, knew a certain amount about Rasch; indeed they must know all that Conway knew. Therefore he was alive because they wanted to know more.

Rasch decided he had a lever. Conway had known a good deal. Conway knew about the reasons for Rasch's visit to Stockholm and what had followed; even in Stockholm, Conway had known a surprising amount about Rasch's soldiering. But Conway had known nothing of other things, things the British would be keen to learn. And for those things there would be a price . . .

Rasch considered the price. There was ten thousand pounds in a vault in Dublin; there was the money Conway had brought back along with his treachery. Thirty thousand.

Money to live on, and live well for a period: money to provide the time in which he could find and kill Conway. He had a sudden ache to kill, thinking longingly of Schellenberg's neatly-collared neck and coldly intelligent smile. For a time he luxuriated in the warmth the thought of those two deaths brought into his mind, but then he checked himself and began again.

Freedom to act. Rasch looked at his nakedness, at the rubber padded walls. Freedom to act was a great distance away, perhaps impossible to achieve, and he realized as he contemplated this freedom, that the idea of self-destruction had gone. In the aircraft, if he could have kicked his way through the skin, he would have been happy to fall through into the night and darkness.

Not now. There were other things.

At first it was a voice out of nowhere, entering his cell through some vent or speaker above his head, a voice that tried to be soft and persuasive, to establish some kind of contact. Rasch ignored it. Then there was another voice, crisper and full of warnings: collaborate with us, or else. He ignored that too.

At last his nostrils sensed the gas again. He didn't fight it; because the gas would win; instead he pretended to succumb quickly. They did not fall for it. He awoke, straitjacketed again and strapped to a table and after his eyes finally opened, they left him for an hour. Then a doctor came with a syringe and something was injected into Rasch's arm. Could it be pentathol, he wondered, to loosen his tongue, or had they something else of which he had never heard? Certainly he was feeling a desire to talk.

Rasch had thought what he intended to say.

'You work for Schellenberg?' a voice inquired pleasantly.

Rasch said, '*Jawohl, mein Führer.*'

There was no gasp of astonishment, but there *was* a short silence.

Then, 'Tell me about Schellenberg. What do you think of him?'

Rasch said, '*Mein Führer*, the Reichsführer says he is . . .' Rasch let his voice die away. It was difficult. His lips itched to speak.

'What does the Reichsführer say?'

Rasch said, allowing the urge to talk full reign, 'I swear to thee Adolf Hitler, Führer and Chancellor of the German Reich, loyalty. I vow to thee and to the superiors whom thou shalt appoint, Obedience unto death, so help me God.' Then he laughed, or rather, he tried to laugh. The sound came as a startling, high-pitched cackle that sounded mad even in his own head.

'Your loyalty is admirable, Rasch.' Whoever was speaking had learned Hochdeutsch, not Hitler's accented Austrian.

Rasch said: 'Yours is not, *mein Führer*.' He wondered how long he could hold on to this insane feeling that made him want to talk and above all to please. More and more his brain was not his own; it felt as though it were cradled in somebody's warm hands, being gently massaged. Sing, he thought to himself desperately. Horst Wessel. '*Die Fahne hoch . . .*' he bawled.

He heard footsteps, two people, feet soft upon the floor as they retreated to whisper.

He sang it through: three verses, the first solo of his life, while they puzzled over him. When the song was done, he recited the oath again, fast and almost out of control, the words tumbling from his lips as though they had their own anxiety to escape. The drug had him now. It was as though the contents of his mind stood in a pile to be shovelled out. He must try and stick, stick, stick to the things . . .

He yelled, '*Jawohl, Herr Reichsprotektor! Jawohl*, it is a beautiful blade. Spanish from Toledo. At four? Of course, *Herr Reichsprotektor!*' God, it was there, the whole scene, Heydrich swishing the damned thing within an inch of him and saying, 'I shall beat you, Rasch,' and meaning it: meaning, defeat me at your peril, Rasch; today I want to win!

He found his lips treacherous now, speaking unbidden, the words out of his mouth before they were formed in his brain: 'I'll tell you about Heydrich,' his lips said, and Rasch fought himself to add the saving '*Mein Führer*,' and gabble on about the Reichsprotektor's counter in tierce, made upon his opponent's second disengagement and the parades of tierce, prime or quinte. He was grasping desperately at nonsense, for even in fencing terms that was what he was parading, but he gabbled on, fighting to hold the line of words.

'What about Heydrich?' the soft voice, and from far away.

'Dead,' Rasch yelled. 'Dead, thank God!' He clamped his jaw to keep the words in, clamped it so fiercely tight that the muscles in his neck went into cramping spasms. If only he could choke, collapse, sleep.

'Too much,' the soft voice said.

'He's said a lot.'

'Not rationally.'

'Dead!' Rasch yelled. He thought about Heydrich and the hospital in Prague. 'Nine days to die, damn him!'

'He knows Heydrich, Himmler, Hitler.'

'We'll try again.'

Sing, damn it, Rasch told himself. Oh God – the words hadn't actually been spoken, had they? Horst Wessel again: '*Die Fahne hoch . . .*'

'Mad, of course.'

'They're all bloody mad.'

He was actually biting his tongue, holding it between his teeth, as they wheeled him back to the cell. No attacks this time; no risks. He sensed others around him, strong hands

146

taking off the restraints. When the door closed, Rasch shuddered with relief. He'd planted it. If he could only be sure he'd said what he thought he'd said!

It had been recorded and transcribed. The envelope was marked Top Secret Glint, the third word signifying an active file, and was delivered by Colvin to R. H. K. Wills. There were several strings to Wills's bow, and one made him the SIS officer responsible for accumulation of information about the enemy leaders. The conversation on the scrambler phone had been carefully brief, but Wills knew the report was coming. He took the envelope and said, 'Sit down, please.'

Colvin waited, studying his master as Wills read the transcription. Wills was slim, balding, bespectacled, fifty; he could have alighted from any commuter train and gone as a clerk to any insurance office. He looked like a clerk when he visited Downing Street, unremarkable and un-remarked. His contact was direct with the Cabinet Office and the Home Secretary.

Wills put down the report. 'Your impression?'

Colvin said, 'He's mad.'

'We're all mad. Beyond that?'

'I'm not sure of anything.'

'You don't have to be sure. I'm asking about impressions. *Does* he know all these people?'

'It sounded that way.'

'Familiar?'

Colvin thought about it. 'Wrong word, sir. Obedient The *Jawohls* were very snappy. Smart officer standing to atten-tion.'

'Not just dreams surfacing?'

'Not the way he spoke, sir. I don't know if Heydrich was a fencer, but . . .'

'He was. The psychiatrist gave Rasch too big an injec-tion?'

'He thought so, afterwards.'

'Bloody man.' Wills looked suddenly at Colvin. 'Experts in infant sciences are all very well. *You* have heard a great many confessions.'

'Not all of them true.'

'Describe Rasch.'

'My own impressions?' When Wills nodded, he said, 'Very tough indeed.'

'Physically?'

'Physically he's hard as an oak plank. Mentally, too, probably, in his own way. He seemed to be fighting the drug.'

'The psychiatrist wasn't sure of that.'

'Well, I'm not sure, either, sir. Nor am I a psychiatrist. I think he's mad, but it's a kind of – '

'Rational madness?' Wills smiled tiredly. 'I know it well. Meet it most days, in fact. Will you get anything out of him?'

'I doubt it.'

'Even with drugs.'

'I think,' Colvin said, 'that he wants to die.'

'Go on.'

'So does the psychiatrist, sir.'

'If you're just agreeing with the psychiatrist,' Wills said, 'I know what he thinks from the report.'

'It wasn't that, sir. It was after he killed Streeton. He was the warder – '

'You saw that, did you?'

'Yes, sir. Rasch just stood there after he'd done it. He was grinning, sort of. He didn't say anything but it was a kind of challenge. Fight to the death kind of thing. I was in the last lot, sir. In Flanders. Sometimes you'd see that expression.'

'I think I know the one you mean,' Wills said. 'Young officers?'

'Not just them, sir.'

'But usually them. I saw it and never understood it. Something to do with the officer class, perhaps?'

Colvin said stolidly, 'Politics isn't my field, sir. But that's the way Rasch looked: he was ready to take on any ten and kill five before they killed him.'

148

'What makes you think,' Wills said, 'that it wasn't the heat of the moment?'

'It wasn't a hot moment, sir. He killed Streeton very coolly.'

Wills picked up the transcript. His eyes flicked through it again. At last he said, 'Hitler, Himmler, Heydrich, Schellenberg. He's disillusioned. He's defiant. He may be suicidal. And I want what's in his head. Even now it could save lives. Any ideas?'

Colvin had an idea. It had come to him moments earlier, as Wills spoke, and he distrusted ideas that came like that; he preferred to examine his fleeting thoughts before he let them out into the open.

'I see you have?'

Colvin said, 'If we offer him death?'

In the early evening there was an informal meeting. The two of them met irregularly but frequently, partly to exchange information, partly to pick each other's brains. Patterson held some puff-of-smoke position midway between the American Embassy and Eisenhower's headquarters and had a steady supply of Bourbon whisky for which Wills was developing a taste. Patterson had studied at Heidelberg in the 'twenties and had a sabre-cut on his left cheekbone to prove it. When the rest of their exchange was over, Wills was tempted to mention Rasch. He did so quietly, *entre nous*, seeking the other's insight.

Patterson said, 'Some have stiffer necks than others. Where's he from?'

'East Prussia.'

'I thought,' Patterson said, smiling, 'you said he wouldn't talk.'

'We know a little.'

'Straight Nazi thug, or what?'

'Soldier. Military family.'

'And tough, huh?'

'Very.'

The American grinned. 'Want me to have a look at him?'

'Not particularly.' Wills felt tired and suddenly irritated with himself. It had been a mistake to let Patterson know even of Rasch's existence. 'Forget him, he doesn't really matter. Just an interesting problem.'

'I agree. How'd you get him?'

'Fished him out,' Wills said carefully, hoping the words carried maritime overtones. Damn it, why *had* he mentioned it? From now on evasions would only serve to intrigue Patterson.

'What was that name again?'

'Rasch,' Wills said dismissively. 'But he doesn't matter, really. Look, I was thinking about those Shaef papers on the Ruhrgebiet people . . .'

Would anything come, Rasch wondered? Had he planted enough? The hours had come and gone and he was still alone, still naked, still unfed and un-watered, and now very uncomfortable. Surely they couldn't ignore what he knew?

The voice through the wall, when at last it came, said, 'Do you want anything?'

He ignored it.

'Nothing?'

He did not reply.

'Some kind of exchange, perhaps?' the voice inquired, and Rasch felt the thud of excitement.

It was time to speak. He said, 'I have nothing to exchange. You have nothing I want.'

'I can't believe that,' the voice said. 'We can offer you a number of things. Food, for example.'

Rasch said, 'I want only to die.'

'Because you have nothing to live for?'

No need to answer.

The voice said, 'If you really want to die, it might be arranged.'

'Then arrange it.'

'You'll want to die like an officer, I expect. Firing squad, that kind of thing?'

'A pistol will do.'

'A pistol, a little privacy, a little time. I know. But for that the price would come steep, Hauptsturmführer. Would you pay it?'

Rasch said, 'There is something I will not do. I will not negotiate with somebody I cannot see.'

The determination to die was his trump, he was sure of that. There was very little to be done to a man determined to die: such a man was beyond threats, beyond persuasion, and could set his own terms. There was torture, of course, but it was doubtful if the British tortured.

'You killed one man,' the voice said reasonably. 'It would scarcely be sensible to give you another opportunity.'

'Up to you,' Rasch said.

'You would give your word?'

'Would you accept it?' They must be face to face; he could not work otherwise.

Silence again. Then, after a couple of hours, the voice again: 'The door is open, Hauptsturmführer. Go through it, turn right and you will come to another open door. Go into the room and close the door.'

'Why should I?'

'Because we can then begin to talk sensibly.'

Rasch entered the room to find a wire screen had been rigged across it. He sat on the chair, looking at the screen and its wall fixings. There was a smell of new-cut wood. They had put the screen up for him. Good, he thought.

A door opened in the opposite wall and a man entered whom Rasch recognized from the room in Dublin. When he sat at the little table on the other side of the wire, he did so gingerly.

Rasch said, 'The Geneva Convention requires only that I give you my name, rank and serial number.'

'That's for prisoners of war,' Colvin said. 'Which you're not. You have been engaged in a conspiracy to extort. Blackmail, in plain words.'

'I was on neutral soil, from which I was removed by force by armed representatives of a belligerent power,' Rasch said coolly. 'Neither you nor I was acting with propriety.'

The man nodded. 'We begin level, then. You want to end your life. I may let you do it in return for information. Whether I allow it will depend on the information. But just to set you straight, I'd better tell you what will happen if you live. You'll be brought to trial as a member of a criminal organization: the SS. Since you are a member, you'll be found guilty. Depending on what you've done, you'll either be hanged or put in prison for a long time.'

Almost the same words Conway had used in Stockholm, Rasch thought. He said, 'I will not betray my friends.'

'I'm not talking about friends. I'm talking about masters. They betrayed you first, from what I hear.'

Rasch said, 'I'm a comparatively junior officer.'

'Of an unusual kind.'

Rasch shrugged. 'How do I know you will keep your side of the agreement?'

'You don't,' Colvin said. 'But I will, when I've pumped you dry.'

'Your word?' Rasch said.

'You don't know I'd keep it.'

'I'm interested in whether you give it.'

'If I do it doesn't alter much. It's my judgment that matters, not my word: if you don't talk enough there'll be no quiet room with a pistol on the table.'

'All the same.'

Colvin nodded. There would be no forward movement unless he conceded, reluctant as he was to do so. 'If I give it to you, I want yours in return: that there'll be no more of your attacks on the people here.'

'Agreed,' Rasch said.

'Right.' Colvin blew his nose. 'We'll start with name, rank and number. After that, we'll have all the details about Hauptsturmführer Franz Rasch. And from there, we'll see what else there is.'

'There's one thing first,' Rasch said. 'Or rather, there are four.'

'Go on.'

'Trousers, cigarettes, food and a little cognac.'

'I can see,' Colvin said, 'that trousers might be necessary to your concentration. The other three come under the heading of rewards. We'll see what progress we make.'

When he began to answer Colvin's questions, Rasch wore his own trousers and socks, plus a khaki shirt and a pair of slippers that had been provided. By the time he returned, under his own steam, to his cell along the corridor, he was concealing his satisfaction He had proved two things. The first was that concessions could be won. The second was that he could exert some control over the direction of the interrogation. Not enough, but some.

ARMED FORCES/SIS LIAISON – ATTENTION
MR R. H. K. WILLS

SUBJECT: Hauptsturmführer Franz Maximilian RASCH, Waffen SS. Debriefing by Commander J. S. Colvin.

1) As you are aware, it was necessary when the subject was first brought to England to confine him in a room in which he would be unable to harm himself, since he was intent upon his own destruction. He is a man of formidable strength and skill and killed the first man to enter his cell alone. He did not respond in any way to conversational overtures. Threats were useless; he seemed to welcome them.

2) Resort was therefore made to chemical methods. Sodium pentathol in this subject, as in others, produced no clear compulsion to tell the truth, and such statements as he made while under the influence of this drug were wild and confused.

3) When it was put to Rasch that the means to kill himself might be made available once he had agreed to make a detailed statement, he at last agreed. The reasons why he wishes so strongly to achieve his own death are not clear, but our psychiatric observer has now come to agree with the prisoner Conway that Rasch's determination is a matter of pride; in other words, if he can no longer live in the way he chooses,

he prefers not to live at all.

4) Debriefing of the prisoner Conway has provided us with a useful basis for Rasch's debriefing.

5) Rasch, in agreeing, made it a condition that he would not betray his friends. This condition was accepted, though with certain reservations. However, once he began to talk, he spoke freely.

6) BIOGRAPHY: Born Berlin, 1910, son of Freiherr Maximilian Rasch.

Home: small estate near Landsberg in East Prussia.

Educated: Imperial Gymnasium, Baden-Baden; Berlin University. SS Cadet School, Bad Neuberg, Mainfranken. (Comment: In other times would probably have followed father and long line of ancestors into Prussian regiments.)

Joined SS in pursuit of military career in 1933, at the time when the SS had a major infusion of blue blood. Rasch says he joined on the same day that the Princes Christof and Wilhelm of Hesse became members. Commented in the course of interrogation that the SS unit Leibstandarte Adolf Hitler, of which he was a member, closely resembled in purpose and discipline, the Household Brigade of the British Army.

Serving with the Leibstandarte, Rasch spent much of the years 1934–40 engaged in personal guard duties. His unit's task was the preservation of Hitler's life.

Rasch claims that on his own request he was transferred to a fighting formation immediately before the German invasion of France and Belgium in 1940. He holds the Iron Cross 1st Class (awarded, he says, during the advance of the von Kleist Panzer group towards St Etienne in 1940). He was wounded, returned to Germany and, upon recovery, to his duties in the Leibstandarte. He was awarded the Knight's Cross of the Iron Cross with Oak Leaves in 1941 during the German advance into Russia. This decoration he received from Hitler personally. Subsequently he participated in three commando-style operations under the command of Sturmbannführer Otto Skorzeny, SS. The first was the rescue of Mussolini from the Gran Sasso in Italy; the second was an attack upon Admiral Horthy's palace in Budapest; the third as spearhead to the German attack in the Ardennes forest on 15 December 1944.

7) VERBATIM: It was felt necessary, from this point, to record verbatim the answers he made to my questions. Upon your instructions, I began by asking him what he knew of Hitler.

INTERROGATOR: When did you last see Adolf Hitler?

RASCH: In person? At the funeral of Reinhard Heydrich in Berlin in June of 1942.

INT: Not since?

RASCH: No.

INT: How well did you know him?

RASCH: I shook his hand twice. He knew me by sight. Occasionally he has nodded to me in passing.

INT: But you were close to him?

RASCH: Nobody is close to him, except perhaps Goebbels and Bormann. I was often near to him.

INT: What did you observe?

RASCH: I saw him get in and out of cars, inspect parades, enter buildings. When he was present I was usually looking elsewhere: my duty was to guard him, not watch him.

INT: This is scarcely helpful.

RASCH: If I asked what you know of Churchill, what would you say? I am willing to tell what I know.

INT: What did you hear?

RASCH: Gossip? I do not listen to gossip.

INT: We all listen. You are bound to have heard things.

RASCH: He has a mistress. Is that the kind of thing you want?

INT: Go on.

RASCH: Fräulein Eva Braun. She has been his mistress for several years. Her sister Gretel is the wife of

	Gruppenführer Fegelein, who is an opportunist.
INT:	Does Fegelein have influence?
RASCH:	On horses only. He's a jumped-up riding instructor.
INT:	We're not getting very far.
RASCH:	My knowledge of Adolf Hitler is limited. I knew Heydrich better.
INT:	Heydrich has been dead nearly three years. We're seeking up-to-date information. What about Hitler's health?
RASCH:	There are rumours that it deteriorated after the attempt on his life last July.
INT:	You know no more than that?
RASCH:	No. I spoke to Skorzeny in January. He told me Hitler remains confident he can win the war.
INT:	How?
RASCH:	The V-weapons, I suppose. I fought in Russia and I fought in the West. I don't see how anybody in his senses could believe Germany can win.
INT:	Are you saying Hitler is not? In his senses, I mean.
RASCH:	I told you, I haven't seen him. But I'm glad his doctor isn't mine.
INT:	Which doctor, and why?
RASCH:	Morell. He *is* a madman. After Heydrich's car was blown up, he was in hospital in Prague. The injuries weren't serious, I gather. At least, they weren't enough to kill him. But Hitler and Himmler insisted only the best was good enough and all the doctors came from Berlin. Bunch of prima ballerinas, they were. They stood round arguing pet theories until sepsis set in, and that is what killed him. Apparently one good surgeon, operating quickly, could have pulled all the bits of leather and horsehair out of his body, and cleaned the wounds, but Morell and Kersten and the rest waited too long, so he died. Nine days, that took. And he suffered.
INT:	How do you know all this?

RASCH: I was in Prague.
INT: I said, how do you know?
RASCH: I was told by Lina Heydrich, the widow. She was as bad as he was – one of those icy blondes. At the funeral I was supposed to give her my arm for support, but she stood as though she was posing for a statue. Heydrich was –
INT: We're talking about Hitler.
RASCH: Well Morell, the doctor, is Hitler's personal physician. As I say, I'm glad he isn't mine.
INT: You have no more to say about Hitler?
RASCH: It's difficult to know what you want.
INT: We'll leave it there for the time being.

'Useless,' Wills said. Colvin had been summoned to London from Surrey as soon as Wills had read the transcript.

'To tell you the truth, sir, I'm a bit out of my depth. I just don't know enough. For instance, I'd never heard of this man Fegelein.'

'Neither had I,' Wills said. 'We need political experts for the fine detail. How frank do you think he's being?'

'I think,' Colvin said, 'that he's answering direct questions fairly straight.'

Wills thought for a moment or two. 'We'll try it another way. Think of this as once-over-lightly. We'll have people study the transcripts and produce further questions. Keep on at him. On and on. But in the meantime, you can tackle him on the others, starting with Schellenberg.'

The questioning went on for days and Rasch was a model subject. When he knew answers, he gave them. When he didn't, he said so. Yet Colvin, listening, and Wills, reading the daily transcripts, began to suspect that somewhere there was more.

They learned a few fascinating snippets about several of the Nazi leaders, some of it good, some not. Himmler had a mistress in Lübeck, named Hedwig, who had borne him two children; Schellenberg was hated by Kaltenbrunner and Bormann but protected by Himmler; Hitler, since the Bomb

Plot in July, had a deep distrust of his generals, with a few exceptions, Guderian, Jodl and Keitel among them; Goering was no longer of consequence, according to Schellenberg.

'If I were writing the William Hickey column in the *Daily Express*,' Wills said one evening, 'this is just the stuff I'd want. But I'm not and it isn't. He knows no more of the Stockholm business than he told Conway, or so it seems. Their statements coincide. The single important current event he seems to know about is Wolff's negotiations in Northern Italy with Alexander's people, and we know about that already – naturally enough since we're involved!'

It went on for three more days. Rasch was questioned at length by military strategists, by political analysts, by psychological experts. He was free with his answers, and appeared to be hiding nothing. He was even anxious to advance information that was not particularly wanted; in particular he was keen to talk about Heydrich, whom he clearly detested, a keenness that none of his interrogators shared. He kept on asking on what date the British would keep their part of the bargain and supply him with the means to end his life.

It was frustrating, but not all the information was valueless. Hitler's distrust of his generals and apparent insistence on conducting the war himself, was valuable intelligence for Supreme Headquarters; Rasch's description of Schellenberg gave a little more insight into the by-now-limited operations of German intelligence. Rasch had known Dr Best, Gauleiter of Denmark, and believed Best would be unlikely to carry out wholesale destruction as the Allied armies approached. The information was duly passed on.

And by now it was not the British alone who were frustrated. The Americans, too, having been supplied with some of the products of Rasch's interrogation, wanted to know if there was more. Patterson mentioned it several times in the course of a conversation with Wills.

'You were holding out on me,' he accused good-humouredly.

'If I was, it didn't do much good.'

'Beat it out of him. What you need is a good Missouri deputy sheriff.'

'No need,' Wills said. 'He answers the questions.'

'Maybe you're not asking the right ones.'

'Possibly not. Though it's difficult to think of anything that hasn't been covered.'

'About the Stockholm business,' Patterson said. 'He hasn't much to say there.'

'I'm inclined to think he's told us all he knows. He was given some papers to deliver, and it was all an intelligence operation. Not what he thought it was. If it wasn't, how much more *can* he know?'

'Could we get to see the papers?' Patterson asked. He was smiling.

'I don't think so.' Not bloody likely, Wills thought to himself.

He was already irritated that Patterson had had to be given access to such transcripts as did not mention the White List. *That* instruction had come from the Cabinet Office as a result of a direct request from Eisenhower's staff chief at SHAEF, General Bedell Smith, and was a consequence of his own ham-handedness in mentioning Rasch to Patterson in the first place.

Patterson said, 'We could make a formal request. Maybe that's what I'm doing right this minute.'

'Seems pretty *in*formal to me,' Wills said.

'Yeah, well . . .' Patterson rose. 'That's about it I guess. By the way, who's Conway?'

How in hell did they know about Conway! His name had been edited out of the transcripts. 'Conway?' Wills said politely.

'If you don't want to talk about him,' Patterson said, 'you shouldn't leave his name around. Transcript Five, where he's talking about getting out of Stockholm. Who's Conway?'

'One of ours.' What on earth had the reference been?

'He helped Rasch out, that it?'

'Something on those lines,' Wills said cautiously, wishing desperately that he could have a quick look at Transcript Five. He couldn't get up and go; that would be suspicious behaviour, especially to Patterson who was suspicious by nature. To his surprise, Patterson dropped the subject. Wills was sure it would be picked up again.

Wills returned savagely to his office to examine the version of Transcript Five that had been sent to the Americans. There it was: 'Conway told me about an Irish ship and said he believed he could get us aboard.' *Us!* Wills swore. He'd edited the transcripts himself, in order to be certain. It was fatigue, or carelessness and it was unforgivable; his fault and nobody else's. Wheels would turn between the American Embassy and Downing Street, that was clear. Very well, he must get in first. Not that there was the slightest prospect of the Americans being shown the White List; that was a British secret and it was vital it remain so, or they'd be doing Schellenberg's job for him. The other paper, once its contents were accurately assessed, might well be just as damaging.

Wills gave instructions that Conway be moved at once to the wing of a mental hospital in Buckinghamshire where SIS housed some of its problem detainees. The Americans didn't know about either document, and could only learn about them from Conway. If necessary, Conway would have to disappear altogether. Rasch, too, though happily *he* was prepared to do the dirty work himself.

Late on the night of Conway's arrival at the mental hospital, he heard the observation slot on the door of his room slide open and then close. He took no notice: the process of inspection was familiar enough. But then the door itself opened, the light was switched on and Conway sat up in bed blinking. He had two visitors. One was the man who had issued him with bedclothes and towel. The other was new to him and this man nodded dismissal to the nurse-cum-warder, came to sit beside Conway's bed and offered him a cigarette. 'Who are you?' he asked.

Conway told him. The man's face seemed somehow familiar, but he couldn't place it.

'Oh yes, I know. The neutral who got tangled. You were a bit greedy, weren't you?'

'I was a bloody idiot,' Conway said. No longer dazzled, he looked at the man carefully. 'Don't I know you?'

'I don't think so. Got everything you need?'

'A lot more than I need, thank you very much,' Conway said sarcastically.

'Interrogation over?'

'How do I know! Who are *you*?'

The visitor smiled. 'You're not allowed to ask, I'm afraid, but you can think of me as welfare, if you'd care to. I see myself sometimes as a kind of sweeper-up of unconsidered trifles. Sometimes there's a little left over that didn't come out in the interrogation. If you think of something like that, you can ask for me. All right?'

Conway grimaced. 'I've told your people everything I know, believe me.'

'I'm sure you have. But sometimes one remembers something.' The visitor rose. 'I'll leave these with you.' He put the packet of cigarettes on the locker beside Conway's bed. 'If you do remember anything, ask for me. The name is – well, to you it's Mowgli. Kipling, you know, a small conceit.'

Then he left and the light went out. In the darkness Conway stared up towards the ceiling, projecting Mowgli's face on to a kind of mental screen. They *had* met, he was sure of it. But where?

Chapter Eleven

The pressure had been growing, and would grow further. Patterson, his voice friendly and courteous as ever on the telephone, had none the less given an uncompromising message. 'Just so you'll know,' he had said, 'we've decided to make it formal. You'll be getting it on paper later today. We want access to this guy Rasch.'

'You'll find there are difficulties,' Wills told him. 'Health for one. In any case, it's completely pointless. We've bled him dry.'

'Always another drop of blood in there.'

'Vampire,' Wills said, forcing a chuckle. He put down the telephone, allowed it to rest for a moment, then picked it up again and asked the operator to put him through to James Tendring in the War Cabinet Office. 'I'd like to come and see you.'

'Urgent?'

'It's becoming so.'

'Twenty minutes.'

Wills walked, thinking hard as he did so. The word 'no' had to be said. It must also be said with some unlikely combination of delicacy and finality impossible in his own relationship with Patterson. Well, that was what diplomats and Cabinet Offices were for.

Tendring was baggy-eyed with fatigue, chewing with distaste at a cheese sandwich. 'More like soap than soap itself,' he said, 'but it's the only chance I'll get. The Old Man was dancing like a dervish till four this morning and there's a meeting at twelve-thirty that'll go on until doomcrack.'

Wills explained his problem and waited for a solution to be manufactured. It was a relief, sometimes, to play pass-the-parcel.

Tendring chewed morosely on the sandwich. 'This stuff grows in volume the more you masticate. You know the Prime Minister's seen the list?'

'Yes.'

'It's to be destroyed.'

'Good.'

'He says it would be foolish to allow the tarnish of suspicion to besmirch the shining silver of victory.' Tendring grinned. 'In other words, keep it quiet at all costs.' He chewed again for a moment. 'All costs,' he repeated.

'Meaning that – '

'Meaning,' Tendring said, 'that you may have to take your little indiarubber and rub it all out.'

'Who is going to explain to our American friends that their reach is no longer quite long enough?'

'It will be done, never fear. Broad shoulders will bear their blows.'

'I can't help feeling,' Wills said, 'that there's more to come.'

'There's always more to come,' Tendring said. 'I can't say I'm keen on this solution, but – how good is Rasch's English?'

'Not good.'

'Would he remember any of the names?'

'A few. Not many. To him they're just names. To Conway they mean a lot more. He's a journalist, remember.'

'Yes. We simply can't risk it. As long as they're alive the Americans will nag and nag and nag. Still, that little arrangement you made with Rasch will save somebody an unpleasant moment. Something to be thankful for, I suppose. Pity for Conway that they know about him, too.'

'My fault, of course.'

Tendring looked at him through calm, weary eyes. 'Yes. We all have our crosses.'

Anticipating that Patterson's formal request would be waiting on his return, Wills stayed away from Curzon Street and instead went direct to Waterloo Station to take the train to Woking. He telephoned from a call box and arranged for transport to meet him.

It had been no part of his intention actually to allow Rasch to kill himself. Colvin had given his word, but Colvin was comfortably outranked and could have been overruled. Among other things, Wills felt strongly that Rasch and everybody like him *should* ultimately come face to face with a court, and justice. About Conway he felt guilty, starkly and personally guilty.

A few minutes after his arrival, he was sitting at the interrogator's table, facing the wire screen and waiting for Rasch to enter the room through the door opposite.

To Rasch the sudden summons had come as a surprise. It was clear to him that the interrogation was complete; the last two sessions had covered only ground that had previously been gone over several times, and now they seemed to have run out of questions for him. So far it had gone as well as he could hope. He had answered all their questions; the fact that they had no more to ask, and furthermore had not asked several important ones, was scarcely his fault. If the British kept their word in the matter of his intended suicide, his strategy was ready, but he was inclined to believe they would not. The British were known for their adherence to the law and he had seen in Colvin's face when suicide had been talked about, that Colvin did not understand his motives.

As he came in through the door and saw Wills, he half stopped. This one was new. Rasch looked at him for a moment, absorbing an impression, before he turned and closed the door and heard the lock click. The man looked junior, some kind of clerk, a messenger with a minor additional question.

'Sit down, please,' Wills said.

Rasch remained standing, looking down at him. Like Conway before him, he was making a swift reappraisal based upon nothing but tone of voice.

'I said, sit down.'

Rasch obeyed and got in first. 'I have co-operated to the maximum. I kept my word. I now expect that you will keep yours.'

Wills watched him as he said, 'We intend to.' Something happened in Rasch's eyes. It wasn't much: a widening, some involuntary movement of the muscles.

'Thank you.'

Wills said, 'There is only one condition. It must be soon.'

'Today?' Rasch said.

'At once.'

Rasch nodded. 'I too have a condition. No, not a condition, a request.'

'If I can grant it, I will. What is it? A letter? I should warn you that there is not much chance of a letter being either sanctioned or delivered.'

Rasch shook his head. 'It is unlikely I shall miss my own brain. However, if I do, I should like somebody to administer the *coup de grâce*.'

'Very well. You gave us your word once before, and kept it. I am personally tempted to supply you with a length of rope and a chair to jump off, but I understand you were promised a weapon. Do I have your word that if the weapon is given to you, you will use it against nobody but yourself?'

'Certainly.'

Wills said, 'I have made the arrangements. You will be taken to a cell in which there is a pistol. It contains one bullet. The door will be locked and you will be left alone for a time. I'm afraid there will be no priest.'

'No need for a priest,' Rasch said. Now came the important thing. 'Who will administer the *coup de grâce*?' He stared hard into the man's eyes.

'I will,' Wills said firmly.

'Then let us do it.' Rasch stood up, the chair scraping on the concrete floor, brought his slippered heels together and bowed. 'Thank you for your courtesy.'

'I shall be outside the door. When I hear the shot I shall enter.'

He told Rasch which way to go. Rasch turned to the door and left the room. He walked slowly along the corridor, listening. No footsteps accompanied his own. He came to the cell that had been described to him, glanced inside and saw

the table with the pistol on it. He was mildly surprised that
it was German, a Mauser. Perhaps they thought he would be
more accurate with a weapon he knew. He stepped into the
cell and waited, and after a moment the door slammed.

Rasch picked up the Mauser, unloaded the single round
and examined the mechanism, in particular the firing-pin.
The pistol had been carefully cleaned and smelled of oil, as
pistols should. He loaded the single round carefully, slid off
the safety-catch and placed the muzzle carefully beneath his
chin, wondering as he did so whether the man was watching,
or merely listening. He said, 'Are you there?'

No answer. He called more loudly, 'Are you there?'

'Yes.' The voice was only on the other side of the door, and
the word perfectly clear. Rasch was prepared to bet the man
was sheltering behind the brickwork, though the door was of
steel.

'Then listen,' Rasch said. 'Listen carefully. There is
something very important that you do not know.'

There was a pause. Then, 'What is that?'

'Something I did not tell you.'

Lost his damned nerve! Wills thought. Now he's got the
gun, he doesn't want to use it, at least on himself. He
glanced at the observation hole in the cell door and grimaced. Put an eye to that and it might very well be filled with
a bullet! 'Concerning what?'

'Heydrich,' Rasch said. 'You should have asked me more
about Heydrich.'

'He's dead.'

'Oh yes,' Rasch said. 'Heydrich is dead. But his files are
not.' The pistol was still beneath his chin, its muzzle no
longer so cold against his skin.

'Why should they be of any value now?' Wills demanded.
He had heard about Heydrich's files; their reputation had
travelled. It was difficult, though, to understand why they
might still be important nearly three years after his death.

'I shall explain in detail,' Rasch said, 'when we have concluded an agreement.'

'The agreement's concluded already,' Wills said crisply.

'Or it will be when you pull that trigger.'

'I mean a further agreement. Having negotiated for my death, I wish now to negotiate for my life.'

'Impossible,' Wills said.

'In return for what I know about them,' Rasch said, 'you will provide me with another identity, with money and with immunity for the future.'

'Impossible,' Wills repeated.

'Is it? Do you know the shareholding in the Focke-Wulf company? Do you know whose ships fuelled long-range U-Boats? Do you know all you wish to know about the personal lives of certain politicians and financiers?'

Wills felt himself beginning to sweat.

'Do you wish,' Rasch continued, 'to prevent major scandals when they fall into the wrong hands, perhaps Russian hands? Have you considered that possibility?' He wished he could see the other man's face. 'My finger is on the trigger,' he called. 'I shall pull it, quite soon, unless you respond in some encouraging way. Then all this material, very valuable material, will be lost.'

Wills half-believed him. There had been rumours in plenty about Focke-Wulf, *and* about tankers keeping rendezvous with U-Boats in the South Atlantic. It was thought they were mainly South American, but . . .

'If you are not senior enough to make a decision,' he heard Rasch call impudently, 'you must put my offer to somebody who is.' Rasch moved the Mauser until he could see the black circle of its muzzle, and found himself thinking how easy it would be to pull the trigger. In a way, the thought was almost attractive. But there was Conway, and possibly even Schellenberg, and both had prior claims upon a bullet. He replaced the barrel beneath his chin.

Wills would have conceded at once if this had been a purely departmental matter. He existed to gain intelligence by whatever means. But the morning's instructions from Tendring and the Cabinet Office had been clear and unqualified. If Rasch were now to remain alive, there was a danger he would have to be surrendered at some point to the Americans. He said, 'Wait,' and went off to the telephone.

Extricating Tendring from his meeting was a lengthy business, and explaining Rasch's demand proved an unpleasant one because it reflected so seriously upon his own and his department's competence. To say that a man had been cleaned out, and then to discover not only that he had not, but that he remained in possession of information of great value, and *then* to be given an ultimatum after the prisoner had been handed a loaded pistol, must sound to Tendring more like insanity than mere incompetence.

They talked on the scrambler phone, obliquely, conscious always of telephone security.

'The arrangement need only be temporary, surely? A postponement, no more.'

'Certainly,' Wills agreed.

'Then offer what is necessary. Reluctantly though, or he'll smell fish. Afterwards we can resume the position which existed this morning.'

'Without his co-operation, I imagine.'

'Yes. Without that.'

A tap on the door of the cell. Rasch said, 'You have decided?'

'We agree. The terms will have to be worked out.'

Rasch smiled to himself and said, 'I have told you the terms: money, immunity and another identity.'

'All possible, if the information is as important as you say.'

'I doubt if you'll be disappointed.'

'Then put down the gun. Return to the interrogation room.'

Rasch returned to the interrogation room. But he retained the pistol, still held under his chin, pointing upward. Wills, watching him through an observation port in the door, called, 'No gun. I won't talk under those conditions.'

'I will talk on no other terms!' Rasch said. 'You can have an army with you. But this is for me.'

Wills thought about it. When he entered the room, Colvin

was with him, armed with a big, clumsy service Webley and they were escorted by one of the warders carrying a Sten.

ARMED FORCES/SIS LIAISON – Attention
J. P. Tendring, War Cabinet Office
SUBJECT: Further debriefing Hauptsturmführer Franz Maximilian RASCH.
Debriefing by R. H. K. Wills; Observer, Commander J. S. Colvin

VERBATIM TRANSCRIPT

RASCH: My terms are fifty thousand pounds in Spanish pesetas, a Mexican passport and a signed guarantee from the British Foreign Secretary that I shall be immune from prosecution.

WILLS: That's really too high.

RASCH: I'm not an idiot. I imagine you think you can take my information and then go back on your word. I have to protect myself, and I have a way of doing so. First you must agree. If you do not agree and today, I shall pull the trigger.

WILLS: The matter will have to be discussed.
(Debriefing ceased for consultation. Resumed seven p.m.)

WILLS: I have authorization. The money will be deposited in the Banco de Bilbao in Madrid. The passport will be prepared. You understand there is no way we can provide you with a true Mexican passport? The document itself will be genuine, but the entries will be forgeries.

RASCH: Where is the letter?

WILLS: Being prepared. The Foreign Secretary is not immediately available. You understand that none of this material will be given to you unless the information you have is sufficiently valuable?

RASCH: I understand that.

169

WILLS: Very well, tell me about Heydrich.

RASCH: Just before Christmas of 1940 I was appointed his adjutant.

WILLS: Christmas 1940? You told us –

RASCH: I know what I told you. After I was wounded in France, I returned to the Führer's guard. After a few weeks I was transferred to Heydrich. He was then Obergruppenführer SS, the equivalent of lieutenant-general.

WILLS: You told us you were a member of a fighting formation.

RASCH: Until that appointment that is what I was. The information I have given you so far is all true, except that I omitted certain details of my service with Heydrich.

(The next part of the interrogation covers Rasch's service with Reinhard Heydrich. Rasch says he served for two periods as adjutant to Heydrich. The first ended in April of 1941 when he returned at his own request to the Leibstandarte for training in preparation for the attack on Russia. He served in Panzergruppe One, in Army Group South under von Runstedt and was wounded in July at the battle of Uman. He was recommended for a decoration and later received the Knight's Cross with Oak Leaves from Hitler personally. He was thereupon transferred back to duties as adjutant to Heydrich. This was just before Christmas of 1941. Heydrich was then Reichsprotektor of Bohemia and Moravia. Heydrich used Rasch as a fencing opponent and riding companion. His duties were light.)

VERBATIM RESUMES

RASCH: I dined with him the night before the partisans attacked his car. I had applied to return to active service again. I was fully recovered. He said I could not be spared and invited me to dinner. It was earlier that day that he talked to me about Ernst Wilhelm Bohle.

WILLS: Tell me about Bohle.

RASCH: We had just finished a fencing bout and for once I had permitted myself to beat him. Heydrich wasn't bad, though not as good as he thought he was, especially with the foil. He was annoyed that day. When we were in the shower afterwards, he gave my shoulder a comradely slap. It was hard and my skin was wet and it was right over a wound, and he laughed. That was Heydrich.

WILLS: What did you do?

RASCH: I also laughed. You would have done so, too, I assure you. He said he had a fine idea and took me up to his office after we had changed – that was in the Hradcany Palace in Prague, of course; we fenced in the cellar – and he gave me a glass of beer, which I drank with a certain hesitation because Heydrich was capable of jokes and there could have been something in it, an emetic perhaps. I'd beaten him badly, you see, trying to get myself out of his service, and Heydrich was always playful when he lost. He asked if I knew Bohle. I said I'd seen him, once in Berlin, at the Reich Chancellery, and knew who he was, and he told me about a document prepared by Bohle for use in the occupation of Great Britain. It was a list of all the people who might be expected to collaborate with our forces. Guess where it is now? he said. I told him it would be in some filing cabinet somewhere. He said yes, that was exactly where it was, and could I think of a better use for it?

WILLS: What did you say?

RASCH: Well, a babe in arms could think of a better use. I said it must provide the basis of an excellent spy network, if nothing else. Espionage, information, anything. Blackmail, too, for that matter. You have seen the list.

WILLS: Where did you come into it?

RASCH: I was to look after the project for him. He always had people looking after things for him. The idea was that I was to be attached to the head of Amt VI, Walter Schellenberg, and to liaise with the Foreign Ministry via Bohle. Schellenberg's overseas communications with Bohle's foreign contacts were what Heydrich was after. Bohle and Schellenberg kept themselves well apart. They were bureaucrats and they behaved like bureaucrats. Heydrich wanted them galloping in harness with himself holding the reins. My appointment was actually made. He got a secretary to type it there and then, that afternoon. Perhaps because I'd beaten him once too often.

WILLS: What was your formal position?

RASCH: I was to be on Schellenberg's staff. They hadn't decided on a title. Indeed, at the time Heydrich was wounded, I doubt whether Schellenberg even knew I was coming.

WILLS: He knew later?

RASCH: He certainly knew before Heydrich died.

WILLS: At that time, while Heydrich was dying, what were your duties?

RASCH: Himmler took over. Perhaps you know? He intended to make Czechoslovakia pay. There was a village called Lidice . . .

WILLS: I know all about Lidice. Tell me about your own activities.

RASCH: The same. Paperwork related to the guard at the Hradcany Palace continued to come to me. Minor administrative work. Nothing serious. Then, on the day Heydrich died, Himmler suddenly summoned me. He was in Heydrich's office on the first floor. I wondered what on earth he wanted! He started by giving me an emotional sermon about Heydrich, though how anybody could feel any emotion about him except fear and hate escapes me. But Himmler called him the greatest SS man of all and I nodded and stood to attention. Then I got my orders. To me was to go the sacred duty – his words, not mine – of conveying Heydrich's body to Berlin for the funeral.

WILLS: We have obtained pictures of the funeral. This is you?

RASCH: Yes.

WILLS: Shaking hands with Himmler.

RASCH: He was thanking me. That was after the cermony. And this is the important matter. It was then that Himmler ordered me back to Prague to collect Heydrich's files.

WILLS: Why?

RASCH: I'd never seen anything of what was in them, but I knew they were there in the castle. Heydrich had dossiers on everybody, including Himmler and the Führer, or so it was said. Those files were the real basis of Heydrich's position. Nobody dared cross him for fear of the things he knew about them.

WILLS: Himmler wanted – what?

RASCH: He wanted them moved. He told me they were under guard in a sealed room in the Hradcany and that I was to move them at once. Himmler wanted his own hands on them and nobody else's.

WILLS: *Your* hands were all right?

RASCH: I was expendable.

WILLS: Explain.

RASCH: I was Obersturmführer, then, a junior officer of a fighting formation. Once the job was done, who'd notice if I disappeared?

WILLS: But you didn't.

RASCH: Because I gave it a lot of thought.

WILLS: Explain.

RASCH: When I flew into Prague, I had everything waiting for me. I had trucks, motor-cyclists, command cars and a company of Waffen SS. My theory was that if I sealed and loaded everything at very high speed, Himmler might believe I hadn't had time to look at anything. Anyway, everything was locked and he had the keys. So I myself tied wire and fixed seals to every cabinet. We moved them in seventeen minutes and I sent a timed signal to the Reichsführer-SS immediately on my arrival in Prague, immediately upon beginning the work, and immediately upon completing it. We then made up a convoy and drove through the night to deliver the cabinets where Himmler wanted them.

WILLS: Where was that?

RASCH: For the moment that is my secret. And please do not think you can either trick it out of me or force me to tell you. I will tell you voluntarily when you have demonstrated your agreement with my terms by supplying me with evidence that the things I require have been carried out.

WILLS: We'll return to it.

RASCH: He was actually waiting when I got there. He demanded to know whether the convoy had stopped. I told him it had, that we had stopped once, for fuel and refreshment at the SS barracks at Halle, which, ironically enough, is where Heydrich was born. The trucks were guarded throughout. We stayed twenty minutes and were timed in and out. Himmler said he was impressed. I think I saved my life by sheer speed.

WILLS: What happened then?

RASCH: He had had a room prepared. He intended to keep the files in there. Nobody else was to enter, ever. The filing cabinets were carried up to the room. It had a special steel door with complex locks. Himmler vanished in there and stayed several hours. When he came out he drove at once to the airfield without a word.

WILLS: What happened to you?

RASCH: I remained there. Himmler's orders. The room was sealed and there was a permanent guard mounted outside it. Himmler came back twice while I was there, each time for a full day, and locked himself up alone with the files. Obviously he was going through them. He used me as a removal man. He called me up to the room when he wanted cabinets moved about. It was very strange.

WILLS: Why strange?

RASCH: What is the point of achieving a position like his and then engaging in menial work? I should have thought the whole point was to avoid it.

WILLS: Was that all you did – to stack the cabinets?

RASCH: At that time.

WILLS: But later?

RASCH: I said I will tell you all I know. May I continue in my own way?

WILLS: Continue.

RASCH: When I was assisting, he broke off a few times and I had to sit and listen to his monologues. The Reichsführer-SS sat there like some common labourer, eating a piece of sausage and drinking water and talked about Heydrich. I think in a way he was relieved Heydrich was no longer there. Even to him Heydrich must have represented some kind of threat. Anyway, when the cabinets had all been stacked, and he had been through them all, the door was sealed again. One cabinet he took with him to Berlin. I had to carry it to his car and I rode with him all the way. We had two armoured cars in front and two behind and motor-cycle outriders. I had a Schmeisser light machine-gun and I rode all the way with a bullet in the breech.

WILLS: Where was the file taken?

RASCH: To the Prinz Albrechtstrasse.

WILLS: Its contents?

RASCH: I have no idea. I returned to collect clothes and equipment, and then joined Schellenberg.

(COMMENT: Rasch's work with Schellenberg and the Foreign Intelligence department of the RSHA – Reichsicherheitshauptamt – are described in the Transcript of Debriefing session IV.)

WILLS: In your earlier statement you said your contacts with Himmler were limited. Were they limited after this?

RASCH: He sent for me from time to time to carry out errands for him.

WILLS: Why you?

RASCH: I was a soldier, and Himmler had always had a romantic feeling about soldiering. I imagine it's evaporating now he's soldiering himself. I'd demonstrated that I could work fast and that he could trust me. I was the gallant young man who'd die for him.

WILLS: Would you have died for him?

RASCH: I'm a soldier. I would have died as ordered. I can think of more glorious causes.

WILLS: We're straying from the point. He sent for you to do some errands?

RASCH: It must have been about May of 1943. Certainly quite a lot of time had elapsed since I'd seen him last. Schellenberg came rushing in to me and said I must go at once to the Reichsführer-SS. He'd sent for me. I went and Himmler stood me in front of his desk and stared at me in silence for a long time. He was frowning and I thought I was going to be shot. Then he told me he wanted me to go to . . . well, to where the files are stored, and to bring him a certain file. He'd caught his fingers in a drawer and they were painful and bandaged and he showed them to me as though they were some fearful wound. Then he said, 'The question is, Rasch, can I trust you?'

WILLS: You went?

RASCH: I was timed in and out of the place. I was in the room about half a minute. No, perhaps a little more because I had to find the cabinet, break the seal, find the file and then replace the seal. But I was quick, believe me.

WILLS: Did you read the file?

RASCH: It was put into a briefcase which was handcuffed to my wrist. It was locked by the man who kept watch on me, and unlocked by Himmler himself. I had no key so there was no way of looking inside.

WILLS: Whose file was it?

RASCH: A man named Allen Dulles, an American. I remember that. He is the American intelligence chief in Switzerland. He's conducting negotiations now with Obergruppenführer Karl Wolff. Did I tell you that?

(COMMENT: See Transcript II for details of negotiations. Schellenberg clearly aware of them. Is Hitler? or Himmler?)

WILLS: You told us, but we knew already. You spoke of errands. Were you sent for files at any other time?

RASCH: Several times. As long as I was with Schellenberg I was used in this way. After a time they even stopped timing me in and out.

WILLS: So you saw some of the files?

RASCH: There was never really time to read them, but I got a good general idea of the range and content of the files.

(COMMENT: Rasch was questioned later as to range and content. See attached schedule.)

WILLS: The papers Schellenberg gave you to bring out of Germany, were they duplicated in Heydrich's files?

RASCH: I saw two copies of the British list.

WILLS: Does Schellenberg know that?

RASCH: I certainly did not tell him. I doubt if he knows.

WILLS: Why do you doubt it? Schellenberg is head of the—
RASCH: The files belonged first to Heydrich and then to Himmler. They were extremely secret and largely personal. It wasn't exactly a public archive.
WILLS: *You* saw them.
RASCH: I'd be surprised if anybody else did.
WILLS: The British list. Do you know where your copy came from?
RASCH: The one I had is stamped Number One of Three. There were three copies only. One was for Bohle as Gauleiter-designate of Great Britain. One was for Admiral Raeder, who was in command of preparations for the projected invasion. The third copy went to Heydrich.
WILLS: Why?
RASCH: He collected such things. He must have obtained Raeder's copy after Sea Lion was cancelled. Numbers Two and Three are in Heydrich's files. Himmler obviously knows they are there but has not had the intelligence to make use of them. Heydrich had.
WILLS: All right, but it's a tall story. You're saying that Heydrich mentioned a document to you and you alone. And then that nearly three years later, Schellenberg did the same. And in the meantime you've seen the document yourself, in the most secret files in Germany.
RASCH: That is true. As to coincidence, what is that? My SS number was the same as my date of birth. These were random events.
WILLS: What about the financial statement?
RASCH: I have no knowledge of it. I can only speculate.
WILLS: Go ahead.
RASCH: If it was intended that through me the statement should reach Ivan – that it should reach the Soviets – and if its purpose was disruption, as it clearly was with the British list, then it refers to some Allied activity.

WILLS: You mentioned Focke-Wulf.

RASCH: That is an example. One of Heydrich's files referred to American shareholdings in the Focke-Wulf company.

WILLS: After the war began?

RASCH: Yes. Some special terms existed about the remitting of dividends, but yes.

WILLS: There were other companies?

RASCH: Several others.

WILLS: Just a minute. Before you begin to tell me about them, let's stay with the financial document. Have you any idea who could have prepared it?

RASCH: I say only that it is a possibility the document is about some such American or British shareholding.

WILLS: British?

RASCH: Yes, British. There are places in the Ruhr which have not been bombed, either by the British or the Americans. Of course, that could be a random pattern, too. I merely doubt that it is. However, there is a financier who has assisted Schellenberg with many transactions. He is also a great supporter of Himmler.

WILLS: Who?

RASCH: I'll tell you about him. When the Nazi Party first came to power, and even before, it received support from many such people. From bankers and industrialists who thought the party would destroy the Bolsheviks. A group was formed called Friends of the Reichsführer-SS, whose purpose was to see that he was never short of funds. The head of this organization is von Klaussen of the Bendler Bank in Köln. He was a personal friend of Heydrich, too.

WILLS: He could have prepared the document?

RASCH: It is the purest speculation, but von Klaussen is an extremely powerful man, and if the information is so secret, very few would know it, eh? Well, he is one who would know.

(At this point, debriefing was again halted for further examination of the document. The letter B – for Bendler? – is watermarked into the paper. An attempt is being made in the City of London to find pre-war correspondence with the Bendler Bank to examine the watermarks of its stationery.) (At one a.m. we learned that specimens of the Bendler Bank letterhead had been found in the correspondence files of Hauser & Co., merchant bankers, of Old Jewry in the City of London. The watermarked letter B is in effect the Bendler Bank's trademark. However, inquiries made by the British Embassy in Switzerland elicited the information that von Klaussen is dead.)

(Debriefing resumed, two a.m.)

WILLS: I formed the impression that this paper was recently-prepared. For whom would it have been prepared? Himmler?

RASCH: Not from what I saw of it.

WILLS: Why not?

RASCH: It is not obsequious enough. If it were for Himmler, there would be a grovel on every line. Probably it was for Schellenberg.

WILLS: For your mission?

RASCH: How can I know? I should say that it does not look like a report as such, though I know little of such things. It looks like two pages which are part of some larger document.

WILLS: All right. Now – who do you say refuelled the U-Boats?

RASCH: There are certain shipowners, Greek and South American, who have done so throughout the war. Certainly I can give you names . . .

Chapter Twelve

Neither man had slept. Wills, who himself felt weary beyond belief, wondered how Tendring kept going at all. The Prime Minister had again worked until three a.m. when he went cheerfully off to bed leaving the War Cabinet staff to record and act upon decisions taken. That happened day after day and year after year.

'Our kind of medal,' Tendring said, 'is a portmanteau beneath the eyes. It's a civil equivalent of mention in despatches.' Tendring never changed. Through the years Wills had known him he had been always tired, always amused, always somehow able to summon the energy to read and listen with concentration.

He also had a penetrating eye for weakness. 'You went,' he said with a degree of surprise, 'to a merchant bank?'

'I went to a man at Hauser's who is security cleared.'

'Money men,' Tendring said, 'are like pet cats. They can appear domesticated, but they are never, never, never tame. Give them half a chance and they gobble up the goldfish and look at you defiantly over the bared skeleton. Did it help, identifying the Bendler Bank?'

'Looks like it. Piece of a jigsaw, that kind of thing. There's something called a company profile. If you get enough figures you can determine the shape of the whole enterprise and no two are alike. A bit like fingerprints.'

'I can imagine,' Tendring said. 'Whose sticky paws are on this?'

Wills hesitated briefly. 'It looks,' he said, 'as though this one is the Co-lect Corporation. They have a major holding in Untersee Elektrische Fabrik. U-Boats.'

Tendring said with relief, 'Thank God they're American.'

Wills corrected that happy assumption. 'They're international. There's a good slice of them that's British.'

Tendring suddenly looked a good deal wider awake. 'Which slice?'

'Union Electric. Big, but a subsidiary.'

'How nice,' Tendring said softly. 'There's even one former director holding ministerial rank.'

'I know. More to come, too. It seems there are parts of the Ruhr, and one or two other places, that have been . . . well, shall we say they seem to have been spared the agonies of air attack?'

Tendring's mouth tightened. 'Any good news?'

'Quite a lot. Rasch knows where the body's buried.'

'Give me another titbit,' Tendring said.

'All right. The gallant Greeks, our brave allies, have one or two disreputable citizens in the shipping industry who have kept the U-Boats refuelled.'

Tendring sat up, eased his shoulders, and lit one of his very rare cigarettes. 'And Rasch knows where this material is, does he? Has he told you?'

'Not yet. Here's the transcript.'

'Sit tight while I read it.'

Ten minutes later, Tendring said, 'Where is he now?'

'In a cell. He's sitting there with that bloody pistol under his chin, holding on to his little secret. Not another word until he has evidence that the money has been deposited.'

'And has it?'

'No.'

'That won't be the end of it, you know,' Tendring said. 'When he tells us where it all is, he'll turn out to be the only man with access.'

'I know.'

'Furthermore, in case you think you're the only one with bad news, *I* will tell *you* something. This can't possibly stop here. The Americans have a right to this information. That's what the Old Gentleman will say – don't forget he's half-American himself. Come to that, I agree with him. We don't want skeletons this size tumbling unheralded out of cupboards at this stage, thank you very much.'

'So we give Rasch to Patterson,' Wills said.

'Certainly not. We offer the information to the State Department at a very high level. That's if they haven't already got it via Hauser's and the international brotherhood.' Tendring gave a sudden thin smile, adding, 'Do you see any reason why they – Co-lect, that is – shouldn't fund Herr Rasch's retirement, instead of the poor hardpressed taxpayer?'

OFFICE OF THE SECRETARY OF STATE
Briefing for Emergency Study 17359-Cv. March 19, 1945.
Action immediate upon:
Report via British Intelligence that Co-lect Corporation investments in German industry have continued throughout the period of hostilities: further, that dividends have been remitted through neutral countries. (Attached)
Requirement:
Assessment of effects if this information becomes public either as confirmed fact or as rumour, under the following headings:
       1. Political – domestic
       2. Political/diplomatic
       3. Financial.
Advisory document required by noon March 20, 1945.

Extracts from report of Emergency Study group 17359-Cv, submitted March 20, 1945.
To: The Secretary of State.
   . . . *Domestic effects* (*political*): (a) There can be no question but that a great deal of mud will be thrown or that a proportion will stick. The matter will inevitably be presented as one of morality, and the administration will be seen to be culpable.

                    (b) In addition to Republican party reaction, the smaller political parties, particularly those of the left, and certain trade unions, as well as the entire press, will react with great hostility. 'While our boys were dying, etc., etc.' Co-lect may well be held out as an example of American business morality.

. . . Financial (industrial): (a) Co-Lect Corporation shares are blue chip stock and will inevitably fall, probably very heavily, as soon as their German activities become a matter even of rumour. There may well be consequent depressant effect upon stock markets as a whole.

(b) Other American corporations will avoid contact with Co-lect. Co-lect has thirty American factories and 100,000-plus employees. Some unemployment must follow any general business boycott of Co-lect Corporation.

(c) Suspicion will fall upon all other US Corporations with pre-1941 German connections . . .

. . . *CONCLUSIONS:* 1. it is highly desirable that the facts of Co-lect Corporation's involvement in German industry be suppressed.

2. All available means should be used to achieve this objective.

ADDENDUM: Co-lect Corporation will fund any necessary negotiations or actions.

It came back at them like a boomerang. Secretary of State to Foreign Secretary in high-grade cypher, processed, discussed, consultation on the Atlantic cable, voice to voice. Gratitude for the information, please inform of proposed action.

Was action proposed?

What action?

For local American consultation, Mr William Patterson available immediately.

Patterson was in at last, smiling and flexing his muscles, in-

formed about Co-lect Corporation and seemingly unsurprised. Not a man to *be* surprised, of course, still less to show
it. But fore-knowledge?

Patterson squashed that notion flat. 'The US Government
did not know. No Government can be aware of every action
of a company with world-wide operations.' Spoken with
utter conviction.

Co-lect Corporation would be brought to book, by God!
But *later*.

First, access to Rasch. No, Patterson knew that had not
been agreed, but it was surely implicit. State would want it.
Insist was a word not used, but also implicit.

'To whom does Rasch belong?' Wills had asked.

'Technically, I suppose, to us,' Tendring had replied.
'But I'm afraid that at this point the question is rather
academic. No access to Conway, though. *He* recognizes the
names.'

Patterson, the global generality disposed of, was now brisk
for the details. 'What's the problem with this German? Why
won't he unload?'

'The difficulty,' Wills said, 'lies in ensuring he will get the
things he wants. He's inclined to think he'll be double-
crossed.'

'Money, passport, immunity, right?'

'Correct.'

'Well, money's no problem. It's paid into a bank in
Madrid, an account in his name. Can't be taken out except
on his signature and the bank's sent a specimen of it.'

'Oddly enough, we thought of that,' Wills said. 'The passport is more troublesome.'

'He thinks once he comes through he won't get the passport, right? Won't get into Spain without it. And even if he
gets it, we'll knock him off because he knows too much.'

'Something along those lines.'

Patterson gave a grin. 'He's got a point. Him against the
great mailed fist. Well, maybe we could help the guy, not
kick him. You taking me to him now?'

In the car he turned to Wills, wearing another of his

assortment of grins, and said, 'Don't look so serious. We got one dirty little secret each, you and us. Kind of binds us together, right?'

Rasch had been awake for more than forty-eight hours. From the moment when he had lifted the pistol from the table, sleep had been an impossibility. It was necessary for him to remain awake and to keep the pistol in place the whole time. Once already, in this place, gas had been used to put him to sleep; that must not happen again. The pistol was his only defence, his only bargaining point. Without it they might strap him to a table and torture him – his earlier feeling that the British were too squeamish had been dissipated by the determination with which his revelations had been pursued.

He had been awake for similar periods before, even longer ones on occasions; but experience did not help. Every passing minute brought him closer to the time when sleep would knock him over. His eyelids drooped involuntarily several times and he knew that at some time in the ensuing hours they would close and remain closed, however hard he tried to hold them open. He had just demanded cold water and a sponge, thus reluctantly revealing his weakness, when the summons came and he went again to the familiar room with the wire screen across it. Two men sat facing him. One he knew, the other was new to him, a man with a cheek scar unmistakably cut by a sabre. German? If so . . .

'American,' the man said in easy German. 'In case you're wondering, I got to wielding the soup plate of honour one day at Heidelberg a long time ago.'

Rasch's weariness became wariness, fatigue sliding back a little . . . It would be back before long, and irresistible soon, but for the moment at least his mind was clear. He sensed that the real bargaining was about to begin.

Patterson had been studying his man. As Rasch had entered the room Patterson had noted the hard, strong face, the light easy movement as the big man crossed to the chair. Now he looked at the sunken eyes, the bristled chin. He said,

'You help us. We help you.'

'I have helped already and received nothing in return.'

'You're dealing with another man now.'

'Who?'

'I'm going to meet your needs. Then maybe you'll meet mine.'

'Who are you?'

'My name's Patterson. I represent the United States Government here. And boy, am I pragmatic! Put it this way: *you* know where the body's buried, *we* want to know and *I* have to find some kind of an accommodation.'

'Once I tell you,' Rasch said directly, 'you will kill me.'

Patterson shook his head. 'I want to keep you alive.'

'Until you know.'

'Nope. Until we have the papers. Or we know they've been destroyed.'

Rasch shrugged. 'So it's for a day, a week, for three months? Useless to me.'

Patterson looked at him thoughtfully. 'Has it occurred to you that once the proof is destroyed, the knowledge that it used to exist isn't worth a good goddam? You rush round shouting it to the world – who's going to believe you? There'll be no *need* to kill you.'

Rasch laughed harshly and dismissively.

'No? Okay, let's talk around this thing. We've got this place in Germany with files in it. You know where and nobody else, right? If you tell us, what do we do with that knowledge?'

'That,' Rasch said, 'would be up to you. However, this is pointless – '

'Stay with me, huh? Logical thing would be: when the Allied armies reach this place, we're with them, right? We scoop all this stuff up. But maybe it's a battleground and something goes wrong. Let me ask you a question. Could we get there before them?'

'I don't understand.' Rasch glanced at Wills, saw him frown.

'Listen and I'll explain. This war has been full of guerrilla actions. Maybe there's room for one more. A raid.'

Rasch shook his head, not to convey a negative, but to clear it; fatigue was creeping over him again. He said, 'How does that help me?'

'I don't know it does,' Patterson said. 'I'm trying this thing out and it depends on a lot of things. Where the place is, for one. If it's somewhere along *Unter den Linden*, then maybe I'm not talking practicalities. But what if it isn't? Maybe it's some place that can be hit before the armies arrive. Is that possible?'

Rasch stared at him, sudden interest clearing the gathering fogginess in his brain, mind clear again, too clear, he knew the signs. He found himself thinking about the open country, the approaches, the airfield.

'Well?'

It was giving nothing away; armies were converging on Germany from every direction. Switzerland excepted. 'Possible,' Rasch said.

'We're getting there. You don't need to tell me any more. Not yet. But listen – suppose we organize a raid. *And suppose you lead it?*'

'I hardly think – ' Wills began.

'Wait.' Patterson, hand raised to halt the protest, was watching Rasch, had seen the eyes react, the scalp tighten. He went on, 'Suppose you had the Spanish passport with you, and maybe this letter you want, though I don't see what use the letter's going to be. And suppose that when you leave you have dough with you. Not pounds or dollars or pesetas – you can run into problems passing money. What if you carried a few diamonds?'

He glanced at Wills, who looked almost as surprised as Rasch.

'We can't,' Wills said.

'Want to bet?'

Rasch's scalp prickled with distrust. There was too much here, too much that appealed to him. It was all being presented to him as a sudden inspiration, but these were clever men and the scheme could have been – probably *had* been –

calculated to appeal to a man who wanted what was being offered: a man who *wanted* money, *wanted* action, *wanted* to fight his own way into his own future. He sat stone still, struggling with it in his mind, seeking the barb hidden in the bait, not finding it. Finding instead the realization that the scheme could only have come after his own admission that a raid might be possible. But there must be a trick, a snag, and he couldn't find it. Because he was weary?

At last he said, 'It's very ingenious. I must think about it with a clear head and I cannot because I need to sleep. He gestured with the pistol. 'But I cannot sleep because this is the only defence I have. Can you think of a way to let me sleep? Because if you do not,' he hefted the pistol again, 'I think I shall have to blow my brains out.'

'I'll stand guard over you myself.' Wills was surprised that Patterson's enthusiasm should lead him to this unexpected naïvety.

'To take the pistol while I sleep.'

'I wouldn't do that.'

Wills intervened. 'I don't see how it's possible for you to sleep. Not now. Not with what you would regard as proper security.'

'Room locked from the inside?' Patterson offered.

Rasch shook his head, the pistol still beneath his chin.

'Why not?'

'How many keys and who holds them?' Wills said. 'In his shoes *I* wouldn't take it.' He remembered something about Patterson and a trace of mischief stirred. 'Didn't you tell me once that you can fly an aeroplane?'

'Yes.'

The mischief turned to a pleasant malice in Wills's mind, though not in his voice, as he said: 'Suppose we can obtain a light cargo aircraft? One without an auto pilot, that's the point, so that when you fly it you can't leave the controls. You stay in the air for three hours or so, and Rasch sleeps in the rear cabin. He has his pistol, you are unarmed, and perhaps there's even a locked door between you. Or is it a bit far-fetched?'

'Far-fetched – Jesus!' Patterson said irritably. 'Also he's got this money in Ireland. What's to stop him forcing me to fly there?'

Wills enjoyed the moment. He knew very well how petty it was, but it was very pleasant. 'He wouldn't, would you, Herr Rasch? In Ireland you'd be a wanted man, and that's not your notion of pleasure. And, of course, you'd be caught.'

'Three hours flying in a circle,' Patterson said. 'It's crazy.'

'Yet practical, too, in its curious way,' Wills said. 'Does it appeal to you, Herr Rasch?'

Rasch considered briefly. The gamble did appeal to him and he was too near the limit now to spend hours negotiating alternatives. He nodded.

'Well, then.' Wills gave his own knee a little pat of finality.

Patterson, aware he'd been railroaded, kept his face under control, but couldn't resist a verbal dig. 'Just so it's a good airplane,' he said.

'I'm sure an American one must be available,' Wills said sweetly.

Four and a half hours later as they drove away from the RAF station at Biggin Hill, Patterson and Rasch could exchange tight smiles. The flight had done more than repair a weary mind; it had built a small bridge of confidence between them. It had also given Patterson the opportunity further to develop his idea.

When they returned to the SIS retreat, Patterson said, 'You get the papers you want. You get diamonds worth fifty thousand dollars. That's a good hunk of dough but it won't last for ever. But if you get to Madrid with the job done, there's another – what is it, Wills? Fifty thousand?'

'Only if you supply it,' Wills said.

Patterson smiled. 'Co-lect money,' he said. 'They got lots.'

Rasch thought about it for an hour, alone in his cell, staring at the barrel of the pistol, knowing that he could not hope for a better arrangement, and that the alternatives were simple: one more exciting operation or a miserable death, now, where he sat. He didn't trust Wills, Patterson, Colvin, any of them. But he had trust in himself.

At last he rose and banged on the cell door. When Patterson came to him, he committed himself entirely by speaking a single word. The word was 'Wewelsburg,' and as he spoke he kept the pistol firmly beneath his chin.

'Wewelsburg?' Patterson said. 'Where's that?'

'It lies,' Rasch said, 'between Paderborn and Büren, in Westphalia. It is a village with an old castle. The castle belongs to Himmler.'

He waited, then, for the double-dealing: they had the crucial knowledge now and could use it without him, could mount their own raid, use their own, excellent commando units. The word had been his defence and he was now defenceless.

He was taken to another room and this one had no screen between them, no guards; instead there were easy chairs, a table, a bottle of cognac, glasses.

'Put the damn thing away.' Patterson gestured at the pistol. 'Have a drink.'

Rasch did not move. The pistol remained beneath his chin.

Patterson seated himself, poured cognac: a Croizet, old and rare. He looked up at Rasch. 'I know what you're thinking. The answer is that you can do it better.'

Rasch nodded. 'I can give no guarantee.'

'Nobody can. But you increase the chances. *You* know the place.'

'Very well.'

'You know where everything is.'

'Yes.'

'So we'd be crazy to use anybody else. Put the gun down.'

Rasch smiled faintly. 'Lay down your arms. That is the phrase?'

'Only temporarily. Keep it by you if you're nervous. We've got talking to do.' He turned to Wills. 'How are you fixed for SS prisoners?'

'We have some classical specimens,' Wills said. He was

profoundly disturbed by Patterson's approach. 'Look, I have no ethical objection to turning them round. But I do wonder if it can be done.'

Rasch looked from one to the other. 'Turn them round?'

Patterson said, 'You're SS. You're prepared to attack an SS establishment. I want some more who'll do the same.'

'I doubt if you'll find them,' Wills argued. 'Better if we sent – '

'Nope.' Patterson stopped him. 'We need them real. Destroy the place – that's one thing. All you need is Rangers or commandos who know how to handle explosives. For this thing, we need the real McCoy.' To Rasch he said, 'Can you find them? Four or five men?'

Rasch blinked slowly, thinking. 'They will be paid well?'

'Yes.'

'Then I imagine there will not be much difficulty.'

'My honour is loyalty,' Wills said with irony.

Rasch turned stony eyes on him. 'Men like that are in every army. Yours, also.' He turned to Patterson. 'Let me talk to them. I'll find men.'

Patterson poured Croizet into a glass and handed it across. 'That's it then.' He raised his own. 'Wewelsburg.'

Rasch looked at him steadily for a moment, then lifted the cognac to his lips and said 'Wewelsburg' firmly before he sipped.

'One more thing,' Patterson said. 'You get to take a passenger.'

Later, alone with Patterson, Wills said, 'It could be very messy.'

'Damn it, you know the guy. You know his history, how he thinks. You only have to look at him. Christ, he's – '

'Dangerous and resourceful. Yes, I know. But he damn well isn't one of ours, is he? *We* may think we have him on a string, but what does *he* think? This we do know, though – he's SS and the SS is strong, *very* strong, in the matter of loyalty.'

Patterson thought for a moment before he said, 'What you do wrong is, you underestimate two things. The first is the power of hate. The second is the power of money.'

Wills shrugged. 'Your decision.'

'Right. And that's the way we'll play it.'

Patterson had fixed the price himself, for the four other members of Rasch's group, as he had fixed it for Rasch. It seemed to Wills that he spread Co-lect money around with positive glee. The men had been selected over a period of three days, from German prisoner-of-war camps in Britain. Rasch had hand-picked them, reading lists of names, then interviewing more than twenty before he decided on four. Hauptscharführer Heiden, the SS sergeant-major, Rasch had spotted with pleasure in a camp near Kendal in the Lake District. Heiden had been on the Gran Sasso drop, a big, bullet-headed Swabian who had seen service in the early 'thirties with the French Foreign Legion in the Sahara. Rasch knew of only one of the others, a Leibstandarte corporal named Mohnke with the Adolf Hitler band in silver at his cuff who, like himself, had been in the Ardennes offensive and had been captured when his scout car ran out of fuel near Houffalize. He knew of Mohnke as a fighting man, but nothing else about him. In particular, he did not know whether Mohnke was devoted to the Führer. Several men had already been rejected because nothing, not defeat, not capture, not the prospect of a bleak and possibly ultim- ately fatal trial could shake their loyalty to Hitler.

To Mohnke he had said, 'The war is nearly over. What then?'

'If I survive?'

'You *may* get the chance. What will you do?'

'Try to make some money.'

'How?'

'Any way I can. Rob banks, maybe, if there's anything left in the bloody banks.'

'Politics?'

Mohnke looked at him as if he was mad. 'After *this*?' He spat on the floor.

'Your oath?'

'Bugger the oath. Bugger politics. Bugger politicians. Bugger everybody.'

Rasch looked at him. Mohnke had been decorated – he could recall reading about it in the SS newpaper, *Das Schwarze Korps* – for some piece of crazy heroism involving a Russian tank. 'Would you fight again?'

'Only for money. For money, enough money, I'd fight like a madman.'

'Where are you from?'

'Russia.'

'What?'

'It's as good as Russia now,' Mohnke said grimly. 'I'm from East Prussia. Right on the Polish border. Never see it again. Why all the questions?'

'Why all the questions, *sir*.'

'Sir.'

'I'm thinking of offering you money.'

'How much?'

'Quite a lot. What would you do for it?'

'Do? Anything. What do you want?'

'Perhaps some killing. Perhaps some theft. Perhaps – '

'I'm bloody good with explosives, too,' Mohnke said.

'Against Germans?'

'Against anybody, if it's for money in the right quantity. Enough to live well for a bit. Against Germans, you say. Christ, I'd tear the Führer's tripes out with my bare hands.'

'He's Austrian,' Rasch said drily.

'What do you want me to say, then? That I'll kill? I've killed a lot of times already, a few more won't bother me. You want to know if my honour is still bloody loyalty? It isn't. You want to know if my nerve's gone? Well, you get them to give us a gun each and hunt each other over that mountainside out there, for a money prize, winner take all, and I'll take you on and kill you. Right, *sir*?'

Rasch said, 'Yes. All right. Here's the project. A small group is to attack a target in Germany. It's guarded by the SS. If the attack's successful, you will get ten thousand dollars American and a passport and you'll be taken to Spain and given a job if you want one.' He had watched Mohnke as he spoke about the SS guards, but Mohnke's eyes hadn't flickered.

'I mean killing SS men.'

Mohnke said, 'I was in Spain with the Condor Legion. Spain's good. Plenty of wine and plenty of sun. Show me the bloody gun.'

The other two were men he didn't know. Heiden recommended one of them, a man named Sauer, with whom Heiden had served in France in 1940 and who chanced to be in the same camp. Sauer was an SS classic; six feet three inches tall, blue eyes, chiselled, fair features. Rasch thought he looked like Heydrich idealized for a recruiting poster. Sauer, too, had been decorated. Like Mohnke he had also put the past behind him. 'My loyalty,' he said to Rasch's question, 'is to myself. Not to anybody else. Not for the rest of my life.'

'It had better be to me,' Rasch said. 'For a few days.'

'For ten thousand dollars,' Sauer said, 'you can buy me for at least a month.'

The last member of the group was younger than the others, only twenty-one, and would not have been interviewed had his name not intrigued Rasch.

When the man entered the hut, saw Rasch's hurriedly made-up uniform and came to attention, Rasch said, 'Naujocks, eh? Any relation?'

Naujocks smiled. 'Not as far as I know, sir. I'd be proud if I were.'

'Nothing much to be proud of,' Rasch said. He looked at the young man and thought the resemblance was really quite close. Alfred Helmut Naujocks was a legend in the SS: the man who, quite literally, had started the war. On August 31, 1939, Naujocks, on Heydrich's orders, had attacked the radio transmitter at Gleiwitz, pretending to be Polish, and thus giving Hitler the excuse to march into Poland. There were other exploits, too; kidnapping and forgery among them.

Naujocks was a dangerous, charming, ruthless thug, and Rasch had known him, if not well, then as well as he wanted to know him.

This one was too young, but he *did* look as if he had potential. The other Naujocks, Rasch thought half-regretfully, would have been the perfect man for this raid. 'Where are you from?'

'Ahden, sir.'

Rasch stared at him.

'In Westphalia?'

'Yes, sir. It's only a village, really; between Paderborn and Büren.'

'I know where it is, Naujocks. It lies between Wewelsburg and the airfield.'

'Yes, sir. You know it?'

'I know it.' Rasch was thinking hard. This could be real luck. Local knowledge: trees, woods, fields, streams – he remembered the view from the castle. This boy would probably know it all, every path, every track, every stream.

'Parents?' he asked.

'Dead, sir. Killed in a raid on Hamburg.'

'Relatives?'

'An aunt, sir. In Hamburg, if she's still alive.'

'But nobody in Ahden?'

'No, sir. It's a small farm. My mother inherited it. It will be mine, I suppose, if I ever get back, after the war.'

'Why shouldn't you?'

The boy looked at him hesitantly. 'They're talking of a trial, sir. I was with Colonel Peiper's force.'

'Malmedy?' Rasch asked. There had been a massacre at Malmedy. Jochen Peiper's Leibstandarte men had slaughtered American prisoners.

'I wasn't at Malmedy, sir.'

Rasch grinned. 'Can you prove it?'

'No, sir.' The boy grinned back. 'I don't think I can.'

He was tempted, and only partly by the boy's familiarity with the area round the castle at Wewelsburg. Young Naujocks, quiet and formally respectful as he was, had about him that light, devil-in-the-eye quality that sets apart the natural military raider. Skorzeny, for all his grim fanaticism, had it too.

Rasch went through it again: the target in Germany. SS guards they'd have to kill. A big money bonus. Immunity. A safe job in Spain. When he'd finished, young Naujocks thought for only a moment, then answered directly. 'Big risks for a big reward. That appeals to me, sir.'

'Hitler?' Rasch said.

'*He's* the target?' Young Naujocks's mouth opened in surprise.

'I wish he were. Remember you swore the oath.'

Naujocks looked steadily back at him. 'There was once a rumour in Wewelsburg village, sir, that Hitler was to be buried there. If it's true I'll volunteer to dig the grave.'

Five, he thought, was the ideal number: a tiny force, which could move naturally and easily, survivors of a platoon, perhaps, on its way to join another force, and with the extra armour of SS black to protect them against inquiry. It was a pity he must take a sixth. Rasch resented it but had accepted the requirement.

They were upstairs now, Heiden, Sauer, Mohnke and Naujocks, cleaning the weapons they would use, wondering what lay ahead. Rasch wondered, too, as he went to meet Patterson and Wills, to make an outline plan. When he entered the room, another man was there, and Rasch, looking him over with care, knew at once that the man was a soldier, despite the civilian clothes. He was tall, lean, grizzled; all trace of softness had gone from his body over the years, leaving muscle and bone and sinew, a skin smooth with fitness, a pale hard gaze full of experience and authority. Rasch recognized this type: without them, armies did not function.

The four sat at a table. The soldier was, it turned out, American. He was introduced as Colonel K, on the staff of General Lawton Collins, commanding the US 7th Corps. 'No name,' he said.

197

'Now you can tell us about the Wewelsburg,' Patterson ordered briskly.

'There's no need, I know it well,' Rasch said. 'What I need is a means of reaching it.'

Colonel K raised a hand. 'Hold it. Be clear on this, all of you: we have a major offensive going on. Your event occurs *inside* the main event and may, just may, have a bearing on it.'

'It will not do that,' Rasch said. 'It will be local and of no military significance.'

'Maybe. If it is, I'll judge. At this moment, there will be no support and no facilities *unless* I am given full details of the target and the plan of attack. General Collins is running a battlefront, not a taxi service.'

Patterson flushed. 'You know about my authorization from the State Department, Colonel. Facilities are to be made available.'

'Where possible.' Colonel K had control here and meant to keep it. 'None the less, I'm here to help. Let me, however, remind you of the structure here. I report to General Lawton Collins. General Collins reports to General George S. Patton. Patton reports to General Eisenhower. It's a short ladder. I'm sure you'll see the wisdom of working with that structure, not against it. Now, gentlemen,' he glanced at Rasch quickly as if in momentary regret at applying the term. 'I know that you intend a commando-type raid on Wewelsburg Castle. I don't know why and I don't want to know why. But I insist on knowing every detail you have about the place before I approve the military plan.'

Patterson remained flushed. His speciality was subtle pressure and he resented his seeming helplessness in the face of military rigidities.

Rasch, too, was sharply angry. Wewelsburg's secrets were *his* secrets: his knowledge of them a major part of his own security. Once reveal it all and the operation could still be taken from him. He snapped, 'It was not part of my agreement – '

Colonel K interrupted him. 'Hauptsturmführer, that's

captain, right? All right, Captain. I accept you're the ranking expert here and I can guess what you're afraid of. I'm making no moral judgments. Things happen in war. But you're going to tell me, or we'll stick so many spanners in your engine you'll never get yourself rolling. We know a little about this location from intelligence reports. You have to add the rest.'

Rasch stared at him bleakly, then abruptly gave in. It was another gamble and he had already taken so many. But this would be the final one, apart from the raid itself. 'How much do you know?'

'Let's say nothing. Tell me.'

'Very well. First the history – what I know of it. The castle is very old and extremely strongly constructed. It belonged originally to the Bishops of Paderborn. It was once destroyed by Swedish troops, and partly rebuilt, for use as a prison, in the 1870s, but never finished. In the 1920s it was decided to use it as a hostel for youth and it was further rebuilt. It was bought by Himmler in the 1930s – I am not certain of the date, but it must have been 1934 or 1935 – and he bought it because he had read an old Germanic prophecy that there would threaten from the East a gigantic storm which would overwhelm the country if it were not brought to a halt at the Birkenwald in Westphalia. When the Wewelsburg was shown to him, Himmler was delighted. How much do you know about Himmler?'

'It's your briefing,' Patterson said morosely, pride still smarting.

'Assume, Captain, that we know nothing.'

'Do you know, for example,' Rasch asked, 'that he is obsessed by the romantic history of a British king and knights of chivalry?'

'King Arthur?' Wills said in surprise.

Rasch nodded. 'It is on such nonsense that the Order of the SS was founded. I read these stories as a boy. There was a place . . .' He snapped his fingers.

'Camelot?' Wills said.

'Wewelsburg Castle is Himmler's Camelot. Almost everything there is modelled upon the legends. There is a round table, which seats only twelve, and at each place at the table there is a chair which bears a name, engraved on a silver plate, of one of the supposed Knights of the Order. The knights are the Obergruppenführer, so there is a chair for Wolff, for Sepp Dietrich, for Berger, for von Herff, Hildebrandt, Daluege, Pohl, and the rest. There was also one for Heydrich. Each of these men had arms, like the knights, and they hung high on the wall behind each man's chair.'

'You *serious*?' Patterson said, absorbed now, despite himself.

'You asked for details of the Wewelsburg. I am giving them. The purpose of the Wewelsburg was to establish a centre at which the high priests of the SS could take in what Himmler called spiritual refreshment. It was also a study centre. There is a department of the SS which has made a study of Nordic history, and the rooms in the castle are shrines to different periods. Himmler used to summon his high priests to the castle for weekend study. Each man occupied a different room on each occasion. There was a room dedicated to King Henry the Fowler, another for Frederick the Great. Darré's idea of Blood and Soil had a shrine, so did the old Teutonic conception of Revenge and Right. Heinrich the First, of course, was Himmler's personal object of worship and his spirit was represented by the room Himmler chose for himself. It was very lavish indeed, though he is not a man of lavish personal tastes.'

'A man of unpleasant habit though,' Wills said. 'Did these men believe all this nonsense?'

'If they did not, they pretended they did,' Rasch said. 'Heydrich, of course, believed in nothing. He used to take detective novels to read, but Heydrich was a law to himself. The rest were required to read the books in their rooms, and were questioned next morning by Himmler to be sure they had done so. Wolff, of course, knew it all. He was responsible for the Ancestral Heritage office which did the research.'

'Jesus Christ,' Patterson said.

'Himmler was brought up a Catholic,' Rasch went on,

'and in a way there is a resemblance to the Jesuits, too, in this SS order, with Himmler as Grand Master. Hitler compared him once, so I am told, to Ignatius Loyola. Now – it is in the North Tower that the "holy" part of the castle exists. There are two chambers, one constructed over the other. The upper chamber contains the table and the arms. The lower chamber's principal purpose is ceremony, in particular, the burning of the arms of a dead knight. It was built for this purpose. An eternal flame burns there. There are twelve stone plinths round the walls which are intended for urns holding the ashes when arms are cremated. A special ventilation system removed the smoke. You see the parallel with the Vatican?'

Wills, fascinated, said, 'Were they used?'

'Heydrich's arms were burned. Beyond that, I don't think so. But to continue, since you are so anxious for detail: there is a suite of rooms for Hitler's use, though he has never visited the Wewelsburg. The point is that everything was done in the expectation that he would. Everything was of the best. Fine woods, precious metals, every room, every desk, every chair individually designed and worked by the finest craftsmen.' He looked at Colonel K, who sat alert and un-moving, making no notes. 'It all cost eleven million marks. A great deal of money. Some of the walls are four metres thick. Wewelsburg is very strong indeed.'

'Not so strong,' Colonel K said gently, 'that it couldn't be pounded down.'

'In time,' Rasch agreed. 'But it could be defended with great determination.'

'In that case, how do you propose to get in?'

'There are several possibilities,' Rasch replied. 'I have not yet decided.'

'You'd better decide.'

'Nor will I decide,' Rasch said with harsh emphasis, 'until I see it. I don't know how it is defended. I don't know how many men are there. What I do know is that there is more than one possibility.'

'Name them.'

'The Wewelsburg stands on a great rock of roughly triangular formation.' Rasch rose and crossed to the blackboard. To it was pinned a map labelled 'Bürener Land' which showed the area for roughly twenty miles round Wewelsburg. The map was dated 1926, and was the most recent that Wills's colleagues in SIS had been able to dig up. Pinned beside the map were a few picture postcards of similar and slightly later date showing the castle itself. Nothing more recent was available, because a clamp had been put on the area from the time the SS reconstruction of the ancient fortress had begun.

'The critical factors,' Rasch said, 'are two. First the presence here to the west – ' his finger touched the map – 'of an airfield. It is the one which Himmler used on his visits to the castle. The distance is approximately two kilometres.' His finger moved across the intervening countryside. 'Here is Schloss Wewelsburg. The country between the airfield and the castle is largely open, though as you see, it is crossed by several roads and the river, which at this point has two, and in places three, separate channels. The fringe of this stretch of country, however, is heavily wooded on both sides, as is the land area to the south and east. Now: the immediate topography, the second important factor. Schloss Wewelsburg itself is raised on its rock over the surrounding territory. On the west, facing towards the airfield, the rock falls away in a shale slope approximately thirty metres high, and almost sheer. To the north, the slope is less steep, but of the same height. On the east, between the castle and the village itself, is a steep-sided, but small valley roughly twenty metres deep. Only at the south, where the empty moat divides it from the village, is the castle on a level with its surroundings. Here there is an esplanade over which motor vehicles approach the moat bridge to the castle gate. The far end of the esplanade is overlooked by the village church, and on the other side by an old building which houses the SS guard.

'There are two principal methods of attack. The first is to go direct, in uniform, over the bridge and into the castle by the main entrance, but we do not know how big the guard is nowadays. Once there were more than a hundred men.' Rasch smiled. 'Many of them may now be on other duties.'

'The second method?' Colonel K asked. 'No, let me guess. You choose the hard way and scale the slope on the west side?'

Rasch nodded. 'It is steep, but it can be done, and the approach is largely through trees.'

'Minefields?'

'I doubt it, unless they have been laid recently which I also doubt.'

'Once you're up the slope, how do you get into the castle?'

'Sunk into the east wall,' Rasch said, 'there are a great many right-angled pieces of iron. They engage with the window shutters to hold them open. They will also provide an effective ladder for ropes.'

'What are the shutters made of?'

'Wood. Oak, in fact.'

'You prise one open and go in? It's that easy?'

'We would be fifty metres in the air,' Rasch said, 'and the fastenings are strong. It will not be easy to exert leverage. However, here,' he touched one of the picture postcards, 'one can just see another kind of window. I do not know the name of such a structure, but it projects outwards, shaped like a small gable of a house. This is the Heinrich the First room. Himmler's own room.' He paused. 'We can blow the whole thing off the wall.'

Colonel K came to stand beside him, inspecting the map and the photographs. He had questions to ask, many of them. Rasch had the answers.

At length the colonel said, 'Okay, you seem to know it.'

'Once, as an exercise,' Rasch said, 'I worked out methods of attack. I didn't believe then that I would ever have to carry them out.'

'What about your men – five of you?'

'Six,' Rasch said.

'Who is the other?'

'With respect,' Rasch said, 'he is no concern of yours, Colonel.'

'The five, then. How good are they?'

Rasch gave a small, hard smile. 'They are some of the best the Waffen SS can produce,' he said. 'And while you may not approve of the Waffen SS, you will perhaps admit they are good soldiers?'

'Good,' Colonel K said, 'is not the right word. They are certainly very effective.'

'In soldiering,' Rasch said, 'the two are the same. How will you get us there, Colonel?'

Chapter Thirteen

After several days' close confinement in the Buckinghamshire mental hospital, Conway was decidedly unhappy. He was needled from time to time by some of the staff and ignored by others. Worst of all, he was left alone, for most of the long, dragging days, to contemplate the bars on the window of his room. He was almost permanently famished. The rations he was given were, it was explained with relish by one of the more unpleasant of the staff, two thirds of those allowed to the British public. To make it worse, food was cooked badly and was invariably almost cold.

The cigarettes given to him by the curious visitor had long been smoked. If Conway had known there would be no more, he would have hoarded them carefully, rationing himself. But in his jumpy state he had smoked without thinking until the packet was empty, and had only then discovered that cigarettes were forbidden. He thought savagely that his warders must have watched him smoke, knowing that the sudden deprivation when the last cigarette was gone would be the harder to bear.

To be hungry and without tobacco were bad enough; the boredom was a kind of torment.

'May I have something to read?' he asked the man who brought his breakfast on the second morning.

'No.'

'A pack of cards, then?'

'Why?'

'To pass the time.'

'You're not here to enjoy yourself.' The man had almost sneered. 'Be thankful you're alive – for the time being.'

'What do you mean?'

But there was no answer, and Conway was left to reflect

on the unpleasant implications of the cryptic little phrase. They surely couldn't kill him? Not for what he'd done! Blackmail was certainly serious, no avoiding that. But not *death*. On the other hand, the subject of the blackmail *had* been a matter involving security; and security matters were always dealt with differently, and more harshly, than common criminality.

Surely, though, he was a neutral and that ought to count. And there was no question of passing secrets to an enemy. Christ, surely they couldn't hang him or shoot him!

For days, alone in his cell, staring out over the bare trees and fields of Buckinghamshire, his mind churned with the question.

Then, without warning Mowgli appeared again, and Conway stared at him with relief, as the man offered him a cigarette, held out a match and watched as Conway sucked in smoke too eagerly, half-choked, and recovered.

'You seem a bit jumpy.'

Conway looked at him beseechingly. 'What's going to happen to me?'

Mowgli shrugged. 'Lap of the gods, I suppose. Somebody will look at your papers one day and make a decision.'

'Yes, but who? On what basis?' Conway didn't want even to allow the mention of punishment, let alone death as a punishment, to enter the conversation; once say it, he felt superstitiously, and it came appreciably nearer.

'I really don't know,' Mowgli said. 'I know why you're here, of course, but not the details. Difficult to judge, you see. Are they looking after you?'

As though he were in a bloody hotel! 'For God's sake!' Conway said. 'No, they're not.'

Mowgli smiled. 'Usual things, I suppose. Food's filthy, isn't it? Trouble ɪs, you see, you've become accustomed to Sweden's little luxuries.'

'Can you get me something to do? Something to read?'

'Oh, you're bored, too? Have you thought any more about what I said?'

'I don't know anything else,' Conway said. 'I told them

everything I know. There's nothing more, I promise.'

'It always seems like that,' Mowgli said. He took out the cigarette packet again. 'Not many left. Only four. I'll leave them with you, though. In the meantime . . .' He looked at Conway speculatively. 'How would you like to write it all out for me – pass the time, wouldn't it? I could give you paper and pencil.'

'Typewriter?' Conway said hopefully. He had always hated writing by hand.

'Not allowed, I'm afraid. All those nasty sharp bits of metal. You might take it into your head to do yourself some mischief.'

'Kill myself? Not bloody – '

'No. But that's how the official mind works. So it has to be paper and pencil. Write it all out for me, will you?'

'All right.'

Mowgli nodded amiably. 'And when you've done it, I'll see if I can't get you another packet of those things. Oh, and by the way, while you're about it, you might give me your observations on the Stockholm picture. I'd be very interested.'

Conway frowned. 'What kind of things do you want?'

'Oh, you know. It's a neutral capital with everybody ferreting round for advantage. In your time there you must have noticed a lot. Who works for who, that kind of thing. The tipsters and the passers-on. Where embassy leaks come from. Will you do all that for me? You can name names, of course – don't worry about doing *that*, will you? Nobody will ever know it was you.'

He smiled and left and the paper and pencils came a few minutes later, accompanied by a cup of hot coffee.

'Anybody'd think this was the bloody Dorchester,' the man who brought them said with a rough laugh. 'Enjoy it while you can, chum.'

He worked hard, and did, in fact, enjoy it. His writing, like his tongue, had always been facile with no labouring over words. He had never deceived himself that he wrote well, but he could certainly write quickly, and his practised reporter's mind fed the facts down the pencil in a steady stream. For the first time since his capture, the day held some pleasure for him. He retold, for Mowgli's benefit (and who else's, he wondered?) the story of Rasch and the papers from Germany, right through to his own debriefing, which he found he could remember, if not word-for-word, none the less with great clarity.

When he had completed it, he read it over, thought for a little while, then added one or two small details he had omitted. He had smoked two cigarettes, and now lit a third as he began to think about Stockholm. Where the first set of notes had been written as narrative because they fell easily into that form, he found that the second task would be accomplished more easily if he made a list of names.

Since his life in Stockholm had been spent among these people, it was not difficult for him. He simply listed the names, the jobs the people held, their countries of origin, their friendships. As he worked, his mind kept returning to Mowgli, and where he had seen him before. He was sure it had been either in Spain or in France, one of the two. But however hard he tried to remember, he could not think *where* it had been, or in what circumstances. He kept seeing Mowgli's face in his mind's eye, but never the surroundings, nor even the clothes. Sometimes he thought that perhaps it was an illusion, Mowgli's was a very English sort of face; you'd see one much like it in any photograph of a cricket team, or a group at a wedding.

Conway was even a little surprised, as he worked on, to discover how many people he had encountered in Stockholm. By the time he'd finished, the list ran to almost a hundred: some entries no more than a single line, others quite long and, in a few cases, detailed. These were the ones about whom he'd written stories or articles, or whom he'd known well. When it was done, he wasted no time looking at it. He'd been without a cigarette for three hours, and his body ached for nicotine. He banged on the door and, when the guard came, asked for Mowgli.

'Not here,' he was told.

'When?'

'Tomorrow, maybe. Or maybe not.'

Conway could have wept.

Two days later, Mowgli made up for it. There were two packets of Players and an afternoon walk in the grounds, in pale sunshine and a chill wind and Mowgli said, 'I must say you've done very well.'

'Thanks.' Conway inhaled tobacco smoke and cool air in delightful combination.

'Quite a memory you have. Wish I had. Always forget the odds and ends.'

'It's those that make the story, sometimes,' Conway said with a trace of smugness.

'Yes, of course. By the way, you were quite wrong, you know. There were a few things you hadn't mentioned before.'

'What?'

'Oh, I forget.' Mowgli laughed. 'Proof, as you see, of my rotten memory. But it was all checked against the list, you see, and there were one or two things . . .' He stopped and faced Conway. 'I'd like you to know I appreciate your help.'

'I appreciate this.' Conway held up the cigarette. 'And this,' gesturing round him.

'Yes. Sometimes it cuts two ways.' Mowgli paused. 'Look, I don't know what the future holds. Well, how can I, after all? But if it should turn out that one of these days you have something, I'll always be ready to listen. Useful to have observant people.'

Conway's heart bumped. This, surely, was an indication that he actually *had* a future of some kind. Mowgli obviously had standing, and wouldn't have said it otherwise.

'Of course, your movements may be somewhat restricted for a while,' Mowgli said. 'But a phone call to the Ministry of Defence will always bring you in contact. Extension one thousand and one, like the Arabian Nights, eh? If you ask for Mowgli, they'll always let me know. And you'd better have a name, too, hadn't you? Keeps everything neat and personal. What shall we call you? Better stick to Kipling, I think. You can't be Sher Khan, I'm afraid. What about the

Elephant's Child, eh? After your memory.'

Two hours later, Conway left the hospital. They had come for him as he sat on his bed, smoking and almost happy, because he at last felt some small sense of security. Mowgli's words, above all Mowgli's amiability, had pointed directly to a return to his own life, if not immediately, at least in some reasonable time.

When they came, the brief near-complacency evaporated. The door of his room swung open suddenly and there were two of the staff, grim-faced and harsh. 'Come on, you're leaving.'

'Where – ?'

'No questions. Move!'

Conway rose and began to pick up his few belongings: the toothbrush, the cigarettes. He was marched swiftly along empty corridors, down the concrete back stairs, outside into a thin drizzle that fell soundlessly on a waiting van. One of the men opened the door. 'Inside.'

The door closed and he heard the lock turn; he was alone in the van.

In the following hours he was cargo: a small animate shipment in transit between two points. The van stopped, reversed, its door opened. He was ordered out, led by a silent man into a low building, taken to a lavatory and told to use it. As he did so, he heard the cough and then the roar of big engines starting up.

'Right. Follow me.'

He followed, out by another door, on to an airfield where a battered-looking Airspeed Oxford, rigged as an air ambulance, stood ready for take-off.

'Where am I going?'

'Get inside.'

'Please – '

A push. 'Get in.'

The Oxford taxied at once, then roared into its take-off run. Isolated on the cold rear cabin, Conway sat on a stretcher and wrapped himself in blankets. He was not handcuffed or otherwise restrained and there was a window through which, as the ground fell back below him, he tried to judge the aircraft's course and make some attempt at guessing its destination; but he had no expertise and soon the plane climbed into cloud.

Where were they taking him, and why? With no means of measuring the passage of time, no light, and beneath him only the grey and uninformative cloud blanket, he was quickly disoriented. As time passed, as what he thought might be an hour stretched into two or even three, he began to think of Stockholm again. Mowgli had described his Stockholm material as useful, so perhaps they were sending him back there. He grasped gratefully at the thought and prayed it was true, then found hope suddenly damped. Had the Oxford aircraft sufficient range to reach Stockholm? The wartime service from Britain had always gone from Leuchars, in Scotland, and the aircraft in recent time had been Dakotas and Mosquitos, not Oxfords. Maybe they were taking him to Leuchars? The plane's nose tilted downwards towards reaching wisps of overcast and Conway thought with a lurch of apprehension that he would soon know.

When the Oxford had taxied to a halt and he stepped down on to the tarmac, he looked around, trying hopefully to prove to himself that this was Scotland. It was impossible, in the dark, to have any idea and he was not, in any case, left standing long enough to pick up any indications. An army truck stood waiting, its doors bearing the big white star of the Allied forces, and he was ordered briskly into the back. There, once again, he was alone and in the dark, as he sat uncomfortably on a hard and narrow bench that ran down the side of the bumping, swaying truck.

After twenty minutes or so he got his first clue as his ears picked up the sound of another engine, accompanied by a harsh, roaring clatter he'd heard before and was unmistakably made by a moving tank. The noise receded and reappeared several times, and with the certainty that the truck was passing a column of tanks came the realization that he could be in France!

France?

Conway shivered and tried to reason the thought away. Britain must be full of tanks; it was, after all, the arsenal of the Allied armies, so the ones the truck was passing could be on a test run, or on exercise. Yes, that was it! Why, after all, would he be taken to France?

The truck left the road, bumped sharply over rough ground for a few moments, reversed, then halted. When the rear door opened, Conway jumped down to find himself again facing a door. He glanced quickly round him at what looked like a farmyard, though no animals were to be seen or heard. He went into the farmhouse as ordered, entering a dark passage. Behind him the door slammed and a second later a light was switched on.

'In here.'

Still blinking, Conway went through into a smallish room stripped of ordinary furniture but seemingly full of men. As the pupils of his eyes contracted and focus returned, he saw first that they were all in uniform, and then something else . . . several of the uniforms were black!

Astonished, abruptly cold with fear, he stared from one man to another, recognizing the silver flashes that decorated the uniforms, the silver Death's Head rings on several fingers. And there was a man by the fireplace, also black-clad who, though facing away, looked none the less familiar. That broad back . . . *Rasch!*

That terrible moment of recognition was only the beginning. He knew at once, as Rasch turned and looked at him with hard eyes, that he was in deep and desperate trouble. It quickly became worse. He looked at the assembled men: one American in uniform, one, two . . . *five* Germans, and one of the Englishmen who had interrogated him. He it was who spoke.

'Over there, Mr Conway, on the trestle table, you'll find some of your things.'

Conway crossed the room, feeling their eyes on him, his own gaze flickering uncertainly from one face to the next. Some papers were laid out on the trestle, among them his passport. He grabbed it quickly and with relief.

'Yes, we're returning it,' the Englishman said.

Conway swung round to face him. 'Why? What is all this?'

'Afterwards, you may keep it.'

'Afterwards? After what?' Conway's legs were starting to tremble.

'There's a little job for you to do. After *that*.'

Clutching his passport, Conway said, 'What job?'

'We're coming to that. First you'd better check the papers.'

Reluctantly Conway turned back to the table. The papers were the ones taken from him after his arrest, including the Swedish press permit specifying his accreditation to an Argentine newspaper, and his vaccination certificates. But there were others that were not his, though his name was on them, and he examined them with increasing horror: a German ration card of current date, an entry permit stamped at Tempelhof Airport, Berlin; a Propaganda Ministry press pass, also current; a return rail ticket from Berlin to Hannover, a return air ticket from Stockholm to Berlin.

There was also a brief-case containing pyjamas, shirt, socks and a couple of notebooks. He stared at them, baffled and apprehensive. 'I don't understand.'

'No? Well, all will be explained. Sit down over there, please.'

He took the seat, feeling numb, and watched as a tripod was erected and a big blackboard draped with a cloth was lifted on to it.

The Englishman looked round the room. 'Ready? Good.' He turned to a tall, lean military figure in American battle-dress, colonel's insignia at his collar. 'All yours, Colonel K.'

The American lifted the cloth carefully from the black-board and faced the group. From that moment, German was spoken. 'This,' he said quietly, bony knuckle rapping once at the map pinned to the board, 'is Landkreis Paderborn. And right here . . .' the knuckle straightened and his finger pointed to a red-headed pin stuck in the map, '. . . right here is Wewelsburg Castle.'

Conway saw the SS men glance at one another in surprise. He looked at Rasch, whose face showed nothing. Wewelsburg Castle? Conway had heard the name somewhere . . .

'Tomorrow,' the quiet voice went on, 'the castle will be attacked by six of you. Hauptsturmführer Rasch leads. The others are Heiden, Mohnke, Sauer, Naujocks and – ' he paused, his eyes moving over the assembled men until Conway found himself looking into them, ' – and you, Mr Conway.'

'Me?' It was less a question than a squeal of outrage.

The colonel nodded.

'But I'm not a bloody commando!'

Colonel K gave him a small, thin smile. 'You,' he said, 'go as a non-combatant. It will be explained. Listen, now.'

Conway's mental turmoil was now such that he was quite unable to take in the details as the logistics and techniques of the operation spilled crisply from Colonel K's lips. Another and larger map of Germany was pinned to the blackboard, and on it Colonel K began to draw with a black wax crayon. There was talk of armies and army groups, of targets and encirclement. Around him heads nodded understanding. Conway could only sit, rigid and cold as marble, as he tried to take in the appalling fact that he was being sent on a commando attack on Himmler's own citadel. It was crazy! He wasn't a soldier, even, let alone a commando; he had no training, no skill with arms; he had nothing to contribute! He must find a way to avoid it, he thought wildly. Damn it, they must realize he was useless to them; they must be *made* to realize he'd be a handicap. Christ – !

'. . . the encirclement of the Ruhr,' Colonel K was saying, 'will then be complete. At that point, you have the choice of directions, north or east. Maybe south, too, though it's a longer trip. But east or north will, in fact, be American. You understand that? Do not, repeat *not* travel west. Our estimate is that Field Marshals Model and Kesselring will have a quarter of a million men in the Ruhr pocket when it's sealed. Okay, questions?'

'Why me?' Conway said, and was ignored. There were no other questions; the briefing had been detailed and complete and the men being briefed were experienced.

'Why me?' Conway repeated.

'There's food in hot boxes in the kitchen,' Colonel K said. 'Better get some now.'

The men rose and Conway began to rise with them, but a hand on his shoulder held him in his chair. He glanced up to find Rasch staring down at him. 'Not you,' Rasch said. 'For you there are further instructions.'

Conway's presence in the raiding party was the product of trading. Wills, who had quietly conceived the notion of sending him, had contrived to raise the matter in such a way that Patterson thought it his own idea. It relieved Wills of the alternatives Conway represented, either of unpleasant disposal or malodorous public trial. To Patterson, therefore, he fed the idea of Conway as insurance, as a second line of retreat: here was a well-documented neutral speaking fluent German who could, if it became necessary, carry the papers away after the raid. If Conway disappeared, well, that was that. Nobody's nose lost skin.

Rasch resisted vigorously when it was put to him. Conway was weak, unreliable, contemptible, a betrayer. They had no idea of the demands of such an attack, of the weakness Conway represented. Without him the raiding party was a small but strong team. His inclusion would endanger them all.

They explained. Conway *might* be needed. If he was not, then who was to know what happened? Rasch had, after all, a score to settle. Furthermore, and to be blunt about the matter, it was an order: *Conway was to go.* Rasch saw the point, disliked it, but could see no real alternative to acceptance.

So now Conway was alone with them: with Rasch, Colonel K, the Englishman and the American and his role was explained. For him as a neutral civilian, with the papers he had, movement might be difficult but it would at least be legitimate. They told him about a house in the little town of Büren, a few kilometres from the Wewelsburg, where an Irish-woman, the widow of a German diplomat, might be expected to offer shelter to a compatriot. If it became necessary, he was to reach her house and lie low until Allied troops arrived. It wasn't far and he could walk and shelter in the woods; the whole area was well-wooded.

When at last he was left alone he thought at once of escape, but the windows were heavily shuttered. The big oak door securely locked. Then the American civilian came in and Conway asked despairingly why he had been chosen. The American made no bones about it. 'I guess because that guy Rasch wants you along.'

'It's his idea?'

'Yup.'

'To kill me,' Conway said hollowly. 'He's going to kill me because – '

'I know why.'

'And you're still sending me?'

The American picked up a brief-case that lay beside the wall, and took from it a leather belt which he handed to Conway. 'Wear that.'

'Why? It won't protect me.'

'It might help you. There are diamonds sewn into it. Here, you see.'

Conway could see where the leather bulged a little. *'Diamonds?'*

'Ten thousand pounds, negotiable anywhere. We get the papers, there's more, right?'

'Papers?' Conway asked disingenuously.

'You know which papers. There's others like them on file at the Wewelsburg.'

He said, 'Who are you?'

The American ignored the question. 'We want the papers. If you get a chance at the files, look for anything to do with Co-lect Corporation.'

Light dawned then. Conway said softly, 'That's who they are, then? Co-lect – '

The American raised a warning finger, then opened the

brief-case again and reached into it. When his hand emerged, it held a grenade.

Conway looked at it, horrified. 'What's that for?'

'Mills grenade. You pull out this pin. Let this lever fly free. It goes off in just under five seconds, so they tell me.'

'I meant – '

'I know what you meant. Think. You haven't any defence, have you? What if Herr Rasch gets, well, difficult? This kind of evens things up.'

It was all unreal. Conway watched his hand take the grenade and put it into his brief-case. The grenade felt as cold as his intestines.

The American rose. 'Our little secret, right? Bring those papers and you can stop worrying. For life.' He slipped quickly, almost furtively, out of the room, locking the door behind him.

Life, Conway thought wretchedly, probably meant for him no more than a few hours.

Chapter Fourteen

The old Heinkel 111-H had been captured in France when a Luftwaffe airfield near Roubaix had been overrun by advancing Allied forces after destruction of fuel stores had grounded its aircraft. The Heinkel was one of three planes in which explosive charges set by the ground staff had failed to detonate. Its KGR-100 formation emblem – a map of the British Isles crossed by the lines of a gunsight – still decorated its sides. There was a Swastika on its tail and the Luftwaffe cross in black edged with white on wings and fuselage. The pilot, an American, was the only crew for this trip. The gun turrets above and below the fuselage were unmanned though the turret guns and those in the nose remained in position.

At five a.m. on March 30, 1945, a single US Army Air Corps truck, its headlights dimmed to slits to meet blackout regulations rigorously enforced, hissed out through a light pre-dawn drizzle towards the Heinkel. The driver halted it, climbed out of his cab leaving the engine running, and slid back the bolts which held up the tailboard. He watched as the truck's occupants jumped lightly down, and tried to keep his face expressionless. The driver had had a brother, killed near Bastogne by these black-uniformed bastards just before Christmas, and could not understand what Uncle Sam was doing handing out arms and equipment to them.

For they bristled with weaponry. He looked at the light machine-guns and machine pistols, at the hand guns and grenades, all German, with distaste, and at their hard faces with disgust, wondering what was in their packs and what was in their minds. He wondered too, most of all, about the single civilian, in raincoat and soft hat, who was clearly neither soldier nor German, but who stood, brief-case in hand, watching the others remove their equipment from the truck and begin to load it into the Heinkel's belly. He might, the driver thought, have been a nervous office worker waiting for the commuter train to the city.

When they'd finished, the driver slammed up the tailboard, noisily to indicate his disapproval, slid the bolts back into position, returned to the driving seat and drove away.

As the Heinkel's twin 1200 horse-power Jumo engines roared their chorus across the dark airfield, Conway looked round him, trying to decide whether, even now, it might be possible to make a break into the darkness and somehow stay clear of pursuit. He had learned the night before that he was not in France but in Germany – on the Western bank of the Rhine behind Coblenz. It was desperately tempting; he knew that no time would be wasted searching for him, because the timing of the raid allowed no delays. The Heinkel would take off with or without him. But, as the driver had done, Conway looked at the massed weapons with dismay. These men wouldn't hesitate. The moment he bolted, they'd fill the night with bullets and they were expert. He hesitated, keying himself up to take the risk, to duck beneath the wing and race for the darkness, then losing his nerve as a new rattle of weaponry dissolved all resolution. In the end he hesitated too long. A large figure loomed beside him and a German voice said, '*Komm*,' took his arm and led him to the Heinkel's door. After he had climbed aboard, and when the door slammed, he felt as though the coffin lid were closing on him.

He took his seat on the side-wall bench, fastened the strap, and sat sweating in the cold air. There was no avoiding it now, nothing he could do to save himself. If only he'd *run* . . .

The twin Jumos were winding up now, and the plane lurched forward to begin its take-off run. Half-fuelled and underloaded it came off fast and stayed low, now throttled back a little, for its eastward dash. It was no plane for tree-hopping in the dark, but tree-hopping had to be done: warnings had been sent to American forces on the route ahead, but it was still a German bomber with German markings and there'd be plenty of men on the ground below who would shoot first and remember the warnings later. Rasch, feeling the buffet as the Heinkel hit an air-change over the Rhine river, smiled to himself. It was good to feel the tingle again, to sit in a plane tense but controlled, and listen to the speed of his heart beat.

Somehow, as he sat, a change took place and the confusions that had ravaged his mind seemed all at once to fall away, to be replaced with a sudden, driving certainty of purpose. For weeks the future had seemed to be merely a blur of warring needs. He had ached for revenge, yet had wanted, too, to spend his life on a small country estate as was his birthright, and allowed himself to think that in Spain it might be achieved. Now he saw clearly how unthinkable it would be to drift away, to seek peace in vineyards. He had wanted to cut free from the years and forget them; now he knew it was impossible – the years were part of him. To escape into the future without revenge would be no escape at all.

He was in uniform. Soon he would be on German soil, and in Germany were the ones who had betrayed him. When the plane landed, he could slip away into the forest and . . .

But no. No, he could not do that. He had agreed to carry out the raid. His agreement, his given word. And the raid on the Wewelsburg was in itself an act of vengeance. So it must be *after* the raid. He'd be free then! And then, Walter Schellenberg, he thought with satisfaction, you may expect a visit . . . Rasch's hands tightened on his gun. With a bit of luck, a little ingenuity, he ought to be able to get to Schellenberg, and perhaps even to Himmler! Not to both, that was unlikely. But he could try, and at least one of them would pay for his betrayal. He would hunt them down in the collapsing ruins of their kingdom.

'Herr Rasch?'

Conway. Rasch's eye picked out the dark figure. Another candidate for vengeance, betrayer, though a miserable one, scarcely worth the bullet, sitting there with his watery bowels, seeking even now to worm his way out. To Rasch, now with a clear vision of the way his own life must go, came the contemptuous thought that to destroy Conway would be almost demeaning.

'I must talk to you.'

'We have no time.'

'Please, Herr Rasch.'

Rasch slipped across the fuselage to take the seat next to him. 'Well?'

'I just want you to know about Dublin. I had to tell them. There wasn't any alternative.'

'Threats,' Rasch said. 'Or red-hot needles?'

'They'd have shot me. Believe me, *please!*'

'Sensible men.' Leave him now, go back to the seat and wait in silence. The final silence, Skorzeny had called it, when body and mind come through their tensions to a relaxed alertness in the minutes before action explodes.

'Do you think we'll survive?'

Half-way between anger and contempt, Rasch sighed. He thought, *are* you worth a bullet? – and said, 'We must be efficient. That's what gives men luck.' As he began to rise, Conway's hand on his arm detained him.

'I didn't hear . . . didn't understand, really, all that briefing. All the military stuff. What are we going to find?'

'Find?' Rasch said. 'We'll find a fortress. When I was there, the guard was eighty to a hundred men. Now, I don't know.'

'But what about the Americans? The army, I mean. The colonel said – '

'I know what he said.' Rasch had been thinking about Colonel K and his neat, matter-of-fact briefing. It had been detailed and informative; too much so. K had said the great strategic aim was to encircle the Ruhr, and cut off Germany from its industrial heartland, and Rasch believed him. What Rasch did not believe was the colonel's description of the direction of Allied thrusts into Germany, with the Ninth Army in the north and the First Army south of the Ruhr driving to a meeting near Hannover. Why enclose hundreds of square kilometres of unnecessary ground? No reason; none at all. They wouldn't contemplate it, let alone do it. But there were excellent reasons for a false briefing on that point: if they were captured and tortured – and if they were captured, torture was as certain as death – then the information they gave would be false. The mission might fail, but advantage would be gained. Well, they must avoid capture. Win – or die: that was the equation. To Conway he said, 'Don't think about strategy. Concentrate on living.'

Back in his own uncomfortable perch on the wooden seat, Rasch deliberately allowed his mind to wander over the Wewelsburg, recalling every detail of the castle, its situation and surroundings. He still had not decided on the final method of approach. Colonel K had been assured that they would go for the west wall, covered all the way by trees, but there might, Rasch felt, be a substantial advantage to be gained from a direct, frontal approach. To scale the wall would be to leave the guard, in whatever strength it now existed, free to attack. If the guard were eliminated quickly, at the beginning, then the problems might be simplified. He tried to recall distances, to measure in his mind how far it was from the church to the guard house, from the guard house across the esplanade to the main entrance. And then there was Rupprecht: much would depend on Rupprecht.

Rupprecht was Warden of the Wewelsburg: a big man, fleshy-faced, with small alert dark eyes deep in their sockets. Rupprecht believed every word Himmler had ever spoken; he walked endlessly round the SS shrine, velvet cloth in hand, to ensure that the artifacts of Aryan culture were never contaminated by dust. Rupprecht would defend the cathedral of the SS Order to his last drop of blood, as a sacred duty; to him the end of Himmler's world would be bearable only if he fought the final flames until they consumed him.

In a way, Rupprecht was a caricature figure, but he was formidable, no doubt about that. Even some of the Obergruppenführer had been nervous of him. He had always had the Reichsführer's permission to search the rooms and report on their contents, and once had brought down

Himmler's furious reproof upon the head of Obergruppen-
führer Maximilian von Herff, head of the SS Personnel
Department, in whose baggage he had discovered a copy of
Gone With The Wind.

In the darkness, Rasch half-smiled to himself. Rupprecht's
world was disintegrating round him, yet probably he didn't
know it. The Warden's virtues were loyalty and dedication;
intellect was not conspicuous. Something in his eyes and
stance always put Rasch in mind of a forest boar. *They* were
not over-intelligent either, but by God, they were dangerous,
and at their worst when hurt and cornered.

The roar of the engines filled the cabin. Nobody talked.
All six sat silent, the soldiers keyed up, anxious now only to
begin, to go like hell, to get it over. Rasch, unable to see their
faces, could picture them: stiff, brows bent down a little over
eyes narrowed with concentration. The question remained
whether all could be trusted; whether among them there
might be a fanatic, a Rupprecht, to whom the SS oath was
the most important thing in life. They had been picked with
care, but there was no way to be certain that at some unknown critical point, one of them might turn his skill and
weapons once again to the service of the black corps.

The Heinkel tilted, turning on course for the third time in
its short flight. Rasch glanced at his watch. Only minutes to
touch down, little more than an hour and a half to dawn. He
stared at the pale green of the luminous hands, watching the
seconds tick by, waiting for the Heinkel's nose to tip down to
signal the approaching landing. A minute went by, and then
the floor tilted and Rasch slipped quickly into the seat of the
upper gun turret to watch as the plane came in.

At one point in the preparations, it had been suggested
that the Heinkel should radio the Sudostwestfalen airfield
control tower as it approached, and attempt a conventional
landing. If it had worked – in other words, if the British
radio intercept experts had succeeded in predicting accurately the German call signs and frequencies in use that day –
then the Heinkel would have had lights to land by. The
notion had been abandoned; the dangers had been too

great: a wrong call sign would alert the airfield's defences, and the Heinkel would then have been destroyed easily on the ground and the raiding party with it. Rasch, preferring as always to put his trust in individual skill rather than the workings of a system, had asked the American pilot whether the Heinkel could be put down there safely by moonlight. The pilot had thought about it, tried a similar landing in France, and got away with it. He was prepared to try again. So they were coming in in the dark, under the radar, into a wind from the north-east which was nearly perfect for their needs. The worry was about the moon, full only a day earlier, but now obscured by the heavy overcast.

Swivelling his head, he looked first ahead and then to the sides, over the nose and along the wing surfaces, at the darkling countryside. The Heinkel was coming in, very low now, over the small forest four kilometres or so from the runway. The trees, rushing past beneath, seemed almost to brush the aircraft's wings as it hurtled down towards the more southerly of the twin runways. To the north, beyond the horizon, Rasch twice saw the distant flicker of gunfire. The Ninth Army's advance north of the Ruhr was clearly going well.

Suddenly the trees were gone and there was open ground beneath them. To the right he saw the road, and then . . . the plane lurched abruptly, shedding height, and they were tearing down towards the concrete, pale against the dark grass, of the south runway. Rasch held on tight to the gunner's grips; there was no time now to return to the bench and strap himself in. He heard the engine note drop sharply and a moment later, with a jolting thud, the Heinkel's wheels touched and bounced, then bounced again, awkwardly, one wheel high . . . then they were racing down the concrete.

He clambered down swiftly: 'Ready to exit.' And positioned himself beside the fuselage door. The Heinkel was braking hard and moments later began to slew into a rapid turn.

Rasch flung the door wide. 'Out!' He grabbed Conway by the shoulders and virtually flung him to the concrete, watched as Heiden, Mohnke, Sauer and Naujocks followed. Jumping down after them, Rasch turned to slam the Heinkel's door. The two engines were already picking up power for a downwind take-off run and the plane had begun to roll.

The others were already sprinting for the edge of the runway, seeking to get on to the downslope of the hill before the airfield's defences began to ask one another what was wrong. Heiden was dragging Conway with him as Rasch ran crouching after them. A minute later, he flung himself flat in the grass as a searchlight cut the darkness and wavered, too high, as its crew fought to lower it to find the source of the engine noise. He saw the black silhouette racing along, then lifting, and the whole plane was off the ground, the searchlight stabbing after it. He could imagine gunners winding frantically at elevation wheels, trying to bring their flak to bear on so low a target. All attention, for the moment, would be on the plane, but it wouldn't be long before they stopped asking themselves whether to fire at a Luftwaffe Heinkel and began to wonder frantically why it had made its unheralded landing and then gone immediately into a downwind take-off.

'Move,' he grunted to the others, and led the dash towards the trees that began a hundred metres or so beyond the end of the runway. They reached the perimeter fence, climbed it rapidly, and almost dived into the woods. Had they been spotted by guards? Normally there would be sentries on the airfield, but with American troops so close . . . Rasch could remember a day when Himmler had come to Sudostwestfalen and there had been a battalion of Waffen SS to guard him.

Now there appeared to be no one. If any sentry had been standing at the runway's end, he had been sensible enough not to challenge them. The Heinkel's engine note, with its characteristic throb, was vanishing now into the distance and the searchlight, still too high, pursued it with hopeless determination.

Rasch watched for a moment, then turned away. They

were down and uninjured and the castle lay two kilometres away on the far side of the shallow valley. They began to move swiftly and quietly through the trees, Sauer twenty metres ahead and the target for the first tripwire, the first mine, the first patrol, if any of those things existed. Rasch had calculated, and the American colonel had agreed with him, that troops would have been drained from this empty countryside to guard the Ruhr cities or to fight at Paderborn twenty kilometres or so to the north, where the sandy territory of the Senneland was the Wehrmacht's, and particularly the Panzer troops' favourite training ground. There would be fierce fighting at Paderborn, no doubt about that, with the defenders fighting over ground they knew intimately and could use with skill and experience.

Not all the troops would have gone, however, and possibly none at all from the Wewelsburg unless Himmler himself had given permission. As he flitted down the hill through the trees, Rasch thought that he would not have cared to be the man who had to seek Himmler's approval for the removal of the castle's guards.

No, guards there would be. Some, at least.

They came to the first road and crossed it quickly, six abreast in the best infantry style, Conway gasping as they dragged him along at a pace he hadn't kept for years. The trees ended and they were dropping down the short, sharp incline towards the Alme river which wound from here, like a long, slender serpent, across the countryside over which Himmler's fortress watched. There was a small bridge over the river, a little way to the north, and Rasch debated as he moved, whether to risk the dry crossing. It was not a matter of comfort but of practicality: to wade the river would mean arriving at the castle looking half-drowned and would rule out an approach to the gate.

He whistled for Sauer to halt, and hurried towards him. 'This way.' Rasch pointed. 'We'll use the bridge and the railway track.'

'It's in the open, sir,' the experienced Heiden warned beside him.

'There's more cover than you think,' Rasch said, 'and we're in it as soon as we get under the ridge. Come on.'

No guard on the bridge and they raced across, five men fast and silent, one unco-ordinated and gasping, his feet hitting the metalled road flatly and noisily. Conway was dragged along with the irritation the fit always feel for those who are not.

They reached the railway track and followed it, running bent, to the shelter of the high ground upon which Wewelsburg village sat. Here, for a moment, they stopped and listened, hearing only sounds of the night: the river burbling nearby, their own hard breathing. They were close now to the road which would curl, five hundred metres or so ahead, beneath the western wall of the fortress.

Rasch looked at his watch. It was only a little more than twenty minutes since they had dropped from the Heinkel. Dawn was three-quarters of an hour away. No need to hurry, now; more sensible, in fact, to move naturally this close to the castle. It was far more important to move quietly. If they were seen, too bad. Rasch hoped to be able to talk his way past a challenge, but it was better if no challenge appeared.

'From here,' he ordered softly, 'we are silent. If there's a sentry on the north tower, he'll be looking outwards, not down. We ought to be able to get by unless some fool makes a noise.'

They moved on, in single file now, close to the trees and scrub that grew haphazard on the slope up to the village. When the North Tower came into view over the lip of the slope, he halted them with an outstretched arm and used his binoculars to search the top of the tower, looking for the sentry's head against the sky. He saw nothing, but was not convinced: in the thin moonlight, it would be all too easy to miss seeing anything.

Chapter Fifteen

Among the trees they halted and looked up through the budding branches at the south face of the Wewelsburg. Twin round towers stood at either end of the great castle wall, which was still decorated with the inset ownership marks of the Bishops of Paderborn. The fortress looked now as it must have looked for centuries; grey and strong and impregnable.

'How the hell,' Conway asked, almost with indignation, 'do you expect to break into that?'

Rasch ignored him and gestured the others closer. He could see that, like Conway, they found the old fortress daunting. It was one thing to look at plans, to draw lines on paper, to theorize about the best means of assault; quite another to face the vast granite fortress on its high rock.

'First,' Rasch said, 'we establish means of retreat while it remains dark. I want two ropes fixed on the west wall. After that . . .' he left the sentence uncompleted. 'You, Sauer, with Mohnke, will climb to the last window on the third floor, where the wall joins the North Tower. You, Heiden, will guard me as I climb towards the Heinrich room, in the middle of the wall. The right-angled iron brackets I described are set into the wall to secure the shutters.' He gave a tight smile. 'Almost like climbing a ladder.'

'What if there's a sentry on the North Tower?' Mohnke asked.

Rasch eyed him. 'I expect you to be so quiet he won't hear.'

'If he does?'

'Sauer will be covering you. But a shot reveals our presence. Remember that.' He turned to Naujocks. 'You remain here with Conway.'

'I could reconnoitre the front approach, sir,' Naujocks said. 'I can go up through the trees and use that narrow street that leads to the churchyard.'

Rasch shook his head. 'Stay with Conway. Don't move from this spot and don't let him move.'

Conway watched the four men slip away through the trees, climbing obliquely up the sharp slope. 'Can they do it?' he asked Naujocks.

'Very difficult. Not to climb, but the silence. The slope is partly shale.'

'How do you know?' Conway looked at him sharply.

'I was born near here.' Naujocks pointed south-west. 'At Ahden. You can see it when it's light.'

'You know this whole area, then?'

Naujocks nodded, holding a warning finger to his lips. They listened, and after a moment heard quite distinctly the movement of stones beneath someone's foot. Naujocks unslung his binoculars and focused them on the rim of the North Tower, looking for the sentry. Again shale slid on the slope, but still no head appeared at the top of the tower.

Twice more, distantly now, they heard sounds from the scrub-covered slope beneath the wall, and Naujocks continued to stare with concentration through the binoculars. At last he licked dry lips and said, 'Maybe there's nobody to hear.' But he sounded doubtful.

'No sentry?'

'I can't see him. But there's always a sentry there. Since I was a boy.'

'Maybe they've cleared the place out,' Conway said hopefully. 'Shifted everything somewhere else. That would make sense, with the American advance coming this way.'

'It's the best observation post for miles around,' Naujocks said. 'So I doubt it.'

But there was no sentry to be seen, and now there was no sound to be heard, either.

'Hiding places?' Conway said.

'What?'

'If the worst comes to the worst, I mean. If everything went wrong and we had to hide. Do you know somewhere?'

'It won't happen. Herr Rasch is a fine soldier. He's done these things before.'

'But if it does go wrong?'

'Then running is better than hiding. The forests are thick.'

'Have to reach them first,' Conway said, 'and there's too much open country before we could reach the trees.'

Naujocks grinned. 'There's a little culvert down there. Empty nowadays. Down by the bridge, I used to play there as a child, until they stopped it.'

'Why did they stop it?' Conway had turned and was looking towards the bridge. The river ran across the open ground, almost parallel with the castle wall and about a hundred metres from the foot of the slope.

'The SS cleared the village, or most of it,' Naujocks said. 'Wewelsburg was to become an SS town. They moved a lot of people out and restricted access.' He tensed. 'Look!'

On the grey wall, a small dark shape had appeared, level with the first-floor windows. For long moments it seemed to remain motionless, then moved up again. Naujocks said, admiration in his voice, 'He's a fine soldier.'

'He's a bloody madman.'

'That kind of madness is a soldier's greatest weapon.' Naujocks sounded as though he was quoting a manual.

Soon another dark figure appeared on the wall, and they watched as the two inched upwards, thirty metres or so apart. Rasch slightly higher than Mohnke.

'Ever been inside?' Conway asked quietly.

'Only when I was small. The castle belonged to the village then. After 1934, nobody went in without the Reichs-führer's personal invitation.'

Rasch had reached the level of the third-floor windows. He stayed there a few moments, presumably fixing the rope, then came down quickly, half abseiling. Mohnke was slower, but two or three minutes later, he too descended, and soon afterwards the occasional movement of small stones on the slope indicated the four were returning.

Conway had spent minutes trying to decide. This young-ster Naujocks seemed to have the hallmarks of SS dedication. But if he was so bloody dedicated, what was he doing in Rasch's group? What the British called a keen type, he thought sourly. Still, if he was to make an approach, it would have to be quick, before Rasch returned. He said, 'What happens to you afterwards?'

Naujocks grinned. How, Conway wondered, could a man grin in this situation?

'They have promised me money,' Naujocks said. 'I am going to Spain.'

'Enough money? I could see you got more.'

'You?' Naujocks looked at him closely. 'How?'

'I have money.'

'What is it you want?'

'Bright boy,' Conway said. 'I want to get out alive. I'm no soldier. You'd have to help me, guide me out of here.'

'How much?'

'Ten thousand. English pounds.'

'When?'

'Now.'

'But – ' Naujocks hesitated, blank-faced. 'We can't – '

He'd left it too late, anyway, Conway realized with sinking heart as Rasch and the others seemed to materialize out of the countryside a few yards away.

'The ropes are in position,' Rasch said. 'The back door is ready for use. I have cut the telephone wires. Now we will approach the front.'

Dawn was minutes away as four of them took up their positions: Heiden and Mohnke in the churchyard, hidden from sight behind gravestones and a stone wall; Conway and Naujocks were in the edge of the trees at the top of the slope. From there they could see the edge of the churchyard and the whole length of the castle's great west wall.

Rasch and Sauer, moving swiftly through the silent village in an arc which took them close to the main road, halted as soon as they saw it. They remained still, for a moment, in the shadows, looking round them in case there was someone to see their movements. When Rasch was satisfied, he rose to his full height, stepped boldly to the middle of the road, and began to march towards the castle. His machine carbine was slung at his shoulder; his pistol was in his belt; his briefcase contained plastic explosive, time pencils and three hand grenades. Sauer, similarly equipped except for the briefcase, fell in behind.

'Pride,' Rasch muttered out of the side of his mouth. 'After today there will be no more marching. One last time: let's look like Waffen SS.'

They strode, feet placed precisely, heads up, shoulders straight. But for the quiet of their footfalls it could have been a parade, but they wore rubber-soled boots, partly for silence, partly because the rubber soles had been part of the Skorzeny Kommando legend, and Rasch was part of that legend. Down the little hill that rose again, abruptly towards the church, swinging right to the foot of the slope that led up to the castle's esplanade. Now they could see the guard house, grey and old and turning silver in the watery sun's first rays. To the right, over the wall, was the wide stone stair that led to the guard house's end door: a stair that had often rung to the crisp and complex rhythms of treading jack-boots as the Wewelsburg guard turned out with flags and banners for the Reichsführer-SS. It was empty now: thirty metres to the main door of the guard house.

Twin sentries had always stood there, flanking the stone steps, rigid as statues for two hours at a time: a day-and-night duty of some honour and great tedium. Rasch could remember the stony young faces, the gleaming leather and silver.

Today the steps were unguarded, the tarmac of the esplanade empty; beyond stood the looming ancient stone of the Wewelsburg. He marched briskly to the door and was unsurprised that the curiously sensitive echo bounced even the soft sound of his boots off the walls of the guard house. Himmler had been proud of that fortuitous echo; to him it was the supernatural granting additional protection to his cathedral.

Rasch turned the brass handle, still well polished, and entered the guard house bone-stiff, to look round with arrogance.

Behind the table, a grizzled and middle-aged Rotten-führer was hurriedly buttoning his collar, and getting to his feet.

'Name?' Rasch said.

'Stahmer, sir.'

'Place is a pigsty, Stahmer. Who commands the guard?'

'I do, sir.'

Rasch glared. 'Inform Warden Rupprecht that I am here?'

'Yes, sir. He'll be asleep, sir. May I know – '

'Waken him. Hauptsturmführer Rasch, from Berlin.'

'Yes, sir.' The corporal picked up the telephone, almost dropped it, and began to jiggle the receiver hook.

'How many on guard?' Rasch demanded, eyes roving disapprovingly over the table with its full ashtray and crumpled magazines.

'Three. The castle's locked up, sir.'

'The other two?' Rasch sniffed disapprovingly at sweat and cigarette smoke.

'In there, sir. Sleeping.' Stahmer rattled again at the telephone. His eyes kept flicking to the Knight's Cross at Rasch's throat.

Rasch strode into the side room. Two men lay breathing noisily on wooden cots; he prodded each with the barrel of his carbine. As their eyes opened he snapped 'Raus!' and ordered them sharply into the guard room, where they snapped to attention and stood bootless and tunicless. Both over forty, Rasch thought. As was the corporal.

'He doesn't seem to answer, sir.'

'Get brooms and get this place swept out. It's a disgrace!'

'Yes, sir.' The two men, relieved, hurried away.

'Still no – Ah, here he is, sir.' The corporal, confused, held the telephone out for Rasch.

'Then report to him,' Rasch said with quiet menace.

'Yes, sir. Herr Warden, sir, Hauptsturmführer Rasch is in

the guard room and wishes to see you, sir. Yes, sir. From Berlin.'

The corporal put down the telephone. 'He'll come to the gate, sir.'

Rasch nodded. 'When I come out of the castle, corporal, this guard room will shine like a gigolo's eyes, do you understand?'

He wheeled about and stood, facing the door. The corporal hurried round to open it for him.

'Remember,' Rasch said.

With Sauer on his heels, he stalked down the stairs and turned right, across the esplanade, blood thudding behind the stone face. Rupprecht might have been told, from Berlin, of his supposed treachery. He doubted it, but the chance was there, and he'd know the answer the moment the castle gate opened.

'Pistol cocked, Sauer.'

'Ready.'

Rasch glanced to left and right, confirming his recollections. On this east side, the castle was guarded by a small, steep-sided valley and over the low wall to the right of the approach was a drop of twenty metres. To his left, over another low wall, lay the empty moat, drained long ago and planted with trees. An old, gnarled oak stood at the corner, where the road turned left towards the castle gate and crossed the moat bridge. He remembered Himmler talking about that oak, boasting that the Reich would make the oak's great age seem puny. 'In a thousand years, where will the oak be? But the Reich can only grow greater and endure.'

They crossed the bridge, Sauer behind Rasch and to his left. Rasch's leather overcoat lay over Sauer's arm concealing the pistol. They halted smartly and stood facing the old gates with the twelve circles of the diocese cut into the timbers.

They waited. Footsteps sounded on the cobblestones on the other side of the gate; bolts slid back. Rasch swallowed, and waited. Sauer's finger curled to the trigger.

The door was opened – and by Rupprecht himself, tunic only half-buttoned, and red in the face from hurrying. Things had certainly changed.

'Good morning, Herr Rupprecht,' Rasch said formally. 'I regret having to waken you at this hour.'

Rupprecht straightened from securing the bolt. 'Heil Hitler!'

'Heil Hitler!' Rasch performed the salute as though he were on the parade ground at Lichterfelde, arm rigid to the point of quivering. Rupprecht was always punctilious, a man who noticed things. And he'd noticed something now, looking over Rasch's shoulder.

'The petrol we get these days,' Rasch said, 'is disgusting. My car broke down just this side of Niederntudorf. Blockage in the fuel line or the carburettor. We've had to walk.' Rasch watched his face carefully.

'Come in, Herr Rasch. I can offer you some coffee. Ersatz of course, dandelion. Loosens your bladder, but it's not as bitter as the acorns.'

So Rupprecht *didn't* know! Rasch said, 'I don't know if I have time. If I'm to get back to Berlin – '

'What's the situation?' Rupprecht asked.

'Situation? The Americans are trying to surround the Ruhr, that's the situation. They're driving for Paderborn from the west and the south. I got through on the way here, and with luck I'll get through on the way back, but it will be close.' He stepped forward, past the gate, through the arch into the triangular courtyard and paused there while Rupprecht refastened the gates.

'You mean we're surrounded?'

'Not quite. They haven't joined forces yet. The battle's on the Senneland. I don't give much for the Americans' chances there, eh, Rupprecht?'

Rupprecht looked at him. 'It depends on the strength of – '

Rasch laughed. 'The Senneland, man. The cream of the Wehrmacht there. All the instructors, all the experts, and fighting on ground they know like the backs of their hands!

I'm glad I'm not an American, fighting there.'

'You said it would be close.'

'Battles are fluid these days, Rupprecht. Especially
Panzer battles. Don't worry – there's more than a quarter
of a million men in the Ruhr. Field Marshal Model and
Field Marshal Kesselring. They'll roll them off the Senneland
eventually. Meanwhile, as I say, I have to get through in the
current situation. And take the papers with me.'

Rupprecht stopped. 'What papers?'

'Why do I always come here, Rupprecht? Because the
Reichsführer wants something from the files.'

'I have no orders.'

'No? I have.' Behind him he heard Sauer's hand move, a
little sliding sound from the leather coat. He said carefully,
'The Reichsführer is at Lübeck.' It was an open secret that
Himmler's mistress, Hedwig, lived at Lübeck. 'He telephoned
me yesterday.'

'So you have no authorization?'

'Telephone him. I'll tell you exactly what my orders are.
You can confirm them. I am to take certain papers from the
files. The rest are to be burned, in case the Americans get
here. We don't want the Reichsführer's files falling into their
hands, do we, Rupprecht?'

'Even so . . .'

'Telephone him, man, but do it quickly. Would I have
driven from Berlin, through all that, unnecessarily?'
Deliberately he let his face soften. 'I'll tell you what he said.
He told me he could trust me, and I was honoured. He told
me he could trust you, and you should be honoured, too. He
said, "Give my old comrade Rupprecht my warmest
regards."'

'He is a great man,' Rupprecht said.

'He said, "I rely on Rupprecht to destroy every last sheet
of paper, and I rely upon you, Rasch, to bring these documents to me if all the devils in hell are in your way!" And
it may be,' Rasch added grimly, 'that for the moment they
are.'

'All right. I'll telephone.'

'While you're doing it, the keys.'

'What?'

'Give me the keys, man. Let me get on! What transport have you here?'

'The Reichsführer's Horch, that's all.'

'I expect he'll be glad to see it again. Get the castle staff to collect all the sacks you can find. And petrol or paraffin to start the fire.'

They crossed the courtyard and entered the main door of the Wewelsburg in the west wall. Inside, in the great hall, Rupprecht's office was to the left of the door. He unlocked it, hesitated, then handed Rasch the keys and reached for the telephone.

Leaving him to it, Rasch hurried up the wide wooden staircase. The room which had belonged to Heydrich and which now contained Heydrich's files, was one high floor up from the hall, at the end of the corridor that led to the massive North Tower. He turned the key in the lock on the steel door, entered the room, and stood looking at the filing cabinets for a moment. There might be other papers he could use. Everything had gone beautifully and it would be a pity to waste an opportunity.

In the churchyard on the far side of the esplanade, Heiden and Mohnke crouched. They had watched Rasch and Sauer approach the castle gate, had seen them admitted, and had relaxed a little. If Rasch could talk his way in through the front door, and leave the same way, the task would be simple. With luck, now, the money was almost in their pockets. A few hours, and they might begin to imagine the warmth of the Spanish sun on their backs.

Suddenly they heard the engine, gears changing as a vehicle negotiated the steep, narrow streets of Wewelsburg village, then a lorry came noisily up the slope to stop outside the guard house. Behind the sheltering tombstones they kept very still, and watched.

A sergeant climbed quickly down from the cab. Heiden noted the uniform flashes: SS Engineers.

The guard corporal, on his toes after Rasch's dressing-down, came swiftly out.

'Detachment from Arnsberg,' the sergeant said. 'Has Major Macher arrived yet?'

'No.'

The sergeant looked at his watch. 'We are to rendezvous with him here.'

'Nobody told me. He hasn't arrived yet, I can tell you that much. What did you say his name was?'

'Macher, for Christ's sake,' the sergeant said angrily. 'He's only the Reichsführer's adjutant, that's all!'

'Another officer came, but he's not called Macher. How's he getting here?'

'He's supposed to be flying in,' the sergeant said.

'Well, I heard a plane at the airfield an hour or so back, but he can't have been on it, can he? He'd have been here in a few minutes even if he'd had to walk. Wait here and I'll telephone the Warden.'

Rupprecht, in his own office, insulated from outside sound by walls two metres thick, was standing with the telephone in his hand, reluctantly accepting that it was dead, when the other phone on his desk, the direct line to the guard house, rang. He picked it up.

'Guard corporal, sir. There's an Engineer detachment just arrived from Arnsberg.'

'Engineers?' Rupprecht said. For months he'd been trying to get the bloody engineers to do something about the hot water supply, which was intermittent at best, and its best was very infrequent. And they chose to send the men *now*! 'Tell them to wait. I'll see them when I'm ready!'

'Yes, sir. They're supposed to be – '

Rupprecht cut him off short. 'I know what they're supposed to be doing. Tell them to wait.'

'Sir.'

Rupprecht hung up and bustled out of his office. It went hard against the bureaucratic grain of his existence to allow anybody, even a much-decorated SS hero like Rasch, whom he knew Himmler trusted, to go near the files, or even enter the castle, without proper written authorization. Damn it, a month or two ago, he wouldn't have let in Obergruppen- führer Wolff himself on those terms, and Wolff was respon- sible for the Wewelsburg! Still, Rasch *was* here to do some- thing that he'd done plenty of times before, and if Rupprecht stood in his way, the Reichsführer would be furious. Rup- precht swallowed at the thought of Himmler's fury, and left his office to dig out of their bunks the half dozen cooks and cleaners who nowadays constituted the castle staff. Once there had been squads of men, all immaculate. He felt a powerful nostalgia for the days of the Wewelsburg's glory, when the twelve places at the round table had been occupied and the Reichsführer had been able to relax here and draw strength from the strength of the fortress and the stability of the SS Order. It had been wonderful then, with the banners and the formality and the sense of place and propriety, and Rupprecht had snapped his fingers and been obeyed by skilled servants. Now . . . half a dozen people too old or in- firm for service in the Volksturm, difficulty even in keeping the place clean, and nothing available when he wanted it. Those damned engineers come to repair the heating, when it had been left unrepaired through the winter!

He banged open his batman's door, hard so that the noise would awaken him, and brusquely told him to get a pile of sacks together and find some paraffin for a bonfire, then went to wake the others. There was sense, he supposed, in burning the papers. They were Heydrich's files, after all, and notoriously dangerous. Often he'd wondered what was in them; occasionally he'd been tempted to find out. But a man didn't do that – not a man like him, anyway, with responsi- bility for this fortress that was the heart of the Order. It was unbelievable that it was all coming to an end, that the Reich's sacred territory was no longer inviolate, that the boots of British, American, French, even the inferior Russian troops were now marching into Germany from east and west. If any man on earth could stop them, it was the Führer, but the long retreat that had begun in North Africa and in Russia, and had seen the Wehrmacht fall steadily backward upon the Fatherland, had never been halted, and there seemed no likelihood of its being halted now. The Saar had gone. Now Rasch said the Ruhr was almost encircled. The troops would fight, but the materials of war could hardly be sent to them.

No, the Reichsführer was right, as usual. The papers must be burned. And after that? It would then be time for Rupprecht to discharge his duty. If the invaders came to the Wewelsburg, well the castle was strong and he had weapons. It had been assaulted before, through history, and sometimes been taken, but always it had risen again. National Socialism would rise again, too. It was a nation's belief and the fact that the nation was in the process of defeat did not mean that beliefs would disappear. After a little while, they would rise; the Wewelsburg would resume its place of glory. For that time, he must put together the ornaments of the SS, and place them securely, so that even under bombardment, there could be no destroying them. When the papers had been burned, then the flags and coats of arms, the books and the standards must be gathered and placed in the base of the North Tower, in the cremation chamber, where the walls were four metres thick and set in rock. Yes, immediately the papers were burned, *that* task must be fulfilled . . .

The SS engineers were grumbling. Heiden and Mohnke could hear every word in the still air of early morning.

'We'll have to wait,' the sergeant announced, returning from the guard house.

'Wait?' one of his men said. 'What for?'

'The Warden says so,' the sergeant said sourly. 'He outranks us.'

'He doesn't outrank Major Macher! And it's his orders we're under. Christ, sergeant, if we're going to blow the place up, what's the point of delay? We could be fixing the bloody charges while we wait.'

'We wait because we're ordered to wait.'

Blow the place up! Heiden glanced at Mohnke, who shrugged.

Mohnke, Heiden thought, wouldn't care who or what was blown up, as long as it wasn't Mohnke. More important was Macher, Himmler's adjutant. Rasch had entered the castle as Himmler's messenger; Macher would know he was nothing of the kind.

He leaned close to Mohnke and whispered: 'I've got to let him know.'

Mohnke lifted a finger suddenly to his lips. 'Listen.'

Heiden, head tilted to one side, heard it too: an aircraft engine, somewhere to the north. As he listened, it came closer, became louder.

'I'll have to tell him. Wait here.' Heiden, moving at a crouch, began to back through the churchyard. Out of sight of both the guard house and the engineers, he straightened and hurried across the south front of the castle to where Conway and Naujocks waited.

'Did you get the signal?'

Naujocks nodded. 'He opened the shutters and waved. He's up there.'

'There's trouble. SS engineers are here to blow the place to bits. They're just waiting for the officer in charge. Watch out.'

The castle's windows were all shuttered, so there was no danger of being spotted from inside. Heiden ran to the corner, where the moat wall turned in front of the round West Tower, went a few feet down the slope, then followed the line of the west wall to where the ropes dangled. He could see the aircraft: a little Feiseler Storch spotter plane, high-winged, flimsy as an insect, was dropping towards the runway on the horizon. That had to be Macher! Furthermore, if he had any kind of wheels beneath him, he'd be at the castle in no more than minutes!

Glancing up, he saw that the single pair of shutters remained open. Perhaps the window was open, too. He whistled, waited, then whistled again, more loudly. Damn, Rasch obviously couldn't hear. He whistled again, still louder, and waited anxiously.

He'd have to climb.

And quickly, too, because Macher would be coming down the road from the airfield and now, in daylight, a man climbing the castle wall was bound to be spotted.

Slinging his carbine across his chest, Heiden grabbed the rope and began to walk up the wall, thankful for the long hours of training that had taught him this tricky skill. It was a long climb, too, but urgency set adrenalin flowing and in three minutes he'd reached the room beside the North Tower and, breathless from the exertion, was rapping the window hard with one hand while clinging to the rope with his feet and the other hand.

Rasch opened the shutter so swiftly as almost to knock him off the rope, but asked no stupid questions; he reached down, grabbed Heiden by the belt, and hauled him quickly over the sill.

'Macher!' he said, when Heiden, between gasps, had explained. He looked from the window across the open countryside to the airfield. The Storch was almost hidden by the ridge, but after a few moments with his binoculars, he saw its high wings, and they were stationary. As he looked, a scout car appeared over the ridge, coming swiftly down the straight road towards the castle.

'Kill him?' Heiden said.

Rasch stared at the speeding car. He knew Heinz Macher, a burly SS major of considerable ferocity, utterly devoted to Himmler.

'Not out there. There may be other troops in the area and the sound of shooting would stir them up. We'll get him here, *in* the castle.'

'Two of us against the castle staff?'

'Old men,' Rasch said. 'And there are three of us. Sauer's outside in the corridor.'

There was a tap on the door at that moment from Sauer. Rasch opened it. 'Well?'

'The Warden.' Rupprecht was approaching along the corridor.

Rasch gestured to Heiden to move behind the open door and, as Rupprecht stopped, said, 'I'll be only a few minutes.

Have you got the sacks ready?'

Rupprecht nodded. 'All in hand. When will the Americans reach the castle?'

'I don't know if they *will*. But they're not far north of Salzkotten. We can expect them to send patrols south.'

'God help the first patrol to approach the Wewelsburg,' Rupprecht said grimly. He turned, unlocked the door that led into the North Tower, and disappeared.

Rasch closed the steel door and returned to the files. No time now to do anything except be quite sure he'd got all the papers relevant to American and British investment in Germany. Hell would break loose soon!

Rupprecht, meanwhile, was descending the stairs that circled the wall of the round chamber on the third floor of the great tower. If he was to defend the castle, it was from the massive fortifications of that tower that the final shots would be fired. He wanted to check what arms were there already.

There were two racks on the second floor: both placed near the narrow windows that looked out to the north. He pulled one of them, loaded with half a dozen Gewehr 33/40 rifles and a pair of the newer Mauser semi-automatic rifles, to the window overlooking the courtyard. Using one of the keys from the bunch at his belt, he opened the cupboard in the base of the rack and brought out ammunition clips for the Gewehrs and a dozen of the short curved magazines for the Mausers. There was also a box of stick grenades. Drop those from the slit windows of the tower, and the Americans would certainly get a nasty surprise! Unless they had artillery to pound the castle down, and patrols tended to precede artillery . . .

With the weapons in position, he went on down the stairs to the first floor, and out into the courtyard, heading for his office again. He'd barely reached it when the telephone from the guard house went.

'Yes?' Those damned engineers, no doubt, getting impatient.

'Major Macher is here, sir. From the Reichsführer-SS.'

'Macher?' Rupprecht repeated, blinking. What was the Reichsführer doing, sending one after another of his aides to the Wewelsburg?

He rose and went out into the courtyard, across to the gate, and slid back the bolts.

Macher stood there, hands on hips, impatient. Behind him on the far side of the bridge that spanned the moat, a lorry stood with its engine running, SS engineers beside it. Rupprecht said, 'Heil Hitler!'

'Heil Hitler.' Macher's arm barely rose in acknowledgement. 'Why did you keep these men waiting?'

'The engineers? Because I had other things – '

Macher turned and waved an arm and the lorry began to move forward, across the bridge.

'That lorry's far too big,' Rupprecht pointed to the scratches on the stone entrance. 'You'll never get it through. It'll jam under the arch.'

There was impatience in every line of Macher's face. He turned and called to the sergeant engineer. 'Unload it by hand. Pile the stuff in the courtyard, over there by the main door!'

'What's going on?' Rupprecht demanded. 'I thought they were here to do the . . . well, the heating.'

'Heating?' Macher said incredulously. Then he laughed. 'Well, you could call it heat. A lot of it, all at once. We're here to blow the place up!'

'*Blow it up!*'

'Not one stone must stand on another. The Reichsführer's orders,' Macher said crisply. 'And it won't.'

'My God, you can't destroy it,' Rupprecht protested. 'Do you know how much it *cost*? Eleven million marks!'

One of the engineers, carrying a wooden crate covered in stencilled warnings, came at a half-run across the bridge. Rupprecht moved to block his path.

'Out of the way,' Macher said sharply.

'But you can't. You *can't*!' Rupprecht's voice rose. 'Good God, this is the Wewelsburg! It's the shrine of the Order of the SS; the living spirit of the *Schwarze Korps* dwells here!'

Macher put a hand on Rupprecht's shoulder to move him aside. 'Out of the way,' he repeated. Looking at Rupprecht's angry eyes, he added, in the hope of mollifying him, 'the Reichsführer built it. He can surely destroy what he built.'

'No!' Rupprecht insisted urgently. 'It's bigger than that. It's like the Roman legions with their *numen* that lived beyond the lifetimes of commanders. It is the *spirit* – '

Macher hit him, hard across the mouth with his gloved hand.

'Nothing must get in the way,' Macher rasped as Rupprecht staggered back, blood at his mouth. 'That's what the Reichsführer said. Not even you! Now stand aside while these men do their work. Get your own valuables while you have time, and warn the staff to get out. You have only a few minutes.'

He was a large man, but Rupprecht was bigger, and at that moment he looked as though he would attack Macher with his bare hands. Macher clipped open his pistol holster, meeting Rupprecht's glaring eyes with the threat in his own.

Rupprecht hesitated, then turned abruptly and swung away across the courtyard into the castle entrance. He slammed and locked the great oak doors behind him, and Macher, watching, hearing the lock and the bolts, swore aloud. He should have shot Rupprecht: the man was impossible and the job would be held up, and he must get back to the Reichsführer at Hohenlychen.

He snapped to the engineer sergeant: 'Those phosphorous grenades, bring them in.'

The sergeant dashed back through the gateway to the lorry and returned quickly, carrying a green-painted wooden box stamped with warnings in English, for the grenades had been captured. Using a short lever bar, the sergeant ripped off the lid, revealing rows of canisters like fruit tins, matt-painted. Macher bent and took one out of the box. 'What's the delay on the fuse?'

'Four seconds, Herr Major. The pin releases here, you see?'

'Smash that window.'

The sergeant swung the lever, breaking a single pane of glass, and Macher ripped at the pin, which flew off hard to one side, clanking on the stone. He reached and carefully thrust it through the glass.

'Back, sir!'

Macher stood, back against the wall as, with a crack followed instantly by a violent hissing noise, the grenade exploded. A single globule of the phosphoric mixture, flung by chance through the broken window, fell a few feet away to land like the splashings of hell on the cobblestones, sputtering malevolently and giving off gouts of dense white smoke.

Inside the building flames and smoke had instantly filled the room. Macher, leaning out from his place by the wall, watched with approval. 'Better than explosives,' he said. He looked round him at the castle walls. 'To blow up the castle will take a long time. We can burn it quickly, eh, sergeant?'

The sergeant nodded. 'We've two cases, forty-eight in each.'

Macher thought for a moment, going over in his mind the layout and contents of the castle. The ground floor was of stone but the upper floors were wooden. His orders were to use explosives to bring down the castle, and large quantities of explosives, placed with care, would be required. But it would certainly burn, and these British fire bombs the engineers had brought from Arnsberg were the perfect instruments.

Damn Rupprecht! Damn his stupid, pointless resistance, which would make everything so much more difficult. Couldn't he understand that orders were there to be obeyed; that it was the Reichsführer himself who had ordered this, and that the loyalty to which they were all sworn obliged them to carry out the Reichsführer's orders?

'Right,' he said, 'we'll – '

246

His words were cut off by a shot, and beside him one of the engineers gave a little grunt and collapsed backward, the box he was carrying falling beside him. Macher bent over him, but the man was dead.

'Take cover!' he ordered loudly, cramming himself into a narrow doorway to the left of the entrance, then peering cautiously out. He'd heard the tinkle of glass immediately before the shot and now tried to spot the broken window from which the shot had come. He saw it almost at once; Rupprecht's office in the main hall, just beside the castle doors. And it was clear that from there he could cover the entrance arch that led from outside into the courtyard, the arch where they now tried to shelter. Crammed into the doorway, Macher found that his back was becoming uncomfortably hot. Behind the door lay the room in which the grenade had exploded, and the fire had rapidly taken hold.

'Sergeant.'

'Sir?'

'Another grenade. Lob it to land under that window, to the left of the main doors.'

With its sinister click-and-tinkle, the pin flew off the grenade and the sergeant bowled the canister underarm across the courtyard. The briefest pause, while they flattened themselves against their small places of shelter, then it went off.

In the open, the grenade's detonation was even more impressive. Gobbets of fire spat in every direction over a radius of five metres or so, and when they had all landed, to lie spitting and hissing on the stones, a massive cloud of dense white smoke was already obscuring a wide section of the western wall.

'We'll have to blast the main door down,' Macher ordered. 'High explosive and percussion fuse.'

Beside him, the sergeant fumbled with sticks of blasting gelignite and a fulminate fuse. Macher watched impatiently as the bomb was hurriedly put together, then thrown through the gouting smoke towards the door.

The blast was tremendous and a shock wave bounced back

at them, funnelling itself into the entrance way and rocking them as they stood, hands over their ears. They waited impatiently for the smoke to clear.

Rupprecht, meanwhile, was already off and running. After closing and bolting the doors, he had gone into his own office, tapped out the glass of one window pane, and loosed off a single accurate round. He watched the engineer fall, then grabbed the telephone linking his office with the guard house. Waiting for the answer, he crouched on the floor beside his desk, where several feet of solid stone protected him from return fire.

'Guard house.'

'The castle is under attack,' Rupprecht shouted into the receiver. 'Major Macher's men are trying to destroy it. Attack them from the rear!'

There was silence.

'Did you hear me? *Attack!*'

Hesitantly the guard corporal's voice came back to him. 'Sir, Major Macher is the Reichsführer's . . .'

'Fool! He's going to destroy the castle. Kill him. And the others. Do you hear me – those are *orders!*'

'But sir,' the corporal almost wailed, 'I can't – '

'Attack, or you'll be shot,' Rupprecht snapped. 'Do you understand your orders, corporal?'

'Yes, sir.'

'Repeat them.'

'Attack Major Macher's detachment, sir.'

'Good. Do it.' Rupprecht slammed down the phone and hurried out into the hall.

Chapter Sixteen

The crack of the first exploding phosphorus grenade, muffled as it was by the massive masonry, none the less reached and alerted Mohnke where he crouched behind the gravestones in the churchyard. The sharpness of the sound was familiar to him – he'd encountered those damned British fire bombs before and had unpleasant memories of them. What the hell, Mohnke asked himself, was going on in there?

When, a moment later, he heard the faint but unmistakable crack of a shot, he decided Rasch must be in trouble, and if Rasch was in trouble, then according to the plan, he must be assisted. Mohnke's job, in that case, was to deal with the men in the guard house.

He ran crouching among the gravestones, vaulted lightly over the wall, and crossed to take shelter behind the end wall of the guard house.

Ever since Rasch had left it, frantic cleaning had been going on inside. Windows had been opened, dust had been brushed out over the front steps. Even Macher's arrival had merely punctuated, not halted, the efforts of the guard. Now, crouched low behind the wall, Mohnke found he could hear through an open window, the ringing of a telephone.

'Guard house.'

Mohnke listened intently, heard the corporal's voice rise in protest: 'Sir, Major Macher is the Reichsführer's – '

Then, 'But sir, I can't – ' Stopping as he was interrupted. Then, 'Yes, sir.'

And finally, 'We are to attack Major Macher's detachment, sir.'

A click as the phone went down. Then a babble of voices inside the guard house, and the corporal saying, 'It's orders.

Warden Rupprecht says we'll be shot if we don't!'

'We'll be shot if we do,' one of the others protested. 'Macher is the Reichsführer's adjutant!'

'Rupprecht says he's going to destroy the castle. We're the bloody guard. We have to . . .' A deep sigh. 'Come on, let's get out there.'

Mohnke put his head cautiously round the corner. At the end of the approach road, where it turned on to the bridge, the engineers' lorry stood, back open, as two men unloaded its contents. The engineer sergeant had now joined them, sub-machine-gun at the ready, to guard his men.

Mohnke gripped his carbine, listening to the scuffling inside the guard house as the three prepared to emerge. He heard the corporal's muttered, 'Right, fire at will. Come on!' And watched as he appeared on the top step, and began cautiously to descend, the other two behind him. For the moment, the engineer sergeant had not seen them; he was still facing the entrance, watching whatever was happening in the courtyard.

Mohnke picked his instant. The three men of the Volk-sturm, rifles at the ready, stood in line abreast facing towards the castle, hesitation in every line of their bodies, every doubtful movement. From behind them, Mohnke loosed off a single shot that flicked through the canvas upperwork of the lorry. He ducked quickly back behind the corner.

The three surprised guards hardly had time to begin to turn. The SS engineer sergeant, alert and experienced, pivoted upper body and weapon swiftly in the direction from which the shot had come, saw the guard advancing on him, pulled the trigger and held pressure. The three men were at long range for a sub-machine-gun. Had they been more experienced, they might have flung themselves flat, returned fire, and survived. But they were not. The bullets were sprayed a little, the weapon circling characteristically, but the effect was like a shotgun. In seconds, the three men were down, dead or wounded severely.

Mohnke grinned to himself. The sergeant engineer must know there had been only three men in the guard room, and had dealt with three. He watched with satisfaction as the sergeant, after a single long glance at his handiwork, turned away again to see what was happening in the castle yard.

As the chatter of the sub-machine-gun sounded behind him, Macher turned his head in quick apprehension. He saw the sergeant's face, jaw tight as he killed, gun bucking in his hands, then stopping.

'What is it?' Macher demanded.

'Castle guard.' The sergeant paused for a moment, then turned towards Macher. 'Bloody fools came to attack. Nothing to worry about now.'

'Good. Keep watch.' Macher turned to look again at the courtyard. Behind him the old oak door was getting very hot; he couldn't lean against it much longer, but to emerge from the shelter of the doorway was to risk a shot from Rupprecht's office through the smoke that was slowly beginning to clear. Macher couldn't yet see whether the castle doors still stood, or whether the blasting gelignite had destroyed them. Until he knew, he could not determine his next action.

But it was essential to get into the castle. Himmler had been specific about the destruction of the files. Privately Macher was astonished that he was even to be allowed near Heydrich's files. For so many years their deadly importance had been known and understood. Only Heydrich . . . later, only the Reichsführer, wondering neurotically whether they were safe, even in the Wewelsburg. Now they were to be destroyed on almost a casual order.

Nor would destruction be easy. He'd been told the files were bulky, and paper in quantity was notoriously difficult to burn. That was why he'd had the phosphorus bombs brought, but it looked now as though they would have other uses. In his shallow doorway, back beginning to burn through his coat and uniform, Macher sweated and waited, praying the doors had gone . . .

The moment he had ordered the guard corporal to attack, Rupprecht moved quickly out of his office, into the castle's main hall which lay immediately behind the main doors. There, for a moment, he paused and looked round, deeply conscious that this would probably be his last look, at the huge hanging banners, the Swastika black on its white circle in the middle of the great sweep of crimson; the huge portrait and the busts of the Führer, the double-lightning-flash of the SS in woven silver thread on its banner. Everything pristine, gleaming, shiny, pressed. He snapped to attention and said, 'Heil Hitler!'

He had hoped one day the Führer would come to see the Wewelsburg. The Reichsführer had always said Adolf Hitler would come.

The Reichsführer!

Damn the Reichsführer who wanted now to bring it down! Rupprecht's upraised arm wavered and lowered as the castle staff came running into the hall. All he had now: a cook, two cleaners, his batman, and the one-armed sergeant from the SS Division *Das Reich* who had come here after fearful wounds in Russia and spent his days happily and carefully polishing metal. Six altogether, including himself.

Well, they'd see what six could do!

'They're trying to destroy the Wewelsburg,' he told them. 'Come with me!'

He ran down the corridor that led to the North Tower, ripping at his belt for the key to the tower door, opening it, ushering them through; he was about to close it when an enormous blast hammered at the main doors and glass smashed everywhere. Momentarily numbed and deafened, Rupprecht watched with horror as the great doors slowly fell inwards and smoke poured in after them to fill the hall.

Ears ringing, he forced himself to move, closing the door and locking it, entering the circular chamber of the tower. Thank God he'd had the forethought to check the weapons! He crossed to the window that overlooked the courtyard, reaching for one of the Mauser semi-automatic rifles from the rack, slapping the magazine into place. From here the whole courtyard was covered. The old Germans who had built the Wewelsburg had known what they were doing: this tower had been designed as a place of last defence, and was perfectly fitted for its purpose. An invader might breach the outer defences and enter the castle, but the North Tower remained, its walls metres thick and its narrow windows so placed that every inch of outside ground could be covered. It was at the apex of the triangle and an angle of fire of only thirty-five degrees covered the entire courtyard. Try to get in here, you bastards, he thought!

But in the courtyard nothing moved. They were sheltering in the entrance way, he thought, before they made a dash for the main doors. He turned to his batman and gave him the other Mauser. 'If anybody moves out there, get him!'

The man was hardly a soldier, but at least he'd been through the training course, and with a semi-automatic at thirty yards, he could hardly miss! Rupprecht dodged across to the window which covered the east wall of the castle. Here was the advantage of the triangular structure: from this tower it was possible to cover not only the courtyard, but both outer walls.

He could see the lorry, nothing else. No – he looked again – was that a body he could see? A leg, certainly. Where was the guard? He'd ordered them to attack, damn it! Could it be that Macher had killed the guard? Rupprecht slipped open the narrow window to try to improve the angle of his vision, but could see no more. The visible leg did not move.

Something else moved, though. Rupprecht raised the Mauser, slipped the lever to single-shot, and lined it up on the man who had just emerged from the entrance way and was going towards the lorry. The engineer sergeant! Lovingly he squeezed the trigger and watched the sergeant, catapulted backwards by the heavy 7.92 mm bullet, somersault helplessly over the wall into the empty moat. That left Macher with four men; four: all trapped in the entrance way. If they moved forward, he'd get them. If they tried to retreat, he'd get them.

'Your move, Major Macher,' Rupprecht murmured, eye squinting hopefully along the Mauser's sights.

'Sir, there's a fire.' It was the one-armed sergeant.

Rupprecht's head snapped round. 'Where?'

'Room next to the old armoury.'

Rupprecht went reluctantly to look, ordering his batman to replace him at the window. The fire was half-hidden, but unmistakable. Those damn fire bombs! The remnants of one of them still snarled and sputtered in front of his office window, the smoke thinning now but hanging like a wall of cotton-wool across the inner west wall.

'Try a shot or two into that lorry,' he told his batman. 'See what you can hit.' Modern military explosives, he knew, were largely insensitive to rifle fire, but a lucky shot might touch off detonators or even the fire bombs!

He listened as the man fired. Six shots, aimed and spaced.

'Any luck?'

'No, sir.'

'Try the petrol tank.'

'Can't see it, sir.'

'Must be on the other side.'

Maybe it was, but he'd better look himself. The man was a good batman, but not over bright. Rupprecht shifted across to see.

There was barely time to look out of the window before the one-armed sergeant said quietly, 'Sir!'

'What is it?'

'Fire bomb, sir. Right in front of the tower.' Rupprecht felt like a rat in a cage, running endlessly back and forth, as he crossed again to the window that overlooked the court-yard and found he could see nothing except dense white smoke rising to blot out all vision. In an instant, the commanding view of the courtyard was lost and instead of controlling it, Rupprecht found he couldn't see so much as a cobblestone.

'Spray the yard with rifle fire,' he ordered, thrusting the window open and loosing a hail of bullets from the Mauser. He heard them ricochet off the stones, but knew how unlikely it was that they could have any effect. As he lowered the rifle, the butt snagged against the keys at his belt, and a thought struck him.

'Guard the door,' he snapped. 'I'm going outside.'

At the rear of the tower, a small staircase led to the chamber below. Rupprecht paused to grab two spare magazines then clattered down the steps, unlocked the door at the bottom and stepped through. For a second the stillness inside stopped him. He stood for a moment looking at the great circular table, so carefully specified and so lovingly crafted, at the twelve pillars with their coats of arms, the twelve chairs, each with its occupant's name on its silver plate. Everything that could gleam was gleaming. The chamber had not been used for many months, but had been always ready. The thought of its desecration by fire made Rupprecht want to vomit and he crossed the chamber quickly, thrusting the thought from his mind, towards the door that led from the chamber to the moat on the east side.

Opening it, he glanced quickly out. Here he was eight metres below the courtyard and on the outside of the east wall; the lorry stood at the turn of the bridge, but nobody moved beside it, or anywhere else that he could see. Ahead of him, through one of the bridge's two arches, the sprawled body of the engineer sergeant lay on the smooth, close-cut lawns of the moat. Rupprecht, bulky body bent almost double, ran quickly forward to the foot of the narrow stair that was set into the wall, and led up to the bridge. If he could get to the top, he'd have the lorry *and* command of the entrance to the castle.

He had almost reached the foot of the stair when the man came into view, creeping cautiously forward towards the lorry. Futilely Rupprecht flattened himself against the wall; if the man happened to glance his way, he'd be seen. But the man did not; he was intent upon the courtyard, creeping forward towards the rear of the lorry. Rupprecht could see his helmet and collar but little more. But it was a target. He raised the Mauser, aimed, allowed for the uphill shot, and squeezed the trigger with a marksman's steady finger. The helmet vanished at once. Dead, or not? Rupprecht stayed where he was, rifle at his shoulder, trained on the rim of the bridge's low wall. He let a minute go, counting the seconds, then began to mount the staircase with slow care, conscious of his own vulnerability.

The man lay unmistakably dead. The bullet had gone in beneath the helmet and through the collar: a perfect shot. Briefly Rupprecht wished somebody could have witnessed its perfection.

In his first minutes in the file room, Rasch, knowing the files he wanted, had been unable to find them. He had thought he knew which of the fourteen cabinets they were in, but either memory had let him down, or the cabinets had been moved about. Even by the time Heiden arrived, he had still not succeeded in finding them and had been reduced to sliding out the long file drawers one by one and fingering his way impatiently and laboriously through the marking tags. Heiden's news of the arrival of Macher and his demolition detachment had added urgency to his search, but not luck.

From the beginning he had been unable to remember the wording on the tag of the file and had intended to rely on what he thought was knowledge of its location. He had been sure that the card folder was orange in colour, but the cabinet he had opened first and with certainty had contained only green folders.

Drawer after drawer was opened, examined and slammed shut, and his impatience increased.

'We'll have to be fast now,' Heiden said warningly.

Rasch swore at him. He was trying to remember . . . and, damn it, he couldn't! There was a word, if only he could recall it: a typical Heydrich word, too. What the hell was it?

Another drawer, orange folders this time. He went through them quickly and with concentration, but the file wasn't there. The word. The word! Fencing came into his mind. Something to do with fencing, wasn't it? He ran quickly over the familiar terms: quarte and tierce, circle, octave, prime, quinte, parade . . . No! Feints, disengagements, the three attacks . . . No! Heydrich had had a favourite gambit, with the feint, one, two made as a return after the parade of . . .

'Got it!' He almost shouted. 'Chess!' he said over his shoulder to the mystified Heiden.

The file was White Knights, pure Heydrich, and with the return of the words came the memory of location. Within a minute the file was in his hand. After that the others were easy.

Good. Now one more: Heydrich's file on Schellenberg if it were here, if the Reichsführer had not taken it away. Whatever discreditable secrets there may have been behind Schellenberg's immaculate Party face, Heydrich would have rooted them out, and if he could arrange for the file to reach Kaltenbrunner's bloody hands, or Gestapo Müller's . . . It was there! He grabbed it from the cabinet with a swift, fierce joy, and was about to open it when the first, muffled crack of the exploding phosphorus grenade penetrated the walls. He straightened, rammed the Schellenberg file inside his jacket and stuffed the others into his brief-case.

He ripped open the door and was crossing the corridor to the room which overlooked the courtyard, when the cracks of other grenades were suddenly followed by the deafening blast of high explosive, and even the castle seemed to shake.

This room was set out for lectures on early Germanic history, runic symbols on the walls, with explanations on charts and the walls lined with books. Rasch crossed it quickly, wrenched at the window catch and gazed down into the triangular castle yard. Smoke everywhere, but after a few seconds he saw a pattern to it. One smoke bomb had gone off beside the entrance to the North Tower, another near the castle entrance. There was also darker smoke from the HE blast near the entrance.

As he watched he heard a stutter of fire come from the North Tower, looked instinctively for its target and saw dimly through the smoke that men were running towards the main doors.

'They've blown in the doors! Why?'

'Maybe the Warden's resisting,' Heiden said. 'Would he – ?'

'He's mad enough!' Rasch stared for a moment. If Rupprecht was doing the firing from the North Tower, and firing at Macher's men, then he was certainly resisting. Bullets ricocheted from the old stone walls, whining and screaming round the courtyard, and a sudden murderous thump on his upper chest sent pain in a sudden sick eddy through his body.

Rasch knew Macher. Not well, but well enough to know his determined ruthlessness. Rupprecht's absurd defence would merely increase Macher's determination to carry out his orders. He tried to flex his arm. Collar bone broken! He gritted his teeth, and felt the place. No blood.

'Does Macher know we're here?'

'I don't know,' Heiden replied. 'Maybe not. You all right?'

'Then he won't be expecting anything. Yes, I'm all right. Heiden, take Sauer and go to the head of the stairs. Shoot down anyone who tries to come up!'

Heiden nodded and turned to Sauer. 'This way.'

Rasch heard their footsteps move away down the corridor. The pain in his shoulder was bad but not incapacitating.

Seconds later came a single shot followed by the bangs of two exploding grenades. Rasch raced to the door and glanced quickly down the corridor to see Sauer, uniform aflame, lying prostrate near the top of the great staircase. Heiden he could not see at all. But there were shouts and running footsteps on the stairs. If Heiden and Sauer had been together, as they must have been, then Heiden, too, would have been caught by the grenades.

In either case there was nothing Rasch could do. He tore into the file chamber, slammed the steel door and crossed to the window. With one arm useless, what good was the rope? He couldn't climb down it, not with the briefcase and his damned arm! He stared wildly out of the window. Naujocks and Conway were by the South-West Tower but there was no way they could help him. Christ, he'd have to try to fight his way out, past Macher's men . . .

As a sudden thought struck him, he swung back the

window shutter and looked to his right. It might be possible, just possible, to swing one-handed on the rope to the flat roof of the North Tower. It wasn't far. With difficulty he unfastened his belt, passed it through the handle of the brief-case, then climbed out on to the sill. No, it wouldn't work: the arc of swing would be too short and he'd be left hang-ing. He climbed in again and hauled in the rope. If he could attach it to the shutter itself . . .?

From the corridor outside, he could hear doors slamming and the crack of the fire bombs. In a moment they'd be out-side the steel door of the file room. One-handed, the loop was impossible to tie. He made a knot in the rope, jammed it between shutter and wall and climbed again to the sill. This time he'd have to go!

Rasch wound the rope round his arm and gripped it tightly, leaned back and out, then launched himself forward with a hard thrust of his legs to set the shutter swinging, and, as his body came arcing out almost horizontally, reached with scrabbling feet for the parapet.

From the beginning neither Naujocks nor Conway had moved from their place of concealment among the trees beneath the South-West Tower. Naujocks, trained through-out his youth for war, had been impatient at times to find the action, and had to be restrained.

Where restraint of that kind was needed, Conway was a deeply conscientious advocate. 'We have orders,' he kept repeating. 'We're to remain here. Nobody else can see the window.'

Naujocks fretted, but remained where he was; his hands, though, fiddled endlessly with his carbine, checking that the magazine was fully home, then releasing it, ramming it home and checking again.

Conway, terrified almost out of his wits by the sounds of battle so close by, had none the less put the time to use. With three factions joined in combat, he had a strong feeling that Naujocks's knowledge of this countryside was the most important weapon available and had devoted himself to extracting as much of that knowledge as he could.

'I wish I knew what the hell was happening!' Naujocks kept muttering. 'I ought to go and see. Maybe Rasch is in trouble.'

'Rasch,' Conway said tightly, each time, 'is in that room up in the corner by the North Tower. We're here in case he wants us.'

'But Christ, anything could be happening!'

'None of it concerns *us*. Not yet.'

'But – '

'Wait,' Conway repeated. 'That's our job. We *wait!*'

'If only we could *see* . . .'

If they had been able to see the far side of the castle, they would have seen Rupprecht, standing motionless close against the side of the lorry the SS detachment had brought from Arnsberg. Rupprecht now controlled the exit from the Wewelsburg, and was trying to work out how to use his control. His determination to preserve the Wewelsburg was warring now with an ache to destroy, and a glance over the lowered tailboard of the lorry had shown him that it contained the means of destruction. Not all the explosives had been unloaded.

He had also finally remembered that Rasch was in the castle. Macher's mission had driven Rasch from his mind and he was struggling to apply a brain racing with adrenalin to what had become a three-sided equation. Not that Rupprecht had much time for Rasch. To Rupprecht, men like Rasch were scarcely SS at all; they were merely soldiers who wore different uniforms and SS badges. Rasch and the Waffen SS people were not really interested in the *spirit* of the Order. They had, if anything, a contempt for it. The Waffen SS were elite fighting formations, but had rarely been imbued with true commitment to the SS ideal. All the same, Rasch was in the castle with his own permission. He could hardly defile it by destroying those he himself admitted.

He looked round, trying to calculate the destruction if the explosives in the lorry went off. He had little knowledge of explosives, and the lorry was hardly more than ten metres from the gates. Though destruction of Macher and his invaders was the Warden's clear duty, if he touched off the lorry's cargo of explosives, he might even be helping Macher's treacherous attempt to destroy the castle.

Torn by the pain of a decision that would be wrong whatever it was, he glanced up and saw that the sky was filling with smoke. They had started their fires! It was then that fury made the decision for him: he would destroy the bridge and thus trap them in the castle. Let their own fire destroy them! He climbed quickly into the lorry, grabbed a case of blasting gelignite and some percussion detonators, then scrambled down and ran to the stairs that led down to the moat. Blast away the bridge pillars – that was the answer!

In the shelter of the inner arch, he worked quickly. The gelignite was bound in bundles, six sticks to a bundle; he fitted three bundles with fulminate fuses, then took his SS dagger from his belt, and dug away the soft earth at the foot of the central bridge support, to make a small hole. It seemed appropriate to him that the dagger, ceremonial in purpose, should have this final ceremony to perform. With the explosive in position, he packed the earth back round it then raced back to the shelter of the wall and unslung the Mauser from across his chest. Gelignite, he reflected, might be proof against rifle fire; fulminate of mercury was not.

He sighted, squeezed the trigger, and ducked his head quickly. There was no explosion. He frowned and fired again, looking for the puff of earth as the bullet struck.

The padding at the front of his cap saved his life, but not his consciousness. A flying chip of granite, driven by the blast, took him high on the forehead, smashing him backwards, to lie like a corpse at the foot of the steps.

Inside the castle, the fire had now taken hold, as the SS engineers, protected by thick walls from the castle's defenders, raced from room to room. Where every room had been different, fire now brought a fearful uniformity as the loving work of craftsmen, the assembled fine art, the exquisite carpets, the historical relics, alike surrendered to the uncompromising phosphorus. Doors were opened or, if locked, forced with bullet and boot, a grenade was slung in, the door closed, and the grenades left to scatter their fizzing incandescent showers upon the work of fine German woodcarvers, great painters, long-dead Persian and Chinese carpet weavers. The banners went, too, and the SS flags, the war trophies and the collections of the historical papers. The fire, making no distinction between the fine and the meretricious, intensified its hold with every passing second.

The steel door, however, still survived.

Macher shouted for explosives and blasted it down, then tore into the room and began to pull out drawers from the filing cabinets and tip their contents on to the floor. In minutes the hoard of information that had taken years to assemble was a pile of scrap paper into which, from the doorway, more phosphorus bombs were tossed. Soon, like the rest of the Wewelsburg, the long-dreaded files of Reinhard Heydrich were burning.

Macher had seen the open shutter, but taken no notice of it. An additional draught of air would assist the fire. What, after all, was an open shutter in a wall sixty feet high?

When the last of five grenades had exploded, he took one final, careful look round the wrecked doorpost, saw the intensity of the inferno he had created, and yelled, 'That's it. Let's get out!'

The staircase was in flames and impassable, but the long corridor was still open. Macher and his two men raced along it to the entrance to the Treppenturm, the staircase tower, in the south-west corner of the courtyard. There was no wood in the Treppenturm, built as it had been to resist fire. The stone spiral of its staircase ran down inside circular granite walls to the courtyard and even there, the angle of its door provided protection.

Once again, phosphorus grenades, hurled towards the North Tower, provided covering smoke for a dash to the castle gates.

And the ruined bridge.

On the far side, the lorry was wrecked, too. Its load of explosives had not detonated, but the collapsing masonry beneath it had dropped its front axle and suspension on to the ridged stone and there was no hope of moving it.

Laboriously Macher and his men climbed down into the moat, ran round to the south front of the castle, and climbed up to the deserted esplanade by way of the ancient tree that grew from the moat's bed at a corner of the wall. There they stopped for a moment to look back at their handiwork. The ancient pile was burning now from end to end. Only the great North Tower was not affected, and the North Tower was unimportant, its contents only ceremonial, its structure impossible to burn. Everywhere else, flames poured from shattered windows and the air was filling with drifting particles of smoke and carbon. A light wind drove eddies of smoke into a flattened mushroom that hung over the great castle like a vast black cloth embroidered with stitches of fire.

'Get back to Arnsberg,' Macher ordered. Leaving the engineers a little bewildered, he himself set off at a run for the streets of the village to find something, anything, that would carry him back to the airfield. A bicycle would do; indeed a bicycle was all he expected to find. He ran with his Luger Parabellum in his hand, in case some honest burgher might be reluctant to part with a bicycle.

Chapter Seventeen

He seemed to have been hanging there for ever. They stared up at him with a kind of horrified helplessness.

They had watched as Rasch came out to the window sill. Had seen him climb back and reappear, tying the rope awkwardly to the shutter, had seen him gather himself and swing forward and outward to try to reach the tower's rim.

He reached it, too, and a fraction more forward momentum would have carried him far enough to scramble on to the stone work; but that extra momentum was missing and Rasch succeeded only in hooking his heels over the edge. For a moment or two, while there was strength, he fought to use his feet and legs to drag more of himself over the edge of the tower and managed to jam his calves against the stone work. But the strain had been tremendous and soon he had been reduced to hanging, as he hung now: one arm bound into the rope, lower legs holding desperately to the tower. His torso had been rigid as he fought, but the strength went visibly and quickly as his body began to bend until he hung sagging between the rope and the tower's rim.

'His left arm is limp,' Naujocks said urgently. 'We must try to get to him.'

'No,' Conway said. 'Look at the other windows. There's a bloody inferno in there. We wouldn't have a chance.' Even if there had been a chance, Conway would have had no intention of taking it.

They watched, as the strength left Rasch's body. The grip of his legs on the stone, always precarious, began to slip as his muscles spasmed. One foot slipped into space and Rasch, with a vast effort, forced it back. But the ordeal could have only one ending and soon both feet had slipped and his body fell back into space, to hang dangling from his right arm, into which the rope bit ever deeper, cutting off the blood from muscles which needed blood with a terrible urgency if the grip of his hand was to be maintained.

Beside him as he struggled, the explosions had taken place: the deep blast of high explosive as the door was blown in; the cracks of the fire bombs detonating as Macher set fire to the papers. Now fire streamed from the window, licking at the shutter, at the rope, and soon at Rasch's arm.

Even in those hanging moments judgment, not emotion, governed his brain. A further swing would fail. Beside him the file room was a red-white furnace impossible to enter, even if he could climb again to the already-charring oak of the window frame. He glanced downwards. The long fall would smash his body; if he survived by some miracle, it would be as a cripple. The heat on his hand was intense now, blistering the skin, unbearable. So here was his death. *His*, not Himmler's. *His*, not Schellenberg's. But when they found him, they would find also the file inside his uniform and it could yet bring disaster to Schellenberg. Himmler would not outlive the Reich. And Conway? Conway would probably survive anything: the rats always did.

His death . . . So why delay?

He indulged himself with brief, deliberate memories of his home in East Prussia, of Grenadier, his horse, finally of Lisel, his wife. Could it be the priests were right and that he might meet her? He would know soon. He let the rope unwind from his arm until only his hand gripped it, and began a pendulum swing. The fall must be efficient. Three swings. Four . . . and with a clean gymnastic twist, he thrust his legs towards the sky, upending his body. *Now!* Rasch released his hold upon the rope.

He fell silently. The black figure that at one moment had a tenuous hold on life, a moment later had none. He fell head down, without a cry. There was no last scream, no announcing of despair. They heard the fearful thud and raced towards him along the narrow path at the foot of the west wall.

In the North Tower, the one-armed sergeant, veteran of a

hundred encounters in the snow and mud of the Russian front, had tired of firing round after round through a curtain of white smoke at targets which were probably not even there. Rupprecht had not returned and there was nobody else, it seemed, capable of giving orders. Meanwhile the window covering the west wall was unguarded. Bloody incompetents, he thought. It wouldn't have done in any decent unit he'd served with. He clipped a fresh magazine into his rifle and moved to cover the window and as he looked out, his eyes widened. Below him a body lay on the path beneath the wall: a man in uniform, a Waffen SS officer, and two others were bent over it, one slashing with a knife at the officer's belt. The man straightened holding a briefcase.

The one-armed sergeant smashed the glass out of the window with his rifle butt and leaned forward quickly to get in a shot. Instantly the two men jumped for the slope, trying to get into the trees, slithering quickly for cover. The rifle was self-cocking, and because it was not necessary to work a bolt, the one-armed sergeant was able to get off two shots before they vanished. He wasn't sure, but he thought he'd winged one of them.

Conway, crashing panic-stricken down the shale slope through the trees, saw Naujocks appear to trip, then fall, then slide forward a few feet, rolling over, to finish spread-eagled on the slope. Conway stopped long enough to see the open, sightless eyes then, with a little whimper of fear, grabbed the briefcase and ran. Any second, he expected a bullet, but he reached the edge of the trees unscathed. He stopped then, staring out across the open ground that rose towards the airfield, his mind whirling with the knowledge that he was now utterly alone.

He glanced down at the briefcase with loathing, not even sure what instinct had made him pick it up. He was tempted to hurl it away, in the irrational hope that all dangers could be hurled away with it, but something stopped him: perhaps the same instinct that began, a few moments later, to direct his feet towards the abandoned Naujocks farm.

He was in the fringe of trees bordering the road to the village when a figure in black raced past, ludicrous on a bicycle, sped across the bridge, and began to pedal furiously up the slowly-rising hill towards the airfield. He wore the rank badges of an SS Sturmbannführer and must, presumably, be Macher. Even at this remove, proximity to the dread name of Himmler made vomit rise in Conway's throat, and he spent a full minute retching before, pale and sweating, he slipped across the road and moved at a ragged, stumbling trot, to the south-west.

Alone, alone, alone . . . the word drummed into his mind. With Rasch and the others alive and competent, his terror had been leavened by faith in that evident competence. Now that they were no longer there, he had no faith at all in himself. This was German territory; he a civilian with deeply incriminating papers. There could be no doubt what would happen if the Germans caught him.

Yet as he ran on, crashing through the woodland, it became clear that only he and the now-distant pedalling figure seemed alive in the whole landscape. There wasn't a cow, a rabbit, a goose, scarcely a bird.

After a quarter of a mile he stopped exhausted, dragged himself into a clump of bushes, crouched down and began to think about surviving. Was he right to head for the Naujocks farm? There was the other alternative: the house in Büren, occupied by the Irishwoman. He'd been told she would probably shelter him. *Probably!* They didn't know and neither did he, and probably Büren crawled with troops, German or American, and the prospect of encountering either made his blood run cold. The Germans, if they caught him, would search and shoot him, but that was predictable. The Americans were not. There had been plenty of reassurance, but Conway distrusted them profoundly. There was a war going on, and he was on a battlefield, no matter how peaceful it might seem. Furthermore, with Rasch dead, he was the only man who knew the significance of the documents he carried. From the Americans' point of view, Conway's death would be not only convenient, but easy to accomplish.

He was trembling all over as he rose to his feet and began to move again towards the hoped-for temporary security of the Naujocks farm. The Irishwoman in Büren had been put out of his mind. He would find a place to lie low. Trouble would have to come and find *him*.

Less than an hour after the little Feiseler Storch aircraft had lifted off from the Sudostwestfalen airfield, the first American patrol, consisting of men of the Ninth Army, tearing down from near Salzkotten in the north, appeared on the edge of the runway and began to pour machine-gun fire into the control tower. When there was no answering fire, the patrol ventured closer and found the place deserted. The junior lieutenant in command radioed the information to his company commander and headed, as instructed, towards the smoking, burning fortress on the hill on the other side of the valley.

A second motorized patrol, striking northwards from the banks of the Edersee, arrived almost simultaneously. On the outskirts of Wewelsburg village, near the road to Brenken, they encountered a small party of SS engineers who, confronted suddenly by jeeps fitted with heavy machine-guns, immediately surrendered. The patrol had been briefly delayed while the SS men told a tall US army colonel riding in the second jeep, that they were responsible for the column of smoke that climbed into the sky behind them. Yes, it was the Wewelsburg. Yes, they had destroyed it. Yes, there had been fighting. The castle had been defended for some unaccountable reason, by the Warden and his staff. Certainly, the orders to destroy had come from the Reichsführer himself: hadn't his own adjutant, Sturmbannführer Macher been in charge of the demolition?

Had they, the colonel demanded, seen anybody else there? Another SS group? The engineers were honestly puzzled. Why should there be another SS group? It was enough that SS had fought SS.

The colonel left them in the charge of two men, and raced on towards the burning castle. Behind him, church bells in Brenken began to toll, and he wondered why. The Catholic infantryman driving the jeep was able to explain: it was Good Friday.

Colonel K reported personally to Patterson later that day. Patterson listened quietly.

'Which three?'

'Mohnke was dead beside the bridge,' Colonel K said. 'Naujocks and Rasch on the slope below the west wall. The way he looked, Rasch must have fallen. Nobody saw it.'

'And the other three got away?'

'We think Conway got away, sir,' Colonel K said. 'One of the defenders, who shot Naujocks, said there was a civilian with him. They were taking a briefcase from Rasch's body when he shot at them.'

'And the other two? Heiden and Sauer.'

The colonel shrugged. 'There were badly burned bodies, sir. The place was just about burned out. It's impossible to know. We found two bodies, or what was left of them, but they were just husks. Phosphorus grenades were used. They don't leave much to look at.'

'So Conway's on his own?'

'If he got away.'

'He got away,' Patterson said. 'He got away and he got the papers. We've got to get him. I want every unit in the area notified to look out for him. That clear?'

'Maybe,' Colonel K said, 'he'll come to us. That was the deal.'

Patterson looked at him. 'Knowing what you know,' he asked, 'is that what you'd do?'

'No,' the colonel said. 'I don't think it is.'

Fanning out behind the army spearheads, troops began to flood into the area, as the encirclement of the Ruhr was completed. The quiet countryside between Büren and the still-raging battle on the sand-country north-east of Paderborn was criss-crossed by patrols. Farmhouses were searched, and farm-buildings. In the villages, special detachments of military police 'snowdrops' went from house to house with news of a reward for the capture of an Irishman who was loose somewhere in the district. The hunt was as efficient as it could be made. Inevitably, however, as the days passed, and the Irishman not found, its priority decreased. In a theatre of war, war itself is the ultimate priority, and with the fall of Paderborn, there were two fronts to fight on, and troops were needed both in the battle for the Ruhr, where three hundred thousand encircled German soldiers stood their ground, and in the great drive east and north for the Elbe and the heart of Germany. The hunt for Conway was never called off: he remained an open file with both the military police and the intelligence organizations. But as the days wore past, the urgency died. Too many other things were happening and the administrators, who moved in behind the advancing troops, had too much to do in handling and feeding the refugees, the released prisoners, the streams of people on the roads, to have any great hope of finding one man among them.

Chapter Eighteen

Just before the war, the old septic tank system at the Naujocks farm, which had been constructed in the early nineteenth century, had become blocked and unpleasant and a new system had been installed. With the passing years, the fluid effluent in the old tank had filtered through the blockage, and the solid matter had lowered and hardened until it was like a concrete floor. The entrance to the tank, long overgrown, lay beneath a plum tree in the farm's kitchen garden, just as Naujocks had described it and there Conway had taken refuge.

He almost starved. The equipment for the Wewelsburg raid had included two packs of compressed rations. Conway made them last a week. At night, sneaking carefully out of his hiding place, he had obtained brownish water from the farm's old well. He remained frightened; oddly, he was also bored. In addition he was dirty and unshaven. But to his own surprise, he remained alive. More than that, he had an idea: an idea constructed out of a newspaper story he had done and the floor on which he stood. Once, in Stockholm, he had interviewed an escaped Polish prisoner of war who had pushed a wheelbarrow laden with stolen cabbages half across Germany to one of the Baltic ports, and stowed away on a ship to Sweden. Conway had found a battered wheelbarrow at the farm. He wondered what he could put in it. It was the wrong time of year for cabbages, he thought, but probably the right one for manure. Who, he thought, would worry much about a man pushing a load of crap?

The prisoner had said that whenever he was stopped and asked where he was going, he had pointed and said, 'Home. The farm over there.' Papers? 'That's where they are. That farm over there.'

Conway forced himself to wait. He was desperately hungry, with no means at all of finding food. Several times, in the dark, he prowled the deserted farmyard, hoping to find something: an old turnip, oats or even bran. But there was nothing.

It was hunger that finally drove him out. As much as possible, he kept to the woods, and walked at night, hiding himself by day in clumps of bushes. On his first night, he stopped at a farm and begged for food, posing as a refugee, and was given hot vegetable soup and a fairly wide berth, because he stank.

Afterwards, pushing his barrow off into the night, he was terrified that the woman at the farmhouse would notify somebody of his presence in the area, and, warmed and strengthened by the soup, tried to hurry a little. The following evening, crossing a road, he found a spot where some American unit must have halted to eat, and found half a pack of K rations tossed carelessly on the ground. Later, still stumbling south, aching with weakness and hunger, he came across a Salvation Army canteen van, drawn up in a clearing, and had his first real meal for ten days. His clothes hung on him now; he looked shrunken and half-starved, and the Salvation Army men, familiar enough with the needs of the displaced, fed him, gave him a little food to take with him, and tried to offer other help. When Conway did not respond to gentle questioning, they did not pursue it, and simply wished him luck as he staggered away.

Gradually, though, he was covering ground, and becoming more expert at foraging. Twice he managed to steal a chicken and risked lighting fires to cook them. In the garden shed of a shattered house he found onions strung from a joist. They were sprouting and sharp but they seemed to clean his mouth. To his surprise, his strength began to increase, rather than the reverse. He wasn't smoking, and pushing the wheelbarrow gave him more exercise than he had had for years.

He had dreaded river crossings, but found to his surprise that this far behind the lines – he had no idea where the front now lay – the smaller bridges were not guarded. As he crossed the Main, he watched the barges with envy and contemplated finding a skipper and trying to strike a bargain with the diamonds that were still in his belt, but resisted the idea. The diamonds were too important. Without them, there was no future at all. Once, however, he found money. He came across a burned-out tank, as he not infrequently came across damaged military vehicles, and searched it, as usual, hoping for food. What he found instead was a wallet containing forty-two American dollars.

When he had set off from the farm at Ahden, he had thought that it was probably about four hundred miles to the Swiss border, but he had walked more than that before, one night in the middle of May, he abandoned the wheelbarrow and succeeded in crossing. By then, as he quickly discovered, the European war had actually ended.

The American dollars, welcome as ever in Switzerland, bought him a suit. He found a small pension where he stayed cheaply and quietly for two days, while he wrote and rewrote the letter. He did not shave his beard.

On the long walk, he had had plenty of time to think about the future, and had decided that no future existed unless he could find assistance, and the more he considered it, there was only one place that assistance could be sought. It was no use returning to Stockholm, even if he could: British and American intelligence had Stockholm comfortably buttoned up, and Co-lect Corporation had a powerful Swedish subsidiary. Equally, Dublin was impossible: he had bitter memories of the ease with which the British had operated inside Eire.

There remained Mowgli: a single hope, if a slender one. One night, sheltering in the Bavarian pine forests, a memory had come to Conway of his days in Sapin, during the Civil War, reporting from the Franco side. He had tried many times to remember where he had seen Mowgli before, and had failed. That night, for some reason, a picture had surfaced in his mind of a briefing on a hillside, a mental snapshot of one of Franco's commanders talking to a group of foreign correspondents. Conway had been one, Mowgli another.

Mowgli, therefore, had once been a newspaperman, and in a way Conway found slight, irrational reassurance in that. He had thought about Mowgli a good deal in the days of walking, remembering that he had never condemned, had even seemed sympathetic, and had said, casually but with emphasis enough to leave the words clear in Conway's mind: 'Anything, old boy. I'm always interested.'

The letter he wrote so carefully was to Mowgli. Lacking an address, he sent it to Mowgli's telephone extension, at the Ministry of Defence in London, and wondered if it would reach him.

The answer was air-mailed, prompt and reassuring. Mowgli was glad to hear from him, held no malice for 'that other bit of bother' and would be in Zurich himself within a few days, staying at the Osborne Hotel. If the Elephant's Child would care to telephone him there (Mowgli even made a little joke: 'No trunk calls necessary, I think') Mowgli would be delighted to discuss what he had to offer.

Conway viewed the coming meeting with lively apprehension. But when he spoke to Mowgli several times on the telephone, he found him pleasant and most helpful. Mowgli understood very well what Conway had to offer and would be delighted to take the material from him. Indeed, he was prepared to pay handsomely for it.

Conway, concerned more about future safety than immediate large rewards, wanted only to get out of Europe. The diamonds would let him feed himself if he could only escape.

It transpired that Mowgli could arrange travel. A certain amount of money was available, and immediately too, here in Zurich. Conway really was not to worry.

But Conway did worry. He worried as he finally handed over the papers at Zurich airport, just before catching the Swissair DC-3 which took him to Beirut. He worried in the ensuing weeks as he travelled south through Africa, and on the ship which, in October, after the fall of Japan, took him eastwards to Hong Kong.

Even as the years passed, there was no escaping the worry. Conway worried as he moved into middle age, and from place to place. More than once he changed his identity, buying doubtful passports for sums he could not afford, from furtive forgers in Far Eastern seaports. He moved from Hong Kong to Indonesia, and finally to Bangkok where, as James Henderson, white-bearded and using the Liverpool accent of his boyhood, he worked as a correspondent for some of the English language newspapers published in the Far East.

To his own surprise, he was never caught, never even questioned. But the habit of looking over his shoulder, of being constantly on the alert, persisted until, on a morning in 1963, he happened to be in an airline office in Bangkok, waiting for the arrival of a man he was to interview about a new air service to Singapore. The airline official was late, and while he waited Conway read the new edition of *Newsweek*, thoughtfully provided for clients with time to pass.

Opening it idly, he suddenly saw a face he recognized, stared at it for a moment in disbelief, and then began to read the accompanying story. *Newsweek* was proud of its exclusive, and gave it a great deal of space. It concerned the disappearance, from Beirut, of one H. A. R. Philby, nick-named Kim, who had helped the British spies Burgess and Maclean to escape to Russia, and had now followed them there.

When he'd finished reading the story, Conway stared again at the face. Though almost twenty years had passed, there was no mistaking it. This was the man he had known as Mowgli! Then another thought struck him. The papers Schellenberg had intended for the Russians, all those years ago, *would* have reached the Russians, via Mowgli. Too late to serve their original purpose, of course. He wondered, as the laughter began to rise in him, what other purposes they had served over the years . . .

Author's Notes

Dr Ernst Kaltenbrunner, with whom this story began, was one of the Nazi leaders tried before the International Military Tribunal at Nuremburg. He was found guilty of crimes against humanity and died at the end of a hangman's rope in October 1946.

Walter Schellenberg was in Sweden when Germany surrendered. He stayed for some time with Count Folke Bernadotte, writing his memoirs: a vivid and enthralling, if perhaps questionable, account of his exploits. Later he returned to Germany, was imprisoned for a time, and died of a liver ailment in 1952.

Ernst Wilhelm Bohle gave evidence at the Nuremburg trial, where he was principally concerned to deny that his Auslandsorganization had engaged in espionage. The trial record shows his examination to have been undemanding, even lenient. He was later tried on other lesser charges, and imprisoned. He died in 1956, some years after his release.

Sturmbannführer Heinz Macher was one of the small group of Heinrich Himmler's subordinates to accompany him on his ill-planned, almost pathetic attempt to escape through the British lines in May of 1945. When Himmler surrendered, so did Macher. He did not, however, follow the example of the Reichsführer-SS, who took poison. Macher was much criticized, years after the war ended, by SS Obergruppenführer Karl Wolff, for bungling the destruction of the Wewelsburg. For Wolff, fire was not enough.

Warden Rupprecht survived the conflagration of Good Friday, 1945, to tell his story to historians at his comfortable home in the valley of the Rhine.

Admiral Wilhelm Canaris was hanged at Flossenburg concentration camp on April 9, 1945, after trial by a summary

SS court, on charges of complicity in the July 20th attempt on Hitler's life.

It is possible that the Wewelsburg documents may have reached Moscow earlier and by another route. Bureaucrats being bureaucrats, the original documents would certainly have been copied in Berlin, and Kaltenbrunner's close associate, Heinrich Müller, head of the Gestapo, may well have taken copies with him when, as is widely believed by British and American intelligence, he escaped to and was welcomed by the Russians after the fall of Berlin. We can, of course, never know how much pressure was put on how many people as a result of Russian possession of the British 'white list' and the evidence against Co-lect Corporation.

Co-lect Corporation: giant companies are less vulnerable than individual human beings. Co-lect (that is not its name, but it does exist) has continued its expansion through the years.

Finally, *Wewelsburg Castle*: As has happened many times through the centuries, the castle has been rebuilt. The Wewelsburg is now a youth hostel and a particularly handsome one, its interior light and cheerful, commanding magnificent views over the peaceful, wooded countryside of Westphalia. Walls that echoed to jackboots now cheerfully bounce back children's voices. Only in the great North Tower can the remnants of Nazism be seen; the two chambers constructed for Himmler's SS rituals are locked and unused, but are almost wholly intact.